Distinction of Realms

By Ben Soto

DISTINCTION OF REALMS

Second Paperback Edition: February 2023

ISBN: 978-1-7321851-4-2

This is for my father, Emiliano E. Soto, and my mother, Ada Esparza.

He taught me how to be a man and so much more. He believed in me even when I didn't and never let me stop dreaming for a single moment. He is dearly missed every day.

She showed me how to stand my ground and taught me how to be strong. She believes anyone can achieve anything but also knows not to sugarcoat it. Thank you, mom, for the honesty only a mother could provide.

Their love shaped me for the better, and it is a gift I can never repay and will always be grateful for.

Table of Contents

Part Six: Facing New Realities

Part Seven: Final Preparations

Part Eight: Before the Night Falls

Part Nine: When Plans Come Together

Part Ten: The Aftermath

PART ONE:

ENDINGS AS
BEGINNINGS

"Time is an illusion." – Vestor, the Time Bender.

1

THE DARKNESS OF the gray and somber storm clouds that dimmed the midafternoon sky eclipsed the sun, creating the look of early nightfall. A dry, hot wind blew, picking up odd bits of trash mixed with discarded paper, gently raising them into tiny tornadoes. On the horizon, broken rooftops of dilapidated buildings created a jagged and peaked line stating most emphatically that the heavens were *with* but not *part of* this earth. With a bird's eye view, one could see movement on the road below that twisted and turned like uncoiled rope. From this view on high, a car traveled the path: an antiquated navy-blue Ford Escort. It rattled along the barren streets in a forgotten part of the city, long condemned to the emptiness and absence of ordinary human life.

The old man, who was the owner and passenger of the ramshackle vehicle, sat in the backseat, hoping sunshine would break through the dark grey sky. He closed his eyes, wanting nothing more than to feel the warm embrace of the loving sun wrap around his skin one final time before events came full circle.

While the Escort puttered along, leaving random puffs of black smoke in its wake, Vestor allowed himself the massive sigh of certainty that only a Time Bender could convey, "...Hmmm,"; the deep texture of his voice filled the car. He had seen and studied in great detail all the possible outcomes of this day. Did he "see," or did he "create"? Sometimes, even Vestor did not know. The wrinkles on his weathered face stressed the great displeasure (or was it fear?) of *knowing* the end beforehand. There would be no sunshine during his final moments.

Vestor approached two-hundred and twenty-two years of age and carried himself well, considering his birth year was 1995. His geriatric body left him somewhat feeble at first glance; he maintained a young man's ambulatory sensibility in conjunction with a keen intellect. Vestor's extended lifespan was primarily due to the Founding Magic that ran through his blood. The aid of the Supernatural Magic, a power born of the Founding Magic, also had a role. Sacrifices through supernatural means had been granted in his honor along the way, immensely benefitting his current geriatric state. The endearing assistance of a valued friend also counted for much, and he was driven to his final destination by this loving companion. It also helped that the flesh encapsulating his soul wasn't the body he was born with.

The operator of the sentimental vehicle was a woman whose graceful beauty radiated from below the surface of her human shell. The names associated with her were many, and her influence upon humanity spanned the ages. To Vestor, she would always be Valerie. He had nearly forgotten the unique perspective of being a young man. Still, when he looked upon Valerie's agelessness, he vividly recalled their initial encounter lifetimes ago. The old man had no choice but to surrender to the uncontrollable feelings of youth as they erupted. He chuckled as he reverted to the bumbling kid intimidated by a strong, attractive woman. He had barely survived his job interview without sounding like a complete buffoon, and much to his surprise, she had hired him the following day. That was in the year 2012. He had only been seventeen at the time.

Sometimes, he envied her immortality and wondered how her life would have played out had they not met. She would never have regained her magical status as a goddess, and he would never have transformed into Vestor, the Time Bender. It was a possibility he knew existed but could never envision due to the nature of his abilities. How could he view a possible future if he were never to become a prophet of Chronos in the first place? Regardless, it was a strange notion that realities existed, never knowing him as a creature of magic.

With a casual posture, seated next to the old man in the back seat was another individual whose physical appearance betrayed his actual age. He was the corporeal manifestation of eternity; the title of Forever Man had been bestowed upon him in various prophetic circles. To Vestor, he would always be Matthew Gomez. *Call me Matt,* the Forever Man told Vestor when true natures were first revealed. *It's my name, the one I was given before I... well... I couldn't care less about this Forever Man crap. My name is Matt.*

Matt's raven-colored hair and five-o'clock shadow portrayed a carefree vagabond. He, too, had an extended lifespan. In addition, he was indestructible and unable to die, no matter the circumstance. Immediate regeneration made him immune to any attack, weapon, poison, or drop from incredible heights. When he came of age in the early days and the implications of his new abilities were discovered, he had tried, in vain, to destroy himself. He thought he was going mad.

This gift of incredible durability was born of the Founding Magic, as were Vestor's prophetic abilities. The Forever Man was eternity incarnate. Time Benders saw the infinite possibilities of every outcome and influenced the course of events. Some were even gifted with sight to Eternity's Endgame: the end of everything.

Valerie was birthed by the dynamic forces of the Supernatural Magic, harkening back to a forgotten time when gods and goddesses were commonplace. She initially carried the name of Aglaia, living up to her role as one of the Three Graces with a devotion lost and replaced by the demands of a changing universe. Vestor marveled at how the times changed her and the nature of her powerful abilities from divine mythic origins. Like many of those belonging to the ancient pantheons scattered about the world, she had adapted and allowed her magic to mold to her needs.

"We're almost at the country club - or what's left." Valerie broke the silence with her soft contralto voice, a bit loud so that she could be heard over the rambling of the Ford Escort, which had usurped most of the journey. She knew all too well that they were transporting Vestor to his death. "You're absolutely certain that this is the only way it can happen?"

Vestor cast a casual grin and nodded to her reflection in the rearview mirror. He coughed slightly before speaking and felt the full weight of his age. "It's the only way, Valerie. The nexus points demand that I am here. No other alternative is available. Besides, I have lived for two hundred and twenty-two years. I'm well past my expiration date. It's time to be rid of me."

Matt chuckled, and Valerie glared at him through the rearview mirror. She was not amused he had found humor in Vestor's casual dismissal of death.

Matt and Valerie had been immortal lovers for the last century of Vestor's life, and the old man saw the possibilities of this union unfold like a river branching out into endless streams. He kept his revelations secret, not wanting to spoil the sweet feeling of surprise and discovery that he hadn't experienced for far too long. *If they only knew,* the thought made him smile. The old man would allow them to decide their own fate.

Matt took a moment to convey the depth of his emotions through a caring smile. "It'll be strange carrying on without you. I'll have to make my own choices now. There'll be no more giving me a heads up in your roundabout kind of way."

"You know just as well as I that you never really listened to me anyway." Vestor reminded.

A boisterous laugh emerged from Matt as he nodded in agreement. Vestor joined Matt with an aged, raspy laughter of his own. The car rattled through the desolate streets, and he regarded his protégé with the fondest of smiles.

"We've arrived." Valerie felt the vehicle jostle over the uneven road as she drove the car into the parking lot of the former Brightwood Country Club. The establishment had been absent maintenance for over a century, and the shell of the former glory it once held was anything but pleasing.

The Escort parked with lazy indifference in a random spot on the black pavement of the abandoned lot. The engine shut down with a great banging rattle as Valerie turned the key to the off position. That old engine continued to make a clanking noise before thoroughly relaxing to the point of absolute stillness. They shared an uneasy silence after the comforting putter of the engine vanished. All were aware that it was almost time for Vestor to die.

Matt reached out and held Vestor's hand, unable to verbalize the emotions that grew taxing. With wise compassion, Vestor squeezed Matt's hand in return. The message was clear. Vestor understood. With slight hesitation, Matt released his grip, opened the door, and exited the car.

Valerie turned her head to face Vestor from the driver's seat. She studied the old man just as he was, and for a brief second, their experiences together danced at the forefront of her mind. She did her best to hide the sorrow brewing within her deep blue eyes and even managed the semblance of a smile.

"Are you going to be okay, Valerie?" The old man asked.

"Yes and no, but you already know that. You've accomplished much with your time. But I must say, Jared, I've watched you grow into quite an impressive man. You'll surely be remembered among your kind until the end of time." She spoke with pride.

Vestor chuckled. "You flatter me, and no one has spoken that name to me in so long. *Jared*... It feels even stranger to hear it with my own voice."

"It seems appropriate to call you by that name, being back here. It was your first true name." An image of Vestor as a youth came to Valerie. He was so young and full of potential.

Vestor hesitated before continuing to speak. "Our bond is still strong, and I've never felt any different. On all my journeys, I could still feel you with me. I could always feel where you were and always knew I could find my way to you because of that bond."

A tear trickled from Valerie's eye, forming a small river of sorrow along her cheek. "I know. Your presence was always there for me as well. I'm going to miss it dearly. An excellent and true part of me will be gone once you...."

"...die." Vestor finished the sentence knowing she couldn't bring herself to speak the word.

She nodded while wiping away the tear. "Yes. I guess we better get on with it. I... I just..."

"It's okay, Valerie. I love you too." He smiled and somehow seemed as young as when they first met.

The door on Vestor's side of the Escort opened. Matt reached his hand out for support, and Vestor took hold of it, exiting with cautious steps. He stood next to the navy-blue clunker as Matt closed the car door and smirked at the remains of what was once the Brightwood Country Club. The vegetation had run wild, creating a verdant shell upon the concrete landscape. The structural integrity of the building was in poor condition, with sections caved and collapsed. The parking lot surrounding them was covered with potholes and littered with abandoned vehicles.

Valerie stepped out of the driver's seat, closed the door, and walked over to where the two men stood. "Shall we move closer?"

"This spot is as good as any. The two of you should ready yourselves. *They'll* be here soon. It's their last attempt to stop me. It always happens this way. Mere moments ago, it was revealed to Renee and Develin that this is how I'm reborn in the past." Vestor closed his eyes and concentrated his magic. "Goodbye, old friends. I love you both dearly."

Valerie and Matt hardened their gazes and steeled their emotions before taking a position on either side of Vestor. The Time Bender's words were accurate, as always. Valerie sensed a magical distortion in the space nearby, ascertaining that the former Fury turned sorceress would appear as predicted. The sensation of the magic behind the portal had the signature of their common enemy.

"I can feel her, Matt," Valerie warned.

"Let her come. We're ready." Matt replied, confident.

Valerie focused on her magic. "We hold the shield. They mustn't break the barrier."

"I'll make sure of it." The magic Matt had acquired over the years was partly due to Valerie's training though he was nowhere near as strong as she.

A ripple in the air on the other side of the parking lot began to manifest, causing that particular space to wave like the surface of a pond. The ripple transformed into a tear giving a glimpse of a darkly lit chamber. Stepping through the portal from that chamber was a blonde woman whose features were average compared to Valerie's. Long ago, she had been born as a Fury sharing the same pantheon as Valerie. Vestor first encountered her at this very country club when she carried the guise of a typical member. During that period and since he has known her as Renee Dempsy.

Another figure in a classic red suit emerged from the tear, stepping out with a confident swagger while surveying the crumbling landscape. He was an old vile creature, not even human in origin. For most of Vestor's existence, the demon wizard Develin had worked diligently with the former Fury. They had combined their skills and resources in numerous attempts to exterminate or control the Time Bender.

Vestor sensed the tear in space his enemies had constructed, ignoring the magic. Instead, he concentrated his energy on the nexus point that began to form and was confident that his loyal friends would hold Renee and Develin at bay long enough to complete his final act. Then, with even greater confidence, he reached out with his will through the nexus point, extending his essence to the point in space and time where his powers were first manifest. It was the exact moment when Jared transformed into the Time Bender known as Vestor.

Renee's angry dark blue eyes locked with Valerie's as she approached the trio. Her long black coat flowed in unison with her dark blonde hair as the wind wrapped around her body. "Let me kill him. He was never worth your protection in the first place. All things end even for prophets like the one you shield."

Renee's defenses shot up as an invisible wave of pure energy rippled through the air from Matt. The kinetic energy of the magical force was diverted to either side by Renee's instinctive shielding. Stray energy waves struck an abandoned car and black pavement, causing debris to burst from the ground and for the vehicle to ignite into violent flames.

"You're too late, Renee." Valerie focused more strength into the shield around Vestor as Develin shot a burst of demon flames from the palm of his hand. The fire curved in blue hues around the invisible barrier erected inches away from the old man. Vestor remained standing in concentration with his back to the group.

Additional flames shot forth from Develin, this time directed at Valerie. Matt stepped before his lover and, in an instant, became engulfed in bright blue flames. He yelled in agony as his clothing incinerated within milliseconds. His flesh burned off with crispy chunks showing hints of white bone beneath what had melted. Valerie held steady with her shielding though it pained her to witness the physical torment. She focused her strength and expanded the shielding to encompass her and Matt.

Seconds after the apparent death, Matt's body began to regenerate. The charred flesh expanded to proper proportion covering the bare bones, and peeled away like the skin of a snake, revealing the smooth texture of his ordinarily tan skin. His face abruptly became animated as the raven-colored hair grew upon his head. He winked at Valerie, who carried a disapproving glare. As a result of the instantaneous combustion, Matt's clothing was entirely consumed by the flames, and he had no choice but to stand by Valerie's side with all the confidence that a naked man could muster.

"That was unnecessary!" Valerie bellowed.

Matt took in a deep breath with his newly formed lungs. "If those flames hit you, you would have lost your focus on the protective barrier around Vestor, or you would have maintained the shield while sacrificing your life. I couldn't have allowed that. The demon wizard's magic is older than you, and those flames would have been deadly."

"Thank you..." Those two words were never easy for Valerie to speak.

Matt noted his nakedness as he stood in defense. "I guess I should have brought a change of clothing. It would have been a nice gesture on your part to let me know about this particular incident, Vestor! I know you saw it coming!" Matt stood his ground unashamed. It hadn't been the first time he regenerated without clothing, and even though Vestor had his back turned, Matt was confident the old man carried a childish grin.

Renee Dempsy bombarded the protective barrier with slight bursts of energy, prodding for a weak point. She refused to admit defeat. The Time Bender could not be allowed to complete his final act, and her anger at the existence of this prophet grew insatiable with each passing second.

Matt focused his magic on strengthening the barrier's weak points before the former Fury could break them. Combined with Valerie's magic, it was more than enough. From the corner of his eye, he witnessed the desperation on Renee's face and responded with a confident smile. After nearly two centuries of constant bombardment, their enemies ultimately failed.

Develin relaxed his posture and regarded the trio as respected rivals rather than mere enemies. "We're more than capable of breaking their shielding, but it doesn't matter at this point. Vestor will have completed his final act by the time we breach. It's over." The demon wizard knew how much this failure would cost, but then again, he was no stranger to the darkest aspects of existence.

"No!" Renee used all her might, focusing and discharging a massive burst of deadly energy. Yet, the magical barrier remained secure. It held steady deflecting the waves of violent force in either direction; this caused more debris to explode from the energy's impact on the pavement.

"Our pact is finished, Renee. I owe you nothing since the end goal wasn't met. I thought we had a real chance of taming him; I thought we could even kill him. We've both had our share of experience with Time Benders, but this little shit was never like the others." Develin turned from the confrontation and began walking away, giving the human impression that he would enter one of the abandoned cars and drive off.

"You would give up on this now?!" The anger darkened her skin a few shades, and she lashed out, attempting to paralyze the demon wizard by restricting his bodily movements.

"Your emotions have always clouded your judgment even after centuries of being alive long enough to temper them." Develin continued to walk away, unaffected by her magic. "I'm a demon, remember? So you need to do far better if you're going to try and break me with paralytic spells."

Renee bellowed at Develin. "All those years spent trying to manipulate and break him, and this is how it ends?! He gets to be reborn and do it all over again!"

Develin shrugged. "It was fun while it lasted. The problem is Vestor just always saw it coming."

Vestor smiled as he overheard the comment made by his adversary. He recalled speaking similar words to Develin when the demon wizard had almost successfully ended his life.

Renee scowled at Develin, cursing the day fate saw fit to bring them on the same path. Her essence raged with the raw energy of extreme hatred as she witnessed the demon wizard transform into a black mist until nothing was left.

"It's over, Renee! You've failed! Admit defeat and leave!" Matt's voice echoed throughout the parking lot.

"You're both fools! You always have been! I can't go back to *him*. Not like this...." Fear shot through Renee's entire body, replacing every dominant shred of anger. "He'll torture me without end. This was my mission. This was my only purpose. He made sure of that. I can't simply go away. He will create for me an existence of pure agony."

"It was your choice to serve *him* in the first place." Valerie's voice was without sympathy.

"And what I do now is also my choice. I'd rather remember you as we used to be here at the end, so I use the name you were given so long ago. Goodbye, Aglaia." Renee closed her eyes, focusing the energy of her being within itself. She self-imposed all the magic that ran through her blood, and a faint glow began to take over her skin.

Alecto, no! What are you doing?! Valerie cried the thought, shocked by Renee's choice. Alecto had been Renee's first true name as she was born as one of the Furies from the mythical age. Her current form betrayed the idea of her inability to be looked upon. Still, during those ancient times, Renee Dempsy was the beast with snakes for hair and blood-dripping eyes.

"What the hell is she doing now?" Matt studied Renee's body, never having witnessed a god commit suicide. He caught glimpses of her various forms and, for a second, saw her as one of the actual Furies of old. The glow of magic grew in intensity with each passing second.

"She's killing herself, but it's more than that. She's erasing every trace of her energy and every form she's ever taken. The pain must be unbearable." A pang of sorrow rushed through Valerie's chest. No creature should suffer the horrific fate of erasing oneself from existence, but that was precisely the act Renee was undertaking. The severity of who she was under the employ of struck Valerie with great force. *Is he indeed so powerful that Renee would wish nonexistence over punishment?*

Matt averted his gaze as the glow became too bright for his eyes to withstand. An agonizing cry of intense pain was followed by a burst of illuminating energy that launched vibrant waves rippling in all directions. With trepidation, Matt let go of his hold on the barrier at the same time as Valerie. They stared at each other, startled by Renee's suicide, and quickly remembered why they were at their current location. The two observed Vestor standing near them, and the old man remained wholly focused on the task.

"Dying? That's the easy part. It's coming back to life that really hurts. Birth equals pain. It's the price of being what I am." – The Forever Man (Matthew Gomez, physical incarnation of eternity)

2

"IT'S HERE. I can feel the nexus points merging." Vestor spoke softly, letting the wind carry his words. He could perceive all the timelines merging into the same moment for the tiniest fraction of measurement allowed; all realities froze during that briefest instant.

He opened his eyes, studying Matt and Valerie. They stood nearby unmoving as if they were mannequins on display, and the sharpness of his naked masculine body contrasted the beauty of her elegantly clothed figure. The clouds in the sky were entirely still as if brushed into place by a brilliant artist, along with the motionless birds trapped in midair. Even the more powerful gusts of wind froze, creating patterns no mortal human eye would ever appreciate.

Vestor took a few steps forward and sat down on his knees like a Zen master in meditation. Once positioned to the point of comfort, he reached out with *all* his energy and felt his younger version back in time where these two nexus points connected in the fabric of space-time. His life was not a string of linear events like most creatures in the universe. Instead, he was a circle that expanded and contracted depending upon choice. That was the existence of Time Benders.

In the parlance of physics, Vestor was the living reality of a Closed Timelike Curve (CTC), able to travel at will through infinite timelines. He was everywhere at once, and he was only in one place. He had tried explaining the process to Matt and Valerie, but the two hated mathematics and chose to stick to magic incantations and the like... not Vestor. He had been comfortable with both.

Vestor was almost within the mind of his younger incarnation. He called out mentally to the young man that would soon begin an incredible and unexpected life.

Jared...

"There was a vision; it was blinding and brilliant in ways that made mortal men tremble. It was an idea celebrated with new-ness while firmly anchored to the old ways. This vision – this idea, had a name: Vestor." – Former Grace Aglaia (*History of a Time Bender* by Omoikane – Japanese God of wisdom and intelligence. Quotes collected during Aglaia's time on Earth as Valerie).

3

FOR MATT AND Valerie, a fraction of a second had passed. One moment Vestor was standing near them, explaining that he could feel the nexus points merging, and the next, he was lying on the old black pavement of the country club parking lot. A peaceful smile adorned his wrinkled old face. The two lovers held hands and took note of how their old friend was more than content in death. The mere sight of the smile helped ease the pain of loss that ran through their souls.

"We should get out of here. I know this side of town has been abandoned for a while, but we can never be too careful. After all, the only thing we know for sure that stopped living here was the humans. Just about anything else could be lurking in the shadows." Matt lovingly squeezed Valerie's hand.

"What of the body?" Her eyes stayed true to Vestor's smile. "We can't just leave him here like a random victim. His life was spent defending the balance of this world. He deserves more than this."

"We come from nothingness, and to the nothingness, we shall return." Matt let go of Valerie's hand, extending his senses with the Founding Magic and directed energy at Vestor's body. He manipulated the underlying atomic structure touching each atom until they separated and reformed into the surrounding air. Eventually, no trace of Vestor's aged body was left behind. Having regenerated countless times gave Matt a unique understanding of the basic structure of everything.

"I supposed you could have kept his clothing before you did that." She grinned while staring at Matt's nakedness.

Matt responded with a sheepish grin, having forgotten that he was naked in the first place. "Yes, well... I suppose I should have thought of that."

The trunk of the navy-blue Ford Escort popped open as if the vehicle had a life of its own. The car's sudden movement startled Matt and Valerie, and they studied the trunk with defensive postures expecting a trap. The duo cautiously approached the vehicle with curious expressions and peered within the trunk to find a set of clothes neatly folded on the spare tire. Next to the clothing was a note written by Vestor.

Dear Matthew,

In case you were wondering, I did have a good laugh about this particular scenario when I envisioned it. I took the liberty of having some clothing ready for your departure. You didn't really think I would let you leave here as naked as the day you were born, did you? I placed a timed lock to open and release the trunk at the appropriate moment. No magic is needed for that one. And many thanks for disposing of my body like you did. It was a fitting end for a Time Bender.

Love,

Vestor

Matt and Valerie laughed aloud as they read the note together.

"Now what do we do?" Valerie asked.

Matt looked over his naked body, gesturing. "First things first, I get dressed."

Valerie smiled. "And then?"

Matt took in a breath of fresh air. He looked to the sky and noticed that the overcast clouds were beginning to allow rays of sunshine. "And then we live our immortal lives full of surprises like Vestor wanted."

"Until the day of Eternity's Endgame?" She asked, already knowing the answer.

"Yes. Until the day of Eternity's Endgame. But that won't be for a very long time." Matt winked at her as he reached for the clothing in the trunk.

PART TWO:

JUST ANOTHER
MONDAY

"Normal. What does that even mean? When I was normal by societal standards, I felt anything but. There was always a disconnect – like I never belonged. True normal is knowing who you are and where you fit in with your chosen purpose – the one that feels right. It wasn't until I became a Time Bender that I understood this." – Vestor, the Time Bender.

1

JARED HERNANDEZ STEPPED with weary feet and hunched shoulders while navigating the Brightwood Country Club's parking lot. His father, Andres, had dropped him off near the entrance to the parking lot of the lavish establishment. Jared's first vehicle, an 89 Ford Escort full of rust holes and a broken window on the front passenger's side had ceased operating several days prior.

He checked his waiter's uniform as he dragged his feet, feeling the total weight of work upon him with each step. The black vest covering most of the formal white dress shirt was neatly in place except for the small stain near the bottom. He hoped to God that Mr. Drake, Old Merdith, or Valerie failed to make a note of it.

He entered the club from the rear entrance as instructed since the aforementioned management took control of Brightwood. Policy claimed it would be disastrous to the club's corporate image if the members were to see the staff that served them under unnecessary circumstances. Familiarity breeds contempt, and Brightwood sought to enforce its de-facto caste systems at every opportunity.

Jared strolled past the women's restroom and was soon outside the door of the men's. He bumped into the door with his left shoulder forcing his way in. The mirror's reflection greeted him with an indifferent expression as the routine check began. It started with his teeth; they needed to be clean and food free. He then proceeded to inspect his tongue. Jared despised the muck that would build up on top of his. The third phase was the nose inspection; he needed to ensure he was free of any embarrassing hairs protruding with defiance. Finally, all that remained was the hair on his head.

He toiled with the dark-brown-on-the-verge-of-black strands without much emotional investment. From whatever position he brushed his hair into, the strands would only spring back into the original shape. It was an exercise in futility, but he wanted to be presentable.

When satisfied with his hair, Jared made his way to the urinal. He unzipped, ready to unleash that which had been building up. But, instead of experiencing a satisfying decrease in pressure on his bladder, he snapped his head up as the door to the bathroom opened. Carl Remington sauntered in dressed like Jared. Startled by Carl's sudden appearance, Jared ran to the stall where the more comfortable toilet was ready and waiting.

"Jared?" Carl stood before the now vacant urinal, wasting no time unleashing the buildup. The affliction of shyness when urinating in front of others was not inherent in Carl.

"What's going on, Carl?" Jared asked as he began to urinate in the toilet. He had always felt more comfortable there.

"I guess you still have trouble performing under pressure with the captain, huh?" Carl zipped up and moved to the sink to wash his hands. He turned the faucet off, dried his hands on a paper towel, and wet them again, running his fingers through his long blond hair.

"What's it to you anyway?" Jared shot back.

Carl laughed as he spoke. "You're the only guy I know that can't piss in front of anyone."

"Why the hell are you so obsessed with my dick and how I piss? It's not natural. Get a hobby." Jared finished, zipped up, and flushed the toilet by lifting his left leg and pressing down on the handle with his foot. He stepped out from the stall and waited for Carl to finish checking his reflection in the mirror on the wall above the sink.

Carl dried his hands on another paper towel with a faint grin. "If that little pecker of yours is a dick, then the whole male species is in trouble. Any woman that sees that thing is going to laugh and bail."

"Funny you should say that because your mom seemed to enjoy it just fine last night." Jared could always fall back on the mom jokes.

"Gee... I never heard that one before." Carl's facetious tone slightly echoed in the bathroom while he stood halfway outside the entrance, his sizeable muscular body propped open the door. The playful mask faded, and a serious expression took hold. Carl hesitated as he struggled with words, and it was evident that the topic on his mind was difficult to share. "Do you want to hear something crazy?"

"That depends on the kind of crazy." After washing and drying his hands, Jared crossed his arms, relaxed his shoulders, and raised an eyebrow at Carl. "Everything okay?"

Carl held his hands up, pleading for an open mind. "I think so. Look. It will sound crazy; you'll think I'm nuts."

"I already do," Jared smirked.

"I'm serious, Jared." Carl pleaded.

Jared gestured that he would listen. "Okay. What is it?"

Carl took a deep breath. "You have to keep an open mind here, okay? I think a little corgi has been following me around. This dog is showing up everywhere I go, and I can't explain it. It's fuckin' weird; I mean, that's weird, right? It seems to be watching me like it's waiting for something or wants to tell me something. The little shit gives me the creeps every time I see it."

"You're freaked out because you're being stalked by a little dog. Maybe you should go to the doggie police and file a doggie restraining order? That might help." It was difficult for Jared not to laugh.

Carl had hoped to confide in his friend but knew he would only be met with further mockery if he continued. As a response, Carl gave Jared the middle finger laughing at his concern. "I have to run upstairs and help set up the formal dining room for tonight. I'll catch you later."

Jared waved. "See ya, Carl. Watch out for corgis; they're sneaky little bastards."

A muffled "fuck off" was heard through the closed door as Carl walked away.

Jared wrapped up his final mirror check with a laugh and exited the bathroom, ready to face his other coworkers.

"Having abilities hasn't changed me much. I'm still me, but with the upgraded package – so to speak." – Joseph Chan, Medium/Manipulator.

2

AFTER WALKING PAST the woman's restroom, Jared took a right and moved up the stairs to the next level in the club's employee section. He exited the hallway's silence and was enveloped by the hustle and bustle of kitchen life. Every chef moved with a distinct purpose, and Jared felt the temperature rise from the use of all the stovetops and ovens. He could never withstand the heat for eight to twelve hours like most cooks in the kitchen did, and he imagined that the extra body heat from rushing around made it even worse. The kitchen was always that busy, especially before the noon lunch rush.

Jared carried out the usual assortment of greetings, saying hello and waving the gesture as he passed fellow employees. When he arrived at the time clock to punch in, he greeted the dishwashers nearby. One of them paid particular attention to Jared. He wiped his hands on his wet apron and waved to young Mr. Hernandez with a tall, thick posture. Beneath the apron and white shirt, one could tell that Memo was frighteningly fit and muscular.

I hope I never end up on Memo's bad side. That guy could break me in half. Jared took an extra second to smile and wave to the muscular man. Memo's younger sister had shown interest in Jared, which made the man all the more intimidating.

With another smile, Jared exited the hectic kitchen. He was surrounded by the serenity of the central wait station connected to the large dining hall. He studied the wait station and noticed that the large coffee maker to the refrigerator's left was still on from the night before. The decaf valve overflowed with the liquid making a mess on the stainless-steel table giving the room a Folgers best part of waking up kind of smell.

He cringed, knowing he would have to be the one to clean it, but before he could function, Jared's slight OCD obligated him to perform one more task. So, like clockwork, he stepped over to the schedule on the board near the wait station entrance.

He ran his finger down all the names until he found his own and studied the times he would have to come in that week. He had memorized his schedule the night before but looked at it again, wanting to make sure those times were correct. Once verified, Jared continued to move his finger down the schedule until he found *her* name printed in black ink.

Sara White.

He checked to see if Sara was on the same schedule for that shift. Work didn't seem so bad when she was around. Sure enough, she would be arriving within the hour, and a half-smile formed on his face at the thought of just being able to see her.

The door to Jared's right that led into the hall between dining rooms swung open to steal him from his simple moment of delight. Mr. Drake stood for half a heartbeat before approaching Jared's side of the wait station. The thing with Mr. Drake was that he never merely walked. No, this man would tower over you with every step taken, and each step he made had a distinct air of dominance.

"Good morning Mr. Drake." Jared loathed the encounter with all of his being. He had quickly developed a hatred for his new boss, given how he chose to interact with the employees.

Mr. Drake wore a neatly put-together expensive blue suit with a black tie resting beneath the suit jacket, which was always buttoned save the very bottom one. His gold tiepin sparkled from the light and looked as though he had spent all night polishing it, and his short haircut seemed to be the very definition of perfection. Not one strand appeared out of place for fear of what Mr. Drake might say if caught.

The man who thought he was the Brightwood Country Club reached into his right pocket for a large gold watch connected to his belt by a decorative gold chain. He noted the time and glanced over at the schedule. Then, satisfied, he looked at Jared, uttering, "Hello, Jared."

Jared gazed upon the coffee maker only for a split second, but it was long enough for Mr. Drake to notice what his eyes were fixed upon. He tilted his head to the left to find the puddle of coffee that had formed on the table. "Could you be a good sport and clean that up for me there," and the word Jared dreaded most shot forth from the man's mouth, "buckaroo?"

"Sure thing, Mr. Drake. I'll get right on it." Jared jumped to the task and held in the contempt he felt for being called that every time their paths crossed.

"I'd like to keep this wait station clean before the lunch rush begins. You know how hungry those members get after a good golf game."

"No problem, Mr. Drake. You got it." Jared nodded his head while rolling up the sleeves of his shirt. He moved past Mr. Drake, who kept a watchful eye on him, and lifted up the drain cover unclogging the clump of tea bags. The coffee now flowed freely without interruption through the drain and poured into the pipe connected beneath the table. "Who put all these tea bags here?"

The question went unnoticed as Mr. Drake moved into another conversation with Jared. "I almost forgot to mention this."

Jared stopped what he was doing. He turned to face his boss as though he were about to be executed.

"Arturo is out sick today, so I need you to set up the expediting station and run that from the kitchen. Think you can handle that?" Mr. Drake asked.

"I'll do my best. Shouldn't be a problem, Mr. Drake." Jared returned the same fake smile he received.

"You're an excellent sport there, buckaroo." Mr. Drake patted Jared on his back with awkward sincerity, happy to have adequately given the appropriate gesture of appreciation. He exited soon after.

Once satisfied that his boss had vanished, Jared gave the man his middle finger holding it up in all its pristine glory. Then, Sara White entered the wait station, casting an amused expression in Jared's direction.

"I was a passenger for so long. What should have been the best years of my life were taken away from me. Do you know what it's like to be trapped in your body? In your own mind?" – Sara White

3

"WHAT ARE YOU doing?"

Jared immediately ceased his hate dance and turned to face Sara. He watched her for a handful of heartbeats as she ran her fingers through her long black hair. "Me? I'm not doing anything." He cleared his throat, becoming fully engrossed by her simple beauty. "Hi."

"Are you okay?" She asked.

"Yeah, I'm good. How about you?" Jared continued acting like he wasn't caught doing a hate dance.

"Really hungry. I had no time to eat anything before I came to work." She placed her purse on the stainless-steel counter in the wait station while paying attention to the schedule.

"So..." Jared inched closer with clumsy confidence.

"What is it?" Her attention remained on the schedule.

He did his best to portray a casual nonchalance. "Your graduation was this past weekend, right?"

"It sure was." She wrestled through the contents of her purse, ignoring the schedule momentarily.

"Mine too. It was kind of boring, but whatever. It's over. That's all that matters. How did yours go?" Jared asked, genuinely interested.

"It was fun. The valedictory speech was hilarious. I'm going to miss that kid, Eric. He was always so funny. The way he can do an impersonation of pretty much anybody is amazing." She stopped exploring her purse for the following few words and stared off into nothing as she spoke them. "It was kind of sad too."

"Really?" Concern was in his tone.

"Yeah. It's strange how you realize you'll miss certain things you never thought you would. You tend to forget the connections you make, whether you want them or not. In the end, those connections are *there* regardless." She returned to the excavation of personal effects after the brief moment of reflection.

"I wish I could say I felt the same, but I don't." The thought made Jared feel empty.

"Why not?" She asked.

"I've been in an all-male high school for four years. Graduating was like the end of a long, painful prison sentence. Minus the rape, of course, but there were a few close calls." He gave her a playful smile.

She laughed at the comment. "It couldn't have been all that bad."

"You're right. It wasn't." He considered. "After all, I met Carl and Joe, but I never really made any other close friends. It's just been me hanging out with them, coming to work, and seeing... you."

"Just me?" A playful grin formed on her face.

"The others too – of course, I mean, everyone... really." Jared stepped over his words wishing he could be as suave as his friend Joe.

"Where the hell is my pen?" Sara slammed her purse on the countertop, frustrated.

Without hesitation, Jared searched in his pocket, removing a black pen. A connection was made when she reached for the writing utensil; their hands gently brushed against one another. That pure moment seemed like an eternity to Jared as he felt her soft skin move against the rougher texture of his own.

He soaked in every second of her simple beauty and watched her take a sheet of paper on which she wrote her schedule down. Her face's always smooth skin wrinkled in an expression of utter disgust for the number of hours given to her, and it was a cute wrinkle.

"Do you have the usual assortment of slave shifts?" He broke the silence.

"You know it." She wrote down the last of her schedule.

"Doesn't it bother you that you get more hours than anybody else? Rachel and Nicole come close with how much they work, but you know what I mean. You seem to work a hell of a lot of hours now that I think of it." Jared wondered why he had never noticed this before.

She dismissed it with a smile. "It doesn't bother me at all. Things just wouldn't flow so well if I weren't here." She handed the pen back to Jared. "I guess you can say that people around this place have come to *worship* me a little, and there's absolutely nothing wrong with that."

As he deposited the writing utensil back into his pocket, Jared leaned over the countertop placing his hand in a puddle of coffee from the previous night. He shot his hand upright as soon as contact was made, shaking away the feeling of disgust. Sara moved fast, throwing him a white rag while giggling at his clumsiness. He wiped the liquid from his hand as she laughed. He loved when she laughed, even if it was at him.

"I have to help set up the porch for lunch. Are you going to sit and eat during the break this time, or will I have to track you down?" There was a sternness to her question.

"I'll be up there. All I have to do is finish cleaning this damn coffee maker, and then I have to set up the expediting station in the kitchen. His greatness, Mr. Drake, has deemed me the expeditor." Jared rolled his eyes.

"Just remember it could always be worse." She pointed out.

Jared winced. "You shouldn't say that."

"Why?" She asked with a shrug of the shoulders.

His anxiety grew. "Because when someone says that, things get worse."

Sara gave a reassuring smile to Jared and gently brushed her fingertips up and down the small of his back. "You'll be fine. If you need my help, I won't be that far away. Just let me know, okay?"

Jared nodded, taking in the relaxing sensation. "Thanks."

"I'll save you a seat in the break room." She promised with a wink.

He smiled in return. "See ya there."

With those words, she took hold of her purse and promptly exited the wait station.

"Imagine going to a movie theater and seeing all the movies playing simultaneously. You're sitting there in each theater. Now imagine you can pay attention to every detail of each film playing simultaneously. You can pay attention to each theater, noting what it smells, feels, and looks like. Imagine doing all of that and keeping your identity and thoughts separate at the same time. If you can understand that, you can start to understand what being an Animal Speaker is like.

"Being what I now am, I've realized that humanity has lost something along its journey. This world is full of life, but no one pays attention. All the animals and creatures that surround you- all that life! They speak to each and every person every second of every day. Start listening!" – Carl Remington (Animal Speaker)

4

AFTER INDULGING IN a brief daydream of being with Sara, Jared turned his attention to the coffee machine. The damn thing always seemed to give him grief; for some reason, he was the only one who could fix it. Jared finished draining the coffee from the decaf valve and watched as it swirled down the stainless-steel drain. He then focused on the top of the apparatus, attempting to remove the lid covering the large filter where the ground coffee was placed for brewing.

"You can be really stupid at times, Jared." He spoke to himself as he often did when working alone.

Jared realized he had forgotten to move the hot water faucet that towered over the giant machine and covered the circle in the center of the lid. He yanked on the stubborn spigot jostling it out of place and forced it in his direction. While repositioning the faucet, it dawned on him that the machine had been left on. The hot water happily poured from the spout before he could close the gushing flow; consequently, a fair amount of the hot liquid eagerly splashed across his chest, leaving a darker shade on the already black work vest.

"Shit!" Jared danced about in response to the heat of the water on his chest. After the liquid cooled down, he studied the wet spot feeling incredibly silly.

At that moment, another person entered the wait station in a waiter uniform. "What's up, Jared? What the hell happened to you? Are you lactating or something?" Joseph Chan chuckled as he placed his nametag on his vest and straightened out a few loose strands of his short black hair.

"It's from the coffee machine." Jared took the rag from earlier and wiped his chest. "The damn thing is clogged up again. What's going on with you?"

"Same old same," Joe smirked, ready to launch into his friendly insults. "You're Mexican, right? Shouldn't that water be on your back - being a wetback and all?"

"You got jokes today, huh? At least I'm a hundred percent something. I don't even know what to call you; you're Chinese and Puerto Rican. What do I say? Spink?" Jared patted the liquid from his vest with a white towel.

"Touché, my friend. Touché." Joe moved closer to Jared. "I had a crazy night last night."

Jared rolled his eyes. "Don't you always?"

Joe leaned on the counter across from Jared, relaxing his posture. "Okay, I was hanging with Enrique and the guys, and we were down by Tony's place. Everything was cool. We were kicking back, drinking a few beers Tony's cousin brought over, and having a good time."

Jared nodded. "Sounds like a normal night."

"Well, J.C.'s girl starts acting up and turns into a real pain in the ass. This bitch is always killing the damn mood with her drama. So, she storms out, and J.C. starts drinking really heavy because he's pissed off about the bullshit she's pulling."

Jared nodded again, not surprised. "Like I said, that sounds like a normal night."

Joe held a hand up. "Patience, Mr. Hernandez, I'm getting to it. Anyway, J.C.'s girl also decides to start drinking a lot. She isn't used to drinking anything but water and whatever else skinny bitches like her drink. I don't know - fuckin' - green tea or whatever."

Jared raised an eyebrow. "What's wrong with green tea? I drink green tea."

Joe shook Jared's shoulders. "Just focus on the story!" Joe then returned to storyteller mode. "Anyway, she showed up about half an hour later with a big-ass baseball bat and was ready to bash J.C.'s car up, but *good*. She starts going to town, smashing away at the damn car like there's candy inside, but the thing is, it wasn't J.C.'s car. It was a neighbor's car. And this dude, a real big guy, about as big as J.C., steps out of the house yelling, 'What the fuck is wrong with you? Get the hell away from my car, you crazy bitch!'"

Jared shook his head from side to side, laughing in disbelief. A sense of relief also washed over him for having stayed home. He wasn't keen on the drama surrounding many people he knew.

"Now this motherfucker runs over to J.C.'s girl and smacks her right in the face. I mean, it was a good straight-face blast." Joe cocked his arm back to reenact the punch. "Now you know that J.C. wasn't going to let this stand. He and his girl were fighting, but he wasn't about to let some asshole hit her like that. So, he jumps out of his house, his big ass, and starts pounding on this guy like he ain't shit. I mean, J.C. is beating the shit out of Tony's neighbor like he's a fucking heavy bag on the ground being pummeled. I've never seen a beating that bad."

Jared stood with his jaw dropped as the laughter mixed with a silent shock. "Holy shit. Did the cops show up? I mean, what happened after the fight was over? Did he send that guy to the hospital?"

"No," Joe reassured. "The guy J.C. put the hurt on just went back inside his house, holding a bloody nose and screaming threats while spitting out teeth. J.C. and his girl made up, and we all await the next explosive eruption of drama. On the other hand, Tony is now looking for a new place to live with his cousin."

Jared couldn't believe the last part. "Why would he move? He just got that place. When he turned eighteen, he couldn't wait to be on his own."

"Turns out the guy J.C. beat down runs with a gang or some shit. I don't know all the details, but Tony is hell-bent on finding a new place right away, and so is his cousin. Cheap places to live are usually cheap for a reason Jared. That was never the greatest of neighborhoods. It was about time he decided to get out of that area. That whole neighborhood is trash. Hell, *I* can't even stand living there anymore." Joe admitted.

After finishing his story, Joe straightened his posture while stepping over to the refrigerator and opening it. Armed with a smile, he grabbed a soda intended only for the club members. Joe pulled the tab with a relaxed grace, allowing the pressure differential to equalize into that all too familiar hiss. He took a refreshing sip and placed the soda can on a shelf behind a small stack of white plates. It happened to be his time-honored hiding spot.

Joe dawdled near the plates and observed Jared carrying out the menial task mandated by Mr. Drake. Confident no one would descry his work policy violation, he reached behind the dishes and sipped more of the forbidden soda. He stared at his friend, bored with the silence, and decided to speak. "So, what are you getting into tonight?"

"I'm not really sure yet. Probably a whole lot of nothing like usual." A deflated posture followed the words.

Joe shot up, irritated by this behavior. "I really hate it when you say shit like that."

Jared turned to face his friend. "Joe, you know for a fact that I don't have a life."

"No!" Joe hid his soda and walked closer to Jared as he placed the faucet back into the correct position. "I will not hear this rant about you being a fucking loser again."

"I don't rant!" Jared shot out defensively.

Joe nodded his head up and down. "Yes, you do."

Jared's irritation grew. "No, I don't. That's bullshit. I don't rant."

Carl burst through the wait station door, passing the two and moving toward the kitchen on a work-related mission. "Is he ranting again?"

"When isn't he?" Joe responded.

"Screw you guys; that's bullshit!" Jared yelled as Carl vanished into the kitchen and looked at Joe, who stood beside him.

"All I'm saying is that it wouldn't hurt to change your perspective. You have to let shit happen." Joe hoped he was getting through.

The door from the main dining hall on the other side of the wait station swung open at a fixed speed, demanding attention. Valerie joined the duo with a controlled, calm demeanor that spoke volumes about her character. "What's all this standing around for? There's work to be done. We don't pay you guys to lounge about all day and chitchat. And Joe, I better not catch you drinking another soda. If I do, I'll have to write you up. You're well aware that sodas are for members only."

"Hello, Valerie." A rich, suave tone emanated from Joe. "I'm doing well. Thanks for asking. I appreciate the concern. How are things with you?"

Valerie grinned. "I'm good, smartass."

Joe stepped closer to Valerie. "So, have you given any thought to what I said?"

Valerie cast a suspicious glare his way. "And what might that be, Joe?"

Joe smiled. "Don't act like you don't remember. You said you've been stressed out these days, and I suggested you get yourself a nice, just-got-done graduating, eighteen-year-old man to help relieve that stress. And my God! Here I am! Stress can be incredibly unhealthy if you allow it to fester. It builds up and makes life very difficult. So it's good to have someone to help with that kind of thing aiding in, you know, relieving said stress."

Jared tried not to laugh as he noted the overt flirtations between the two and shifted his eyes to Valerie. She was thirty years old. The woman had only come to Brightwood because she had been highly recommended to Old Merdith by a previous employer. The food service/hospitality industry was nothing new to Valerie. She handled that aspect of the country club with vulpine ingenuity.

Valerie was a captivating woman with an allure that spoke of a maturity that seemed far more significant than the thirty years she admitted to being. As Jared looked at her, he couldn't shake the feeling that there was something quite magical about the woman that intrigued his deepest desires. Her smile could talk you into just about anything if you let it, and her body language hinted at an overpowering seductiveness that lay dormant. In many respects, the woman seemed to be the very essence of graceful beauty.

"You need to get a life, Joe. And you better watch what you say to me. You might catch me when I'm not in a good mood, and the consequences would be unkind." Her tone was serious.

"Valerie, I'm telling you it's impossible not to be in a good mood around me." Joe threw another smile her way.

"Watch yourself." She poked his chest. "Jared, did Mr. Drake tell you Arturo is out sick today?"

Jared nodded. "Yes, he did. I was just about to get the expediting station set up."

"Good. And after that, make sure you go on break. I always find out you didn't take one, and you better punch out this time when you do. I know how much you guys like to milk the clock." She turned to Joe. "I almost forgot. There's been a change in the floor plan. I want you in the formal dining room for tonight instead of the main hall. We're short a waiter there, and Merdith will be able to handle the main hall just fine with one less waiter."

"Anything that will get me closer to you consider it done. All you have to do is say the word." Joe winked and smiled.

"Then how about you try acting like a professional young man tonight instead of a horny old one?" And with those words, Valerie exited the wait station using the door that led into the hallway.

"Damn, I'd just love to have one night...." Joe finished the sentence in his head.

Jared couldn't believe his friend. "You can't be serious. She's our boss, and she's older than us."

"That's part of it, man. Older women are hot." Joe reached for his soda hidden behind the plates on the shelf finishing it. He crushed the can between his hands and tossed it in a garbage receptacle beneath the countertop. "I'll catch up with you in the break room, and since you're not doing anything tonight, you're coming out with the guys and me." Joe's voice trailed off as he walked away.

Jared turned to the coffee maker as Joe left and looked at the contraption like a father ashamed of a disappointing son. Then, he glanced back to the schedule and studied Sara's name. Jared stared at the printed text as if it were the most beautiful picture of her ever taken. Then, after a few heartbeats of wanting, he sighed and made his way into the kitchen to set up the expediting station. Mr. Drake's orders had to be done, and besides, he didn't want to be called buckaroo again tonight if he could help it.

PART THREE:

TIP OF THE ICEBERG AT THE END OF THE DAY

"Timelines exist where I never became a Time Bender. They are places where I only exist as Jared Hernandez. They are hidden from me. I can't see them. They are the only realities out there that will always remain a mystery. I hold on to that whenever it feels like I know too much about what will come. It is a reminder that even I can't see everything." – Vestor, the Time Bender.

1

"SHE LIKES YOU, Jared. There's no denying it." Joe locked the driver's side door of his mother's black Dodge Stratus. He jogged a few steps to catch up to Jared, who was already several paces ahead of him in the employee parking lot.

"Don't get me wrong, Veronica is cute, but she just isn't my type; then there's the fact that she's Memo's little sister, which makes me really uncomfortable. Memo is a huge guy. I don't want to hurt her and have him kick my ass because of it. He's like the Mexican Thor." Jared considered.

Joe matched Jared's pace after a few quick steps, and the two strolled across the sea of black pavement to Brightwood's employee entrance.

"What the hell is wrong with you?" Joe asked.

"Nothing." Jared shot back.

"Veronica was all over you last night, and you, my friend, are passing up a golden opportunity. Besides, Memo is cool with you; he actually likes you. It's my ass he'd kick if I ever messed around with his little sister - and if anyone asks, I never have. If you'd have stayed by J.C.'s last night, I guarantee she'd have done all sorts of things your sexually deprived ass needs." Joe winked at his friend.

Jared rolled his eyes. "I'm not about *that*, Joe. Not just for the sake of it."

"That's fuckin' weird. Skipping on an ass like that – are you gay?" Joe smirked. "Totally cool if you are, but I must disappoint you and let you know I'm unavailable. I'm a ladies' man."

Jared shook his head while letting out a chuckle. "Shut up, Joe. And if Memo heard you talk about his little sister like that, he would definitely kick your ass." A thought crossed Jared's mind. "Do me a favor right now and be completely honest with me. Have you ever messed around with Veronica?"

Joe's poker face was on. "The official answer is no."

"Unofficially?" Jared pressed.

"It's a definite possibility. But that was a long time ago." Joe grinned.

Jared smirked. "You're something else."

Joe abruptly stopped after a few long paces of shared silence; a sudden realization dawned upon him. "Wait a minute...." He looked Jared in the eye as he stepped closer. "This whole thing here isn't about Sara, is it? I'd be disappointed if that happened to be the case."

A faux innocence washed over Jared. "I don't know what you're talking about."

"Don't give me that bullshit. You're deflecting. This is about her, isn't it? Man, I thought you'd be over that nonsense by now!" Joe cast his friend a disapproving glare.

"I am over it." Jared insisted.

Joe gave Jared an intense stare. "Are you really?"

"Yes. Of course, I am. Maybe I am. Well, I could be a little bit. No. Not really. I'm not at all. I'm not over how I feel, no." Jared hunched his shoulders while looking at the black pavement, ashamed. The words spewed from his mouth so quickly that he couldn't help but feel idiotic.

Joe placed a supportive hand on Jared's shoulder. "Then tell her how you feel. This hiding in the shadows waiting for the perfect moment shit has got to stop. And to be perfectly honest, it's kind of creepy. Not the type of signal you want to send her way."

"I tried telling her once, Joe, but she wasn't interested in me like that. It's no secret how I feel about her either." The self-doubt and frustration were eating away at Jared.

Joe crossed his arms. "So, let me get this straight. You told her how you felt, the bitch shot you down, and you're still hooked on her? Your ass needs to move on."

More frustration bubbled up in Jared. "First of all, she isn't a bitch, and I just can't move on like that. Second, I... Jesus, Joe, I can't explain it! When I'm with her, things just feel right."

Joe leaned in. "Are you in love with her? Is that what you're saying?"

Jared remained silent, knowing no matter how he answered the question, Joe's reaction would be less than satisfactory.

"Oh Lord, here we go!" Joe threw his arms up and shook his head as he turned away from Jared.

"You're one to talk! You're still all screwed up because of Ana!" Jared spat out with a defensive posture.

Joe spun back around to face Jared. "Wait a minute. This Shit isn't about Ana and me. That's a different situation altogether. I have a reason for how I feel about her because I went out with her for two years. You, on the other hand... You never even kissed Sara, let alone had a real relationship with her."

Jared averted his gaze from Joe with a hurt expression and began walking to the country club's rear entrance. He mentally checked his anger as he gained control over his emotions.

"Shit. Jared! Hold on, man!" Joe leaped in front of his friend. "I didn't mean that. You know that, right? I was just talking stupid, alright?"

Jared maneuvered around Joe. "No, you're right. I'm fucking pathetic. I have to realize that and just move on."

Joe frowned. "I didn't say that."

"You didn't have to. It's just the way it is. You know it. Everyone else knows it, but I can't seem to get it through my thick skull!" Jared tapped his own forehead aggressively.

"Will you stop?!" With a gentle force, Joe grabbed Jared's arm and drew him back. "If it's that important to you, talk to her again." He hesitated for a brief moment before continuing. "And I didn't mean to flip out on you earlier. You're my best friend, and I want to look out for you. Now let's get going. We don't want to be late again."

Jared took the words to heart and nodded. He then looked at his wristwatch out of habit whenever the time was mentioned. "Too late."

"Shit! It's five-thirty already?" Joe sprinted for the rear entrance creating a large gap for Jared to close.

Jared struggled to catch up, yelling with each step. "Why do you always have to run like that?!"

"The truth of the matter is, I wanted to die. At the time, I felt that I had lived too long. I was ready to fade into nothingness, let my powers dwindle, and allow the full transformation into being human. But then Jared happened, and with Jared came Vestor." – Aglaia (former Grace – known as Valerie at the time of Vestor)

2

THE DUO ENTERED the main dining hall making the least amount of noise possible, and much to their dismay, the preshift meeting was already in progress. Jared and Joe tiptoed through a small maze of round sixty-inch tables that still had to be arranged; after the meeting, the proper placement and décor of the tables for that evening's festivities would be taken care of with a swift hand.

Old Merdith stood before the group vibrating like a human tuning fork. Her old age gave her a hunched back and caused her to shake while holding still; her formal business clothing was a bit on the baggy side as it draped atop her frail figure. Jared and Joe approached from the rear keeping their eyes on the old woman while pulling chairs up to the sixty-inch table where Carl was seated.

Jared looked at the table beside them and saw Sara sitting with Ana, Rachel, and Nicole. He observed Sara as she removed a piece of gum from a wrapper and placed it in her mouth in an oddly arousing way. Jared couldn't help but see the beauty and sensual allure in the most straightforward tasks Sara carried out. But, of course, he also didn't know if he imagined it or if she did some of those things on purpose.

God, I really am pathetic! Jared thought, aware of his fixation.

"Got an extra floor plan handy?" Joe asked Carl.

Carl slid one over to Joe and addressed Jared. "It looks like we have the same section tonight."

"What?" Jared snapped back into the moment, letting thoughts of Sara go.

"We have the same section," Carl repeated.

"Cool," Jared responded to Carl and raised a curious eyebrow at Joe, sensing the fixed stare he was being given. "What is it, Joe?"

"I was just wondering if you were thinking about popping a question or two her way tonight. I can assist if need be." Joe nodded his head toward Sara.

Carl eyed the two, despising that no one ever kept him in the loop. His voice was eager for information. "Her? Who's she? What are you guys talking about? What question?"

"It's nothing, Carl." Jared barked while keeping his eyes on Joe. "I don't think it'd be a good idea to do that tonight."

"I think it'd be a fantastic idea. There's no time like the present." Joe smiled.

"What the hell are you guys talking about?" Carl's look grew more intense as they continued to ignore him.

"It's nothing, Carl." Joe kept his eyes on Jared. "If you don't do it, I will. I'm tired of you being screwed up over her all the damn time. You know how I do it, bro, and I won't *hesitate* to point things in that direction."

Fear hit Jared. "Don't do it. I'd look even more desperate if you did."

"All the more reason why you should be talking to her instead of me. I'm forcing my hand on this one. It's for your own damn good. And don't doubt me because you know I'll do it. I'll *fuckin'* do it." Joe's glare was somewhat deranged.

"Do what?" The loudness of Carl's voice was drawing attention from the employees nearest.

"Don't worry about it, Carl!" Joe didn't even bother to look at Carl this time and kept his eyes locked on Jared.

"What the fuck are you guys going on about?!" Carl's frustrated gaze demanded a response from the two, but Joe and Jared continued to stare each other down like gunslingers from the Wild West. They finished their conversation with facial expressions as Joe nudged his head in Sara's direction, and Jared shook his head adamantly from side to side.

"Excuse me!" Old Merdith's chipper, aged voice chimed in. "Joseph and Jared, I think both of you ought to show a little more respect after already coming in late to this meeting. You should both pay attention to what's being explained. It's not nice to speak while I'm trying to inform everyone here of tonight's events and go over the menu."

"Sorry, Merdith. It won't happen again." Of course, Jared was always the first to apologize.

"Oh, and Jared, there's been a change with the floor plan. Instead of being paired up with Carl, I will move you with Sara. Nicole can go with Carl. It's just that there will be a lot of trays to carry, and I don't want Sara straining herself trying to take them back to the dishwasher on her own." Merdith's wrinkled face smiled in approval of her decision.

"Not a problem." Jared moved his focus to Sara, who was already looking at him. A half-smile was sent his way.

Carl reached for Jared's head, and the sudden forceful turn took him away from Sara's inviting smile and to Carl's demanding glare. "What the hell is going on? What the hell were you guys talking about?"

"We were powerful. We were gods! Then the Distinction of Realms was enacted, and we were reduced to nothing. The energy these humans provided with worship was a treasure unlike anything, and to lose that direct line was devastating. Many blended with the mortal world only to die like pitiful humans. Others adapted, using their powers to reshape what we can do and who we are. Deep down inside, I will always be a Fury no matter the mask I wear to the mortal world." – Alecto (former Fury – known as Renee Dempsy at the time of Vestor)

3

THE MAJORITY OF the members that belonged to the club flooded the formal dining room; it was a standard turnout for the evening shift. Every table was seated to capacity. Members enjoyed the high-class meals expertly prepared by the culinary masters slaving away in the kitchen. The wait staff zoomed through the maze of tables taking food and drink orders; they carried out this task while accommodating every member and guest with specific individual care.

Jared poured a cup of ice-cold water into a glass for Mrs. Renee Dempsy. As of late, she happened to be a member he spoke to frequently. He poured the water from the metal pitcher and observed her features. Jared recognized the woman's beauty despite the age she claimed to be. She somehow radiated a timeless form similar to Valerie, although Valerie was far more attractive. Renee's golden blonde hair shone brightly in unison with her bright blue eyes. In addition, she wore just the right amount of makeup that enhanced her best facial features and adorned an elegant dress molded to a healthy physique.

Mr. Dempsy, on the other hand, was an obese blob of a man. Jared often failed to figure out why on earth she had chosen to marry such a poor male specimen. He could only guess it was for the money; it was the only logical conclusion Jared could reason out. Yet, deep down, Jared knew that Renee Dempsy deserved better than the grotesque semblance of a man that displayed her as a trophy.

"How are you doing tonight, Jared?" She asked as he placed her cup on the table on the right side of her plate.

"I'm doing well, Mrs. Dempsy. Thank you for asking." Jared responded.

"Did you have your graduation yet? You and most of the other young staff here are preparing to embark upon the *real* world, as the cliché graduation saying goes." She sipped her water.

"Very true, Mrs. Dempsy. And to answer your question, yes, I'm officially a graduate." Jared smiled, not realizing how proud that statement would make him feel.

"Any thoughts on where you'll end up going to college? I know you've discussed a few possibilities, but have you decided yet?" Renee's finger circled the brim of her glass.

"To be perfectly honest, I'm not quite sure. I've been accepted to a few excellent schools, but nothing *feels* right." Jared finally admitted.

Renee was more than intrigued by the young man and leaned closer. "Do go on. What doesn't *feel* right, as you put it?"

He stood tall, bracing for his own explanation. "It's like I'm waiting for something. I'm not sure what it is yet, and I'm not even sure how long I'll have to wait, but that *feeling* is there. Maybe it just comes down to me being too picky, or maybe the future scares me more than I'm willing to admit. God only knows where I'll end up when it's all said and done."

Mrs. Dempsy gave Jared a curious expression. "*God?* Now that's a topic you've never brought up before."

Jared's skin flushed with embarrassment. "It was just a figure of speech, Mrs. Dempsy. I meant no offense by it."

"It's quite alright, Jared. Do you consider yourself to be a religious young man? Do you believe?" She leaned even closer, revealing some ample bosom.

The question threw Jared off, and he stood unsure. Finally, after a few heartbeats, he cleared his throat and figured that the honest approach was best. "There's what I was raised to believe, and parts of it sound good, but

I'm not sure if I can accept it. People have warped it to fit personal agendas, and any disagreement or questioning makes you an outcast. I never accepted things as they are because someone said so – not when it comes to something like what I believe. How you view things and what you believe needs to be figured out in your own way and in your own time."

"What about the idea of God? Do you believe in God, given that you're clearly at odds with the institution created in His name?" She cast a playful smile his way before sipping her water. This particular topic delighted the woman. The smile remained, reflecting the thoughts flowing through her mind. *Soon, very soon, you'll discover the nature of things. You'll find out just how powerful beliefs can be.*

Jared considered. "I'd like to, but some days are better for that than others."

"Faith can be tricky. It's difficult to believe in things outside of you. People often forget the power that belief in what is inside oneself can yield. We aren't always what we're led to believe we are. Sometimes we are so much... *more*. What lies within you is far more potent and powerful than you might think. I'll be sure to keep a very close eye on you. Something tells me you'll be exceptional in the times ahead." Renee's eyes hinted at a truth Jared couldn't yet see.

"I'm not sure how special I will be, but thank you." Jared gave Renee a polite nod as she turned back to the table and feigned interest in the story that Mr. Dempsy was in the midst of telling.

"I arrived in the human world well before my sisters. I was a rogue spirit cast away from Olympus. Ate was and is my true name, but I inhabited a human vessel to interact with the human realm. I felt the world as a human did, and it was initially difficult to deal with their web of emotions. Those emotions are tied to so much of what it means to be human." – Ate (goddess of mischief and blind folly)

4

WITH NO ONE to serve, Jared found his way back to the tray stand, bringing his shoulder blades together for a slight stretch; Sara stood watch over their particular section. He observed her as he placed the pitcher on the stand at odds with his emotions. He focused on the possibilities of what could be rather than the reality of his work. Jared's lack of attention resulted in the pitcher tipping over the tray stand; consequently, his physical blunder allowed water to spill over the tray in every direction. He jumped back with a less-than-masculine grunt as the ice-cold liquid made contact soaking deep into his left pant leg.

"Are you okay?" Sara's eyes locked on Jared as her vigilance over the tables was interrupted by his clumsiness.

"I'm fine; it was just a little spill. I'm going to clean this off real quick. I'll be right back." He muttered the words like a child.

"Okay." She gave him a nod and went back to focusing on their section.

Jared entered the smaller wait station of the formal dining room with a gait that reeked of embarrassment. A commercial refrigerator was the only significant piece of equipment to reside in this secondary wait station. All along the walls near it were cups and plates lined up on shelves above a smaller sink. He grabbed a nearby white rag from a neatly folded stack and dabbed at the water on his pant leg. Luckily the water blended in with the darkness of his slacks.

Joe pushed the swinging door open and stepped through, walking about in full work mode. He grabbed a tall cylinder glass and collected ice with a plastic scoop, stopping the ice near the brim. "So, have you talked to Sara yet?" He removed a pitcher of iced tea from the refrigerator and poured it into the glass.

Jared shook his head. "Not yet."

Joe rolled his eyes in disappointment. "You'll feel better once it's out in the open. Trust me on that."

Jared stepped forward, almost pleading. "I was thinking of waiting until we got to the parking lot. It might be easier to do it there. We always hang out there for a while after a shift anyway, so why not? That makes sense, right?"

"Just remember that the longer you put it off, the worse you'll feel, and it'll be much more fun for me." With those words, Joe placed the glass of iced tea on a tray, gave Jared an evil genius glare, and reentered the formal dining room.

An anxiety-riddled sigh accompanied Jared as he exited the wait station. In no time, he was standing next to Sara. The woman stood in a statuesque pose observing all the members as they dined.

"That dried fast." She remarked while glancing at his pants.

"I rubbed it hard for a few seconds and was done." The minute the words left his mouth, Jared regretted speaking them. He could tell she was trying her best not to laugh. Jared opened his mouth to explain more but stopped as Sara lifted her hand.

"It's okay, Jared." She smiled. "I know what you meant. It just sounded funny, that's all."

A flash of heat and an embarrassing redness conquered Jared's expression. "I really have to think before I speak sometimes. Things don't always sound the way I want them to."

Awkward silence between the two and the consistent background hum of conversation controlled an eternity of tense moments. Finally, the torture of that silence reached a boiling point forcing Jared to continue speaking. "Did you do anything fun last night?"

Sara kept her gaze on the tables like a patient predator waiting for the perfect moment to strike. "I spent time with Nicole and Rachel for most of the night. I guess that's why I'm feeling kind of tired today. We were up pretty late."

"What did you guys do?" Jared asked, wishing he had something more clever to say.

She thought about it. "We started off the night by Rachel's house. Her parents are pretty easygoing. They let her do whatever she wants, and by default, we get to do whatever we want."

"Your parents are the same from what you've told me," Jared noted.

Sara smirked, holding in a slight chuckle. "You're right; they are. They let us do our own thing. I guess it's how they view the whole growing up thing." Another grin formed.

"My parents need to know what I'm doing all the time. Feels like I never get a chance to breathe." He recalled his father Andres clearing his throat while lecturing about responsibility. His mother, Maria, stood behind him, adamantly agreeing with the pointing of a stern finger. Finally, he snapped out of it and looked at Sara. "Sorry about that. I didn't mean to interrupt. You were talking about last night."

"We were hanging out at Rachel's, then Scott stopped by. It was kind of fun. The unexpected fun is always the best kind." Sara's smile grew mischievous.

Jared attempted to keep his face as expressionless as possible. "Scott? Really? I haven't heard you talk about him for a while." The imagery of Scott and Sara together burned at Jared to the core.

"He's got the greatest smile. I know he's really into me when he looks at me. I'm a sucker for being worshiped like that, I guess." She stood picturing the naïve adoration of Scott.

The anger flashing through Jared's mind could never have been read on his face as he took her words in stride. "It was a fun night, then?"

She nodded. "Some of his friends stopped by later. They managed to get some beer, so that was nice. We laughed, we drank, and we danced. I know this will sound completely insane, but each drink was like a promise of being there. Does that make sense? I really hope that makes sense to you."

Jared nodded, not truly understanding.

Sara continued. "The more out of control we got, the more 'one' we all were, and the more appreciated we felt. There's a kind of power there that people have forgotten about. I probably shouldn't be saying any of this to you - I know how ridiculous it sounds." She laughed aloud, appearing far older than she looked for the briefest moment. "I bet it sounds crazy as hell. Words can't properly describe what I'm trying to convey. You just have to experience it. Maybe one day we could have that kind of fun, Jared. I think I'd like that very much."

"I think I'd like that too." Jared grew mesmerized by Sara's presence. Her words' unusual nature went unnoticed as his desire for her blinded him to how she acted. For a split second, that desire became insatiable, and he wished only to please her at all costs. A strange euphoria erupted within the deepest recesses of his mind and frightened his logical sensibilities.

At that moment, a voice seemed to flash within his mind. The voice belonged to Jared, but the tone was older and distant as it spoke within his consciousness. *Be strong, Jared. Focus. The time of change will be soon.*

A member waved a hand in their direction, wanting one of the two to move to their table.

"Duty calls." Sara stepped into action, not allowing Jared to say anything else.

"I'll be right here." Jared faked a smile and felt a bit shaken and confused by Sara's words. The farther away she was, the more the words rang as a warning. He wasn't exactly sure what she had meant by having "that" kind of fun, but his mind took another turn and ran with all the possibilities. The racy activities that could have transpired flew through his mind. Once again, the imagery of Sara and Scott made him insanely jealous.

They had fun. What the hell did they do?

As he stood pondering over his hatred for Scott and his love for Sara, Old Merdith wobbled near his side. "What are you doing standing around? Go clear some tables and get rid of some of those trays. They're starting to pile up, and we can't have that. Go. Hurry!"

Jared stepped into action as the old hag barked out her commands. While moving toward a tray, he noticed a fork gleaming from the corner of his eye on the elaborately designed carpet. As Jared bent down to pick it up, he felt a sudden tear with the appropriate sound accompanying the sensation. His posture darted vertically, and he kept his back to the closest wall, feeling his pants with discretion. The ripped fabric ran along his rear and between his legs.

"Vestor has been and always will be a tool with a purpose. You see, sometimes defeat is a true victory in disguise. After all, it depends on how you use the tools at your disposal." – Develin, the Demon Wizard.

5

THIS IS JUST GREAT, Jared screamed in his mind as he inched along the wall and into the secondary wait station. Once inside, he seized a small tray with frantic hands to cover up his bottom where the tear was visible.

Valerie sauntered into the wait station, focused on her work, and grew curious about Jared's awkward posture. "Jared? What are you doing? You shouldn't be standing around like this. You're needed on the floor clearing off tables. If Merdith finds you in here, she'll be quite upset."

"Valerie. I didn't know you were working tonight." Nervousness saturated his tone.

"I'm catching up on some paperwork I've put off for longer than Mr. Drake would like, but I'm more concerned about you. Are you feeling well? You seem more than a little out of sorts at the moment." She looked him over with motherly concern.

"Um... I'm not really doing so great right now." The embarrassment manifested as his face glowed with a flash of heated redness.

"What's the matter?" She asked.

"You see my pants... They kind of ripped, and it's not the best spot to have a tear." He confessed his distress a split second before Sara joined them in the wait station.

"There you are – wait... What did you say? Your pants ripped?" Sara's amusement was accented by a slight smirk.

"Oh, Jared, that's not good." Valerie shook her head with pity.

The spectrum of redness upon Jared's face shifted to the darker end as Sara's uncontrolled laughter slipped out at his misfortune.

Joe burst through the wait station a second later; the door swung open, giving him a dramatic entrance, and he wiped his forehead from the obstacle course familiar to waiters in a busy restaurant. He set down his tray with a relaxing exhale, and his eyes went to Valerie. He smiled as he spoke: "Valerie, the thought of not being near me tore at your heart, and you couldn't stand to be away from me, right? I just want you to know that it touches me in so many ways to know that."

"Knock it off, Joe," Valerie warned in full manager mode.

Joe smirked and soon recognized the awkwardness that filled the wait station. "So, what's going on? Why do you have a tray on your ass, Jared?"

"His pants ripped." A few more giggles escaped Sara's mouth.

A boisterous laugh emerged from Joe as he swung his head back; the laughter abated as he caught the glare given to him by Jared. He fought off laughter as he spoke, "I'm sorry, man. That really sucks."

Sara cleared her throat and gestured to Joe to leave the wait station with a fast motion of the hands pointing toward the door. Upon their exit, Old Merdith wobbled her way in with her old eyes explicitly set on Jared. She appeared happily disappointed when she found him standing before Valerie.

"Hello, Merdith." Valerie chimed in before the old woman could speak.

The waviness of Merdith's frail voice filled the room. "Hello, Valerie. I didn't know you were working tonight."

Valerie turned on the professional charm. "I'm just catching up on a few things while I have the chance."

Old Merdith turned her attention to Jared, determined to stay focused on reprimanding his lack of being on the floor. Her voice wavered like an audible manifestation of the way her body shook. "Jared, I thought I told you to return those trays to the dishwashers. They're really starting to pile up out there. What are you doing hiding in here?"

"I do apologize, Merdith." Valerie stepped in. "I'm afraid that's my fault. I need to discuss something with Jared that's rather important. Joe's going to pick up the slack, though. So just go ahead and remind him for me."

"Oh. Okay then. As long as somebody gets out there to deal with the mess. I mean, that's what I care about. We can't have the guests surrounded by dirty plates." Old Merdith wobbled back into the formal dining room, leaving Valerie and Jared in peace.

"Come with me, Jared." Valerie gestured.

"Where are we going?" The confusion of oblivious youth filled the question.

"Upstairs," Valerie answered, leading the way.

"Valerie always spoke of her time at the country club with fondness. Aglaia, as I later called her, had a special place in her heart for those moments. Maybe it was because she had resigned herself to the idea that she would let go of her powers and become completely mortal. It made the experience finite and fragile." – Matthew Gomez, the Forever Man.

6

JARED MAINTAINED A brisk pace while keeping the food tray on his backside. He and Valerie entered the hall from the wait station and ventured to the rear dining room. After two flights of stairs, they were alone on the second level. While walking behind Valerie, Jared took note of her shapely posterior, as would any young man with a pulse. His eyes became somewhat hypnotized as the walk led to a switch of the hips that enticed his male lust. He felt a sudden attraction to Valerie that had not been there before this particular encounter, and he finally understood why Joe found the woman so alluring.

"Jared!" Valerie's strong tone ripped him from his arousing fantasy. "Do you think you can focus your eyes on a higher level?"

"Yes. Sorry. I was just... Sorry." Jared blushed as he continued to follow.

Valerie's office door was already open, and she led Jared to sit on a chair near her desk. She moved to a portable coat rack with a wise elegance; the coat rack was filled with uniforms that had been dormant for years. She began to sift through them, searching for the perfect pair of work pants that would fit Jared and match his vest.

"Now, there has to be a pair of black slacks that will fit you. What's your size again?" She asked; her eyes remained on the clothing.

"It's thirty for the waist and thirty-two for the length." Jared's eyes wandered to Valerie's desk, studying the layout of her office. While taking note of the usual knickknacks associated with work desks, he also observed a very endearing picture. From his vantage, he could make out Valerie entangled in a passionate kiss with a man. Both she and the man in the photograph exuded the type of happiness most only dreamt about.

The sound of the wire hanger sliding across the clothing rack's metal bar forced Jared to look in Valerie's direction. As he looked up, a pair of black slacks was already in mid-flight across her office, and he reflexively caught them with his left hand.

"Take your pants off and put those on." Valerie soon noted that Jared was giving her an uncomfortable stare. "Not in here, Jared!" She spoke her following words with regained composure. "There's a bathroom around the corner on the way to my office."

"Right... um... I'll be right back." Jared marched off to do as instructed and found the bathroom. He stepped in, closed the bathroom door behind him, and kicked off his shoes. The ripped pair of slacks slid off easily, and Jared put on the new pants while looking in the mirror; the fit was perfect. After placing his shoes back on, he exited the bathroom and reentered Valerie's office.

She now sat behind her desk, staring at the photograph Jared had noticed; there was a longing in her eyes. "How do they fit?" She asked without taking her eyes off the picture.

"Perfect." He answered.

"Good." She smiled with approval.

Jared took a timid step forward. "Who is he? If you don't mind my asking, that is. I noticed the picture earlier; it's a nice one."

She shot a curious glance in his direction, surprised that he had asked. Valerie stood from behind the desk and circled around the front. She sat down on the smooth desk surface with casual elegance, reached for the picture at her side, and remembered the past lovingly.

"Forget I asked. It's really none of my business." Jared turned from his boss, ready to get back to work.

"It's okay." She waited until he turned back to face her before continuing. "The man in the picture is my ex-fiancé. It's been a very long time since I've seen him - too long, in fact. I don't know why I keep this picture around, to be perfectly honest. It was just a kiss, but it was a perfect one. Somehow, we managed to capture it for all time. It's difficult to let something like that go."

"What happened to him?" He asked.

Her smile faded. "He died."

"I'm sorry." Jared wanted to say more but was at a loss for words.

She dismissed it with a gesture. "It's okay, Jared. It was a long time ago. I regret things couldn't work out for us before he passed away."

"Why didn't they?" His curiosity was genuine.

She considered her words carefully before speaking. "Various beliefs conflicted beyond the point of reconciliation. The two of us were extremely passionate about what we were doing then. Both of us were headed in different directions, and we felt that what needed to be done simply needed to be done. There's no fighting the conviction granted by the truth of a moment. But, ultimately, he died doing what he loved, and that's more than what most people can leave this world with."

Jared stood for a moment taking her words to heart.

"May I offer a bit of advice?" She gave him a knowing expression.

Jared nodded.

The seriousness of her tone was like an arrow to Jared's chest. "Tread carefully with Sara."

Confusion and embarrassment filled the youth's face. "What? How did you know about that?"

Valerie rolled her eyes. "Everybody knows. She might not be what you think she is. I've had a feeling that something might be different about her and not in a way that would make you happy. So perhaps it'd be best to just let this one go."

"I'll think about it." He reflexively threw the phrase out. He knew his feelings ran deep and that it wasn't that simple.

"Make sure that you do." She shooed him away. "Get back to work. Go be productive."

Jared nodded again, expressing his thanks with a quick smile before exiting Valerie's office.

"Cause and effect. It is the most fundamental law on either side of the Distinction. We act, and there are consequences. More often than not, the cost of actions isn't realized until the deed is done. Most of the time, we're ignorant of the gravity of the effect we leave in our wake. It is a powerful thing humankind takes for granted – this ability to choose and act, imparting your will into the universe. And they wonder why the world is the way it is! Bloody fools! The whole lot of 'em!" – Minx (centuries-old vampire – a supporter of the Forever Man)

7

THE NIGHT SKY blanketed the ragtag group of young employees in the Brightwood Country Club parking lot; they gathered around the black Dodge Stratus that Joe had been allowed to drive. Rachel, Nicole, Ana, Carl, Joe, and Jared were present. Sara, however, was nowhere to be seen. Other employee cars scattered about the primarily vacant lot. Still, the youthful group seemed to congregate around Joe's vehicle after an exhausting shift.

"Cheers!" Joe held a bottle of vodka obtained moments before from the trunk of his car. He was proud to have procured it. With a confident smile, Joe untwisted the cap and began drinking. He allowed himself a quick shake as the effects of the alcohol surged throughout his entire body. The aggressive warmness of the liquid was incredibly overwhelming.

"How is it that you can drink that shit like water?" Carl took the bottle from Joe's offering hand and squinted like a child upon feeling the strength of the vodka moments after sipping.

"It's called tolerance. I've been drinking since I was born. I popped out, and the first word that came out of my mouth was 'screwdriver.' Now that would be good right now. Too bad we don't have any orange juice." Joe considered.

Carl chuckled while rolling his eyes.

"Don't you guys ever tire of drinking vodka whenever we hang out? There are other options. Just making a social observation." Nicole whined the words while lying on top of the hood of Joe's car. She was a short gal, cute in her own way, with shoulder-length brown hair and eyes to match.

"Sorry it's not to your liking, but it's the only thing I can ever manage to get my hands on. What's it to you anyway? It's not like you ever have any." Joe dismissed little Nicole with a wave and refocused on the drinking.

Rachel stood over Nicole, leaning on the car with Ana. The two young women could have passed for sisters, with Ana as the blonde and Rachel as the redhead. Anna stared lovingly at Joe while Rachel gave Jared the evil eye.

Carl and Joe stood near the door on the driver's side, resting their bodies on the vehicle. They studied Jared; both were bothered by his downtrodden demeanor. He sat a few feet away on the pavement staring at Sara's dark green sedan.

"What the hell are you doing over there, Jared? Did you rip your pants again?" Joe laughed as Carl took another swig of vodka.

"My pants are fine, Joe. Thanks for asking... jackass." Jared didn't bother to turn around.

"It's true; you're a jackass. He's got you there." Carl smirked.

"How about you come and join us?" Joe called out, dismissing Carl's comment.

Jared fought against gravity to lift his body from the pavement while turning to face his companions. He trudged the distance to the car as if his feet were bound in shackles. Jared took hold of the vodka bottle in Carl's hand with a burst of powerful energy and took a long hard swig. The drink was strong, and he still couldn't figure out if he liked the idea of drinking. He did, however, enjoy the warmth that spread.

"Now that's what I'm talking about!" Joe retrieved the bottle from Jared's hand. "I take it you didn't end up having that talk with her yet?"

"You know for a fact it didn't happen. Ripping my pants kind of ruined the mood." Jared admitted.

"Why put yourself through all of this, Jared?" Rachel twirled her long red hair while chewing on some gum. "I know how much you like her, but maybe she isn't worth all the trouble. Maybe it's time for you to focus on something else or someone else? You don't want to mix things up at work, either. That's just a bad idea."

Ana nudged Rachel with her elbow, annoyed that her coworker would make such a comment. It was no secret that Ana and Joe had been together for nearly two years; their romantic bond began at Brightwood. When things failed to remain copacetic, the working relationship became awkward. Ana was confident that the problematic aspects of being friends after being intimate as lovers were mostly over. However, old feelings did creep through the cracks of the platonic shield they both struggled to maintain.

"Come on, Ana - don't get like that. You know what I mean." Rachel smiled at her friend with innocence.

"Rachel does have a point, though." Little Nicole was still lying on the hood of the car. She studied the small number of visible stars, mentally playing a game of peekaboo as dark clouds floated through the atmosphere covering and uncovering them. "And Joe feels the same way as Rachel. Isn't that right, Joe?"

"It's no secret how I feel, but Jared has to work this out. But I'm backing whatever he decides." Joe nodded to his friend.

Joe's sense of loyalty struck Ana deeply, and she couldn't help but allow her gaze to stay fixed upon him. A slow smile formed at the corner of Ana's lips as she noticed Joe looking at her in return. He winked at Ana from where he stood, and the two shared a silent moment of affection. The on-again-off-again nature of their relationship was difficult to understand by outsiders. Still, it made sense to them because it was what they knew.

So much for the idea that the hard parts are mostly over, Ana thought.

"Wait a minute, is that what all of this is about? Jared, you like Sara?" Carl put together the conversations from earlier and the events of the day. "So that's what you guys were talking about during the meeting! Why couldn't you just tell me that in the first place?! I've been wondering what the hell was going on all night long!"

"Of course he likes Sara, Carl! Do we have to spell everything out for you? Everybody knows." Joe took another swig from the bottle.

"She has to come out here sooner or later, and when she does, I'll say what I need to say. Whatever happens after that can happen however it's supposed to." Jared took a few steps from the group and sat on the black pavement.

"Well, guys, I have to run, but I'll see you all tomorrow." Rachel studied Jared briefly and betrayed her true feelings with a microexpression of anger. The look vanished before it could be noticed. "Try to stay positive, okay, Jared? Hopefully, things will get better."

"Thanks." Jared appreciated the sentiment.

Move on from her, you pathetic little human! You'll only make things more complicated! Let my sister be so we can do as we must! Rachel's thoughts echoed as she headed to her car, parked a few spots away. "Are you coming with me, Nicole?"

"Of course. Wait a sec." Little Nicole answered quickly.

"What about you, Ana?" Rachel turned to her.

"I think I'll stick around." Ana smiled, keeping her eyes on Joe while responding to Rachel's question.

With a cute sluggishness, little Nicole jumped from the hood of the Dodge. "See ya guys later." She spat out the words while rushing to catch up with Rachel, who was already starting her vehicle. The car drove off as soon as Nicole entered the passenger's side.

Joe impulsively took the empty vodka bottle and tossed it across the parking lot. An amused group laugh was shared at his childishness, and those that remained moved to sit near Jared, forming a small circle. Killing time in the parking lot was a beloved experience. But, when it was all said and done, they had nowhere else to go, and they didn't precisely desire to head back to the realities of home life.

Joe rested his head on Ana's lap, and she brushed her gentle fingers through his jet-black hair. He yawned as the sensation soothed him to the core and brought the kind of smile to Joe's face that only Ana could extract.

"I'm getting pretty tired, guys. My ass needs to get home and get some sleep." Joe yawned after finishing the sentence.

"Me too," Ana added a yawn.

"I'll take ya home." Joe sat up and helped Ana to her feet. "You're coming too, Jared. I brought you here, and I won't leave you alone." Joe opened the passenger side door for Ana and closed it after she was comfortably seated. He looked to Jared, waiting for him to stand up.

Jared shook his head. "I'm staying. I'll catch a late bus home tonight."

"Stop acting like that and get in the car." Joe pleaded.

"I made up my mind, Joe." There was determination in Jared's voice.

Joe knew the tone all too well and sighed in annoyance. "Have it your way, but you call if you need me to pick you up." Joe turned to face Carl. "See you tomorrow Carl."

"Later." Carl waved his goodbye.

Joe opened the driver's side door after a fulfilling stretch. He entered, the engine started, and the black Dodge Stratus drove off into the night, leaving Brightwood behind.

"I'm going to call it a night too. You sure you don't want a ride home?" Carl stood up from the pavement, took out his car keys, and proudly walked over to his beat-up station wagon. He knew it wasn't the most beautiful of automobiles, but it was *his,* and for Carl, that was enough.

Jared gave Carl a slight smile. "I'll be fine."

Carl accepted Jared's decision. "Don't wait out here for her too long." He opened the car door, sat in the driver's seat, and the station wagon made a loud rumbling noise as Carl put the key into the ignition and started her up.

Jared waved to Carl and watched as the beat-up wagon drove from the parking lot, following the path to the main street. The loud, rumbling engine trailed away until nothing was heard in the distance. Jared Hernandez was left alone, sitting on the black pavement anticipating his encounter with Sara.

"The Natural Magic Order simply wanted us to monitor Jared Hernandez. At the time, we had no idea he would become Vestor. Even when he became Vestor, it was impossible to anticipate how disruptive he would become to the events unfolding. However, he was well aware of the impact he'd have. He wouldn't have been an effective Time Bender otherwise." – Special Agent Della Myer of the Natural Magic Order.

8

JARED WATCHED AS the bus meant to take him home drove off down the nearly empty street, echoing louder than it usually would during daytime traffic; the sound of it faded to nothing leaving behind the rustling of a faint wind mixed with random passing cars.

His eyes returned to Sara's dark green sedan once the bus was out of ear-shot, and he accepted the vehicle's presence as proof that she had yet to emerge. Eventually, he heard her delicate footsteps approaching as the wind increased. The cloud cover became more severe, and he could smell the moisture in the air. It was about to rain soon.

A brief moment of joy flashed across his face. The footsteps grew louder on the black pavement. A tingling sensation ran throughout his back, alter-ing him to the fact that her presence was growing stronger. Instead of turn-ing to greet Sara with a warm and welcoming smile, he kept his back turned. His body language would speak for him.

"Hey." Sara sat beside Jared, ensuring her skirt didn't hike up beyond the acceptable point. "What are you still doing here? It's really late. Is every-thing okay?"

"I was waiting for you." He admitted.

Surprise flashed across Sara's face. "Me? Why?"

Jared gazed upon Sara with desire in his eyes. "I... I don't know." He looked away, ashamed, shy, and beaten.

"You can talk to me." The soothing tone of her voice made Jared feel at ease.

"I know." He couldn't find words and then, with great effort, began to speak. "I care about you, Sara."

She smiled. "I care about you too."

"Everything is starting to change, and I want to make the most of things and appreciate the people closest to me." He continued.

"I've appreciated everything these last couple of days. You get used to being a certain way, and somehow those habits for show become a genuine part of you. I used to be so different. I never used to care - I was never really in a position *to* care. Rachel and Nicole would kill me if they heard me talking like that." The weight of inner turmoil carried her words.

"Why should it matter how Rachel and Nicole feel?" Jared asked, confused.

She ripped her ponderous gaze away from the stars in the night sky and focused directly on Jared. It was the intense expression someone carried before crossing a point of no return.

Jared's concern grew as he sensed the immediate weight of how she looked at him. "Now, that's a look I've never seen before."

Sara diverted her focus, moving her eyes to the pavement. "Did you ever just wonder what it would be like to be somebody else for a little while? To have things, I don't know - normal for a change? Normal is attractive. I never understood why humanity tends to think the contrary. Normal by your standards is heaven when you've lived normal by mine."

"You're kind of confusing me here, Sara. I'm not really following." He did his best to abate the puzzlement.

She chuckled, sighed, and rested her head on Jared's shoulder as they sat beside each other. "I've been going through some major changes. I've been dreaming about being something different than what I am, and by that, I mean better than what I've been. I don't like who I am, Jared, and that's never happened to me before. But, unfortunately, Rachel and Nicole are too stuck in the old ways to understand."

"What do you mean by old ways, and why do you keep bringing up Rachel and Nicole? And for the record, there's nothing wrong with you. I like who you are." He was trying to understand, but instead, he wanted to return to the original purpose of the conversation: to let Sara know how he felt.

She cast another sad smile his way. "I'm going to miss you the most."

He felt the conversation spiraling. "You're weirding me out talking like that. Should I be worried?"

"Worry is the last thing you should feel." *You should feel fear! Go home, Jared! Go before it's too late!* The thought raged within her mind.

The first of many raindrops landed atop Jared's head, and a million others blanketed the entire expanse of the parking lot within milliseconds of the first. He and Sara both jumped to their feet as if a fire were lit beneath them. The falling rain was now showering over the entire area penetrating their clothes and flattening their hair.

"This is great!" Sara's body language turned into that of a curious explorer. She began dancing about, allowing each drop to touch her very essence, and a smile replaced the sadness that had been prevalent moments ago. "I love the rain!"

Jared watched her dance with a curious smile of his own.

She looked into the night sky, engulfed in the cleansing salvation the rain offered her, feeling the water's raw power. "The rain is powerful! It comes from nature, and nature can never be toppled despite how we try to control her! Humans have danced for the rain as a sign of worship since the beginning of the species!"

Jared observed her with delight. She radiated a powerful grace, offering her physical senses to the pouring rain. In his eyes, it was a moment of pure perfection. He could kiss her right then and there and hold her like he had always wanted. The sight warmed his heart so much that he didn't feel the falling rain anymore.

"Come on!" She ran to Jared, seizing his hands with her own. "Don't just stand there!"

"What do you want me to do?" He clumsily stepped as Sara pulled him with her.

She looked at Jared as if the answer were the most obvious thing in the world. "I want you to enjoy it with me."

He felt a surge of embarrassing silliness as he danced with Sara. Still, much to his surprise, he enjoyed the shared moment. They ceased the festive movements, and after a few heartbeats of exchanged smiles, Jared kissed Sara without hesitation. She kissed him back with the same passion before abruptly pushing him away. She took a few more steps back, terrified by what had transpired.

Confusion and shame filled Jared. Had he misread the moment? "Sara. I'm sorry. I just thought - I don't know, it seemed the right thing to do. I don't regret it."

"It was a mistake. I have to go." She focused her eyes on anything but Jared.

"Don't go. There's so much I've always wanted to say to you." He pleaded.

She turned away, rushing to her dark green sedan while fighting off the rain gravity forced downward. She jumped into the driver's side of the car, slammed the door shut as soon as she was seated, and started the engine. The vehicle sped off, crashing through the raindrops as they fell and leaving a small wake in the water behind the tires.

Jared stood speechless as the loving rain turned into a hateful downpour. He witnessed the car drive toward the street and away from the country club while an empty void began to fill his chest. It was a pain he was unaccustomed to.

To his surprised delight, the green sedan screeched to a stop short of exiting the lot; it slid across the wet pavement before coming to a complete stop. Sara stepped out of the vehicle with a defiant posture. She struggled with the weight of the emotions coursing through her. Jared showed no hesitation in running to Sara's side as she waited for him to come near.

"Jared!" She wiped the rain from her face, but it did little good as more poured down. "It's not supposed to be this way! Why are you doing this to me? It's not fair!"

"I'm in love with you!" The words were powerful as they erupted from his mouth.

A deafening silence was shared as the power of the words settled around them; the magic of the emotions broke through, creating a bond that now intertwined Jared and Sara. Then, the rain slammed down, and for a split second, it felt like time had slowed to a painful crawl.

Sara spoke gently while caressing Jared's face with a free hand. "What did you say?"

"I'm in love with you. I love you!" He stood confident in his declaration.

A sorrowful pain shook Sara to the core. "Damn you, Jared... you shouldn't."

Her reaction was driving him mad. "Why is it such a bad thing? I don't understand."

"There's a lot you don't understand." She locked eyes with him.

"Like what?" His desperation grew.

"Like the fact that I love you too!" The bond grew more potent, and Sara felt it in a way that Jared had yet to realize. Love was one of the most powerful magical forces in the realm of the supernatural; it was also a force of reckoning in the world of ordinary humans. The energy created by this incredible bond made and destroyed mortals and deities.

"What?" Jared was overjoyed to hear the words and confused about the sadness that weighed them down.

"Yes! I love you! I said it! I've said the words out loud, and now you're marked! It can't be taken back because I mean it with everything I am! Things are going to change for you in terrifying ways. I'm so sorry. Your love for me is an energy I can use, but all mine does is mark you. It brings you into a world that was separated long ago for a good reason." She explained.

Jared flung his arms in the air, irritated by the outcome of this exchange. "You're not making any sense!"

"I'm not who you think I am!" She raged.

"Why are you acting like this?" The question was barely audible.

She slammed her fists into his chest, hoping he would understand. "You're not listening to me!"

At that moment, another vehicle appeared through the rain from the dark veil of the lightless street and drove at top speed cutting through pools of water like a shark in the open sea. It was a black Cadillac, and the tires slid across the wet pavement of the lot before coming to a complete stop near Jared and Sara. It was evident by the vehicle's handling that the driver was an adept operator.

"Who the hell is that?" Jared asked, surprised by the sudden arrival.

She sighed. "They've been waiting here for me. I have a meeting planned with them. Unfortunately, I'm late for that appointment because of this exchange you and I have been having. They wouldn't have made themselves known, Jared, but you had to push things to this point. It's like I've been trying to tell you; you're marked now. You're going to become a part of our world."

The surreal nature of her words and the Cadillac's sudden appearance made Jared feel like he were in a dream. "What the hell are you talking about?"

The rear driver's side door to the Cadillac swung open. A tall, brooding man dressed in a black suit exited with one decisive step after another. It was difficult to see because of the night sky, but his skin appeared to have a Mediterranean tan. A stick figure of a man also exited the vehicle being nothing more than a fragile, pale ghost of a creature. From how he carried himself, he appeared to be the thicker man's assistant. He held an umbrella over his boss' head, not allowing a single raindrop to touch him.

"Sara, is it? Of course, we both know that's not your true name, but that doesn't matter. Word is that you wish to broker a deal, Ate?" The thicker man pronounced the name the way the number eighty sounded.

Sara nodded. "I do. A deal needs to be made. My sisters and I want Lord Dracien's permission to operate in his territory for a grand sacrifice."

"Proper respect need be made." The man's voice boomed. "You do right by you and your sisters of former glory by approaching us with tribute. I believe a deal can be made, and I'll be the one to broker it on Dracien's behalf. Come with me, and we'll settle things by discussing the agreement's proper terms. Then, we will seal the covenant's conditions." The large man held his hand out for Sara to take hold of.

Jared stood dumbstruck between Sara and the strangers of ill intent. He had never faced a situation like this but stood before them as though he could. "Leave her alone! Sara, get in your car and drive away! None of this feels right!"

"Who is this?" The large man grinned and looked at Sara. "You've marked him! I can smell it all over his puny essence. I can smell the fear, too; he reeks of it. There's something to be said about fresh meat. He's got balls. I'll give him that."

Sara stepped forward. "Don't hurt him. He doesn't know any better. He's just a kid and doesn't know what this is about. So I'm asking you to please just leave him alone, Vic."

"He better get wise to how things work and fast. It doesn't sound like you're willing to offer protection and claim him as your own." Vic raised a curious eyebrow.

"Believe me," Sara looked to Jared with apologetic eyes, "if I could, I would. But, as it stands, he's on his own. So just please leave him be."

Who the hell is Vic? What are they talking about? Jared was unable to wrap his mind around what he was hearing.

Sara turned to face Jared. "You need to leave now, Jared. Pretend you were never here and that none of this happened until that's what you truly believe. If you concentrate and do that, it just might work, and it might not be too late for you to be safe. The power of belief is incredible."

Vic chuckled at her words. "I highly doubt that. Look at him! He doesn't want to forget."

Sara glared at Vic, not intimidated by the solitary werewolf. "He's not your concern. Let's leave this place so we can settle our business properly."

"As the former goddess wishes," Vic smirked, gesturing for Sara to join him.

Sara reached the large man near the Cadillac; her hand was extended to place it within his.

"Sara! No!" Jared lunged for her arm in desperation, and as soon as he did so, he felt a blunt object smash into the back of his head. Jared lived in a bubble mostly and hadn't known to watch for a man sneaking up behind him. The blow was quick and unexpected, causing immediate darkness to set in.

PART FOUR:

WELCOMING

THE STRANGE

"It is up to us. We are the line of defense that must stand against that which defies logic. The intelligent and animal creatures of this world that are not a part of our world need to be monitored. A system of balance must be maintained to avoid our extinction as human beings. What we don't understand at first glance CAN be understood through scientific means. Our minds are our most powerful tools, and our free will and ability to act upon that will frighten them. The fear on both sides creates discord and leads to dangerous misunderstandings. Let us ALL understand and be better for it." – Leonardo Da Vinci – First Warden and founding member of the Natural Magic Order.

1

SPECIAL AGENT DELLA Myer and her newly assigned partner, Special Agent Sionmen Repus, were operatives of the Natural Magic Order. The supernatural and the natural were opposing forces of the same energy that connected the whole of existence. Natural Magic was what scientists called life and the universe's natural order. It was also considered a new edition compared to its predecessors: Supernatural Magic and Founding Magic.

Within each human was a well of untapped natural magic rarely inured. There were those in humanity's past who had been able to break through and avail a vast amount of raw power. They were regarded as true geniuses, and some had a physical prowess bordering on the supernatural; however, the distinction was clear if examined. These souls were the versions of what humans could become *naturally* through discipline, training, and genetic evolution.

The Natural Magic Order specialized in training such people so that they could reach beyond their full potential. Their duty was to help maintain the balance between realms and act as humanity's voice. Unfortunately, most humans were oblivious to all the fantastic magic surrounding them.

Della Myer was one of the best the Order had ever produced.

Della was in her mid-thirties and every bit as attractive as the younger women that ran about the city. Her maturity exemplified a physical elegance that complimented her more direct nature. Her long strands of black hair were tied in a bun, bringing out her streamlined, no-nonsense facial features. The black suit she wore was form-fitting but allowed the freedom of movement needed for immediate action; it was a standard-issue for those the Order placed in the field.

Her partner Sionmen Repus was new to the job. Like her, he was an orphan and trained by the Order's monks in matters intellectual and combative. The scientific benefits of genetic research allowed these children to draw upon the natural magic that existed in all of them. His muscles were healthy and ready to burst out of his suit. Sionmen could move faster and had better reflexes than most of his kind. He was young but learned quickly. Della appreciated this fact when life and death decisions had to be made with milliseconds to spare.

Sionmen ran his left hand over his bald head as if he had long hair to play with and studied the Brightwood Country Club's layout. It was four in the morning. The rain had stopped pouring several hours ago, and their non-specific black sedan was parked off the roadside. The two special agents observed the lavish establishment's grounds, studying every detail from within the vehicle.

"I don't understand why we're here." Sionmen Repus complained. He had never been a fan of what ordinary humans called stakeouts.

"We're following orders. That should be enough." Della observed the unconscious youth in the parking lot. "This kid's life is about to change so much."

"Is there anything special about him?" At first glance, the boy in the waiter uniform appeared dead, but Sionmen knew better. He could sense the faint breathing, pulse, and body heat that radiated.

"Not that I'm aware of, but you know as well as I that that could change. Sometimes you just can't tell until it happens." Della also noted the faint signs of life. Thanks to genetic enhancements, they could see through the night as if they had state-of-the-art surveillance equipment. This made Della smile. She loved her abilities.

"If he isn't special, why would the Order send us out here? I don't mind starting our day this early, but knowing why would be beneficial so I could react accordingly to whatever comes up." Sionmen commented.

"We've officially been ordered to monitor the area. Notable events are about to transpire as we approach a powerful nexus point. We're unable to intervene directly because of the agreements made by the Order and Dracien's organization. However, if this event expands beyond the agreed-upon parameters, we're authorized to contain it by any means. I just wanted to get a good look at everything and a feel for the area in case we need to step in. I sure as hell wasn't expecting to find a lonely boy asleep out there in the parking lot." She explained, having patience with her partner.

Sionmen nodded gruffly. "Understood, Ma'am."

"For the last time, Sionmen, I'm not your boss. We're partners. Call me Della - even Myer - take your pick. Just stop calling me Ma'am." She ordered.

"Whatever you say, you're the boss." Sionmen's grinning smirk was matched by Della's glare. "So, what's this kid's name anyway?" He continued.

Della returned her attention to the country club, noting how peaceful the young man looked while unconscious. She then eyed the display screen that extended from the dashboard of the black sedan. A file opened in a new window on the display showcasing various pictures of Jared with descriptive text.

Her eyes remained on the monitor. "According to the most recent upload given by the Order, his name is Jared Hernandez. He's recently been marked, about six hours ago, as a matter of fact, and just crossed over into the realm of the supernatural. Unfortunately, it looks like the goddess that marked him offers no protection, so he's pretty much on his own."

It still impressed Della how magic and technology had synthesized to create real-time updates of people when important events transpired. They had files on all people of note. However, some could mask their movements; they tended to be the more dangerous ones.

"Do the laws of the Distinction ever bother you?" Sionmen asked, switching gears. "I hate it sometimes. We're not allowed to help him, Della, but we should be able to."

"The laws are clear. Humans that are marked are the responsibility of those that marked them. If left unclaimed and unprotected, said human is on his or her own to find sanctuary. Our job has always been to stop the powers that be from crossing over into the normal human world. Unfortunately, we can't worry about all the strays that make their way into ours." She realized her tone was harsh, but she could do nothing about it as a regular agent.

"He won't last." Sionmen's head shook with pity.

A feeling struck Della that her partner might be wrong about this one. "We'll see Sionmen. We'll see."

"How do you expect to relate to Develin? The Natural Magic Order sits with moral authority, trying to make human that which is absent humanity: soul and all. A demon a human does not make! It is a façade, an impression of what they believe us to be. Deep down, they are monsters with unknown motives and alien thoughts. We can never and were never meant to relate. That is why they are demons.

"My only question is why this demon self-named Develin is interested in Vestor? The Time Bender is powerful now, but he was once a simple boy named Jared Hernandez. Why did Develin not strike him down earlier? Why keep him alive, and try to kill him later? Alien thoughts. Unknown motives. I've yet to understand them." – Special Agent Della Myer – formal address to the Natural Magic Order (transcript found in the Vestor File)

2

FROM THE MOMENT of his creation, Develin had always been drawn to the raw power of the Founding Magic. He was a primordial demon in origin, one of the first that blurred the lines between demon and god. His influence extended throughout history, and he had seen much of humanity rise and fall over the ages in predictable cycles. Yet, the elusiveness of tapping into the Founding Magic (or even detecting it) had always frustrated the demon wizard. The powers harbored by the ancient deities and creatures that stemmed from the Founding Magic were only experienced by others if they desired it. Now, however, Develin was fortunate enough to be upon a nexus point.

If done correctly, a nearly infinite amount of power could be harvested from such an event. A nexus point connected the raw and powerful energy of all the choices made throughout the unlimited number of existing realities.

Endless will, love, hate, and all the emotions that shaped existence came together for one brief moment, the tiniest moment imaginable.

The sly demon wizard stood in the shadows granted by the darkness of the early morning while dressed in a red suit fit for a Mafia gathering. He always had a soft spot for the golden age of organized crime. The fashion sat well with Develin, and he was unlikely to change it.

Develin grinned from ear to ear while studying young Mr. Hernandez. The boy's body was limp and appeared lifeless as he lay unconscious on the parking lot's black pavement. He witnessed the encounter with the former goddess, werewolf, and young human from afar; he was elated to see that what had been prophesized was coming true.

Vic should have been more careful with the boy. But, then again, he hasn't the slightest idea what he will be capable of; none of them know. He mused.

Time, Chaos, and Order were the trio of the universe. These three ideas were the essence of the Founding Magic that gave birth to newer forms of supernatural power. This, in turn, led to the natural magic of life. At first glance, Develin observed a dull boy, and the demon wizard felt secure that no one else would suspect anything but an average human as well. Those touched by the Founding Magic went unnoticed until their powers emerged in unforeseeable manifestations.

It was four in the morning as he looked up into the sky. Develin had always admired the elegant transition of the night into day. The passing of powers that went unseen by most creatures gave the demon wizard a sense of wonder, and it would have made him feel like a child had he ever been one.

Within seconds, Develin's existence flashed through his consciousness. His current station left much to be desired, but working for Dracien had its advantages. The demon wizard had been so much more than his current position. Still, he was well aware that circumstances inevitably changed. He need only continue wearing the mask of patience while answering to Dracien.

Jared Hernandez...

Develin cast a satisfactory grin while studying the youth foolishly in love with a creature beyond his comprehension. He also knew Natural Magic agents were positioned nearby in an unmarked sedan. Another grin formed. He was fiendishly satisfied with the knowledge that even their heightened abilities could not detect a demon wizard like him.

He kept his eye on the young man's sleeping body. *Jared, you'll soon become Vestor. Your predecessor confessed as much before I ended his life.*

Develin recalled with great anger how he nearly perished when dealing with the Time Bender before the one about to be born. The task was carried out after his release by the dark powers that imprisoned him far below the modern notion of hell. The demon wizard had been banished to the ancient prison that was also a god born of the Founding Magic in Chaos. This god was known as Tartarus.

During those initial moments of freedom, Develin was happy to shed his imprisonment from the god who existed as both prison and entity. However, Develin knew full well that he owed that freedom to Tartarus. Tartarus cast the demon wizard out to secretly do his bidding. He was to serve one of Lucifer's chief operatives in matters of magic in the mortal realm. When the time was right, Develin would begin his true mission in the name of his savior Tartarus and forsake his allegiance with Dracien and Lucifer.

His first task, when freed over a hundred years prior, was to vanquish a legitimate Time Bender. Ultimately the challenge placed upon the demon wizard had barely been met and almost cost Develin his eternal essence. Nevertheless, the elder prophet had proven to be a formidable adversary.

This elder Time Bender Develin killed spoke of a new Time Bender to come. This future prophet would become far more potent than any of his predecessors. Chronos had touched this dying prophet with the gift of full knowledge before his demise, allowing him to see well past his life to the end of time itself. The information from his ramblings was valued. *Most* of that vital knowledge had been passed along to Dracien. However, specific details about other events remained within Develin's mind and were solely communicated to the one he indeed served.

The importance of Jared Hernandez was a secret long guarded by the demon wizard. Then, with a soundless transition, the red of Develin's suit transformed into the pitch black of night. In the briefest of moments, the demon wizard was gone.

"Waking up in a parking lot was strange. At that moment, that was the only strange thing. I had crossed over into the true realm. The Distinction was null and void for me. I didn't feel any different upon waking. Nothing felt different – at least, not at first. During those initial days, I was still the simple Jared Hernandez." – Vestor, the Time Bender.

3

THE BLISTERING SUN shined through the morning sky, heating Jared's face so that his eyes opened with immense pain, and the powerful rays of light were too much for those eyes to take in. His temples throbbed, and the extreme discomfort allowed him to barely focus on anything but his vision's blurry haze.

The rain had long ceased. Jared opened his eyes all the way with the hope that Sara was still near him. But, as the sun smacked into his vision more directly, Jared was struck with the paralyzing fear that the bad dream was an actual reality. Sara was missing, he'd been attacked, and he had no idea what to do.

Ready for action, Jared darted up from the black pavement stumbling from the grogginess; he stood with desperate anxiety that reeked of helplessness. A thought kept flying through his mind like a mantra that none of this could happen, but his memories assured him that the facts were irrefutable. The events transpired as he remembered, and if he were going to find Sara, he needed to act.

Now that he was standing with ambulatory senses intact, Jared noticed that a few cars were parked several feet away, higher up from his current position. They were the vehicles of the management team that kept Brightwood afloat. The elevated view of the cars belonging to the managerial group meant that anyone driving to those spots would not have seen Jared lying on the black pavement. His body had rested beyond that particular vantage point. Luckily Jared recognized Valerie's car parked amongst the rest.

He made a mad dash for the Brightwood Country Club, running on the frantic adrenaline of wanting to save a life. He would find Valerie and explain everything. He was confident that of all the people at Brightwood, she would be the one to listen. Together they could call the police and hopefully find Sara. God willing, he would save her before something horrible happened, and then they could all move on to better days.

"Why? Before he became fully realized as Vestor, Jared would ask me why? Why did I decide to help him? Why did I decide to protect him after he crossed over? My answer is the same now as it was when I was first asked: it was the right thing to do." – Aglaia (former Grace – known as Valerie during the birth of Vestor)

4

THE POLICE OFFICER dispatched to Brightwood stood in Valerie's office pacing back and forth and wondered why he always got stuck responding to "these" calls. The patrolman was dressed in his blues, and the uniform fit every curve of his unshapely body, bulge for bulge. Finally, after a long sigh of annoyance, Officer Clems looked over his notes and moved to Valerie's desk, where she sat. He raised his eyebrows while scratching his chin, not convinced one bit by the story told.

"Are you sure the events of last night happened the way you say they did?" Clems didn't even bother looking at Jared, who slouched in a chair off to the side near Valerie's desk. Jared finished his bottle of water, surprised by the immense thirst.

Valerie kept a cold gaze upon Clems. The professional business attire that adorned her graceful figure seemed to make her all the more intimidating. She was internally gratified when the police officer looked away from her dominant gaze.

Jared set the empty water bottle down. "I'm not making this up. It happened just the way I told you it did." He rubbed the back of his head, tending to the bruise. The pain had subsided little since waking to it. He could feel the skin around the bruise tightening and was grateful that the bump was well hidden beneath his hair.

"Well, my partner is checking in on this," The officer looked at the small notepad for the name. "Sara White. He's calling her home to see if anyone responds, and according to Miss Chari," Clems pointed at Valerie, "she should be on the schedule to work in a half-hour. So we might just actually see her in a little bit."

Jared studied the portly man who had long ago vowed to serve and protect. He could feel the distrust with every passing second and knew his words were not being taken seriously. Jared glanced at Valerie and was having difficulty reading her. He wasn't even sure if she believed him, but his instincts remained true. Something within his soul was telling Jared that he could trust her.

"We'll get to the bottom of this, Jared. You have my word." Valerie gave a reassuring smile and returned another cold stare at the officer.

The patrolman grinned in return and looked at Valerie while licking away a piece of breakfast burrito that had been caught between his teeth. "If I wasn't married already, I might be inclined to ask you out."

"You'd be wasting your time asking. Do you like wasting your time? Given how you conduct your police work, that seems to be the case." Valerie crossed her arms, unafraid to show her lack of amusement.

Clems grinned again. "You know, on second thought, I take that back. You seem like you can be even colder than my wife. The devil you know is always better. Right?"

Her tone remained neutral. "You have no idea."

Before Valerie could utter more complaints regarding Clems' conduct, the door to her office opened. Officer Preston, a young black male fresh to the force and eager to go by the book, stepped in, glancing at Jared with disapproval. "Mr. Hernandez, there isn't a single shred of evidence to corroborate your story. In fact, we have a witness that speaks contrary to what you've stated. We also found a broken bottle of vodka in the parking lot near where you awoke earlier this morning."

"What? Another person saw what happened? Who is it?" Jared stood up and felt an immediate wave of relief as Sara entered Valerie's office. She trailed in behind Preston with a meek posture. She wore her waitress uniform and was ready to go to work as if it were any other day.

"Sara! Thank God you're okay!" Jared rushed from where he stood to embrace her but was held back by the portly officer.

"There's absolutely no need to handle him in that way!" Valerie stood from behind her desk and walked closer to the group.

What hurt Jared the most was the strange look Sara gave him as Clems forcibly held him back. She wanted the policeman to keep him at bay and honestly looked frightened. "Sara? What's going on?"

With a confused expression, she turned her head away from Jared. "I don't know what you're talking about, Jared. Officer Preston told me what you said. None of that happened. I don't even know why you would make something like that up. I went home last night after work like I always do. There was no black Cadillac, and there wasn't anyone named Vic."

"Sara... Don't do this to me. It happened! Did they get to you somehow? You don't have to be afraid, Sara. It's okay. I can help you - I want to help you! This can somehow all be figured out." Jared's tone was frantic as the words shot out of his mouth.

Sara shook her head in pity. "I'm sorry, Jared, but you're wrong. None of what you said happened. You have to believe that, or you'll only get in more trouble. You *have* to *believe* that it didn't happen."

The young woman's words struck a chord with Valerie as she witnessed the conversation. Yet, the former Grace maintained her composure while studying Sara White. *Just as I suspected. She's not what she appears to be. I think she's actually trying to protect him. Why not claim him, though?*

Sara looked at Officer Preston. "Can I go now? I just want to get back to work."

"Yes, you may go. Thank you for assisting in clearing up this matter." Preston stood in the doorway, watching Jared as she left.

Jared did his best to bypass the policemen pushing and pulling with more force than before. "Sara! Wait!" He yelled the words, not even noticing that his elbow rammed into portly officer Clems' face.

"Jared! Stop this at once!" Valerie yelled as the two policemen subdued Jared and pinned him to the carpet floor of the office.

"Alright, son, you've brought this on yourself." The portly patrolman wiped away a tiny amount of blood from his nose. The impact had caused Clems' eyes to tear up, and his facial expression barely contained the anger.

"Striking a police officer is not a very smart thing to do. That was extremely stupid on your part."

"What the hell do you think you're doing?" Valerie demanded as the handcuffs were placed on Jared's wrists and held firmly behind his back. "It was clearly an accident Officer Clems. He didn't mean to strike you."

"I'm going to have to ask you to please step back. We're just doing our jobs, Ma'am." Preston stated in a matter-of-fact tone.

"Don't do anything else to resist them, Jared. I'll straighten this out." Valerie rushed behind her desk and jumped on the phone. She looked up to catch glimpses of Jared being hauled off by the two police officers knowing in her heart that Jared was telling the truth. Valerie had her suspicions about the true nature of Sara, and now those suspicions had been confirmed. She also knew that Jared had no idea how dangerous his world had just become.

"They're my family. There's nothing I wouldn't do for Jared and Carl. I know, Jared calls himself Vestor now - I don't give a shit. He'll always be Jared to me. Sure, we've had our disputes, but what family hasn't? I'd go to hell and back for them... well, again, anyway. Should be easier next time around, you know, given that I've done it a few times before." – Joseph Chan Medium/Manipulator.

5

JOE TRAVERSED THROUGH the main wait station with a lethargic gait allowing his body to sway from side to side. He bellowed a groggy yawn while stretching his chest and arms wide and could sense something was amiss. Finally, he realized what it was; he failed to see Jared bright and early as his friend usually was. Eager to investigate, Joe turned to the exit of the wait station and was immediately smacked in the face by the swinging door. He landed hard and held his nose in pain as his eyes watered profusely.

"Shit! I'm sorry, Joe." Carl reached down, helping Joe to his feet.

Joe looked at Carl with watery eyes; they both wore waiter uniforms. Joe held his face hoping that the sudden impact didn't lead to a nosebleed. "You gotta watch where the hell you're going, man! You're like a fucking freight train when you're moving that fast! Where the hell is Jared anyway? He's usually here by now. I was about to go look for him."

"That's why I'm here; I was looking for you. I just saw Jared get hauled off by two cops not even a minute ago. They threw him in a squad car and took off. It looked like he got arrested." Carl spewed the information with relief; he could finally tell someone what he saw.

"What?" Joe shook his head in disbelief. "Don't fuck with me this early, man. I'm a little hungover and not in the mood."

"I'm not making it up, Joe. I saw it with my own eyes. You can even ask Valerie." Carl insisted.

"No one needs to ask me anything. I'll just give it to you straight." Valerie stood by the swinging door to the wait station. Her appearance was strong, and she gave off that aura of command and readiness that Joe found so alluring.

"Jared was arrested?" Joe still failed to understand how a guy like Jared could end up handcuffed and in the back of a squad car. Boy Scout was synonymous with the image of Jared when Joe thought of his friend.

Valerie stepped closer, explaining with a comforting posture. "All I can say for certain is that there's been some kind of misunderstanding. I'll go down to the police station to try and get Jared out of this mess. However, it will take me a while before I can properly get to him. He may even be incarcerated overnight. I don't have time to explain any of this in great detail, but he's probably safer in police custody for now. I promise I will get him out of there as soon as I can."

"What the hell do you mean he's safer in custody? What the hell is going on?" The experience felt surreal to Joe, and he wanted answers.

"I'll do my best to explain everything later but believe me when I say that it is indeed the safest place for Jared to be. I need you to trust me, Joe. Look at me." Her eyes focused on the young man.

With great reluctance, Joe allowed their eyes to lock.

Her smile radiated as she spoke. "I want you to trust me. Can you trust me?"

While gazing into Valerie's eyes, Joe felt a strong sense of trust grow from the doubt brewing. He melted into her deep blue eyes, and her reassuring smile was more powerful and beautiful than anything he had ever witnessed. At that moment, Joe could believe anything she said without question. He had no idea that her magic was bending him to her will.

"Yes. I trust you, Valerie." The strange calm made Joe feel uncomfortable, but he embraced it nonetheless.

Valerie gave him a comforting smile. "Good. In the meantime, I need you to do me a favor."

Joe nodded. "What is it?"

"Call Jared's parents. They're going to wonder why he didn't come home last night. I have his cell phone on file but not the house number, if there is one." It didn't matter, but she knew Joe needed a task.

Joe nodded with determination. "No problem. I'll just tell them he crashed at my place."

"Good. I'll speak to Jared's parents later and take care of whatever else needs to be done at that point." The former Grace was not looking forward to that moment.

"Damn it!" Carl interjected and shook his head in frustration, causing his wavy blond hair to bounce. Finally, he spoke his following words under his breath. " I should have given him a ride home last night."

Valerie stepped forward and locked eyes with Carl; she extended her will to him now. "It's not your fault Carl. It'll be okay. Trust me and follow Joe's lead."

Carl's wild nature began to subside. Her powerful calming effect took complete hold of him, and he believed her words. "You're right, Valerie. I just want to help. This shouldn't be happening."

"I know Carl. That's exactly why I'm going to help fix this mess. Can the two of you handle things here at Brightwood until I return? Both Mr. Drake and Merdith are aware of the incident. I assured them that it would be taken care of and that they needn't worry about anything today. I've *persuaded* them to focus on office work for the rest of the day, so you won't see much of them. They're here if you need them, but they should be left alone." She explained.

"We've been here long enough. We've got this under control." Joe responded while Carl nodded in agreement.

"I'll see the both of you soon." Valerie darted out of the wait station, leaving the conversation at that.

"What the hell is going on around here, Joe? Why would Jared get arrested? Why is Valerie getting so involved? I mean, I trust her. I don't know why, but I do...." The feelings forced on Carl by Valerie were strong.

From the corner of his eye, Joe noticed Sara walking by one of the doors that led into the wait station. For a brief second, the two made intense eye contact, and she quickly averted her gaze. She walked on from Joe, maintaining an innocent demeanor.

"Joe? Joe? Are you still with me?" Carl shook Joe's shoulder to snap him from his gaze.

Without hearing another word from Carl, Joe stalked after Sara with a determined glare in his eye that bordered on psychotic. His friend was being hauled off by the police, and Joe's instincts alerted every part of him that she was to blame.

Unsure of Joe's intentions, Carl trailed behind his companion as they burst through the wait station's swinging door. The duo cut through the vacant formal dining room.

"Hey!" Joe called after Sara, who continued walking as if she hadn't heard her name. "Sara! I'm talking to you!"

Sara turned to face Joe with an inviting smile at the ready. She appeared relatively innocent as she stood before both he and Carl. "What's up, Joe?"

With a fierce rage, Joe took hold of Sara's neck and pinned the young woman against the nearest wall. Carl pulled Joe away from her, shocked at having seen such a reaction emerge from his friend.

"Joe, you need to calm down!" Carl yelled in the heat of the moment, pulling Joe from Sara and keeping him at bay.

"I know you had something to do with this! I never trusted you! I told Jared to move on so many times, but he...!" Joe closed his mouth, cutting off the unkind words he wanted to express. The outrage and disgust were boiling to the surface, but he contained the anger that swelled.

"What the hell is wrong with you?" Sara took a few uneasy steps back, gently rubbed her neck, and maintained an innocent and frightened demeanor. "I don't know what's wrong with Jared, but he had Valerie call the cops this morning and told them all some crazy story that wasn't true. He thought someone kidnapped me last night in the parking lot."

"What?" Joe shook his head in disbelief. His Wednesday had been getting stranger by the second. "Why would he tell the cops that? It doesn't make any damn sense."

"I don't know Joe. I don't have an answer to that. Jared kept going on and on about how some guy dragged me into a black car. It was some really messed up story that he *clearly* made up. It's not my fault he got taken away by two cops. Something isn't right with Jared, and it looks like something might not be right with you, walking up on me like that! What do you think gives you the right to always act like such an asshole?!" Sara's fear turned into indignation.

"Bullshit!" Joe raged. "Jared doesn't make shit up! He's the most honest person I've ever known! What are you really hiding here?!"

Carl chose that moment to intervene by placing a comforting yet firm hand upon Joe's shoulder. The gesture supported his friend and warned him not to do anything rash. Carl cleared his throat while speaking as calmly as he could muster. "We'll figure it out, Joe, but we should get back to work. We already talked to Valerie, and she's doing what she can to improve it. Jared is going to be just fine."

"What did you say?" Sara looked to Carl, interested in Valerie's involvement.

"Valerie is helping Jared with the whole cop thing." He turned to his friend after addressing Sara. "And Joe, you have a phone call to make before it gets too late."

Joe nodded to Carl before pointing a stern finger in Sara's face. "I'm going to find out the truth."

"The first soul I consumed was that of this body, and it was nourishing beyond words. The essence of this human invigorated me and charged me with power, as the worship of mortals had done in the early days when we were still part of Olympus. My dear sister, I want more." – the goddess Dysnomia addressing her sister Ate upon consuming and inhabiting the body of a human.

6

SARA WAITED UNTIL Joe and Carl exited the formal dining room; Joe remained a cluster of raw emotion, and Carl dutifully attempted to be the voice of reason. When it was evident that the duo had vacated, she made a mad dash through the wait station to the kitchen. Sara moved down a flight of carpeted stairs and turned a corner in a hallway that led to the basement linen room. Her sisters had been waiting for her arrival.

Rachel and Nicole jumped to their feet in anticipation as Sara entered the linen room and straightened their human bodies' posture, having sensed the disturbance within Sara. Rachel and Nicole soothed Sara with gentle hands and calmed her down. With kind smiles, they guided her to sit on the thick burgundy carpet, forming a circle.

Sara kept her eyes focused on the color as she ran her hands across the carpet's surface. Her human feelings were nearly impossible to control at this point. Far too much time had been spent in these bodies. "Jared was taken by the police this morning. They arrested him because he struck a police officer in the face."

Nicole shrugged, having expected such an outcome. "That's a true shame, but it had to be done. He bore witness to far too much last night. The fool waited for you on purpose because he *loves* you." The word was spoken as if it were a vile thing. "He brought this on himself. I find it odd that Vic showed up while Jared was still there. They usually don't appear before a normal human unless this normal human has already been marked."

Rachel studied Sara with piercing eyes as she tied her red hair in a pony-tail. "Don't tell me you're in love with him as well? The energy of your affections would have been more than strong enough to pull him onto this side of the Distinction."

Silence mixed with defeated body language on Sara's part was answer enough.

Nicole leaned backward, holding a hand over her mouth to hide a shocked gasp. Sara's involvement with a mortal soul would jeopardize everything the trio had worked so hard to accomplish.

"We are not like them! We never have been! I think maybe you've become too comfortable in this human body. Now the fool boy is marked, and there is no turning back. There may have been a chance, but now his life, as short as it may be, will never be the same." Rachel's disgust accented every word.

"We've been in these bodies for far too long! I can barely stand it anymore!" Sara kept her eyes on the floor before her. The thick carpeting became an anchor of sorts. "It's hard not to feel human when we inhabit this form. And I believe that Joe is also noticing that something is amiss. We also have Valerie to contend with. She appears to have taken a special interest in Jared's welfare and is doing whatever is within her power to free him of his current predicament with the police."

"Let them do as they please. They don't matter. Our time is upon us." Rachel grabbed Sara's hands, forcing her to make eye contact. "Don't allow your feelings for Jared to betray what must be done. We need the blood for the sacrifice. Then and only then shall we retain some of the former glory we once held, and at that point, we may cross back to where we've always belonged. It will be as before the Distinction when our stations were clear and undeniable."

Little Nicole chimed in, moving closer to Sara. "I take it things went well with Vic after the fiasco with Jared? Has a covenant been made with Dracien? Are we free to operate in his territory and carry out the grand sacrifice?"

"The werewolf and I were able to negotiate a favorable outcome once proper tribute was paid. Dracien is no longer concerned about our current activities. He has granted us the freedom to do as we must and asks only that we move on from his area of influence once the deed is done. Also, our actions are not to expand beyond the country club grounds. The grand sacrifice must take place and remain within the walls of Brightwood."

"A covenant is a covenant. It shall be carried out as agreed upon. This land is sickening enough as it is. I yearn for our true home. I wish to dance in the chaos as we once did without restrictive form." Rachel touched the flesh of her arm, disgusted by how *human* it all felt.

"What about young Scott Riley?" Nicole's eyes grew intense.

"Yes," Rachel licked her lips with hunger. "Is everything in order?"

Sara nodded. "It is. Scott fully worships me. I manipulated him to include some of his friends, who are just as ripe for the taking. Their blood will be ours, with the individual essence of each one making us stronger."

"I so look forward to this!" Little Nicole licked her lips as well.

"We all do." There was reluctance in Sara's voice that went unnoticed by her sisters. "After feeding on Scott and his friends, we'll be strong enough to carry out the grand sacrifice."

Rachel bounced her gaze between the two as she spoke. "Those caught in our net will gladly bow to our needs, and all of their blood combined will make us what we once were. Then we can move on and return to the chaos. Perhaps we could even rule Olympus instead of being summoned there on Zeus' whim, like in the first days. The grand sacrifice will be our salvation. We shall continue to allow everyone to think that we're indeed these young women but remember that we're not; we never have been. We existed once in a purer form, and to that form, we shall return. Do not let these bodies control you; we control them."

"If we're not what we are acting as now, then what are we? We exist in each moment as we are. If we don't exist as we are, we're nothing in the end." Sara's inner thoughts spilled out without regard for consequence.

A stiff, quick slap to Sara's face from Rachel's hand forced her to cower. Rachel towered over Sara with the might of a titan; her eyes grew intense with fury. Spittle flew from her mouth as she bellowed angered grunts of rage.

"Apologies! My tongue spoke without consent!" Sara crawled to a corner of the linen room, wanting only to melt into the carpet.

"We are the children of Eris! We live in the energy that creates chaos! The human form does not befit what our true natures entail! We must return to Olympus and be free of this restricting flesh once and for all!" Rachel decreed.

"It will be done." Both Sara and Nicole spoke simultaneously.

Sara (the goddess Ate, known as Blind Folly), Nicole (the goddess Lethe, known as Oblivion), and Rachel (the goddess Dysnomia, known as Lawlessness) were all children of Eris, the goddess of strife and discord. Hence, they were granddaughters to Nyx, the goddess of night, and great-granddaughters to Khaos, or Chaos as the world has come to know her. (Chaos was the first Supernatural Magic to be born of the Founding Magic with the same name). Their actual names and forms were a closely guarded secret.

Rachel glared at her sister and spoke with great authority. "You are never to question nor forget what we are ever again. We are goddesses! We're meant to be free of this wretched exile and continue as we once did with endless glory! The energy these weak human creatures create has always rightfully been ours to feed upon, and believe me when I say that we'll make it this way once again."

"I'm an orphan like all the Natural Magic Agents that operate in the field. How does that make me feel? I don't think about it. This is the life I was given. There's no point fantasizing about what may or may not have been. No point in dreaming up parents that never existed. I deal with what is and live to do my job." – Special Agent Sionmen Repus of the Natural Magic Order (annual psychological evaluation dated July 2016)

7

BLOOD WAS SPLATTERED in every corner of the apartment, from floor to wall to ceiling. The early morning sun allowed rays of light to shine through small cracks of old dusty curtains. The cheap lifeless curtains draped over dilapidated windows, and the dark, dried liquid that once sustained a human life glistened the color of red rust. A few odds and ends in mismatched disarray decorated the rest of the space. That was to be expected with the type of lowlife that had inhabited this dwelling. Andrew Callmun survived by scrounging together whatever he could to get by. Ultimately, his curious eyes of profit from opportunity gazed upon something he should never have witnessed: an Aswang.

"I really hate how messy the aftermath of an Aswang attack is, especially when they're in a hurry. That's how it is with the newer ones, anyway. At least vampires tend to keep things neater. They have an old-school sense of professionalism." Della Myer let out a frustrated sigh as she peered into the open cavity of Andrew's chest. The heart of the victim had been taken out and eaten. Andrew's liver had also been removed from another exposed torso area, and both organs were nowhere in sight.

Sionmen studied the scene in great detail. He took note of the struggle and saw how the victim had unwittingly invited the creature into his home. There were no signs of forced entry, but things quickly escalated, and the poor soul named Andrew was now just a dead body sprawled across his bed with bloody sheets beneath. The metallic odor of the dried blood was amplified by Sionmen's genetically heightened sense of smell.

"I take it you've encountered one of these Aswang before?" Sionmen studied his partner. Every day he learned something new about her.

"Yes. It was my first field assignment for the Order." The annoying buzz of her cell phone took Della from the brief recollection. She answered, hearing the voice of her superior on the other end.

Sionmen watched as she nodded her head while carrying a face of disapproval. Whatever she was being told, it was clear that she didn't care for it. He waited until she put her phone away before speaking up. "Bad news?"

"Annoying news." She turned to face him. "There's not much else we can do here. The regular police should arrive soon, so we best be on our way. Some homicide detectives will roll through after the uniforms discover the scene. They won't find anything here since we cleaned up all traces of the creature. It'll just be another unsolved case. In the meantime, I want you to canvass the area for butcher shops."

He gave his partner a questioning glance.

"Aswang love to work at butcher shops by day. Given how the body was ripped open, I'm willing to bet that this one works at one in the area. Look for bloodshot eyes. They rarely sleep because the night is when they hunt. Also, pay attention to your reflection in people's eyes as you interview them. It'll be inverted. That's how you distinguish them. They may appear human during the day, but they're not." She turned from her partner and eyed up the dead body. "Most feed off of the recently deceased nowadays, so I also want you to check the local funeral homes that make trades on this side of the Distinction. There might be a lead there."

Sionmen sighed, disgruntled about the busy work. "While I'm doing this, what'll you be up to, if you don't mind my asking?"

"Someone called in a favor with the high-ups of the Order. So now I get to be a messenger and deliver some information." Della hated running these types of errands.

"Who gets the message?" Sionmen asked.

Della looked at her partner while raising a curious eyebrow. "Some woman named Valerie Chari."

*"The truth? The truth is a lie. That's why we're always search-
ing for it. It doesn't exist in a way we can relate to. The truth is
outside of ourselves in a place we can't see or be because the
moment we see it, it's no longer free. It becomes trapped by the
notions of our will and becomes solidified into what we think it
is. The truth turns into the lie we want to see."* – Detective John
Lycros (handwritten note discovered in the apartment of Detective Lycros
days after his sudden disappearance)

8

DETECTIVE JOHN LYCROS had witnessed his share of strange in a career littered with murder investigations. Having to deal with homicides allowed for the sinister aspects of humanity to become the everyday norm.
The job often left the man enervated, but he persisted in performing his duties to the best of his abilities. Some days had been better than others, and
as he faced the morning, an embedded, underlying premonition nagged at
his very being. Things had been strange, but his instincts as a seasoned detective informed him that events were about to worsen.

His recent caseload had been filled with murders that expressed savage
brutality that went beyond psychotic and dipped into the essence of pure
evil. The more superstitious in his precinct were beginning to believe the far-
out myths of magic and outdated religious rhetoric. The severity of the recent crime scenes started to override the logical reasonings of those on the
force; the gathering of hard scientific evidence no longer seemed to provide
sound explanations.

John buttoned his white collared shirt in the bedroom of the home he
and his wife Jenny purchased after the honeymoon. He caught his complete
reflection in the body-length mirror. He stood a good five feet ten inches tall
and was muscular enough to act as a detour sign to any would-be attackers.
Something, however, remained absent. He could see it clearly in his eyes;

those eyes were only thirty-eight years old. This fact was painfully observed during every instance of solitude where he was forced to gaze upon his reflection.

He turned his attention to the queen-sized bed as if it would help fill the void discovered by the reflection. There was a time when Jenny would be sitting up with a grin and an elegant nightie covering her smooth porcelain skin. She would happily watch him get ready for work and be with him during every step of his morning routine. John had always heard the nights were the hardest to get used to. However, he found that the mornings were even more challenging and wondered if anyone ever grew accustomed to the void left by a loved one's death.

His cell phone rang, vibrating the wooden top of the nightstand near the head of the bed. He answered, happy to be removed from the numbing thoughts crashing through his mind.

"This is Lycros." He spoke into the phone.

Diana Knight spoke softly on the other end of the line. *"Good morning John. I know you're on your way to the station and all, but I just wanted you to know that it would be okay if you took the day off. No one would think any less."*

"Diana, I'd expect that kind of conversation from the department shrink, but you know me better than that." John heaved a sigh as his eyes caught the bed again. He could almost see Jenny lying down, reading one of her science fiction novels in a comfortable pose.

"I'm your partner, John, and your friend. All I'm saying is that it'd be okay." Diana's voice reassured.

"The only time I'm any good is when I'm working. I'll be in soon. Do me a favor. Make sure I get some coffee before it runs out; the first batch always seems to be the best. Do we have any new leads while I have you on the line?" John redirected the conversation preparing his mind for another day of work. There were far too many unanswered questions, and he loathed not knowing. The nagging persistence to need answers is what made him a good detective.

Diana's tone returned to that of a professional detective. *"Right now, we're waiting on forensics to get back to us. I hope I never have to walk into an apartment like that again. Reports should be in within the hour. Do you think we might be seeing the first in a serial? We're finding a lot of similarities."*

"It's hard to say right now. The condition of the body makes for a very deranged and disturbed individual. It's too early to tell if this is the beginning of a series or if it's isolated. If it is, we must do everything possible to stop it." He took a deep breath, preparing himself for the dark side of his city: New Gilead.

"I'll start the team and brief you when you get in. See ya in a little bit."

Lycros ended the call and placed the cell phone in his pocket. He tucked in his white shirt after buttoning the last button, slid on his suit jacket, and ensured his sidearm was secure in the holster at his hip. Finally, he grabbed the badge on the nightstand near the bed and looked about the room as if it were a living person.

"Goodbye, Jen. I'll be home before you know it." He closed his eyes, leaving the pain in the bedroom, opened them, and left for work.

"You think yourselves free? Please! You're slaves to your hab-its. You are slaves to the day-to-day. I've been alive for centu-ries. I've seen enough to know that humans can't function unless it is in some way free of accountability answering to another person, entity, or daily routine. You were created with the pa-thetic condition of needing to be told what to do. Bloody fools! The lot of you!" – Minx, Vampire, and supporter of the Forever Man

9

DIANA KNIGHT HELD her cell phone in hand, contemplating the well-being of her partner John Lycros; the brunette tucked the mobile device in her pants pocket with a concerned sigh before sitting at her desk. The wom-an's career as a detective had been a few years shy of John's. Being married to the job had been her intention from the beginning; naturally, the job al-ways came first.

Her clothing granted the freedom of movement needed while pointing out her position of authority. The stereotype of a tough woman on the force had served her well, but often, she wished that the people she spent so much time with could see her for who she was. However, a more profound aspect of her ran deeper than what she let people see. This was the part of herself she wished she could let John experience, but the consequences were far too significant.

The sounds of hot coffee pouring into Styrofoam cups mixed with wake-up yawns and whispered chatter filled the air in the precinct that morning. The shift change at dawn had already taken place, allowing the night owls to find rest in whichever nest they called home. Dark curtains with tinted win-dows and eye masks kept the day at bay, allowing the sleep-deprived a peaceful daytime slumber.

Diana sat at her workstation, studying the empty seat on the other side of the conjoined desks. Her partner John was still consumed by the demon of Jenny's unfortunate death. He tried desperately to hide it, but it was written all over his face. His wife had taken her own life a year ago today, and Diana felt the void of emptiness that swallowed her whole when recalling that tragic afternoon. Her instincts as a detective and empathy as a friend informed her that John must have felt that exact emptiness times ten.

You'll get through this, John.

At that moment, two officers dressed in patrolmen's uniforms marched along the outer walkway of the station. She had seen them before at various crime scenes. The portlier was Officer Clems, and the younger rookie was Officer Preston. They had a young man in custody; they marched him along on display as their latest catch. He couldn't have been older than eighteen and wore a waiter uniform that had seen better days. The young man was utterly terrified about being publicly shown off in cuffs as he avoided eye contact with everyone he encountered.

It must be his first arrest. Diana raised an eyebrow. *Hopefully, it'll be his last.*

The young man oddly struck Diana. Once he was removed from her line of sight, she couldn't shake the feeling that something was different about him. It was as if the youth were important somehow. All of her innate instincts were alarming her to this fact.

Get your mind right, Diana. With that thought, she stood from her desk and went to make sure there would be enough fresh coffee for John when he arrived. She also needed to assemble the team and get them going for the day.

"Detective Knight." A voice called out, distracting her from her current task.

"Yes." She turned to see Jameson, a tall skinny detective. His clothing style was far too new and proper for the job, but he wore the suit well and was damn proud of his promotion. "What is it?"

He cleared his throat. "We've got a report of a homicide in an apartment district downtown on the east side. River Town. The victim's name is Andrew Callmun. After receiving a tip about a disturbance, a few uniforms went to investigate."

"And?" She patiently waited for him to get to the point.

Jameson took a few uneasy steps closer. "It follows the pattern of some of the murders we've seen lately. It's pretty gruesome. From the preliminary reports, it's almost as bad as the last few scenes we've arrived at. There's blood everywhere —all over the walls and even on the ceiling. The first responders reported that internal organs are missing."

Shit, another bloodied-up scene made her stomach churn. "Let's get a team down there right away and have the uniforms block off the area; follow the usual protocol. I'll let Lycros know to meet us there."

Jameson nodded as he moved into action.

Diana reached for her cell phone, calling Lycros again. "And here I thought it would be an easy morning."

"Blending in after the Distinction of Realms was enacted – that was easy. Language is easy. Humans are easy. Tempting, pushing, and pulling them how I see fit has ALWAYS been easy. I can sound like I belong, I can sound like an authority figure, or I can sound like someone in need of saving. I'm a demon, after all. Which one? That's the question you truly want an answer to, right? Let's just say that I go WAY back. Back before anything was. In reality, your perspective is skewed. Demons weren't always considered an instrument of evil as you now define it." – Develin, Demon Wizard (Origins unknown. True demonic name unknown. From a debriefing with Special Agent Della Meyer of the Natural Magic Order.)

10

THE ALARMING PANIC Jared Hernandez felt from being arrested and placed in handcuffs began to subside as he sat in the police station's holding cell. He had lost track of how long since the portly Officer Clems deposited him within the holding cell. But, if he had to guess, he would say it was sometime in the early afternoon.

Jared did his best to maintain a sense of isolation in the cell as he hoped his parents would arrive; the phone call to them was unsuccessful. He grimaced in defeat as his father's voice picked up on the voicemail after a few rings, and he realized that they were both likely at work by this point. Jared never bothered to memorize their work numbers, and it didn't help that his parents were adamant about turning off cell phones while on the job. The fast-paced tone in which he left the message was an attempt to stave off his frantic nature, but he still delivered the news of his arrest truthfully.

As he sat still, dressed in full waiter uniform, an unknown figure approached the youth from within the holding cell. Jared observed the red suit that adorned his body and thought it odd that he hadn't noticed the man standing around earlier. The stranger carried a grin and sat beside Jared in a relaxed and comfortable pose. It was as if the two were old friends preparing to catch up on years spent apart.

"It doesn't take an observant soul to see that this is your first bout with incarceration." The man in the red suit spoke nonchalantly as he stretched his arms.

Jared nodded in agreement hoping the conversation would end at that.

"Not much of a talker, but that's okay. I can talk enough for both of us. I kind of actually need an opinion on something. I'm looking for a fresh perspective, and you appear to be as fresh as they come." The man in the red suit leaned a bit closer.

The invasion of his personal space left Jared with a sense of unease. "I'm not sure I can help you."

The stranger leaned even closer. "Humor me. I have a bit of a dilemma and two viable options. It's all a matter of choice. I can either choose to act or choose not to act. The problem of it all lies with the unknown factor in this equation. The value of and how I deal with this unknown factor determines the choice. If I knew for certain what the outcomes would be, I'd know which path to take; however, given that I don't have that kind of power, I'm forced to work with what I have in the present moment."

Jared nodded reluctantly. "So, what's the choice?"

"Right now, it's all about what's best for my employer. My boss, the one I report to, isn't in the country at the moment. He's very patient and wants nothing more than to be in the country, especially New Gilead. It's a city of interest to him. A lot of things tend to happen here. It's not called the city of crossroads for nothing." The man laughed, slapping Jared on the back. Jared jostled forward, not expecting the blow. "You see, the choice I make right now - one of two - will determine how that happens. I just can't figure out which choice is the proper one."

"And that has to do with this unknown factor?" Jared asked.

The man smiled. It was unsettling. "Yes, it does. If properly managed, the unknown factor can help my boss get into the country later on. That means manipulating, grooming, and pushing things to that point. It's a delicate process, and if not handled with the right amount of finesse, things can go south and work against my employer."

Jared furrowed his brow confused at how this man thought he could help. "What happens if you decide not to try that?"

"I'd get rid of the unknown factor altogether. It wouldn't be a factor in anything anymore." The smile disappeared, leaving an even greater sense of unease. The man's eyes penetrated Jared to the core with ill intent. "Do I take no action and invest in the idea of control, or do I resolve the problem straight away and take the unknown factor out of the equation? Like I said, my boss is patient, and there might be other ways to get what he wants despite how he may feel about this unknown factor."

Jared cleared his throat and leaned back, suddenly claustrophobic with the lack of space in the cell. "Well, um... It might be better to see where this unknown factor goes and use it to your advantage. Sometimes doing nothing is doing something."

The strange man burst out into unexpected and joyous laughter. He patted Jared on the back, concluding his boisterous episode, and nodded in approval; the forceful jostle nearly knocked Jared from where he was seated. "You see, that's why I love fresh perspectives. There isn't any bias in what you said. It's pure honesty."

"So, what are you going to do?" Jared wanted to know.

The man in the red suit shrugged. "I'm going to see how things play out. It might just be well worth the risk after all."

The guard on duty at the police station waddled up to the holding cell door with a clipboard and pen in hand. He surveyed the group of misfits before speaking loudly. "Mr. Lin? Mr. Dev Lin?"

The man in red stood up with a slight yawn while straightening his suit jacket. "That would be me."

"Your bail has been posted, Mr. Lin. So you're free to go. I just need a signature." The officer explained.

"Thank you, officer. Impeccable timing." Develin turned to face Jared one last time. "See you around, kid."

Perplexed beyond words, Jared nodded to the stranger in the red suit and watched as the guard opened the door to the holding cell. Develin smiled while signing the paperwork and broke into a casual whistle as he strutted out of view. As soon as the mystery man vanished, Jared returned his thoughts to the status of his parents and eventually to the baffling reaction of Sara White.

Why did she lie about me to the cops? Was she scared into doing that? Did they threaten her? It just doesn't make any sense. None of it makes any damn sense!

After having known her for so long, he thought he had a handle on Sara. The previous night's events kept playing over and over in his mind. She had willingly left with the man named Vic, and in hindsight, she seemed to have known him better than Jared would care to admit. However, one thing was sure, and that was the fact that no matter what events may have transpired, he still harbored strong affection for Sara. Those feelings ran deep. That alone made the situation all the more difficult for him to understand.

Why did you lie about what happened to us, Sara? Why are you covering it up?

He remembered the kiss. The warmth of Sara's affection during those moments before the strange encounter with the men in the limo was genuine. Her feelings for him were real. Weren't they?

"Love is magic in its own right. It is blissful and painful. The bliss of the moment is overpowering; the pain of knowing it can never last crushes the soul. I have lived lifetimes, and I have loved men and women alike. Each love was unique and special. Each loss is a scar I carry in my heart. The burden of immortality is that I must carry them with me in every waking moment. I stay the same, and their flame vanishes in the blink of an eye with the promise of eternity echoing in the void left by their absence." – Former Grace Aglaia (Valerie Chari)

11

THE LUSH GREENERY of the park gave Valerie a nostalgic sense of what life had been like in the early days when most of the Earth was covered in varying shades of glorious color. The world was exorbitant with incredible vigor and very inexperienced during those infantile moments. The freshness and allure of first life tantalized her puerile senses.

Modern parks like the one Valerie sat in were still alive with that primal beauty, and it was an ancient power that few mortals ever noticed. Nature's firm grasp still held sway over the different trees, from the Red Oak to the Turkey Oak and the Silver Linden. But, as Fate would have it, the Flowering Dogwood enticed Valerie's essence, or soul, the most. The vibrant leaves left her higher functions benumbed as she felt the power of Nature's design.

"I assume you're Valerie." The female voice spoke up behind the former Grace.

Though Valerie had been startled, she dared not hint at that fact. Instead, she turned her head as if she had been expecting the woman. Valerie's eyes followed Special Agent Della Meyer as the NMO agent stepped from behind her. Della's posture was relaxed yet ready to act; she sat on the park bench next to the former Grace.

"A mutual friend sent me to speak with Miss Chari. You fit the description." Della explained.

Valerie nodded in confirmation. "I'm the one you seek."

Della studied Valerie allowing a slight smile to form. "What are you?"

Valerie was unaccustomed to such directness. "Excuse me?"

Della used her heightened genetic senses to study Valerie. "I've met many supernatural creatures in my day, but none quite like you. I can tell you're not a normal human. The fact that the Order sent me out to explain the information you requested in person tells me you've been around long enough to have a decent amount of influence."

Valerie laughed elegantly, befitting a queen, as she, in return, studied the NMO agent. Della's black suit fit her well and was tailored around an athletic figure. She was in superb physical condition, which rekindled for Valerie a memory of the Amazons of old.

"Are you going to answer my question?" Della smiled, finding it difficult to not be enticed by the former Grace's pheromones. Her heightened genetic awareness could be deadly if she were so immersed in it that she lost control. *Stay focused!*

"I'm a very old friend to the Natural Magic Order, and I have been around for a long time." The former Grace left it at that.

"Since before the city of New Gilead was founded?" Della pushed.

"Trying to discover a woman's age so aggressively is still considered rude unless I'm mistaken," Valerie smirked.

Della blushed a bit. "I apologize. My curiosity got the better of me."

Valerie nodded in acceptance. "I simply wish to gather information regarding events likely to transpire at the Brightwood Country Club."

"What makes you so certain that such events are likely to occur?" Della was impressed by the woman's deduction.

Valerie returned her gaze to the trees surrounding the two. "I've felt it in the air. The energy is undeniable. The thing is, my everyday guise requires me to be an intricate part of that establishment. Changes have begun, and I wish to know if anything has been sanctioned. I'm well aware that Dracien controls the area, for the most part, and that anything sanctioned would be his decision. However, the Natural Magic Order does keep a close eye on things. You've also been known to step in occasionally."

"You're correct in your assumptions." Della leaned back on the park bench, relaxing into it further. "Three rogue spirits brokered a deal with

Dracien to carry out a grand sacrifice within the confines of Brightwood. That's all we were told."

Valerie's eyebrow rose. "That would explain the boy's crossing over."

Della leaned in. "By boy, do you mean Jared Hernandez?"

"I do." Valerie nodded.

Della sat back. "Yes. Regrettably, young Mr. Hernandez was in the wrong place at the wrong time. We noticed him several hours after the deal was brokered between the two parties. Our files on such individuals are updated regularly; science and magic are working together at their best."

"What is the Order's official stance?" Valerie asked.

Reluctantly, Della gave her an answer. "We're not to intervene. The distribution of areas after the Distinction was enacted speaks for itself. It's Dracien's territory, and we abide by his rules. However, it was agreed, by the Order and Dracien, that if events spread outside the country club during this grand sacrifice, the Natural Magic Order is authorized to end it by any means."

Valerie contemplated her options, and she could sense that Della was not happy with the stance the NMO took. "There are a lot of innocent lives on the line."

"Maintaining balance outweighs innocence for us all, and this is especially true with the Distinction of Realms in place. You know that; we all do. Without balance, everything would fall apart. We'd be in another dark age before the sun sets." Della admitted.

A thought occurred to Valerie. "What if I were to enforce the old Edict of Innocence to step in and stop this sacrifice?"

This time Della's eyebrow rose with curiosity. "You'd piss off the Praetor Projector Council, Dracien, and perhaps even the Natural Magic Order, but none of them could stop you. Invoking such an edict gives you the right to protect any life that can't properly defend itself against supernatural means. Technically speaking, this sacrifice fits the definition of the edict, but you'd be on your own. No one from the Order would offer assistance."

"I've been on my own before. Please be kind enough to let your superiors know that I am invoking the Edict of Innocence. I intend to stop this sacrifice from happening. They can send word to the Praetor Projector Council and Dracien. I'm also claiming Jared Hernandez since the one responsible for his marking has abandoned him. From this moment on, the boy is under my protection." Valerie stared at Della, challenging the NMO agent to question her decree.

"Consider it done. Good luck." Della smiled, leaning in a bit closer. "Perhaps one day you'll tell me what you really are?"

Valerie leaned in as well. "Perhaps I will...."

"Myer. My name is Della Myer. Apologies. I should have started with that." Della admitted.

"Thank you for your assistance, *very* Special Agent Della Myer. You've been most gracious." Valerie smiled. The two women exchanged a cordial nod, stood from the park bench, and walked away in opposite directions blending in with the public.

"Just because we're supernatural doesn't mean we have all the bloody answers. In many ways, it makes existence that much more intolerable. Imagine your basic understanding of physics. You're aware of how gravity works. There are laws. You might come to some conclusions about how those laws came to be. You form theories, and there's some supporting evidence. But definitive proof may be lacking as to the why – and by why, I mean the big WHY. Now imagine your understanding of things on that level is ripped apart when a spell is cast, levitating you from the ground. You're further away from understanding things because what was supposed to be a certain way isn't. And there's still no concrete answer for the why! There's no mighty power telling you that it's supposed to be this way or that. So, bugger off and leave me be! Figure it out for yourself!" - Minx (centuries-old vampire – a supporter of the Forever Man)

12

THE LAST RAYS of sunlight vanished from the sky, and the night awoke, casting the city with an eerily unique ambiance that those who lived in the light found uncomfortable for primal reasons. Senses were naturally heightened when the stars and moon appeared, and Valerie was no exception. The transition from day to night was pure magic that commanded respect.

Her confident gait carried her through a grungier part of New Gilead where residents remained aloof of one another, and strangers were fiercely ignored. Then, while turning into an alley after sensing nothing was amiss, she felt a pang of disgust from within her stomach. She was about to meet someone she had not spoken to in ages, and it was a reunion she could have done without.

Valerie ventured deeper into the alley's darkness, where the streetlights allowed for a painting of shadows to cover the faded brick walls of old buildings. The rusty green dumpsters scattered about gave off an aroma that would lead one to believe their contents hadn't been emptied in years.

She froze in her steps and closed her eyes. The sound of a neck snapping and the animalistic slurping and sucking that followed could have only resulted from *him*.

"You, my dear, are a bit early. The sun had set not even twenty minutes ago. I'll be with you in a moment, finishing my breakfast. It's the most important meal of the day, innit?" The shadows carried the voice after the wildly barbaric sounds of struggle ceased revealing the slightest British accents. It was a weathered voice aged with centuries of violence and bloodshed.

"It's a shame you've come to this, Minx." Valerie did her best to subdue her growing disgust. She never did like vampires all that much.

Creeping from the shadows stood a man approximately four feet tall. His clothing was contemporary but hardly of the upper class. His head was nearly bald, and he held a bottle of vodka in his hand, almost as drained as his latest victim. He took a swig allowing his bloodstained lips to cover the tip of the bottle.

"You used to be so proud, but now look at you. And the fact that an immortal creature like you, which thirsts only for the blood of a living soul, would still drink mortal liquors is somewhat perplexing. I never did understand that about you." Valerie sized up the little vampire.

"Judge not, my dear Aglaia. The alcohol makes the blood taste better in a way that can't be expressed with words. It's quite delicious. If you ever decide to change your status and join the vampire ranks, I highly recommend it." Minx took a few more steps toward Valerie. "I've also changed with the times. Foolish pride and status with how things used to be, are behind me. My purpose is as it has been for centuries now. The Forever Man is out there, and I shall find him."

"Still holding on to a lost cause? What happened that turned you into such a devout follower of this prophetic nonsense?" Valerie asked.

He offered the bottle of vodka out to Valerie and took another swig soon after she declined with a slight hand gesture. "It may be nonsense to some, but it is a fact to me. So I do as I must. On the other hand, you have denied what you are to the last. You relinquished your godhood to become a normal human, and for what? Ah, yes, I remember now... it was for the love of a mortal. I'll grant you that he was a rather powerful magician, but he's gone now. So why continue to deny what you truly are? There isn't much sense in being mortal and growing old if the person you planned to grow old with is already dead."

Irritation flushed through her. "I didn't contact you to discuss my choices, and I go by the name of Valerie Chari these days."

"I enjoy revisiting your choices, like choosing the hospitality industry. The rumor mill speaks of you carrying out managerial duties at a country club. How quaint. It's all so very *human*. How does it feel? The agelessness of being one of the Graces hasn't completely left you yet, but I can see that your denial of what you are has made you weaker. If you keep this up, you'll turn completely human. Far too many of your kind have perished that way after the Distinction was enacted." Minx finished the bottle of vodka and tossed it aside. The violent burst of the breaking glass caused a hiding cat to scramble in fear.

"The magic that remains ages me slowly, and I still can conduct a proper spell or two." She admitted.

Minx smirked. "Yes, but even that will fade if you continue this mortal path. Is that what you truly want?"

Annoyed by Minx's prodding, Valerie shifted to the reason for her visit. "I believe there are rogue spirits at work. What I *want* is help with this."

"Rogue spirits?" Minx levitated to a dumpster near Valerie and stood atop it at eye level with the woman. "Is that why you contacted me?"

She nodded. "I've lived a quiet life for a long time now. The last thing I want to do is re-enter the world I left behind. But, as you've stated, for all intents and purposes, I'm on the road to becoming human."

"You do realize that by talking to me, you're back on the radar, as the saying goes. Others will seek you out, and the more involved you become, the more your powers will reemerge. Have you forgotten how things work for your kind? You are of the First Supernatural, the ones born from the age of myth." Caution filled his tone.

"I'll take my chances, Minx." Valerie took another step closer to the little vampire. "Now, can we move on to the matter at hand?"

"What makes you think you've come across rogue spirits?" Minx asked with professional candor.

"I can still sense things of power, and my intuition was verified earlier today after speaking to a Natural Magic agent. It turns out that there are at least three at work, and innocent people are at risk. These are people that I've come to care about." Valerie admitted.

He balked at the statement. "Come now, Valerie. We both know there's no such thing as innocent. Do you truly believe that?"

"You know I do." She answered without hesitation.

"Free will destroyed innocence, my dear. The choice is all that remains for any of them - for any of us, for that matter. Choice leaves no room for innocence: just accountability." Minx sighed, pitying the former Grace.

"I didn't come here for a philosophical debate!" Valerie's eyes flashed with a fire not seen in ages. She grew more impatient with each passing second.

Minx chuckled boyishly as he peered into her blue eyes. "Yes! You hunger for the power you've lost! I can see it in those beautiful eyes of yours. Yet, even now, the essence of what you once were is growing stronger."

Valerie radiated acceptance. "Then so be it. What will happen will happen. Now, will you help, or am I wasting my time?"

"Apologies. How exactly may I be of assistance?"

"I need a bowl. Not just any bowl, mind you, but you already know this. I need an authentic sacrificing bowl. If they're planning what I fear they're planning, then I need a way to counter it, and if all goes well, the boy will be spared of his connection to them." She explained.

"There's a boy involved? Living as a human has made you soft indeed." Minx noted.

"He is a good young man and deserves a fighting chance. But, he doesn't belong in our world." Her posture was adamant.

Minx shrugged. "Does this good young man have a name?"

"Jared." She said.

Minx leaned closer in a playful manner. "And his true name? The one that gives him power? Do you know it yet? Have you touched inside of his soul and taken it from him?"

Valerie shook her head. "I do not concern myself with such things any-more."

Minx shrugged again. "Of course you don't. Return to me tomorrow at the same time. I'll have the requested item in my possession by then."

"Thank you." She allowed her posture to relax.

"You know me, Valerie. I'm always happy to repay my debts, but after this, I owe you no more." His gestures accented the point.

Valerie nodded. "It is as you say; what you owe will be settled."

"Good." A smile revealed the vampire's fangs.

Valerie nodded again as a sign that their interaction was complete and turned away from the little vampire on a clear path to the main street.

"Valerie!" Minx called out, waiting for her to turn back and face him. "I say this because I respect you. Your love for humans will only destroy you. We were never meant to be a part of their world. We were meant to live in a world within the one ordinary humans know. This boy, Jared, spare him if you can. When some human crosses over into our domain, there is no turn-ing back. That human is forever cursed."

"I'm well aware, Minx, but I fear it's too late. He's in love with one of the former goddesses. If I'm reading things correctly, this entity fully recipro-cates the emotion." Sorrow filled her tone. It wouldn't end well for Jared and the rogue spirit.

Minx considered the situation. "I see. The boy is marked. Love... It's such a wretched magical concoction, innit? There's been far too much pain caused by love."

"What is life without love, Minx? What are any of us without it?" Valerie admitted.

Minx scoffed at Valerie's comments and blended back into the comfort of his loving shadows.

"The Praetor Projector Council passes judgment however they see fit. They claim to protect the balance between realms at all costs, but does it truly seem that way? They protect their own interests and dwindling influence. They are powerful, each one, but they are stale, existing as shells of what they were before they agreed to enact the Distinction of Realms. They can create many wondrous things with the magic of their will! Projectors were tasked with CREATING WORLDS from the Founding Magic that brought them into existence! They waste the power granted by the High Celestials and the God of gods! If the scales of this precious balance were to tip in their favor, what then? Who could stand in the way of creatures this powerful? Besides me, of course." – Nina Wols (Projector/Soul Eater. Last of the young projectors.)

13

BARELY STANDING ATOP the remains of a once thriving suburban block was the home of Edward Wols. This formerly lavish estate had once catered to the grander side of life, being a treat to the senses for the well-off of New Gilead's former elite. Now it stood as one of the few homes inhabited in a decaying radius of city blocks that the well-to-do did well to avoid. Yet, despite the grim surroundings, the estate insisted upon enduring the hardships. The Wols family was just as stubborn in their tenacious nature, having maintained the home for generations.

Upon entering the rundown estate, one would instantly be privy to the odor of decades without cleanliness. It was an odor so putrid that it would enfeeble the nostrils of the unprepared that were brave enough to step through the front door. But, for Edward Wols, it was a smell as natural as a flower in bloom and was one he came to expect day in and day out. The dead knew this house well, and the smell reminded them that their corpses had long been unattended. It was a matter Edward intended to remedy but was too lazy to fix.

The kitchen light was the only one that remained on during these late hours. Edward sat at the small round table placed in the center, as he often had, smoking a cigarette and yearning for his situation to be anything than what it was. Broken beer bottles and unfinished food were strewn about the kitchen, with a small path in and out tailored by Edward.

Sufficed to say, the house's appearance complimented the appearance of its owner. Beaten, broken, and unappealing to the eye, Edward lived his days in an idle state of loneliness. Each moment of his existence blended into the next.

Within the living room, which was directly connected to the kitchen, the shadows became alive with swirls of movement. Hands formed out of the pitch-black, reaching for where Edward sat. The hands varied in size, growing more menacing with each transformation. Finally, the forces behind the hands began to whisper his name, letting the darkness carry it to the edge of the living room where the kitchen started.

Edward snapped from his daze, having heard the call. The last remaining male Wols dismissed it feeling his cigarette warranted more attention than his surroundings. Three puffs later and Edward felt normal again. Still, at that moment, faint, unsettling laughter broke through the loud silence and echoed behind him, destroying the temporary peace.

"Is anyone there?" Edward asked, thinking it was a prank from the neighborhood children. The little runts lived on the other side of the tracks where the decaying state of being was absent. The only answer reaching him was a silence as unsettling as the darkness.

The noise that soon followed was barely audible. Slight breathing almost made the house seem alive, and it drove Edward mad as it began to crescendo in volume with each passing second.

"Stop it!" Edward moved about the kitchen, knocking over empty beer bottles and stepping on rotten food. The berating breath grew heavier. "I said to stop it!"

Knowing what must be done, Edward summoned his strength and took a few steps toward the living room's darkness. He stood at the edge where the linoleum floor met the dark carpeting. Unable to move, Edward reached his arm to the light switch, and it was no surprise that the light was unresponsive. Instead, small shadowy figures flickered across Edward's view, making him jump with a petrified sensation that ran through his entire body.

"I have to do this." He whispered while forcing his first step.

The house seemed to welcome Edward into the darkness as he walked into the living room, barely lit by the light from the kitchen. In particular, one door stood out to Edward; it was the door to a bedroom that belonged to his sister. A strange noise could be heard brewing from behind the door, and it was in that room that the source of the peculiar occurrences waited.

The doorknob fit comfortably in the palm of his hand, and he turned it as the eerie noise from within the bedroom grew louder. Then, after a split second of hesitation, he whipped the door open. He jumped inside the room, looking directly at his little sister.

"Nina! Wake up! I need you to stop it right now! You know I have to go to sleep before you do, and it simply can't be the other way around!" Edward yelled as loudly as possible.

Nina shot up from the bed, and the dark shadowy figure behind Edward dissipated. After a yawn, she rubbed her eyes and looked at her brother. "I'm sorry, Eddy. I thought you'd already gone to bed. I assumed it would be okay to turn in for the night."

Edward huffed. "Well, I didn't, Nina. I'm still awake, and you fell asleep on me. You started using your gift doing that unconscious projector thing you do whenever you go to sleep. It's quite unsettling!"

An innocent smile flashed across her face. "You can stop yelling now, Eddy. I'm wide awake, no thanks to you. No more out-of-control power for the night. I promise."

Edward wiped the sweat from his brow. He looked to Nina, who gave a smile on the verge of laughter as she sat upright in bed. Her pale skin and dark hair were attractive in an unorthodox way. Though her pajamas were somewhat baggy and juvenile, it was evident that an adult female figure was covered up beneath them.

"This isn't funny." He growled.

"You're absolutely right. Not funny at all." She kept a straight face.

"I'm going to bed now," Edward warned.

"Good." She nodded.

"Don't fall asleep until I do." He demanded.

"I won't." She mocked his tone.

"I'm serious!" He insisted.

Her serious demeanor cracked as laughter snuck out. "I know. And Eddy..."

"What?" He rolled his eyes.

Nina grew quite serious. "We have to do something about the bodies. The decaying flesh is starting to smell very bad. I don't mind, but others near the house might catch on, and we're just starting. I wouldn't want anything to interrupt our fun."

He sighed and gestured for her to relax. "I'll take care of it, my dear sister, as always. I promise. Now, wait until I go to bed."

"Good night Eddy." Her tone sounded childlike.

Edward exited the bedroom and slammed the door shut behind him with irritation. At that moment, Nina burst into laughter so much that she had to wipe a tear from her eye.

A yawn reminded Nina of the rest her body craved. If she concentrated on focusing hard enough, she was sure she could be asleep in seconds. It was intended as a lesson, after all. She wouldn't get rid of the dead bodies that were the cause of the putrid odor all on her own. So instead, she kept Eddy alive with her power as a projector so that he could have a purpose and take care of such menial tasks.

A sudden knock at the front door caused Nina to sit up with childlike curiosity. She could hear her brother answer with a hidden tone that yearned for an actual death. She also listened to a familiar voice greet Edward as she set her feet on the hardwood floor of her room while sitting at the edge of the bed. With supernatural ease, Nina glided across the floor to the door and opened it. A smile from ear to ear formed on her face as she saw a little vampire standing with her brother in the living room.

"Uncle Minx!" Nina flew to the little man disregarding the act of walking and lifted him up in the air with a mighty hug.

"Bloody hell, Nina, I hate it when you do that to me!" Minx wiggled about in Nina's arms like a helpless pup. He was intimately aware of how powerful she was. If she had wanted to, the woman could erase him from existence indefinitely by merely thinking about it with a focused energy that only seasoned projectors could muster. Projectors, in their own right, were a rare breed and monitored closely by all the powers that kept a balance between realms. The primary source of policing was the Praetor Projector Council. Rarer still was a creature like Nina; she was a projector and soul eater.

"It's so good to see you again! It's been ages!" She placed Minx back on the ground with a childish grin and patted his head with a hint of condescension.

Edward looked at his sister and back to the vampire. "It's been far too long, if you ask me, for just about everything."

"You look absolutely horrible, Edward," Minx noted.

Edward shrugged. "Thank you, Minx. It's the price you pay when you're forced to stay out past your expiration date. Technically I died... I don't even remember how long it's been. In fact, I think I've been *dead* alive longer than I've been *alive* alive. Go figure, but my good old sister here keeps me going with her precious gift nonetheless."

Minx sniffed the house and formed a grin of his own. "It smells like death in here. You two up to your old tricks again?"

"When haven't we been?" Edward let out a sigh feeling the strain of forced life. "I tire of it, however. I'm the one always left with cleaning up the mess."

"I have to feed if I'm to stay strong, Eddy. You know that. I'm a projector and a soul eater. My projection powers come from feasting on the essence of living things." Nina crossed her arms, huffing.

"I know, my sweet sister, I know." Edward turned his attention back to Minx. "So, what can I do for you at this hour? I imagine it isn't a social call."

"I need to procure a particular item. I'm looking for a sacrificing bowl. So I figured you would be the one to turn to if I needed to find one on short notice. Besides, the two of you have always dabbled in such things." Minx explained.

Edward was puzzled. "Why would you need something like that? Have you fallen in love with a goddess or something?"

Minx sighed, irritated by the idea. "I'm not the type to fall in love. But, if truth be told, I'm requesting it on behalf of another party. I'm repaying a debt. She happens to be entangled with rogue spirits of some sort and wishes to put an end to some kind of sacrifice."

"Rogue spirits, hey? Sounds like fun. I haven't fed on a deity in such a long time. So many have gone so deep into hiding or given up godhood leaving the main responsibility of balance to the Praetor Projector Council. I could never imagine giving up what I am for any reason." Nina fell deep in thought and carried a face of insatiable hunger at the idea of feeding upon a rogue spirit. The essence of a deity was far more potent than lesser creatures.

"The item you requested should be in the basement - a few of them, come to think of it. I'll make sure to get the strongest one. Make yourself at home in the meantime." Edward Wols exited the living room at a zombielike pace leaving Minx and his sister alone to catch up.

"Uncle Minx, I have a favor to ask of you?" She stepped forward with the enthusiasm of a teenager asking to borrow the car.

Minx stepped back with caution. "What kind of *favor* did you have in mind, my dear?"

"It pertains to these rogue spirits. If it's agreeable to the person you've come here to gather the sacrificing bowl for, I believe I could be of great assistance. It would be a mutual payoff. The person you represent and I would both get what we want." Her hunger shone through the human façade.

Minx grinned. "I'm sure the payoff for you would be far greater."

"You know me far too well, Uncle Minx." The smile of desired hunger on Nina's face created a fear in the vampire that almost made him feel human.

"My parents were the hardest working people I ever knew. They were a fine example of the American dream. They came to this country with little, worked up to respectable jobs and positions, and built a family here. Because of my crossing over, their lives were changed forever. The idea of family was transformed because they were unknowingly given a new set of circumstances where I never existed as their son. I could never see them again as Jared, but helping them as Vestor, well, that I could do and have done. What's the point of seeing the future if you can't nudge good people in the right direction from time to time?" –
Vestor, the Time Bender

14

VALERIE STOOD AT the front door of the Hernandez residence struggling with the decision she had come to. The proper course of action seemed wrong as she contemplated the details of what needed to be done with a somber expression. The cool night air gave the front porch a welcoming appeal despite the neighborhood's depravity and helped clear her mind.

The portico was void of any outside furniture because it would probably have been stolen by morning, and the exterior light above her head flickered randomly with lazy indifference. In general, crime was a significant factor; most people wouldn't be caught outside at this late hour, but then again, most people weren't ancient goddesses.

Deep within her essence, Valerie knew it was too late to spare Jared from the consequences of being marked; his soul was forever crossed over. For now, young Mr. Hernandez was safe and sound in a not-so-cozy jail cell. She felt terrible for having left him alone with the experience of incarceration. Still, he was far safer with the human degenerates than the supernatural ones.

Valerie took advantage of the moment to exclude the ones Jared loved without his hurt, angry opposition standing as a barrier. If the boy failed to tread carefully, his parents would cross over due to his unwitting involvement with powers beyond his comprehension.

A sad sigh preceded the inevitable knock at the door. Valerie had no choice but to clean the minds of Jared's parents and expedite a process that would happen naturally if Jared remained absent from everyone he knew. However, the patterns of Jared's behavior dictated he would run to those he loved as soon as he was free of his confinement. The fallout of those marked as a result of the initially marked was typically limited to immediate family.

The former Grace stood her ground and knocked on the door again. The hour was late, and the visit was unexpected. Andres, Jared's father, opened the house's front door, surprised to find a beautiful blonde woman at his doorstep. She greeted him with the kindest of smiles, and he returned one reflexively.

"Hello. I truly do apologize for the late hour." Valerie maintained her warm demeanor as she spoke. "I'm here to talk to you about your son Jared. It's important."

"Jared? Where is he? Is he okay?" A woman's voice, Jared's mother, Maria, perked up, rising in volume from behind the door. The face behind the worrisome feminine grunts was soon at the side of the door next to her husband.

They were an average married couple in their late middle years of life. Their matching robes spoke volumes about how connected they were; both had an unrivaled work ethic that carried them through most of their time together. They continued to maintain the status of hard-working individuals. They were incredibly proud of their accomplishments and triumphs over the hardships endured as a family.

"Is Jared okay? Is he hurt?" Maria's voice was concerned.

"He's okay. May I come in for a moment?" Valerie cast another smile in their direction. She knew the magic of being a former Grace aided at this crucial moment. It only took an enchanting smile to disarm the untrusting guard most carried upon meeting her as a stranger.

"Sure. Come on in." Andres' stubbornness felt the need to fight his willingness to accept her request. He was somewhat baffled at how quickly he granted her entrance. "Who are you again?"

"My name is Valerie Chari. I'm one of Jared's supervisors at the Brightwood Country Club where he works." Valerie explained as she walked through the front door.

The living room was adorned with knickknacks collected over many years and mix-matched broken-in furniture to keep them company. The décor maintained the strong impression that a *family* lived here, and it was a family full of love.

Andres took a step closer, wanting answers. "Joe called earlier. He said Jared spent the night at his place and that he would do so again tonight. The thing is, Jared left a weird message about being arrested before Joe called. When we asked Joe about it, he said it was just a joke. Are you sure everything is okay? I mean, it's not unusual for Jared to spend the night at Joe's, but Jared didn't answer his cell phone; it went straight to voicemail. So I figured he forgot to charge the damn thing like usual. Is my son okay?"

"Yes and no." Valerie's reassuring smile vanished. She sobered up to what had to be done.

"What does that mean?" Maria stepped forward, making sure her robe was adequately secure. "Where is my son? I want to know why you're here and what's happening, and I want to know right now! Andres - call the police! I don't like any of this!"

"There's no need for any of that, Maria. He'll be taken care of. On this, I give you my word as a former Grace. However, the fact remains that both of you should never see your son again. This way, you won't be marked by his love for you, and you'll be safe to carry out the rest of your lives in peace." Valerie explained, knowing the truth of what she explained would soon be forgotten.

Andres and Maria grew angry and frustrated by Valerie's cryptic words. Their bodies defaulted to rigidly defensive postures, and Andres snapped out of the enchantment Valerie had placed on him to gain access to the house. The raw energy held by a father's love was far more powerful.

"You need to tell us what's going on right now!" Andres furiously demanded, emphasizing the words with his body language.

Valerie extended the magic dormant within her essence for so long with calm composure. She felt the significant influx of ability come alive with a resurgence that almost made her giddy with joy.

"Where is my son?!" Maria also demanded.

"You better start talking now lady!" Andres was about to reach for Valerie's arm but ceased all movement standing perfectly still. A calming sensation engulfed his entire being, and he saw that his wife was similarly affected.

"The two of you need to listen to me very carefully. You never had a son named Jared. You've been happily married this entire time without him. He never existed." Valerie pushed the idea into the deepest parts of their minds.

"But..." The magic was too strong, and Andres stopped speaking.

Valerie extended her magic further and touched the home's essence amplifying the effects of the natural cleansing spell. She could feel the atoms representing a physical space, such as Jared's room. She also sensed other objects like clothing, meager possessions, and pictures of the family throughout various stages of Jared's life. The revived magic within her blood amplified the cleansing spell causing an immediate change.

Jared's belongings were reshaped as if a Master Projector had been at work constructing an entirely new universe. The remnants of Jared's identity disappeared item by item. His room reformed into a den that Andres would remember having had in his house the entire time they lived there. His recollection would include vivid memories of building and putting the room together by hand. Maria would recall being annoyed at the time he spent working on the project when he could have hired help to finish it sooner.

Atom by atom, all the household material possessions changed, leaving no trace of Jared Hernandez. This was the way of the cleansing that accompanied a marked one's crossover between realms. Long ago, the decision was made for such a distinction by the most powerful projectors: the Praetor

Projector Council. Thus began the Distinction of Realms that was now the law.

I'm so sorry, Jared. I hope one day you'll understand and forgive me. The thought remained with Valerie as she continued amplifying the spell.

PART FIVE:

BEYOND THE
ICEBERG'S TIP

"The Natural Magic Order and the Praetor Projector Council tend to draw a line in the sand. On the left, only the magical creatures are allowed to play. On the right, ordinary humans live and can't know what's going on across that line. The powers that be forget that many sentient creatures live in both worlds and have to walk the line used to divide them." – Ming Chan – descendent of Chu-Jung, the god of fire

1

MING CHAN'S TOUGH beauty resulted from years spent learning to cope with an existence that teetered between realms. Her family's bloodline dates back to China's mythical age. Through this magical bloodline, her father and grandfather made a living as illusionists in the ordinary human world. The common public viewed their performances as great spectacles. The fantastic feats enacted were nothing more than amazing tricks explainable by the laws of science and logic; the Chan family, however, followed no such laws. Instead, they obeyed the true realm of magic where the fantastic was, in actuality, the norm.

Ming's powers manifested when she was the same age as her son Joseph Chan. She expected that an uncomfortable talk about the true nature of their lineage would be on the horizon. Like many people of magic, she existed in both worlds living amongst normal humans while interacting with creatures of a higher power. The delicate balance was taxing at times. Her late husband Emilio had always understood the dance she occasionally had to perform. If anything else, it created an interesting family dynamic.

The pressure and confines of Ming's lineage created an identity she hadn't been ready to accept. Her youthful self fled to the island of Puerto Rico. She vanished, quite literally, from her eighteenth birthday party and had done so in a way that baffled the top human illusionist and magicians of the time. The responsibility of wielding and practicing true magic in the name of her family left her fearful, empty, and ultimately lost. As happenstance would have it, the lost girl was found by a boy the same age, and an unbreakable bond was formed between Ming and Emilio. The two were quick to fall in love and never looked back.

Emilio soon discovered Ming's true nature and was left to ponder how it would affect his relationship with her and others. He was left with a choice. Emilio could continue with his everyday life forgetting that she existed, or he could leave everything he knew behind and crossover to be with Ming as she was. The decision would mean cutting ties with loved ones in the normal realm so they could be spared unnecessary dealings with the undesirable aspects of the magical plane of existence. Sufficed to say, he chose the latter. The two were eventually gifted with a beautiful son named Joseph Emilio Chan.

Arriving at the decision to move to mainland America had been a natural progression for the budding family. Ming's father had already spent much time in the states, and the two had reformed the lost bond between father and daughter. Her father would visit on occasion showing little Joseph phenomenal card tricks. Some of those tricks were even real magic.

Soon after Emilio's tragic death due to an encounter with an evil demon wizard, Ming demanded that her father never return and leave her and little Joseph in peace. Years after the devastating family schism, her father passed away, joining Emilio in the land of spirits. She hoped against all the odds that the latent powers in Joe's blood would never manifest and that he would live everyday life oblivious to that part of his heritage. Deep down, Ming learned to accept that this was never meant to be.

Develin...

The name was a curse she only acknowledged within the confines of her mind. The demon wizard had taken away the love of her life and the father of her son. Joe had grown up believing his father's death to have been an accident chalked up to nothing more than bad tires in a thunderstorm. The truth of it all was far more sinister.

While she sat in her kitchen littered with thoughts of past choices, Ming's son was upstairs in his bedroom, sleeping off another typical day of work.

Consequently, it was perhaps the final ordinary night of sleep he would ever have. An urgent message had been delivered to Ming, and the sender was someone her father had once loved dearly.

The lover in question had been a goddess from a very ancient pantheon. Ming had always thought this woman far too old to be with her father, but she had given up godhood for attempted normalcy as a human. Nevertheless, circumstances had brought her father's love back into the fantastic realm without delay. Valerie had requested to meet with Ming at this late hour, and Ming reluctantly accepted. She sensed the importance of the message as it reached her through supernatural channels.

A slight tapping at the back door window broke the kitchen's silence where Ming awaited Valerie's arrival. Ming stood from the small round wooden table and moved to the kitchen door; she briefly stared at the ageless face through the glass cutout before opening it. Emotions erupted as Ming allowed the former Grace entrance to her humble abode. The late-night hours were ending, and soon the morning would greet them all with the newness of the day to come.

After a few heartbeats of silence, Ming said: "When I found out you were working at the same country club as Joe, I almost made him quit. The last thing I wanted was for him to be exposed to any of this. I think maybe I should have forced the issue. He's going to be caught right in the middle of everything. It just can't be avoided; it comes with the blood."

Ming walked back to the round wooden table fashioned to comfortably seat four. Only she and Joe lived together, so she saw little point in large extravagant furnishing, and the house they shared was already plenty small enough. Mustering up the elegance of a gracious host, Ming gestured for Valerie to be seated across from her and waited to sit down until Valerie was settled.

Valerie cleared her throat. "I had to speed up the cleansing process with the parents of Jared Hernandez. There wasn't enough time to let it happen naturally."

Ming sighed. She had met Andres and Maria during Jared's deep friendship with Joe. They were good people. It was a shame they had to lose a son and an even greater tragedy that they would never know they had lost him. "As you know, there's no need for any cleansing here. We're of magic blood."

"And powerful magic it is." Valerie dreaded bringing up the next part. "Joe's abilities are likely to manifest soon. He's very close to Jared, and that friendship will cause an awakening. The birth of such magic is always painful."

Ming nodded. "I feared as much. When I got your message, I knew things would inevitably go down this path. I recall how painful it was for me. I was seventeen when it happened. After that, the world was never the same."

"Things rarely remain as they are," Valerie spoke the words absently.

Ming studied Valerie taking in that the former Grace had barely aged a day since her childhood. "You look as young as when I first met you. I was a child then. You and my father were always together. I hope you don't plan on stealing away my son's affections as well."

Valerie let out a slight laugh. "Perhaps you should tell him to stop the advances. I've already tried, but Joe does what Joe wants. He's insistent with the flirtations."

Ming smiled in return. "In that regard, he's exactly like his grandfather. It must be the male side of my family. Emilio's side was never so bold when interacting with women."

Valerie grew more serious. "Ming. The last thing I want to do is step in uninvited. I know you'll be there for him as a mentor, but I wanted to stop by and let you know that I'll do what I can to help guide him. Your family line is important to me. I know we've had our differences in the past and that you fled due to my involvement with your father but know I do care for you as if you were my own flesh and blood daughter."

Touched by the sentiment, Ming reached out for Valerie's hand. The sensation of affection grew stronger between the two women, as did the loyalty one would expect of family. "I know. You always meant well, and my father thought the world of you. I could have accepted you if I'd been more tolerant back then. Unfortunately, I was too hardheaded and prideful. I didn't want the magic in my blood. To this day, I still struggle with that power. I'm surprised you continued to allow your powers to fade after my father's death. You really wanted to remain mortal even though he's long been dead? It's been over a decade."

Valerie looked about the kitchen, unsure of how to respond. "I grew tired of outliving everyone. The stamina needed for such an existence wasn't in me anymore. I thought that was the case anyway. It seems the universe isn't done with me yet. Circumstances have forced me back into action, and I promise I'll help you and your son through this. I'll also help his friend Jared. Their bond is great, and Jared is a good young man. He has my protection."

"They're the best of friends." Ming smiled, recalling how the two boys were as children. The duo had been inseparable; one was always with the other, usually getting into trouble. Then, she turned her attention back to Valerie, releasing the memory. "Are you hungry or thirsty? A daughter should offer her mother food or drink when she visits."

Valerie nodded appreciatively. "Thank you. Tea would be lovely. Mint green, if you have it."

Ming smiled. "Consider it done."

Ming stood from the table and continued to speak while preparing the mint green tea; it had been a personal favorite of Valerie's. Ming still preferred the blood orange and opted to have some. The two moved on to speak in great detail about various topics. They bonded as a family should while the water boiled. The steam rose from the kettle, and Ming pulled it from the burner before it could make a noise. Quiet laughter was shared between the two. She poured into the cups savoring the aroma as the water soaked in the flavors of each tea bag. Valerie enjoyed the pure scent as well. During such moments, the universe seemed peaceful, and both women needed that.

"Prisons are simply a state of mind. As long as you can choose, you can always find freedom." – Matthew Gomez, the Forever Man.

2

IN ALL HIS years, Jared Hernandez never imagined that one morning he would open his eyes and awaken in the jail of his local police station. The cramped holding cell the police officers had confined Jared within was sparsely populated by a motley crew of misfits from varying degrees of criminality. Having only witnessed this scenario played out in movies, the young Mr. Hernandez thought it best to remain isolated.

He made sure to have a clear, vigilant vantage of his surroundings by maintaining his back against a corner of the cell. His slumber had been restless. Paranoia continued to wake him every hour of the night. He rubbed his eyes with a yawn while beginning another weary day of nothing. The monotonous snail's pace of time dangled before his awareness, and trying to mentally disregard it only strengthened its existence.

The ever-faithful tick-tock of the clock had been excruciatingly painful to his ears. The long, tedious passage of time left him wondering if the perception of time was an illusion that grew stronger the more he held on to it. More abstract thoughts cluttered his imagination as he sat, stood, walked about, and sat again. He tried unsuccessfully to use the shared toilet of the holding cell in front of the others. He sat down some more, trying to focus on anything but his current situation. Finally, his mind began to go crazy, waiting for anyone to rescue him from his torment.

His waiter uniform grew rancid with the smell of nearly two days' perspiration seeping into the fabric. The fact that he had been placed in this particular precinct shortly after confessing what he had witnessed left an ill feeling in the pit of his stomach. It was a feeling that amplified the nagging sensation of how unclean he actually was. The stress endured caused Jared to fixate on the fact that he needed a shower, and undeniable anxiety began to build around that pestering realization. He loathed feeling unclean, and the unkempt cell did little to alleviate that anxiety.

"Jared Hernandez." The familiar voice of the guard on duty called out his name.

"Yes." Jared shot a glance at the officer with hopeful eyes.

"Your bail has been posted. So you're free to go, kid." The guard spoke the words and pulled the sliding cell door open, gesturing for Jared to vacate.

Jared observed the portly man in uniform and studied the scenario as if the guard were playing a cruel joke. His uncertainty of what lay beyond made Jared think he was safer in the cell.

"Hurry up, kid!" The guard barked.

Standing behind the guard was Valerie. Jared had not noticed her before the guard opened the door, and he stepped out of the cell, confused as to why she was here to meet him instead of his parents.

The guard pushed a clipboard with a pen into Jared's chest and closed the door to the holding cell. "Sign this."

Jared signed his name in the appropriate spot and studied his boss cautiously. "Valerie? What are you doing here?" He returned the clipboard to the guard on duty while keeping his eyes on her.

"I've come to collect you. You're with me now, and we must be on our way. There isn't any time to waste. I'll do my best to answer your questions, but we have to go." Without another word, Valerie turned to exit the police station; her body language demanded that Jared follow.

"Wait! Have you spoken to my parents?" Jared rushed after Valerie bumping into the guard in the process. "Sorry."

"Just get the hell out of here, kid!" The guard barked. "Get!"

With the second command, Jared quickly ran after Valerie.

"After all of this time, I still find it incredibly amusing how lost the young are when they're confronted with a terrible reality." – Matthew Gomez, the Forever Man.

3

IT WAS JARED'S first experience riding in Valerie's car. The sleek design seemed magical to the eye. Though he could consciously think the make and model, he found himself stumbling over his words when attempting to recite the information aloud. He would spout out incorrect details with clumsy syntax painting the picture of a very different vehicle. It was one of Valerie's favorite confusion spells. The incantation worked for almost anything you wanted people to be incapable of describing, making the car ride all the more frustrating for Jared.

"I need to get home. My parents are probably freaking out right now. I've been gone for a long time, and my cell phone is dead. So they sent you to get me, right?" Jared hoped to get some answers as to why he'd been left in jail for so long.

Valerie shook her head. "No, Jared, they didn't send me. I came alone, and there's a reason for that."

Like an unseasoned soldier that has seen too much too soon, Jared placed his fingers upon his head, attempting to rub out the images burned into his memory. A lack of proper hygiene left his hair greasy, and thoughts of a warm shower ran wild in his mind. Nevertheless, he kept his head down as the car continued to drive along the street.

"I'm not sure what happened with Sara in that parking lot a few nights ago, but something crazy is happening. I need to get home and get my head straight because I'm beginning to think I imagined some pretty screwed-up stuff. Really crazy shi...." Jared cut his word short, uneasy with the idea of swearing around his supervisor.

Valerie directed the car off to the side of the street and parked along a quiet city block, turning the engine off very casually. Then, with graceful wisdom about her, she turned her head to look directly at Jared.

Young Mr. Hernandez didn't know what to make of the stare. "What's the matter? You're making me uncomfortable looking at me that way - no offense. I mean, you're an attractive woman, but you might be a little too old for me, and I don't really think that...."

Jared suddenly found that he had lost his ability to speak. He also noticed the odd positioning of Valerie's hand. It took the form of a puppet with a closed mouth. Jared grew frantic and began pointing to his throat while reaching for the car door, unable to undo the lock. The door handle refused to budge, no matter how much he struggled to make it work.

"Jared, I need you to calm down and listen. You did not imagine anything that you saw. You shouldn't have seen any of it. The fact remains, however, that you're a part of something now, and it's something that can never be undone." Valerie paused to let those words sink in. "The girl you're in love with, Sara White, she isn't a normal human. She may have taken on human form, but I'm certain that she is a rogue spirit; it is a term used to describe an ancient deity. I know this is all very difficult to process, but there are forces and powers at work that you are ignorant of. You're going to have to learn how to properly deal with these forces and powers."

Upon hearing Valerie's explanation, Jared grew even more frantic. He ceased the spontaneous body movements due to a paralyzing fear that usurped control. The sincerity and honesty of Valerie's speech frightened him to the core, and he could feel his flesh turning pale. His heart began to beat rapidly and felt like it were about to burst through his chest.

"I'm going to release your voice to you again." Valerie continued. "You'll be able to speak freely. I'll do my best to answer any questions you have but know that your well-being is my responsibility from now on. There is no going back to the life you had."

Valerie opened her hand and lowered her arm, doing away with the puppet form. She watched Jared gasp for breath as if he had narrowly escaped drowning. "How...? How the hell did you do that? How the hell was any of that possible?"

"Magic from my former life has reemerged within my blood." Valerie hesitated for a moment before continuing. "I was on the verge of becoming fully human when you met me, but I'm slowly reclaiming my previous status."

Jared couldn't believe what he was hearing. "What the hell do you mean by former life? And *magic*? What the hell is that all about?"

"A very long time ago, I was a goddess. I was one of the Graces, to be exact." She finally admitted.

Jared's face contorted into utter denial. "No fuckin' way... This can't be real - none of this can be real! It has to be some kind of sick, demented trick! I'm so out of here! I'm going home, going to bed, and going to forget that any of this crazy bullshit ever happened! Either let me out of this damn car or take me home right now!" Jared tried with great force to open the car door again but still couldn't.

Valerie continued, ignoring Jared's frantic nature. "Jared, you fail to realize that you've been marked. Sara marked you by loving you in return. When that happened, she was supposed to claim you as her own, but she didn't. As a result, Sara can't protect you. For whatever reason, she's forfeited the shelter she could have provided and cast you out to fend for yourself. Because of this, you must stay by my side. I was able to get to you in time. I'm sure others were beginning to notice."

"Others were noticing? Noticing what? What others?" Jared felt his chest grow heavy. Each breath was riddled with panic. "What the hell is going on here, Valerie? Why would I need protection?"

She attempted to be delicate with her words. "Certain creatures love when a human crosses over and sees the world that was once worshiped by all humans. It's mostly the savage eaters that survive on the essence of the living that keep an eye out for such things. Thankfully civilized eaters are around as well."

"What the fuck is an eater?!" He kept pulling on the door handle to no avail.

"They're like vampires, but instead of blood, they feed on a creature's life force or essence: souls. You shouldn't worry about that now, however. Just do your best to remain calm." She looked sternly in his direction, gauging his ability to handle the truth.

Jared focused on what he knew. "What about my parents?"

Valerie shook her head. "Home is the last place you want to go. The people you're closest to are no longer safe when you're near them. You'll mark them because of your love for them, and you should spare them from such a fate."

"I don't care about any of this! I want you to take me home right now!" Jared pounded his fists on the car door.

Valerie turned her gaze forward. Then, with slight reluctance, she started the engine. "Seeing is believing, as the saying goes." After checking her blind spot, she returned the vehicle to the street. Finally, she turned the car around and headed toward the Hernandez residence.

"What happens after you die depends on what you believe. Most of us just wake up." – Cheung Chan (Master Magician – mortal practitioner)

4

JOE'S INNATE NEED to watch over Jared was in his DNA. Their relationship began when they were children, and he never treated Jared as anything less than a blood brother. The shared influence upon each other's lives was so strong that Joe was at a loss for words regarding how helpless he felt in aiding his friend during this challenging moment. Jared had been arrested and in jail for far too long.

That day at work, Joe went through the motions without experiencing the slightest trace of Valerie's managerial influence. The woman vanished, and no one around Joe seemed to care or know what was happening with Jared. To top it off, Carl had the day off of work. This left Joe unable to even confide in him.

The house his mother owned resided in an undesirable neighborhood where the crime rate was higher than most law-abiding citizens would care for. It was a small two-level home, run down for the most part. Yet, his mother, Ming, continued to make the best of it. During his childhood and teenage years, he forgot how much they didn't have by how much she made him feel they did. This home was purchased by Joe's mother and his late father, Emilio. It was one of the last things his parents had done together.

A knock on the door took Joe from his moment of introspection. He watched the bedroom door creak open; the noise disrupted the overwhelming silence. Ming entered, casting a motherly smile that hid the curious nature of wanting to know what her son was up to. She wore comfortable jeans and a blouse that covered a figure that was once very firm; the effects of childbirth and aging had altered that.

"Hey, mom. What's going on?" Joe asked.

Ming took a few casual steps over to the bed where Joe sat. She hugged him while sitting beside him and sighed like mothers do. "I came to check in on you. I heard about what happened at Brightwood with your friend Jared the other day. Getting arrested doesn't sound like him at all. We didn't have a chance to talk earlier. I got called into work. I'm sorry about that."

"It's okay. No worries. I know how the routine goes. You usually work when I'm at home, and when you're at home, I'm usually at work or school. So it's actually weird that you're here right now. Did you get fired or something?" Joe gave her his charismatic wink and smile.

She rolled her eyes. "No, you smartass, I didn't get fired."

"How did you hear about Jared?" He asked.

She cleared her throat. "Carl mentioned it when he called the house. He lost your cell phone number. You should call him back when you get a chance. There's something else. Jared's parents were worried sick earlier yesterday. They said you called and told them he'd been here with us the whole time."

Panicked worry ran through Joe's body. "Mom... Let me explain...."

Ming held up a hand to stop him from speaking. "It's okay. I went with the story you told them. I have a feeling they've calmed down by now. That's how things tend to go with this sort of situation."

"What's that supposed to mean?" He studied his mother.

Ming smiled, ignoring his question and taking in the moment. She stared at him with an intensity that soaked up every detail, and he stared back, unsure how to interpret her behavior.

She placed a loving hand on his back. "Do me a favor, Joey. I want you to remember things. I mean, I want you to *really* remember things. Remember your father, Emilio, and how he was. I know that might be hard to do at times. You were very young when he passed away. But I just want you to remember how good and simple things were before this craziness started with your friend Jared."

Confusion filled Joe. "Ma, you're starting to freak me out with the emotional speech. It's not like you. You sure you're okay?"

She smiled. "I'm fine, Joey. It's just that I've tried to protect you. I've only ever wanted for you to live a normal life. I sometimes wonder if I did the right thing by you."

He smiled in return. "Ma, you've got absolutely nothing to worry about. You've always been great."

Ming gave her son another side hug before standing from the bed. "Are you hungry?"

"No. This whole thing with Jared has been messing with me. I just don't feel like eating." Joe admitted.

"I'll bring something up anyway. It'll be here for you if you change your mind." With those words, Ming exited the bedroom leaving Joe to return to his meditative state.

Joe sat in the cramped space that passed for a bedroom, reviewing the strange events repeatedly in his mind. Nothing added up in a way that left him feeling at ease. Finally, the helplessness grew to an unbearable point, and he stood from his bed, stomping to his desk chair, needing to take helpful action. But what could he do?

In the background of his consciousness, a faint scratching noise soon became the focal point of his thoughts. The scratching grew louder and amplified in intensity within the confines of his mind.

What's going on? The very thought was drowned out by the incessant scratching.

A split second later, Joe was on his knees, holding his head in anguish. The pain that pulsed through his temples was unendurable, making his skin crawl and wave. The thumping beats of his heart became just as loud as the scratching that raked within his mind. The blood within his veins boiled; those veins physically pushed toward the upper layer of skin all over his body. Amidst the chaos, a lingering fear persisted that if he removed his hands from his head, it might explode. This caused him to grip even tighter, cutting into his scalp with his fingernails.

While cowering in a fetal position, a swift magical awareness erupted within Joe's psyche. This caused his body to convulse in a reaction to assimilating unaccustomed thaumaturgic cognizance. As the intense pain began to quell, a numbing sensation remained, with a slight awareness that he was still alive. Whatever had scratched its way out of Joe's head had finally escaped, and now he was left wondering if he was going crazy.

"My, how you've grown. You're practically a man now." A familiar voice spoke up within Joe's room.

Joe opened his hazy eyes and studied the peculiar figure of a man that looked strikingly like his grandfather. He remembered that the old man had been a part of his life when he was much younger. He'd perform magic tricks occasionally, mainly with a deck of cards. Then, quite soon after his father's accidental death, his grandfather vanished from their lives altogether.

"Grandpa Chan? Is that really you?" Joe stood up with a sluggish posture feeling the remnants of the psychic hole in his mind. He attempted to ignore the energy that was escaping. The magical force had no color or substance. It merely rippled through the very fabric of reality. Yet, if Joe focused hard enough, he could visualize this energy falling around him like a drizzle of rain in slow motion. It distorted the ordinarily unmoving space that was his bedroom.

The old man said: "It's me. Joseph, I haven't seen you since you were about five years old."

Joe nodded, still recovering from the experience. "I remember. You used to do magic tricks and whatnot when I was a kid. Heavy on the card tricks." Joe was in awe as he moved to sit on the bed. "I don't know what the fuck is going on here, but if my memory is still working the way it should be, then you're dead."

Grandpa Chan nodded. "That, I'm afraid, is also true. And watch your language. You should show more respect to the dead, especially when the deceased happens to be your grandfather."

"Dogs and humans have an evolutionary bond that spans thousands of years. There has always been an understanding between the two species. It just so happens that I can translate the meaning behind that bond, and not just with dogs, but with every living creature on the planet." – Carl Remington, Animal Speaker.

5

CARL REGARDED HIMSELF as a simple soul. Carl knew he wasn't the most intelligent man alive and accepted that he was slower when picking up certain things; he did so with graceful wisdom. Most often than not, when a problem manifested, Carl could turn a blind eye and let it pass him by. However, the events of the past few days did not sit well with him, and he knew within his deepest self that something was very wrong.

He had spent the morning working out; it had been an intense session of plyometrics and weight training with a reasonable break to refuel between the grueling physical exertions. Carl learned early on that physical activity kept him sane; it helped release overbearing stress and allowed his mind to work out a solution while he focused on the exercise.

The evening hours of his day off from work began to set in as the sun parted from the sky, allowing the moon to reside. He trudged through the kitchen of his parents' not-so-humble abode, which had been purchased a little over a year ago. Being a bit better off financially, Carl had grown accustomed to moving into more luxurious homes with each passing year. The newer houses were supposed to make him feel better for an absent mother and father. But, in actuality, it stirred and created the opposite response.

His father, Henry Remington, had worked hard to gain his status as a company man, and it paid off with a material satisfaction that most only dreamt of. His mother, Elizabeth, had lived off her husband's success, and

Carl had somehow become another possession for the two. He was a polished trophy brought out when they wished to display him as the ideal son.

Early on, Carl had decided to make his own way by working at the Brightwood Country Club. At the club, the monetary gains were his own. This mentality led to the purchasing of a beat-up station wagon. The vehicle quickly became the centerpiece of mockery amongst his family. Regardless, Carl had obtained that car with his hard-earned money, and he would be damned before he let anyone make him feel ashamed.

While standing before the refrigerator, an odd sensation took hold of Carl's entire body. The hair upon the back of his neck stood on end. His eyes began to water ever so slightly, and the thought of turning around to face the bone-chilling sensation made his fight-or-flight response kick in at a high level.

Paralyzed with fear, Carl felt a cold breath on the back of his neck. The breathing fluctuated at a controlled, slow, and steady pace; Carl trembled as it seemed to move near his left ear. Once there, he felt the breath turn into an undistinguishable whisper, and at first, it seemed to be gently moving through the open cavity that led into the eardrum.

Relief swam through Carl's senses as the whisper left, and he looked about the kitchen, sure that he was alone. Then, without warning, a piercing shriek boomed within his mind. The breath resurfaced, moving faster, and he held his head in agonizing pain as the shriek and breath became very comfortable inside his head. The pain was maddening.

"What's happening?" He managed to verbalize while cradling his face in his hands.

The intensity of the pain grew, and even though it was a few minutes that passed, for Carl, it had felt like an eternity.

"Experience teaches us all the most crucial lessons and forces us to deal with the reality before us." – Valerie (former Grace known as Aglaia)

6

JARED OBSERVED HIS house with fresh eyes. Dusk had begun to settle, and for the first time, Jared realized how dramatically his circumstances had changed. Magical couldn't begin to describe the extraordinary colors shifting and how the lighting transitioned from the sun's warmness to the coldness brought about by the darker shades of the night. The natural change sent chills through his spine, and he began to understand Valerie's seriousness. He had no choice but to entertain the idea that the blonde woman beside him had spoken a significant truth.

"I need to see them." Jared kept his eyes on the house. "I was in jail. The police said they tried to contact them after my phone call didn't go through. I just need to know that they're okay."

Valerie moved her hand to the back of Jared's neck and caressed it as a mother would. "They're safe so long as you never go near them again. They won't know who you are, Jared. They won't remember you at all. Records of your existence as you used to be, are mostly gone by this point. Soon there won't be any trace left of your old life."

"So, this is how it is when someone that's marked crosses over?" Jared slapped Valerie's hand away and faced her. "We just vanish from everyone we care about? Are we really forgotten that easily?"

She ignored Jared's physical outburst. "Yes and no. It happens naturally if left unaided and if you were to never go near your parents again. We didn't have time for that. You would have run to them and, in your folly, marked them as well. I took it upon myself to intervene for the welfare of those you care about most - it had to be done; there was no other way. I sped up the process and made them forget you sooner."

"You made them forget who I am?" The thought broke Jared's heart.

Valerie nodded. "They're better off this way, Jared. It saves them from having to survive in a realm you are now a part of."

An empty dread filled his chest. "I didn't even get a chance to say goodbye. It can't be like this, Valerie. It can't happen this way."

"This is the way it is." She responded with a stoic tone.

With a defiant posture, Jared opened the door to Valerie's car. He ran to the front door of his old house, nearly tripping over the uneven concrete walkway. Jared fumbled for the keys in his pocket. When retrieved, he tried to undo the lock beneath the doorknob. He soon discovered that the key wouldn't turn the deadbolt, no matter how hard he tried. He pounded on the door, yelling desperately for his parents to open up.

The door was opened cautiously, and Andres stood before Jared with a puzzled look. "Can I help you?"

Excitement filled Jared. "Dad, it's me – Jared! Can you just let me in?"

Andres noted the hysterical nature of the boy and changed his demeanor to be more comforting. He didn't think the young man before him was dangerous but decided to err on the side of caution. He took a defensive posture with his body while trying to come across as gentle and helpful. "Listen, I think you're a little confused right now. I'm not your father. I never had a son."

Jared's eyes began to water as disbelief covered his face. "Dad... Don't do this... I'm your son!"

Another voice called out from within the house. A late middle-aged woman poked her head around the front door and looked just as confused about the situation as her husband.

"Mom!" Jared wanted nothing more than to run inside and hug his mother tightly.

"Andres, what's going on? Who is this boy?" Maria asked.

Andres looked at his wife and held his hand out in a calming gesture to let her know he would handle the situation. "It's okay, Maria. I think he's just a little confused."

"Mom? Dad? Please... Don't do this...." Jared tried to step inside the house but was kept at bay with gentle force by Andres.

Andres' voice was firm. "Look, kid, I don't know who you are, but I don't want to have to call the police. You're not our son. You're very confused right now. Is there someone we can call to pick you up?"

"Jared!" Valerie called out from the car, gauging that now was the time for her to step in. She leaped out of the driver's side door and ran to the front doorstep, acting both worried and relieved. "Jared! There you are! I'm so glad I found you!"

"You know this boy?" Andres asked.

"Yes. I'm very sorry for the trouble. He's my little brother; he's very ill. He stopped taking his medication today, which confuses his sense of what's real. I'm truly sorry for any trouble he may have caused you. I'm just grateful I was able to find him so soon. He runs off sometimes." Valerie grabbed Jared by the hand and slowly began walking him back to the car.

"Valerie..." Jared's voice failed him. The sadness of the situation weighed him down.

Valerie took the opportunity to use Jared's disbelief to aid her story. "That's right, Jared. It's me, Valerie. I'm going to get you home now. You can trust me. Come on."

Jared had no choice but to play along as she led him away from the only home he'd ever known.

"Make sure you keep a better eye on him. He can get hurt or maybe even end up hurting someone else." Andres' voice carried out to the street from his front doorstep.

Valerie turned her head back, looking directly at Jared's father. "I'll make sure to take good care of him. You have my word on that."

Andres closed the door to the house while shaking his head in disapproval. Before the thick wood of the door hit the frame, Jared could see his mother, Maria, talking to Andres about the strange encounter. The sound of a deadbolt turning locked away any hope of entering and sealed the truth of Jared's reality. His parents had no idea who he was and would never remember him as their son.

Jared allowed Valerie to guide him to the passenger side of the car. He waited for her to return to the driver's seat with a dull numbness that ate at his soul. He wiped away the silent tears and gazed upon Valerie with a sunken face of pure desperation. Like it or not, she was his only hope for survival.

After giving Jared a few seconds to process, she said: "I know this is difficult for you, Jared, but I need you to trust me. I'll see you through this, and when it's done, I'll make sure you have the tools needed to survive."

"What do we do now?" He asked, defeated.

She started the car. "I have to pick up a certain item from an associate of mine. You're safer by my side for now, so I'll take you with me."

SPECIAL AGENT DELLA MYER: Mr. Chan, have you ever used your abilities for self-gain?

JOSEPH CHAN: Self-gain? If by self-gain you mean to protect my life, then sure. Of course, I have. You NMO suits know what it's like. It's a dog-eat-dog world on this side of the Distinction.

SPECIAL AGENT DELLA MYER: Mr. Chan, you know what we're referring to.

JOSEPH CHAN: Fine! I admit it! I once made a guy believe I had already paid for a bag of chips.

SPECIAL AGENT DELLA MYER: Mr. Chan!

JOSEPH CHAN: Okay, okay. It was more than one time. I love chips; what can I say? When I can create illusions in people's minds, it's hard not to make people believe something went down a certain way. It's more harmful to me, you know. I don't need to be eating that many junkie carbs. Magic or not, the body can handle only so much unhealthy.

SPECIAL AGENT DELLA MYER: Mr. Chan, the Natural Magic Order, takes this investigation very seriously. The repercussions on you will be severe if it's found that you were involved to the degree that we suspect.

JOSEPH CHAN: *That's the problem with you NMO suits. You act all high and mighty when it's convenient or politically favorable. But when people need you — I mean REALLY need you, you're nowhere to be seen. My conscience is clean, Special Agent Della Myer. How is yours?*

— Natural Magic Order interrogation transcript. The Messengers case year one. Interrogation conducted by Special Agent Della Myer. Person of interest Joseph Chan.

7

"I DON'T FUCKING believe any of this!" Joe paced about his bedroom studying the form of his long-dead grandfather Cheung Chan. "I'm going crazy! That has to be what this is! I'm going fucking crazy!"

The ghost stood before his grandson with arms crossed and a disapproving glare that only the elderly could muster. "You're not going crazy, and for the last time, watch the language! You were raised better than that. Your mother would disapprove of such vulgar profanity, especially when directed toward your elders." Grandpa Chan sat on the bed next to Joe and sighed heavily, allowing his chest to rise and fall.

"Why are you doing that?" Joe asked, confused.

"Doing what?" Chan didn't understand what his grandson was getting at.

"You're sighing! Why the hell are you sighing? You're not even real!" Joe moved his hand through the essence of his grandfather and watched the old man's shape ripple ever so slightly. "Why act like you're even breathing?! You're a ghost, for crying out loud!"

The ghost rolled his eyes. "Because that's how I remember being alive, and that's how I act when I take this form. Besides, it's more comfortable for you to see me like this, making it easier to communicate with you. Of course,

I could simply take the form of pure energy, but that wouldn't get us anywhere, would it?"

"No. I guess not. So, if I'm not going crazy and this is real, why are you here?" Joe demanded.

Grandpa Chan sighed again, exaggerating the movements to irritate his grandson, and licked his lips before speaking. "I always knew this day would come, so I placed a spell on you to summon my spirit when your abilities were awakened. You have magic blood pulsing through your veins; it's a part of our family heritage. It doesn't happen to everyone born of our blood, but some can turn it on. Your abilities have been turned on. I'm here to help guide you. Some in the realm of the Natural Magic world can do parts of what you can do. Still, you have Supernatural Magic, a different beast that makes you slightly more formidable."

"You have to be fucking kidding me!" Joe felt a real slap from his grandfather as the old man's hand made intense contact with his face. Then, with an angered embarrassment, he rubbed the red mark now prominent on his left cheek. "How did you do that?"

Chan glared at Joe. "I can focus the energy of what I am at specific points and make contact with your world. And I'll slap the hell out of you again if you insist upon using poor language."

Joe lowered his head. "Sorry, Grandpa. Can you please just explain what the hell is happening to me?"

Grandpa Chan continued. "The pain you felt inside your mind was like a door opening. It was a door that was always there, but you were never aware of it. Then, something happened to you that opened that door, and as a result, I was summoned. So, tell me, what were the events that led to this? What have you been up to? From then on, I'll do my best to fill in the blanks and explain what you're capable of."

Joe explained: "I'm not really sure what happened. My best friend Jared was arrested. He was taken to jail, and nothing about it makes any sense. He was going on about some crazy stuff that went down a few nights ago in the parking lot after work. I couldn't ask him to get his side of things, but I know it was over this girl Sara. She was there with him that night but denied his side of the story. She acted like Jared was crazy. But I know Jared; I've known him most of my life. He isn't crazy."

Grandpa Chan nodded his head taking in every word. He absorbed them in a way that made the essence of his spirit pulse with a slight glow of concentration.

"So, this is real? All of this is actually real?" Joe asked again.

Grandpa Chan nodded, this time with irritation. "Yes. The catalyst for this is either your friend or the girl he cares about. One was marked because of the other. But why? I'm not directly involved, but you need to be. There's no other choice for you now. This is the world you'll be living in from now on."

"What about Mom? Does she know about any of this?" More and more questions surfaced for Joe.

Chan nodded. "Yes. Your mother has taken great pains to protect you from this, but your life is your own, as are your choices. Normally minds are cleansed when a person is marked and crosses over. There's no need for that with your mother. She's been waiting for this day to come hoping and praying that it never would."

"No wonder she was acting so weird earlier. What do I do now?" Joe desperately needed direction.

Chan thought for a moment before speaking. "First, allow me to explain what you can do. You're a medium. That's why it's so easy to talk to you regardless of the spell cast to summon me. Communication with ghosts can be iffy if someone's mind isn't as open as your mind now is. Secondly, you're a manipulator. You can crack into any normal person's mind, insert memories, and even take them away. You can also create illusions within people's minds and communicate without words. With more powerful creatures, you'll need more practice, and if you can crack a vampire's mind, you'd be the strongest manipulator the world will have ever seen."

"Vampires? Fucking vampires exist?!" Joe sat up and began pacing. "Sorry for dropping another f-bomb, but what the hell else is out there?"

Grandpa Chan lifted his hands in a calming gesture. "There exists far more than a single night with my grandson can afford me to explain. What you need to know is already in your blood, but it just woke up. So let it wake up completely. Doing that lets you know what to do and when you should do it. With time you'll get better and stronger."

Joe thought of his best friend. "What about Jared? You said he was marked?"

"That's what I gather from what you've told me. Whatever happened between this Jared and this young woman named Sara set these events in motion." Chan was confident of this.

"I never trusted her, Grandpa." Joe's anger grew.

Grandpa Chan stood up and focused the energy of his form on his hands. He reached out and grabbed Joe by the shoulders to keep him from pacing. Joe locked eyes with his grandfather and genuinely smiled. He hadn't realized how much he missed the old man.

"While I'm here, I might as well help prepare you as best I can," Chan said.

Joe smiled appreciatively. "Okay. Where do we start?"

Chan's tone grew more serious. "Close your eyes. Your mind is the only eye you need when using your gift. Your mind can connect with other minds and manipulate those minds according to your will. But your will must be strong, and to have a strong will, you must have a strong sense of who you are."

Joe closed his eyes with a calming breath. He wasn't sure how to enact the instructions, but he trusted his grandfather and attempted to feel his surroundings. As he reached out with his senses, the bedroom door opened, interrupting his focus.

Ming stood by the doorway with a tray of food at the ready. She entered, seeing the ghost of her departed father standing next to her son.

Grandpa Chan smiled. "Hello, my darling Ming."

She placed the tray of food on the bed and eyed up the essence of her father with a smug little smile of her own. "Hi, dad. I figured it was only a matter of time before you showed up. So how's the afterlife treating you? Have you seen Emilio?"

Chan considered his words. "I haven't seen him in ages, but I'm sure Emilio sends his love wherever he is. To be perfectly honest, the afterlife is a little too boring for my taste. All the exciting things tend to happen in this realm. Being a spirit has given me a better understanding of why so many ghosts tend to stick around."

Joe interjected. "Ma, you knew about the magic and the stuff our family can do? Why didn't you tell me?"

"There was a chance, albeit a small one, that the magic in your blood would remain dormant forever. If that were the case, you could have lived a normal life. But, obviously, that isn't the case. So I'll leave the two of you be. I'm sure your grandfather is explaining things far better than I could. Whatever happens, Joey, know this place will always be your home. Consider it a sanctuary. Remember that." Ming gave Joe the warmest of motherly smiles.

Joe's mind raced. "What about Dad? He knew, didn't he? He knew that this might happen to me?"

Ming fought back the sudden influx of emotions that welled up when thinking of her late husband. "Yes. He did."

"Grandpa Chan, you said I was a medium. Does that mean I can speak to my father?" Joe's eyes shot back and forth between his mother and grandfather with hope.

"In theory, yes. But you have to be stronger than you are now. Also, understand that not all spirits want to be bothered or brought back for a chat." Chan accentuated the act of taking a deep breath and looked at his grandson with sympathy. "But there will be a time for that, Joe. I promise."

"Let's get started then." Joe turned back to his mother. "I know you did what you did to protect me, but I guess this is what I am now. I have to help Jared. He'd do the same for me. And maybe, just maybe, I can talk to Dad? Maybe I can talk to him for the both of us, Ma?"

Ming held back a tear of joy. "That would be great, Joey. I've missed your father so very much. Just remember to deal with everything one step at a time and listen to your grandfather. There are a lot of dangerous things out there."

"He'll be ready." Grandpa Chan jumped in.

"Don't let the food get too cold." She smiled at Joe with slight trepidation and eyed her father sternly, using that moment to mask her growing fears. "Don't be too hard on him, Dad. I lucked out because you trained me while you were still alive. You actually got tired back then, and I was afforded breaks. As a ghost, I know it isn't the same. Remember that your grandson is still flesh and blood, and don't you dare go disappearing without saying goodbye." Ming smiled at both of them as she closed the door behind her.

"Is Mom like me? Can she do magic?" Joe considered the possibility.

Chan nodded. "It manifests differently for different people of our bloodline. She's powerful in her own way, and I'm sure you'll learn all about what she can do directly from her. Right now, however, we need to get back to work."

"I hear their cries. At first, it was maddening. I didn't want the voices in my head. But now they are a part of me, and I act on their behalf. I do what I can to protect them. Life is precious, and all living creatures are connected. When we hurt Mother Nature, we destroy that bond and disrupt that delicate balance."
– Carl Remington, Animal Speaker.

8

CARL AWOKE ON the cold floor near the island in the middle of his parents' kitchen. The aching pain of the whisper within his mind began fading away like the memory of a dream. As he reconciled his surroundings with his physical body, he felt the presence of life in a strange yet fascinating new way. Images from varying vantage points began crowding his mind, and he found it incredibly difficult to focus on clear thoughts. It was like trying to watch a hundred televisions, all on different channels simultaneously.

What's going on with me?

The barking of a small corgi near the glass doors that led to the patio of his parent's home caught Carl's attention in no time. He had seen the dog around the neighborhood, strolling about as if the canine belonged wherever it happened to be. Now it appeared that the small corgi was intent upon entering Carl's house.

"What are you doing here?" Carl walked over to the glass window and was bombarded by feelings and imagery. He viewed himself from the corgi's vantage point and could feel that the dog was telling him that things would be okay in an odd yet familiar way.

The corgi unconcernedly sat down and looked at Carl with something close to camaraderie. The large bat-like ears pointed up, and as the corgi relaxed into a lying position, the left ear flipped down at the tip while the right one stayed erect.

"Are you actually talking to me?" Carl felt a rush of confusion like none other. It began earlier that night when he walked to the kitchen to quench his thirst with a drink from the refrigerator.

The hour demanded his attention, and he glanced at the microwave. It was two in the morning. Summer allowed for most of his time to be left up to him (mainly due to his parents traveling), but he knew he required rest if he wanted to function properly at work.

"Sleep," Carl said the words aloud so that the noise would break the eerie silence. "I need to sleep."

As he attempted to exit the kitchen, images of the very act bombarded his mind. He somehow knew they were from the perspective of the corgi. The dog waited by the glass doors to the patio, and Carl shook his head, trying to rid his mind of the disorientation.

Stop! A voice blurted out within Carl's mind.

"What the hell was that?" Carl's eyes focused on the corgi.

You... hear me now... in mind... My sound make sense as... words... The corgi looked right at Carl as the voice continued to speak within his mind. The voice came across with the accent of someone unfamiliar with language and had a childlike quality mixed with subtle wisdom.

"Yes. I can hear you." Carl spoke aloud, feeling somewhat foolish. He was very concerned about having a conversation with a corgi. "This is more than a little weird. This isn't normal. It's impossible."

The dog kept his eyes on Carl. *You... call me Bandolar. I... see this thing happen for you. I felt air change around you. Your smell gets different. I knew change... close. Change... happen.*

Carl looked at the corgi, now named Bandolar, with great concern and curiosity. He felt like he was going mad, and an anxiety-riddled worry made him think that feeling would only worsen.

You no crazy. Please... let in. I explain. The corgi let out a tiny bark.

"You're a dog!" Carl yelled at the corgi through the glass doors.

You human! Bandolar yelled back with a loud bark to accompany his determined stance on all fours.

Carl opened the sliding glass door in the kitchen with a reluctant posture, and the small corgi ran inside the second there was enough space to do so. Carl shut the glass door, locking it in place, and watched the creature with curious eyes. He closed his eyes for a second, seeing what the dog saw, and opened them, disoriented by the mental transfer of energy.

Bandolar ran around the kitchen, sniffing about, and when he was sure that all was safe, he moved back to Carl and sat down near the human's feet. He stared at Carl with both ears pointed up and tongue hanging out as he panted his breaths.

"What do you want with me?" Finally, Carl gave in to the oddness of the situation.

An excited bark erupted from the corgi. *I am... guide to you. There are... creatures... like me. We aid with animal... speakers... like you. My thoughts, you understood... in a way, humans make noise with other humans.*

Carl tried his best to understand the jumbled message. "Do you mean talk? Are you talking about how we speak to one another?"

Bandolar barked in agreement.

"Why me?" Carl asked.

Long ago, all lands... were one. All life spoke... freely with all life. No... barriers. Then came what first gods named... Distinction... of... Realms... The dog almost struggled to get the thought to a place that would accurately translate the words for Carl. *This... Distinction... is why magic is keep away... hidden. You have magic. Your human fathers... animal... speakers... also. They talk with creatures... of nature. They made pacts with animals... so all live in good ways. They ask of us... and we follow strong speakers... like you.*

"This is too much. I mean, it's just crazy! Are you telling me that my father can do the same thing?" Carl couldn't imagine anything special about his dad.

Bandolar almost appeared sad as he transmitted the following few thoughts. *Man lives with you not... father. Mother not... mother. Smell not same.*

The words struck Carl to the core and rocked him like a knockout punch. "They're not my real parents?"

As shocking as the revelation was to Carl, all the events in his life began to make sense. It shed much light on why he had been raised as he remembered. He really was just another possession bought by his wealthy providers.

Bandolar barked, demanding attention. He paced about in a circle before lying comfortably on the fancy kitchen floor.

"You're not expecting me to let you stay here, are you?" Carl asked.

The corgi appeared to yawn as he rested his head on the floor between his paws.

Carl shrugged, relenting. "I guess you are. I'll see you in the morning then. Hopefully, none of this happened, and I'll just remember this as a dream when I wake up."

The dog barked again and closed his eyes.

"Right." Carl began taking hesitant steps to his room. He hoped that he would wake up remembering this night only as a strange dream. If only he could be so lucky.

"It's a travesty that humans tell their children that monsters don't exist. They believe there aren't things in the shadows that can swallow them whole. The human species is so unobservant it's a wonder they've survived this long. And while telling their young that monsters don't exist, they become the worst monsters of all." – Minx (centuries-old vampire, a supporter of the Forever Man)

9

JARED SOON FOUND that the things that had scared him in his childhood were to be just as feared in his adult life. At night, as a child, he would run to his bed after turning off the light. He'd been deathly afraid that a monster living beneath the darkness of the bedframe might eat him or that the boogieman would burst forth from the closet to steal him away forever. So, as a protection, young Jared covered his feet beneath the blanket and engulfed his entire body with it. He wondered if the boogieman was real and pondered over what else lurked about that he once thought make-believe.

"Are you sure this is safe?" Every slight noise caused Jared to jump as he asked the question, and in a feeble attempt to protect his neck, Jared flipped up the collar of his white waiter uniform. But, at the moment, he was more than preoccupied with the fact that he and Valerie were waiting in a dark alley to meet with an actual vampire.

"He won't harm us, Jared. He's a friend." Valerie assured him.

A voice called out from the darkness of the alley, joining in on the conversation. "I wouldn't exactly say that, Valerie. I'm more of an acquaintance and a well-respected acquaintance at that."

Valerie studied the shadow play as Minx waddled from the darkness, standing proud. The simple act of walking took away from the little vampire's intimidating image, but she knew he couldn't care less. When needed, his powers were great, and he was a force of reckoning. She was glad to have him on her side at the moment.

"So, this is the boy you've taken great pains to protect?" Minx asked.

Jared stepped back, unsure what to make of the little vampire. "This... I mean... I just wasn't...." Words escaped Jared as he pointed at Minx from near the car. His expression was offensive as he gestured the noticeable height difference between him and Minx.

"Not what you were expecting, hey?" Minx's upper left lip lifted like that of a ferocious predator ready to attack and revealed his fang.

"Not exactly, no." Jared fumbled with his collar some more, and the car acted as a crutch holding him upright as he leaned upon it.

Minx flew through the air faster than the eye could see and pinned Jared to the car's hood. His fangs were fully exposed, and the shock of the blurred movement left Jared paralyzed with a great fear that made it impossible for him to speak.

"Do you know why you can't move or talk?" Minx kept his face close to Jared's. "It happens to be part of what I can do. It took a century, give or take, to master the paralytic gaze. Come to think of it, that's why many vampires these days don't last very long. They think they can master the gifts given to them quickly. No patience. Those of us that have been around for as long as I have, well, simply know better. If you're going to survive, you need to relax, stop making yourself an easy target, and accept the fear you're feeling. When you accept a thing and let it go, it no longer has any power over you."

"Not that I don't appreciate the lesson you're imparting upon Jared, but I'd much rather attend to the business at hand." Valerie stood with her arms crossed and carried a look of annoyance far more potent than any spell.

"He's fresh meat, Valerie. You need to show him the ropes. I just thought I'd imprint him with a little reminder as to why he needs to listen to you." Minx slapped Jared on his cheek with a playful hand; his fangs remained exposed as he let out a jovial laugh. He then levitated from the hood of the car and kept himself afloat to be at eye level with Valerie.

Frightened for his life, Jared sank down from the hood of the car until he was sitting; his arms were wrapped around his knees as he hugged them tightly to his chest. He wanted to run home but knew home no longer existed. His parents had no memory of him. Jared began to wonder about his friends and if they could even recall their friendships with him.

Joe... Carl...

"I have the item you requested." Minx held out his hand, and a pouch floated next to Valerie from behind a dumpster. "Check it over to make sure it's to your liking."

Valerie snatched the pouch from the air and opened it revealing the sacrificing bowl. It was a bowl of basic and straightforward design. One could find an exact copy in any thrift store, but it wouldn't hold the same power for the average person. This bowl had been enchanted, thus giving whatever sacrifices were made in it great power. She could feel the magic emanating from the simple material.

"Is the item to your satisfaction?" Minx kept a watchful eye on a frightened Jared as he spoke with Valerie and laughed a bit on the inside.

"Yes, it is." Valerie nodded.

Minx lowered himself from his levitated position and touched his feet to the ground of the alley. He reached into his coat pocket and pulled out a flask filled with his favorite vodka. He wasted no time taking a long hard swig.

"You're as charming as always, Minx. Your debt unto me has been paid in full. Good hunting tonight. I'm sure many detestable people are roaming the streets just waiting for you to sink your teeth into them." Valerie placed the bowl back into the pouch.

"There is one more thing left to discuss before you depart. I have a proposition. It could aid in the matter to which you're attempting to rectify." Minx took another swig.

Valerie was unsure of his intentions but remained curious. "Go on."

"I think I know what you're planning. You wouldn't have asked for this specific item if you weren't. I might have a more powerful way of ensuring that you can counter the sacrifice these rogue spirits intend." Minx smiled, proud of his deductive abilities. "You alone may fall, but with the proper help, your success would be guaranteed. Let's face the facts, Valerie. No one is going to come to your aid now that you've invoked the Edict of Innocents against an already established covenant between two parties."

Valerie raised a curious eyebrow. "I'm listening."

Jared also listened as he sat on the alley ground propped against Valerie's car. The words being spoken seemed as if they were out of a fantasy story and not based on the reality he had come to expect. He had extreme difficulty believing that what Minx proposed could and would be carried out.

The conversation between Valerie and Minx became background noise as thoughts of Sara invaded Jared's mind. He crouched lower, hugging himself tighter. *She said she loved me. Evil things don't love. Do they?*

Jared allowed his thoughts to wander and awaited further instruction from his new mentor, Valerie. There were things in this world that would tear him apart with the greatest of ease. The brief encounter with Minx had proven that all too well. He had a lot to learn, and for now, Valerie was his lifeline.

"There are times when it's important to shut up and simply do as you are told." – Vic, Solitary Werewwolf. No pack affiliations.

10

THE POSH ESTATE where Mrs. Dempsy resided was intimidating to those unaccustomed to the significant excess that a lavish lifestyle could afford. Yet, it was a lifestyle that the former Fury now enjoyed regularly. Gardeners steadily worked on the landscaping while maids and cooks moved with purpose; they cleaned and prepared top-notch meals within the estate built from scratch with Mr. Dempsy's money. The view from the balcony where Mrs. Dempsy stood with red wine and elegant glass in hand was magnificent, to say the least.

She was poised upon the second level of her exorbitant dwelling, admiring the calmness of the night sky. The clouds were few, and the stars unusually bright. She enjoyed such nights, and the cool breeze that penetrated her dark blue nightgown made it all the more enjoyable. Her golden blonde hair was free and hanging past her shoulders. The wind became familiar with the golden locks running through her hair like a lover's gentle fingers. Renee Dempsy bided her time with patience, absorbing the moment, and sipped her red wine with a grin of satisfaction.

The footsteps were very faint. Renee could barely discern the sound of someone approaching, but she would expect nothing less from a creature such as him. Popular myths happened to be hit or miss when it came to werewolves. The idea that they could become large menacing creatures was very accurate. On the other hand, it was often taken for granted how stealthy the powerful monsters could be; they were ultimately predators.

This particular werewolf was still in human form. Transforming into his more beastly appearance was rare these days. His primary employer, Dracien, frowned upon such reckless use of power. Too much attention was terrible for those that lived in the hidden world.

Vic stood at the balcony's bottom, looking up at the older yet beautiful Renee Dempsy while wearing his black suit. The darkness of the night somehow enhanced the tan color of his skin. Then, with the grace of a supernatural creature, he scaled the wall landing near Mrs. Dempsy without so much as a sound.

"How are you this evening, Vic? May Lupercus protect you and all that." She smiled while taking a sip of wine and admired the impressive specimen that stood before her.

"You spout this Lupercus nonsense every time we meet. It stopped being amusing after the first time." Vic growled as he spoke.

"Lupercus is the god to which your kind owes tribute. The one I'm most familiar with, anyway. We met briefly during my tenure as a Fury. He became the sun. Then again, I gather the sun is big enough to absorb all these creatures that turn into it." The former Fury waited for a response.

Vic said nothing.

"There's also Fenrir, another god attributed with your kind, although the Norse gods and I rarely interacted. Back then, it was easier to keep to those that worshiped us. There were, however, those encounters that I had with Loki, the bastard. Still, he's gotten into almost everything at some point. I don't believe there's a creature he hasn't terrorized. Fenrir was actually born of Loki. Did you know that? He's a very tragic wolf creature. He will kill Odin at the end of the world, you know, only to die at the hand of Odin's son, Vidar." Renee paused.

Vic said nothing.

"Prophecy can be very problematic. Once cast, you're bound to it until what is foretold is completed. Time Benders have been spewing prophecies since the Founding Magic put into action the events that created the world as we know it. I absolutely loathe Time Benders and the power they hold. To control a Time Bender would be to shape the nature of things." *And I happen to have one at my beck and call, the old crone. Clara is all mine.* The thought faded as she looked upon her servant werewolf.

"My powers are my own, as is this version of myself or any other version in any other reality. No one controls me, and Time Benders are nothing more than creatures that manipulate to get the desired outcomes. I'm a free creature and pay tribute as I see fit, not as others believe I am supposed to." Vic grumbled under his breath.

"Then do you pay tribute to me?" She loved testing him.

Vic nodded, recalling how Renee Dempsy saved him from an excruciatingly painful death. The bites were deep, and the attack was sudden when Victor was mauled long ago by a Nazi soldier of the werewolf affliction. When he was a young human, he was intended as a meal for the creature; the feast had been interrupted by the former Fury.

The Second World War had intrigued the former goddess, and she made herself present during specific engagements. The opportunity to have a werewolf at her service struck Renee with delight. She kept young Victor alive, saving him from the soldier planning to devour his flesh. Having been bitten and surviving the attack, however, cursed Victor. He was able to live, but never again as a human. As a result, he was forever in her debt; it was because of this debt that he found himself defying Dracien to do her bidding. He despised playing both sides.

"Were you able to find a suitable water demon for my purposes?" She turned away from Vic and looked up to the night sky while sipping her wine. She honestly did love the stars on such a clear night.

Vic straightened his suit. "I did."

"And?" She took another sip.

Vic continued. "I placed the potion in the essence of her water as you instructed. The water demon is now bound to carry out your orders and will be at the appropriate time and place you specified."

Renee smiled from ear to ear. "Fabulous. You've done well, Vic. You've done very well."

"How do you know that the boy will be there?" Vic asked.

"I have my source. And it's a source that one need not question." The smile deepened.

Vic let the curiosity go, knowing the answer received would be the best response he could hope for. "Is this boy worth it? I had a brief encounter with him when dealing with this rogue spirit business on behalf of Dracien.

So why go through all the trouble for this Jared Hernandez? He's just a normal human marked by a goddess that couldn't care less."

She sighed. "There are wheels within wheels, Vic. He is Jared Hernandez for the time being, but the form he carries and the identity he holds dear will fade. When that happens, Vestor will be born, and Vestor is *very* dangerous. So we kill him before he becomes Vestor while he is plain old Jared Hernandez. If we do this, we prevent what Vestor does later on. My source is certain of this, and my source is never wrong. Founding Magic is at play here after all, and we can't waste any time."

PART SIX:

FACING NEW
REALITIES

"Worship is a source of power. It keeps the gods going. When humanity changed over time after the Distinction, we had to adapt. We blended in, formed legitimate companies, fueled organized crime, infused governments and bureaucracies with our ideologies, and influenced everything down to what a human buys for breakfast. We even went so far as to change the nature of our powers and how they manifest. Make no mistake, we are still here. We are just hidden in plain sight, and perhaps more impactful hidden than we were in the open." – Zeus (address to Olympus Corporation board meeting of gods)

1

OLD MERDITH RELAXED her frail body as she stood before the group of young employees that congregated within the formal dining room of the Brightwood Country Club. They sat scattered across a small sea of tables, unprepared for the evening's festivities. As she gazed upon the group, she had an eerie impression that something had changed. Merdith was at a loss to identify the discombobulating nature of what she was sensing but grew confident the elusive feeling would dissipate. The more her mind attempted to ascertain the source of the change, the more a comforting emotion emanated, allowing her to let the confusion pass.

Carl, Joe, Sara, Nicole, Rachel, Ana, and a few other new hires were gathered before the old woman. Mr. Drake had appeared mere moments before Merdith's opening speech. He checked in on the employees, not from a sense of leadership, but because he wanted to keep an eye on them. He didn't trust them, not even Old Merdith, and wanted to make sure the elderly woman was running a tight ship.

As Merdith stood before the group, she recognized the faces before her. Still, the pestering awareness that there might be a hole in her memory continued. Every now and then, that feeling would surface only to get forcibly pushed back further into the recesses of her mind. She would occasionally glance at Carl and momentarily forget who he was. Luckily this would only happen for a split second.

Joe relaxed in his seat, focused on Old Merdith's speech, and fully prepared for the changes that were taking place around him. The ghost of his grandfather had readied him for the day, and he did his best to hone his skills over a long, intense night of training. However, Joe could also sense that something had changed within Carl and became sure of this fact when Carl continued to remember Jared. In contrast, everyone else had wholly forgotten who Jared was.

Carl felt relieved that he hadn't been going crazy while explaining his transformative experience. Carl even went into detail about his strange encounter with the corgi named Bandolar. The canine remained in the neighborhood near Carl's home while he ventured off to work, and Joe interjected, filling in the gaps.

Grandpa Chan had touched on animal speakers during his night of cramming, and Joe explained to Carl that he was probably now one of them. Carl could communicate with any animal and, with the right focused effort, *will* any animal to do as he commanded. Carl grew uncomfortable with that level of control over other living creatures. Despite that, he found himself easily amused by making two flies in the room buzz around Joe's head during the pre-shift meeting. Joe glared at Carl as he swatted at the flies.

With a deep breath and a serene expression, Joe pushed emotions into Carl's mind to help calm his nervous anxiety. A few days ago, Joe would never have thought any of this possible, but given what was before him, he had no choice but to believe.

Carl? Can you hear me in that noggin of yours? Joe cast out his thought.

Carl vigorously scratched his head. *Yes, I can.* He looked directly at Joe, who kept his eyes on Old Merdith with a bored expression. Carl mentally asked: *How can you be so damn calm right now?*

Joe stared at Carl as he communicated his following thoughts. *Carl, I need you to listen to me. First of all, cut it out with the damn flies!*

Carl chuckled. *Sorry about that.* With a single thought of concentration, he made the insects buzz elsewhere.

Joe continued with the mental communication. *Keep your eyes on Merdith, and play it cool for the remainder of the shift. Everyone else's mind is about to be or has been cleaned. We know Sara is involved, but there might be others. We hold tight and wait for Valerie. Grandpa Chan knew her when he was younger, and he's sure she'll help us. Do your best to remind people of who you are. You're starting to be cleansed from their minds. I think I can feel it. And we stay away from Sara as much as we can. She might sense we've changed if we're not careful.*

Carl tried to hide his panic. *I can see it in their faces, Joe! For a split second, they have a hard time remembering my name! Can we really make it until Valerie gets here? And what about my parents? Should I even be here right now? That damn corgi told me they weren't my real parents, to begin with.*

Do you believe the dog? Can you trust him? Joe felt silly asking; it was a dog.

Carl nodded, paying attention to the shift meeting. *Yes. The feelings were sincere. I don't know how else to explain it.*

Joe let out an audible sigh, passing it off as his usual indifference. *I'm sorry, Carl. I really am. I just discovered my family history was crazier than I would've guessed. We're all having difficulty adjusting to this crazy shit right now. Stay focused. Unfortunately, the only way to contact Valerie is to wait for her here.*

I get that, Joe, but why doesn't anyone forget you? It concerned Carl.

How we're raised decides whether or not people we know are cleansed. Joe recalled his grandfather's explanation.

How the hell does that work? Carl cleared his throat while attempting to feign interest in Old Merdith's speech.

It has to do with my bloodline. Grandpa Chan said it's strong with magic. It's existed in both realms for a long time as a result. I was also raised by my real mom. Since she lived in both worlds from the start, then I can. Certain bloodlines, like mine, help act as a bridge and maintain a balance between realms. That's how Grandpa Chan explained it anyway. If my real parents were ordinary people, I'd have the same problem. They'd forget the version of me they thought was real, and so would everyone else. Joe yawned, keeping up the façade to those watching.

How the hell does that even make any sense?! Carl tried not to look at Joe as the thoughts were communicated.

Another yawn came out of Joe. *I don't know, Carl, it just does! Valerie should be able to explain it better.*

Just how old is Valerie anyway? Did she really know your grandpa when he was young? So what the hell is she? She sure as shit can't be human to look that young and be that old! I'm freaking out, man! This is fucking crazy! Carl wiped the nervous sweat from his brow.

It's new to me too, Carl. It's actually kind of freaky being inside your head. Joe cleared his throat.

I don't like you being in my head, either! Carl shot a quick glare at Joe.

Fine! I'll leave the empty space you call your brain for now, but just remember that Jared needs us, and Valerie will help us get through this. Okay? Joe tried to have the mental projection of his voice appear calm and in control.

That's easy for you to say! Every time you pass an animal, you're not seeing what they're seeing or feeling what they feel! Carl complained.

What are you trying to say? Do you have an irresistible urge to lick your balls right now like your doggie friends? Joe smiled while relaxed on his chair and appeared as though he were listening to Old Merdith as she continued her speech. He was also quite proud of himself for retaining his sense of humor during such a strange and stressful time. If he kept that aspect of himself alive, he knew he could get through anything.

You're always with the jokes. I'll do what needs doing. Just get out of my head! Carl crossed his arms, completing the look of a toddler having a tantrum.

Old Merdith continued on for what seemed to be an eternity. She finally finished explaining what was on the menu for that night in painful detail.

She wished everyone good luck at their particular workstations and nodded with a smile; her frail body vibrated ever so slightly.

Joe and Carl smiled to Old Merdith in return and stood from the large round table they were seated at. They openly joked with each other as they walked together to the nearest wait station as if it were any other day.

"I can change the memories of anyone alive. I can make them believe wonderful things and make them forget horrible tragedies. But I have to live with all of it. Good and bad. That's just the way it goes." – Joseph Chan, Medium/Manipulator.

2

ANA'S CONFUSION AS to where she stood with Joe and their relationship had pestered her since the intimate exchange they shared a few nights ago. After leaving the parking lot, she snuck him into her room with great stealth. It wasn't the first time the two had made love, but that night they explored each other and grew closer in a way that made her confident their love was real. The lazy ease with which he slouched in his chair during the pre-shift meeting deeply bothered Ana. It was as if their latest night together had meant nothing to Joe.

She stepped in front of Joe purposefully, cutting off his path to the wait station. She carried a hurt and confused expression with determined eyes that needed answers. "Joe. We need to talk."

"Ana!" Joe was startled by her sudden appearance. Recent events being what they were, had left little time for anything else. He was ashamed he had forgotten about his rekindled feelings. "How are you?"

"I'm okay, I just...." Ana left her sentence hanging in the air with a stare that begged Carl for some privacy. For a brief moment, she had forgotten who Carl was. She thought it an odd sensation.

Carl nodded in an understanding way and looked at Joe before walking off. "I'll be in the wait station preparing some stuff for tonight."

Joe nodded in return as he kept his eyes fixed on Ana.

Ana crossed her arms, steadying herself. "You didn't stop over like you said you were going to. I tried getting a hold of you, but I was just sent to your voicemail right away, over and over again. So what's going on, Joe? You've been avoiding me these last few days, and I don't understand why."

Joe winced, feeling torn at breaking promises to Ana yet again, but this time those broken promises were for good reasons. "Damn it... I'm sorry, Ana. It's just that things have been getting a little crazy for me lately. I can't really say much more than that."

Hurt confusion filled her. "Do you still love me? Are we really trying to get back together, or was it just a one-time thing the other night? I really thought maybe we could work things out. It felt like that, anyway. Did I imagine that? I mean, was it in my head?"

Taken aback by the questions, Joe weighed his options as he gazed into Ana's wanting and beautiful eyes. He did indeed love her, but if he were to expose her to the world he was now a part of, she would be in more danger than she could ever imagine. He could not allow that, and he knew within his heart that a choice had to be made.

"I do love you, Ana. And that's why I have to do something important for you right now." Joe took a deep breath. This wouldn't be easy.

"What do you mean?" She asked.

Joe reached out with the energy of his thoughts and was soon inside Ana's mind. It hurt him more than words could express, but he pushed away the feelings of affection she carried for him. Then, like an expert weaver, he reorganized her emotions so she would fall out of love and feel only a strong friendship. Joe put it together so naturally that Ana quickly came to believe her feelings had followed the path presented within the construct of her mind. Grandpa Chan and his mother Ming would have been very proud of Joe for accomplishing the first real test of his abilities.

Ana broke from the momentary daze and stared at Joe. "I'm sorry...." She seemed truly confused. "I'm having a blonde moment here; I don't remember what we were talking about just now."

"You were asking me about tonight's floor plan. So I told you I'd help in your section if needed." Joe pushed that memory into her mind, and she nodded in agreement.

She smiled, happy to have recalled. "Oh, that's right. Thanks, Joe. I'll let you know if I need you."

"No problem. I'm always here for you." Joe felt a pang of anguish come and go within his chest. The true meaning of those words would never be understood by Ana. He knew he had done the right thing, but his emotions screamed at him in defiance. Love often defied logic in ways that could make anyone go mad. After taking a few seconds for composure, Joe made his way to the wait station where Carl was waiting.

"We fell into one of the oldest traps in the universe. We wanted more than anything for things to be the way they used to be. That much obsession and devotion to the past destroyed our future." – Ate (goddess of mischief and blind folly)

3

"THIS IS VERY curious." Rachel studied both Carl and Joe from a distance. Then, she stood from the roundtable where she sat for the meeting; Nicole and Sara stood up in the same deliberate manner.

"They're clean. I'm sure of it." Sara yawned, trying to mask her concern for Jared's friends. "Joe carried a face of boredom, and Carl looked as if he were confused. That's how they always are during these meetings."

"I want to be certain that nothing strange is going on with the two of them. Jared crossed over because of your incompetence." Rachel glared at Sara before gazing away to the wait station door where Carl and Joe entered. "Others may have been affected as a result. Make sure that they have been cleansed; if not, we'll take appropriate action."

"What about Valerie? Her involvement is clear; she knows something. Perhaps she is a human who crossed over long ago, or maybe even something more? There is a familiarity with her. She could even be a creature of our pantheon." Nicole suggested with a pensive stare.

"Valerie will be here soon enough. She's on the schedule for later tonight. I'll confront her and determine if anything is truly odd with her." Rachel pondered Valerie's involvement silently. She then looked at her sisters. "Go after them. Find out with certainty the status of Carl and Joe."

Rachel turned away, leaving Sara and Nicole to the task at hand. She had no trouble blending in amongst the Brightwood Country Club employees, appearing as a teenager stalking about angrily for having to be at work.

"You heard her." Nicole led the way.

Sara followed, taking one hesitant step after another. "This is silly. Nothing is strange about them."

Nicole continued her rapid gait, not glancing at Sara as she followed the same path Carl and Joe had taken. Upon entering the wait station, they found Joe drinking from a can of soda; he hid the can behind a stack of plates on the top shelf to his right. Carl grunted as he unclogged the coffee machine that always seemed in bad shape.

"Careful with that. Otherwise, you'll end up with water all over your shirt. Know what I mean?" Joe warned.

"Yeah, I got it, Joe." Carl continued to meticulously unclog the giant contraption. "What were you saying about the other day?"

"I was just saying that things have been kind of weird with me and the ex. Ana came over a few nights ago, and I don't know... It was like we were dating again - how it used to be. Right now, though, I think she just wants to be friends. I have to admit that staying friends is fine by me. That's probably for the best when you think about it." Joe looked up to Nicole and Sara, having just acknowledged their presence.

"What are you guys talking about?" Little Nicole asked, twirling her hair and jumping up to sit on the stainless-steel table closest to her.

"Joe is talking about how much of an idiot he is. So pretty much the usual." Carl breathed in and out, turning his nervousness into angered frustration with the coffee machine. "Why the hell do people let this thing get clogged up all the time?! Where do these tea bags come from?!"

"Listen, it's all good on my end. I'm not an idiot at all. Sara." Joe turned his full attention to her.

"What is it?" She stood timidly while meeting Joe's gaze head-on. She could sense that something was very different about him now.

"Can you help Carl with that coffee machine? You're a whiz at these kinds of things." Joe reached behind the stack of plates for his soda and enjoyed another long sip.

"No problem. Let me reach in there, Carl. My hands are smaller." Sara walked up, keeping her ears open as she reached into the clogged sink that the large coffee machine vented water into.

"Thanks." Carl smiled while keeping his peripheral vision on Joe and Nicole. He felt a strange boost of confidence and found that he could maintain a steady calmness. He then thought about it and wondered if his friend's new abilities had anything to do with the boost of positive emotion.

"Carl, can you get me a towel?" Sara asked.

"One towel coming right up." He reached the lower section of one of the storage tables, where a stack of white towels sat neatly folded. He handed one to Sara and gave a friendly smile as she wiped her hands dry.

"So, to catch you guys up, I've basically had a feeling that I might get back together with Ana. However, recent developments make that seem like it isn't going to happen hence my better off being friends comment earlier. What do you gals think? I mean, you're tight with her. Not as tight as the three of you guys are together, but you know what I mean. Women stick together and whatnot, right?" Joe eyed Nicole and Sara, waiting.

Nicole twirled her hair. "If it didn't work before, why would it work now?"

Joe threw his arms up in appreciation. "That is exactly what has been bugging me. I don't have faith whatsoever that things change with certain people."

Little Nicole raised an eyebrow at Joe's statement and stepped closer after jumping from the stainless-steel table. "What do you think Jared would say about it?"

Joe gave Nicole a puzzled look. "Who?"

"Jared. How do you think he'd feel about you getting back together with Ana?" Nicole pressed.

Joe appeared utterly confused. "Are you okay, Nicole? I don't know anyone named Jared. Do you guys know what she's talking about?"

"No idea. Who's Jared?" Carl grabbed a towel for himself and began cleaning his hands. "Are you guys hanging out with one of the new hires and not introducing me properly? And if so, why didn't anyone tell me? I'm seriously sick of always being the last one to know anything around here!"

Sara noticed the slight mark that was beginning to grow on Carl's essence. At that moment, she could tell that he had crossed over. If they stayed near the two, it wouldn't take long for Nicole to notice once she returned her attention to Carl. She still felt loyalty to her sisters, but at the same time, she wanted to protect Carl from Jared's fate.

"Nicole, we don't know what you're talking about, hun." Sara moved by Nicole's side as a mother would an ill child. "Are you feeling okay?"

"I don't know, maybe I'm not. That was my mistake, guys. I'm not even sure I know what I was talking about. I don't really feel all that good." Nicole feigned fatigue, and Sara grabbed her by the arm.

"Do you need any help?" Joe asked, taking a step forward. In reality, helping the woman was the last thing he wanted to do, but he knew he had to play it safe and stay in character.

"No, I got it. It's probably just girl stuff, anyhow." Sara smiled as she escorted Nicole out of the wait station.

Do you think they bought it? Carl posed the question mentally. He feared being overheard by the others and hoped Jared was tuned in.

Sure enough, Joe had been listening and responded by nodding his head.

Can you tell if Nicole is a part of it too? Carl asked.

Joe looked at Carl while taking a sip of his soda. He nodded his head again and took another drink. *I'm pretty sure she is. She felt different now that I'm able to tune in to things. Her mind felt like Sara's. It wasn't human.*

What about Rachel? Carl asked, already sensing the answer.

"She's probably the one who told Sara and Nicole to check in on us. I never noticed it before; maybe I wasn't supposed to – none of us were, but Rachel really has a hold on the two of them." Joe responded aloud as he was growing tired of communicating with thought. "Let's get back to work. It's going to be a busy night. As long as we stay away from them and find Valerie when she gets here, we should be okay."

"When my powers first manifested, I realized there was a hidden fear everyone else lived with daily: the fear of not knowing. If I were to be cut off from my powers, I think I would go mad not knowing what the future brings. I've grown far too used to it." – Vestor, the Time Bender.

4

"WHAT ABOUT THE people at work? Do they know you're still you? Have you been cleaned from their minds too?" Jared called out to Valerie, who was in the bathroom of her apartment. He paced about the living room with a frantic intensity taking in the details. A simple elegance created a very personal touch to the arrangement of furniture and decor in the apartment. It struck Jared as odd that he would focus on such a thing, given how stressful current events had been.

From the bathroom, the former Grace responded, projecting her voice. "I'm of the supernatural realm. My mind can't be cleansed, and my station as a former goddess grants me the ability to exist in both realms. I appear normal to people on the non-magical side of the Distinction. Sara and her companions will assume I'm another human if all goes well. I'll act like everyone else and appear to have no recollection of you."

"Okay. I think I get it. You live in both places at once kind of thing, right? So, is that how I am now? Do I have a clean slate on both sides? Will people still see me as normal, but I'll see the things they can't?" Jared struggled to rationalize his situation.

Valerie stepped from the bathroom with a towel around her hair and another wrapped around her body. Her skin appeared to radiate an aura of beauty; her exposed skin the towel did not cover teased the imagination.

"Wow, um..." Jared took a few steps back, feeling uncomfortable. He froze like a statue; his frantic pacing came to a halt. "You're practically naked. I um..."

"Relax, Jared. It would have happened long before if I were looking to seduce you." She glided past Jared into the kitchen area, separated from the living room by a small countertop. "And to answer your questions, you're correct. The life you used to have is erased forever. You'll appear normal to regular humans; you'll also begin to gain a sense of which ones aren't human as your instincts sharpen."

"So, this plan of Minx's, do you think it'll work?" Jared forced himself to sit down, realizing his hands were trembling; the little vampire left quite an impression upon him. He did his best to control his breathing and calm his nerves. *I was face to face with a real vampire!*

Valerie poured a glass of water and drank from it before answering. "It should." She placed the empty glass on the countertop. "It's a far better plan than the one I originally intended. Projectors are creatures to be reckoned with. They are few but very powerful. Projectors that are soul eaters are rarer still and even more dangerous. Fortunately, there is only one still around. I'm thankful that the old ways have not lost touch with current times. It's good that everyone respects the balance, especially those that can distort it at will."

Valerie's words resonated with Jared, and a strange feeling overcame him. Memories of a future life that was him flashed through his consciousness for the briefest of moments. Possibilities fanned out endlessly. It was as if a chess game was being played. He desperately tried to outmaneuver an adversary far more intelligent and powerful than him.

"Are you okay?" Her voice was gentle.

Jared snapped back to the present. "Yes. Sorry." He cleared his throat. "So, what am I supposed to do now?" Jared watched as Valerie exited the kitchen area and sat beside him, still wearing the towel. "How do I get back to some kind of normal?"

"Jared..." She looked upon him with great pity.

"I know what you're going to say. It's what you've been telling me this entire time. Normal no longer applies to me, but how do I get close to it? After this is over, what do I do? I mean, what am I supposed to do?" His eyes were desperate for guidance.

"We deal with one thing at a time. Then, after that, we move on to the next step – whatever that step may be." She answered.

"Sound advice from a sagacious and beautiful woman." An older gentleman's voice spoke up in the living room of the apartment. It carried a mature and robust tone with an underlying hint of adolescent mischief.

Valerie smiled with fondness before turning her gaze upon the apparition. "It's been a long time since a ghost has come my way."

"When I placed the spell that summoned me to my grandson, I made sure that there would be enough energy to have an audience with you as well," Chan explained.

"Ming did mention that you would probably appear at some point." Valerie crossed her arms, delighted to see the old man.

Jared studied the apparition that emanated a brilliant hue of green with dumbstruck awe. "What are you? I mean, who are you? How did you even get in here?"

"Young man, you may refer to me as Cheung Chan or Chan. It's entirely up to you, really." The ghost bowed his head.

Jared scrutinized the ghost with a focused eye as he poised himself near Valerie. He soaked in the fantastic imagery before his eyes in greater detail, taking in the manifestation of physical features the energy of the spirit projected. Jared's jaw finally dropped as he recognized the lineage of those features. "Chan? Like Joseph Chan?"

"He's my grandson and a good and loyal friend to you, I might add. Joseph also informed me about how you, my lovely Valerie, plan to look into matters for young Mr. Hernandez. I told him he could trust you. Joseph will seek you out. He is quite determined to help his friend. He might as well have you watching out for him while he does." Grandpa Chan sat down next to the former Grace and focused the substance of his energy on touching her hand with his own. "It's been far too long. You look exactly as I remember."

"Time is different for me, Chan. It always has been, but you already knew that." Valerie smiled, holding Chan's hand within both of hers. She had forgotten how powerful an intimate touch could be.

"You know him? Joe's Grandfather?" Jared chimed in.

"Yes. Chan was the man I spoke of when you asked about my previous relationship. He's the man I tried so very hard to give up my godhood for." Valerie admitted.

Jared scratched his head in confusion. "But that picture on your desk... It didn't look anything like this guy, and it was from our time. The guy in that picture was a hell of a lot younger too."

Valerie kept an endearing gaze on Chan as she explained further. "That's how it would appear to someone who has not crossed over. You were on the brink at that point. The picture makes itself modern to mask the true image as time goes by. As for Chan, I knew him when he was very much alive."

"I know that using the proper tense in any language can get confusing when dealing with the dead, but you still know me. My form has simply changed." His hand lost solidity and passed through hers as he stood up. "My grandson Joseph is safe for the time being. I spoke with him at length and prepped him as best I could."

"I take it the family blood runs strong in him." It was more of a statement as Valerie spoke.

"He's a manipulator and a medium. He can call upon the dead and connect with the minds of the living. He's learned much in a short amount of time. The potential for his abilities is very promising, but he still has a long way to go. He isn't ready for everything that's out there. Not yet."

"None of us were ever ready." Valerie closed her eyes for a split second imagining the world as it was during the Age of Myth when she first came into existence. Back then, she was a young, naïve Grace, genuinely unaware of the power of her beauty. "You're certain he's safe?"

Chan nodded. "I am. Ming keeps a close eye on the boy, and you already know how Ming can be."

"What about Carl? Is he okay?" Jared jumped in, relieved and ecstatic that Joe was alive, and remembered him as the person he used to be.

Grandpa Chan looked at Jared with an apologetic face. "I don't know of any Carl, but I'm sure he's safe and well." He turned his attention back to the former Grace. "There's one more thing, Valerie."

"What is it?" She asked.

The ghost appeared to sigh. "I know that Ming will do all she can to protect Joe, but if something unfortunate happens to her, I would ask that you be there to guide him."

"It's something I would have done regardless, my love." Valerie gave Chan a sad smile as she stood from the couch and walked closer to the apparition. The towel adorning her body almost seemed to become an elegant dress, given how she carried herself.

With the energy left to him, Chan made his entire body solid. His arms wrapped around Valerie's body, holding her tight just as when he was young and alive. "I'm sorry I ever left you. I was a foolish young man who just ended up turning into a foolish old man. I should have stayed by your side. Please forgive me for my folly."

"All is forgiven, Chan." Valerie fought a sudden surge of emotion, keeping a few tears from escaping. She felt the man that was Cheung Chan slowly fade away; the tight grip of his arms vanished from around her body, leaving her alone with Jared.

"I've had ample opportunities to go BEYOND. There is a place past everything – older than the gods and projectors. The dead sometimes choose this place post afterlife – there are many levels you can move through once you die – it doesn't really end with death. But going BEYOND is final. No one ever comes back from that. The energy simply vanishes past that point. And that doesn't interest me. I prefer to stick around and see how things unfold." – Cheung Chan (Master Magician – mortal practitioner)

5

A BRIEF MOMENT was all Valerie needed to regain her composure and focus on the task at hand.

"Are you okay, Valerie?" Jared spoke with genuine concern.

"I'm fine. I need to get dressed. You should shower and try to get some sleep. I have clothes for you to change into. I'm sure you must be tired of wearing that ridiculous waiter uniform. I never did like the design of the new ones." Before Jared could respond, Valerie was out of the living room and in her bedroom.

Jared trotted along until he reached the bathroom. He found the change of clothing folded atop the closed toilet seat and grinned. It had almost made him feel like a child again, seeing the shirt and pants waiting for him in such a neat presentation. His mother used to prepare him for school with what to wear organized similarly back when he was a little boy.

Mom...

His mind began to wander as the reality of his situation struck him hard yet again. He was now a complete stranger to his mother, Maria, and his father, Andres. He was destined to face whatever was coming his way alone, and a base fear fueled that fact, sending chills throughout his body.

Just get in the shower and focus. One thing at a time, as Valerie said. Valerie's words became a mantra to Jared, and they calmed the anxiety that came and went.

The water poured from the showerhead upon opening the valve with an annoying imbalance in temperature. After disrobing, Jared played with the hot and cold faucet handles, attempting to find a happy medium that would be comfortable for his body to endure. Seeing that his desired temperature would never come to fruition, he settled for as close to that as he could achieve and took one foot after another into the shower.

The water flattened his hair when he stuck his head directly beneath the soothing liquid, allowing the cleansing feeling to run down his back as he pulled his chest forward. His hands were firmly positioned on the shower wall directly before him and beneath the showerhead.

Oddly enough, the water upon Jared's body grew a life of its own, fighting gravity and beading upwards around his skin. At first, Jared attributed this to simple paranoia; however, he soon realized that water beads were moving in various patterns and forcefully held his body steady like the tightest of ropes. As he began to struggle, the liquid strings constricted even tighter around his torso, and he heard sporadic muffled laughter bursting from sections of the water.

"It's Vestor before Vestor! How glorious it is to find you!" The voice reaching out from the water was distorted and caused Jared great fear.

"Vestor?! What are you talking about?!" Jared demanded.

"I've found you, and now I'm going to kill you! I stop you before you meet yourself, and then you can't change things in the future. When I fulfill this cursed impulse, I'll be free of the spell placed upon me!" The water demon began laughing hysterically as the beads of liquid rope tightened with intensity around his chest, making it a great struggle to find breath.

"Valerie!" Jared managed to muster the cry for help before water was forced around his mouth in an attempt to enter through it. He had shut his mouth just in time and continued to fight the liquid that was engulfing his senses.

"It will be easier for you if you do not struggle. Open up your mouth, and let me drown you. It'll be better for you that way." More distorted laughter followed the words.

With a great burst of strength, the door to the bathroom flung open. Valerie stood now fully dressed and ripped the curtain and rod from the shower. She assessed the situation within milliseconds watching Jared struggle with the water demon, and held out her hand in a powerful gesture. Small controlled waves of fire flew forward, touching the water creature that had entered her home, bypassing certain magical safeguards.

"No! I had him! I had him!" The distorted voice screeched in pain as the fire evaporated the liquid surrounding Jared.

Jared watched with a sense of wonder as the fire engulfed the water that held him in place. The evil liquid transformed into pure steam giving the impression that his body was radiating large amounts of heat. He stood in awe of how he hadn't felt the flames; his skin had remained untouched without a single burn mark. When Jared was free, he scrambled to turn off the water from the showerhead.

"Are you hurt?" Valerie asked, looking over Jared's body for injuries.

"I'm okay, I think." Jared suddenly realized he was naked and covered himself with his hands. The near-death experience had run its course, and now he only felt embarrassment for the lack of clothing upon his body. "What the hell was that thing?"

"I believe it was a water demon. Why it was after you is beyond me. Did it say anything?" She asked.

He nodded, still panicked. "It said that it had been looking for me and said something about Vestor before Vestor. Do you have any idea what that means?"

Valerie raised a curious eyebrow. *Another mystery.* "It's something we'll have to look into. Finish getting ready. I'll place a few more safeguard spells to ensure your safety. I apologize for not doing so earlier. I wasn't expecting others to come for you in such a bold manner, but now it seems that you're more valuable than I thought."

"Who the hell would want me? I can't even do anything cool! You have the damn fire hands thing going on! On a good day, I can only snap my fingers with my left hand!" Jared tried to snap with no success, highlighting his point.

"One thing at a time, Jared. That's how we approach all of this. Remember?" Her voice was soothing.

Jared sighed and turned red while recalling his nakedness in front of Valerie.

"I'm returning to the Brightwood Country Club. I told Merdith I'd be around to help as the wedding reception ended. You'll remain here. While in my home, you're protected. Don't leave for any reason and await my return. Joe should be waiting for me if he did as instructed by his grandfather. I'll bring him back here tonight so that we can all regroup. I believe Joe's newfound abilities will greatly aid in the plan Minx's friend laid out. With all of these new developments, we should be in an excellent position to stop the rogue spirits." She nodded her head with confidence.

Jared was uneasy about it all. "I'll stay put. You don't have to worry about that. But what if you don't come back?"

"I will." She reassured him.

Jared mustered up as much faith in this as he could manage and nodded in compliance. Valerie nodded in return and left Jared alone in the bathroom to finish bathing. Upon closing the door, Jared sank to a seated position in the shower and hugged his knees to his chest.

What the hell did that water demon mean by Vestor?

"Of course, we don't always recognize each other. Think about how you sometimes don't recognize someone you knew fifteen years ago. Imagine it's been thousands of years, and you've completely changed your appearance. It's effortless for gods to pass each other and be none the wiser." – Aglaia (known as Valerie during the time of Vestor)

6

THE WEDDING HAD been a grand success. The bride and groom celebrated without limit at the extravagant Brightwood Country Club. The families of the happily married couple had been devoted to the club for generations; the thought of another venue never crossed their minds. Brightwood was sacred to the celebrating party and the rest of the country club's socially elite members.

Over time Brightwood had become a place of hope for the people connected to the idea of the sodality that bound them. The money they poured into the institution symbolized their devout worship and faith. The exclusive group inadvertently turned the Brightwood Country Club into a sacred edifice with the immense energy generated by that same worship and devotion their money represented. This fact was why Rachel, Nicole, and Sara had wanted the grand sacrifice to take place within the walls of this particular location.

The last wedding guests stumbled out of the formal dining room, the victims of one too many mixed drinks. The wait staff worked diligently clearing off the remaining tables and moved the dishes gathered into the kitchen, where Chef and Memo tended to their duties with incredible hubris.

One of the employees worked at the pace of a disinterested teenage girl. At times like these, Rachel enjoyed the charade very much. First, she maneuvered about some of the tables haphazardly, folding up the linen and placing it in a large plastic bag at her feet. Then, she spotted Valerie roaming the club from the corner of her eye. The woman was finally all alone.

"Valerie!" Rachel called out with the right amount of whininess.

Valerie's confident gait continued as she made her way out of the formal dining room. Rachel followed, dropping the giant bag of linen. She ran up the stairs to the club's second level after Valerie. She wanted to stop the woman before she reached her office.

"Valerie? Do you have a second?" Rachel asked with a forced staggered breath from giving chase.

Slowly, Valerie turned to face the young woman. Her eyes were disinterested yet attentive. "I'm a little busy now, Rachel, but I can hear you out. Is everything okay?"

"The thing is, I don't really know where to start. It might sound kind of crazy." Rachel appeared somewhat embarrassed to be asking.

"Take your time. You can talk to me." Valerie gave a comforting smile, switching gears.

"Well, um... Have you ever felt like you remember something no one else seems to remember?" Rachel delivered the question with care, studying Valerie in minute detail.

Valerie hid her study of Rachel behind a puzzled expression. If she were not a creature of magic, she would have believed the young woman's ruse of troubled youth in desperate need of help. *She's very good at this.* "I'm not quite sure what you mean by that? Can you be a little more specific?"

Rachel twirled her red hair with innocence as she began to speak. "The thing is, Nicole has been acting kind of strange. She was asking about someone named Jared. I can't remember, but it almost feels like I should. Have you ever felt like that? Like you've suddenly forgotten something you should know, but you just can't seem to remember?"

"Jared?" Valerie looked as though the name were a foreign concept. "I don't recall anyone named Jared, Rachel. Are you referring to one of the new hires? Unfortunately, I haven't had a chance to properly meet them yet."

Rachel nodded as if Valerie had arrived at the proper conclusion. "Maybe it was one of them she was talking about. I'm not really sure."

Valerie feigned concern. "Are you and Nicole not feeling well? You can both leave early if that's the case. We have enough people here to take care of the breakdown of the wedding setup. I know how stressful nights like these can be."

Faked discomfort added to Rachel's words. "Are you sure that's okay? I know I haven't been getting enough sleep lately. I've been stressed about school and how to pay for it, but that isn't your problem. I'm just babbling right now. I think Nicole's been sick all night, but you know her. She'll keep working unless you make her stop. You're sure it would be okay for us to leave?"

Valerie smiled. "Of course it is. Just be safe on the way home. Is there anyone that can drive the two of you?"

Rachel thought about it. "Sara could if that's okay. Of course, she'd have to leave early with us, but she lives the closest."

Sara and Nicole. You rogue spirits sure do like to work in threes. Valerie nodded her approval. "That's more than okay, Rachel. We should let the boys do the breakdown anyway; they can handle it. Tell Sara I said that it was okay to take both of you home, and if Merdith or Mr. Drake ask about it, send them my way, and I'll explain. I'll see you tomorrow. Be sure to get some proper rest."

Rachel smiled gratefully. "Thanks, Valerie. See ya later." She turned and walked down the stairs showing slight signs of fatigue until she was no longer within Valerie's field of vision. Nevertheless, she had paid close attention to Valerie's body language and picked up on the subtle gestures that would have slipped the perception of a mere mortal's scrutiny.

Valerie hides things well. She must know of our true nature. Something will have to be done about that very soon, but first, there is the matter of the minor sacrifice. The thought fueled Rachel's anger.

A minor sacrifice was waiting for the trio of former goddesses. The blood of Scott Riley and his companions would grant the three sisters strength enough to carry out the intricacies of the grand sacrifice that was to take place at the country club. The devoted followers they had been cultivating would lovingly give their blood up. After consuming the power from the minor sacrifice, Rachel and her sisters would be strong enough to deal with Valerie.

"Even creatures of magic have to have something to believe in. Even they need to have faith from time to time." – Matthew Gomez, the Forever Man.

7

VALERIE RESUMED HER ascent to the second level, having sensed Rachel's lack of belief. She knew this recent encounter had blown the cover she attempted to maintain and felt the pressure of time closing in on her the way a panicked mortal might have. The former Grace stepped inside her office and found Carl and Joe ready and waiting as instructed by Valerie via thought to Joe. His newfound power had the advantage of making communication a lot easier.

"So, let me get this straight, you used to be with my Grandpa Chan, and I've been hitting on you this entire time, not aware of that fact? That shit is not cool! You could be my grandma for all I know! That's just wrong!" Joe shivered at the thought.

"That's very unlikely, considering I gave up the ability to have children long ago. It was a term of the covenant when the Distinction of realms was enacted. No new gods could be created, nor could new gods be borne by the old unless permitted by the Praetor Projector Council." Valerie shut the door to her office and sat at her desk as she sized up the two young men.

"Praewhat? Projectors sound familiar, though. My Grandpa talked about them for a little while. They help maintain a balance or something like that, right?" Joe asked.

Valerie nodded. "Yes, Joe, in a manner of speaking."

Carl stood quietly, doing his best to keep up with the constant madness of unfolding events. Every so often, he would run his fingers through his long blond hair to calm his nerves. "So, what do we do now?"

Valerie passed glances between the two young men with each statement. "We return to my apartment. Jared will be there waiting for us. We must implement a plan to deal with these rogue spirits. You both know your lives are forever changed. Joe, you know this more so than Carl. Thankfully, the addition of the two of you and your unique skills will help ensure that the plan is more successful- if both of you agree to help me carry it out."

Carl did his best to keep the desperation from his voice. "What about after all of that? What happens to us? My parents have been out of town for a while now like they always are. You see, Joe got lucky. It was a part of his family from the start, and his mom always knew this day would come. I know my parents were never really around, to begin with, but they're still my parents, even if it isn't by blood. When whatever was inside me woke up, that became pretty clear. But they still raised me. Doesn't that count for anything?"

Valerie let out a sigh of sympathy for Carl. It never became easy explaining the brutal reality of a new life to the recently crossed over. "They're not going to remember you, Carl. Their minds will be cleansed by the time they return, as will any trace of who you used to be. The people here tonight could barely remember you, and we lucked out that the rogue spirits didn't notice. They were too focused on me by the time I showed up, especially Rachel. My interest in Jared raised the alarm for them. Believe me when I say it's better for your parents if they aren't connected to you. The balance must always be maintained."

"How about we get this going then?" Joe leaned his back to the wall near the door and put a foot upon it for support.

Valerie kept her gaze on Carl. "Carl, you have my address. Can you drive there unnoticed by the others?"

Carl nodded.

"Joe, I imagine that you can manage the same." She looked at him.

"You know it." Joe nodded.

She let out a sigh of approval. "Good. We'll leave separately and meet up there. Make no sudden changes in behavior if you encounter the rogue spirits on the way out. They'll be able to pick up on that."

"No need for the lectures, Valerie. We've been doing just fine so far, thank you very much." Joe's smug tone hung in the air as he exited the office.

Carl reached for the door next but stopped as he felt held back by doubt and questions. He turned to face Valerie carrying a very desperate expression. "All of the things we've heard of and the stories we were told growing up... Are they all true? Vampires, ghosts... Is it true? Why weren't we aware of them before this happened to us?"

Valerie readied herself for the explanation she had given countless times. "The Distinction of Realms was a covenant made between worlds. It keeps the balance, and that balance must be maintained. Before the Primordial Era, there was the One Above All who begot The Great Projector. Shortly after came the birth of Time, Chaos, and then Order. These three are the creatures of the Founding Magic begot by The Great Projector. They willed existence as we know it because our universe is energy, and thought is energy." Valerie paused.

Carl remained silent, taking in her words.

She continued. "What people believe to be real tends to end up that way. Belief is all too powerful, whether it is in one's self or others. Some believe in the things you're now able to see, but their faith wanes. Some creatures struggle to get that lost faith back, and others feed upon energy in different ways now that worship isn't what it once was. Keeping things separate keeps things balanced."

"What about God?" Carl's eyes pleaded.

"What about Him?" Valerie shrugged.

Carl seemed more confused than ever. "Are those stories true?"

Valerie looked him in the eye. "Do you believe that they are? Is your faith truly placed in them?"

Carl nodded, standing taller. "I do, and it is."

She grinned. "Then they're true, Carl. For you, they are true."

Carl pondered her words and seemed even more confused. "How can it all exist? How can the other things exist with what I believe?"

"The universe is vast." She expressed the sentiment with an exaggerated hand gesture. "This isn't the only reality. Every choice that can be made is made. We just don't see them all play out. Sometimes realms touch other realms, and other realities touch other realities. But, ultimately, what you believe becomes tethered to you, whether it exists in this realm or not. Magic is an underlying force that connects it all. Think of it as a constant."

"I'm not sure I understand." Carl stopped focusing on the conversation and looked at the floor in shame.

Valerie took a few steps closer and gently lifted Carl's chin with her hand. She cast a warm smile at the young man. "You will, Carl. I'm here to help guide you through this."

Carl smiled in return, feeling a sudden sense of security. "Okay." He nodded again, reassured by her words. "Okay.

Her smile brightened. "Good. Let's finish this shift and get on with what must be done."

"Desire is the easiest tool one can use to gain worship. What human doesn't desire? What human doesn't lust? My transition, and those other gods like me, probably had the easiest time adapting." – Aphrodite, goddess of love.

8

GIFTED WITH A genetic makeup that was instantly gratifying to the eyes of anyone with an active libido, Scott Riley learned early on in life that he could get whatever his heart desired by way of this physical blessing. People threw themselves at Scott. With his good looks, a certain charm developed that allowed him to say what he wanted without dire consequences and manipulate those he encountered to satisfy his ends. What Scott Riley hadn't realized was that even he could fall under the same spell his beauty imparted on others. Three rogue spirits happened to be doing just that to the young man no one said no to.

He drove the dark red GTO given to him by his father up to the address the GPS displayed on the dashboard directed him to. In the car were two of his closest friends from the varsity football team, and they were all en route to mingle with three naughty yet lovely girls from their school. Nicole and Rachel were attractive, but Scott focused on placing his hands all over Sara's perfectly svelte body.

Bobby and Derrick were the names of his partners in crime. All three wore their letterman jackets; strangely, they wore them more frequently after graduating. The real world was right around the corner, and a looming fear that the best they would ever achieve had been attained transformed the jackets into a type of security blanket.

"You sure this is the place, Scott?" Derrick looked out the window in the back seat of the car. His blond hair seemed to glisten in the moonlight as Scott turned the engine off in front of the run-down house.

"Yeah, I'm sure." Scott kept his mind on Sara's body. "They wanted to meet here so we wouldn't be interrupted. I know it's pretty late and all, but it's worth being tired over. Trust me. They just got done with work, and now they want to party a bit, if you know what I mean."

Bobby began laughing in excitement. His short crew cut made him look like the marine his father was pushing him to become. "Let's do it. I got dibs on Rachel, guys. Her fine ass is all mine."

"Whatever," Derrick grunted. He knew he had little say in choice when it came to these two. Throughout their friendship, he was always stuck with whatever they happened to leave behind.

"Alright, boys, grab the beer, and let's get to it!" Scott exited the car with exaggerated bravado.

Bobby turned to face Derrick while opening the passenger door. "You heard the man. Grab the beer. We'll meet you in there." Then, with an annoying laugh, Bobby exited the car and followed Scott.

"Asshole..." Derrick muttered under his breath while grabbing the cases.

After struggling to exit the backseat of the GTO with two cases of beer, Derrick caught up to his eager companions. They walked to the house together and stood before the run-down front door; the cracks in the wood were large and severe, with an old, discolored door handle that hung loosely. The porch creaked with a life of its own as they moved about in lustful anticipation.

"This place is kind of creepy, man," Derrick spoke up, taking note of the lack of lighting.

"Don't tell me little Derrick is scared?" Bobby threw his annoying laugh out again.

"Cut it out, guys. We gotta be cool here." Scott proceeded to knock on the door.

After a few moments of silence, footsteps could be heard. The door creaked open, and standing before the three was Rachel. She was still wearing her waitress uniform. Her white shirt had been untucked and unbuttoned, revealing a decent amount of cleavage with a white bra that left little to the imagination.

"Hey Rachel," Scott spoke up first.

Bobby smiled while looking at what he gathered as his prize for making this trip during the late-night hours. "Hey, you. You're looking good."

"Why, thank ya, Bobby. Come on in, boys. We've been waiting for you." Rachel scrunched her nose while a mischievous smile.

Upon entering, the trio could hear music trickling from the upstairs level of the old home. The interior was bare and entirely run down, but the girls had almost made it seem like a magical place. The lighting was dim, and the atmosphere made one want to relax and give in to the more lustful ways of life.

"Where can I put these?" Derrick asked, gesturing with the cases of beer in his hands.

"Open them up, and let's drink right now!" Little Nicole yelled as she ran down the staircase leading from the second level of the house.

Scott could see Derrick giving a beer to Nicole from his peripheral vision. Still, his primary focus was on Sara as she slowly descended from the top of the old, elaborate staircase. His eyes took in every detail, and he felt his heart race with desire and strange worship for the woman walking down from up high. Then, with deliberate seductive steps, she made her way before Scott and smiled with innocence as he stood with a dreamy gaze.

"Can you get me a beer too?" Sara asked in a playful tone while untucking her white waitress shirt and slowly unbuttoning the black vest that covered most of it. As she began to disrobe, a nagging sensation crept forth from the back of her mind. It was then that she thought of him. *Jared...*

Scott was oblivious to Sara's thoughts and did precisely as asked. He looked at Sara fondly while she took the drink from his hand. "So, how could you ladies swing a place like this? I'm diggin' it."

"The house isn't what's so important. It's the land the house was built on." Rachel chimed in, having gained a free moment from making out with Bobby. But, being a persistent one, Bobby continued to kiss all along Rachel's neck, pushing back her long red hair.

"The land was sacred to the original people that lived here; by people, I mean the natives of this particular region from a very long time ago." Little

Nicole also interjected with a voice of ecstasy as Derrick found himself kissing her belly. Without hesitation, he moved those kisses beneath the skirt and between her inviting legs; the way he moved his tongue was solely dictated by Little Nicole's sensual moans.

At first, Scott found it odd but then felt a deep and powerful longing for Sara in a way he had never experienced before. He felt Sara's hand direct his chin so that he was looking at her and only her.

This doesn't feel right anymore. The thought plagued Sara. Her inner conflict was unbearable, but she knew she had to play along for the sake of her sisters.

"What are they talking about?" Scott asked, feeling as if he were in a dream. He hadn't even had anything to drink but felt like he had finished an entire pack of beer alone.

"The universe is energy, and energy is powerful in any form. When you focus your energy on something, it creates something special. The people that lived here long ago made this land sacred with their energy. My sisters and I prefer more chaotic energy given that we're of Eris, who is of Nyx, who is of Chaos." Sara explained; her voice remained hypnotic and sybaritic.

"What are you talking about, Sara?" Scott was ultimately bound to her every word but struggled to regain a semblance of control over his actions. It was a futile effort.

"Chaos is of the Founding Magic; may she forever be blessed. The children of Chaos are supernatural. That's where one of the splits between Founding and Supernatural Magic began. Nyx, our grandmother, is a supernatural creature. Her daughter Eris, our mother, is so very powerful in much the same way." Sara continued.

Scott remained silent, staring at Sara with an increasing lust that made him so hard he was on the edge of orgasm.

"We feed off of energy, Scott. It's the energy mortals have given off since humans came to be. No creature has ever given off such lovely and abundantly versatile amounts of energy before your kind. That is why so many of us exist and have fought over your worship." As Sara spoke, she felt guilt mixed with the satisfaction of having such a devoted human.

"Enough with the history lessons, sister...." Little Nicole spoke up, feeling the tantalizing sensation of Derrick's kisses between her legs. Her voice rang with ecstasy.

"Do you trust me?" Sara asked as Scott's hands moved freely upon her body.

"Yes..." He drunkenly gazed upon her beauty.

It pained Sara to continue. She felt the human spectrum of right and wrong. Those human feelings tormented her, but the creature she once was persisted in staying true to the old ways.

"Do you worship me, Scott?" Sara's voice grew with a bittersweet ecstasy. She could feel Scott's kisses on her neck and the slight touch of his fingers upon the nipple of her breast. Her heart reached out to Jared with pain. A sense that she was betraying him took control, and she fought tooth and nail to maintain her composure for the sake of her sisters.

"Yes! I worship you!" He spoke the words vehemently.

"Then get on your knees." Sara's voice was stern, and she watched as he obeyed her command.

Soon all three young men were on their knees with arms spread from side to side. They were entirely under the influence of their misguided worship. The energy of their souls locked into the essence of the former goddesses, and their minds were given over. The young men were so entranced by the spell they hadn't even noticed the glowing dark blue eyes that each of the girls now carried. Nor did they note the transformation of razor-sharp fingers designed to cut flesh. This was how these once proud goddesses fed on energy in a world that had forgotten them.

Rachel ripped the clothing to expose Bobby's bare chest, and the other sisters did the same to their sacrificial humans. Then, in a language long dead to humanity, Rachel began speaking, singing almost, before cutting a line with her sharp index finger down the middle of Bobby's chest.

The pain registered as joy, and Bobby freely gave himself over to Rachel. Blood poured from his open wound, and the razor finger that cut so easily reached inside his chest. He could feel her hand around his beating heart and the excess blood spilling from the gaping wound. The red liquid of life spewed out only to be licked up by the now serpentine tongue of Rachel.

Rachel drank the blood and eventually began to feast upon the heart. Her sisters had carried out the same ritual, and each one grew stronger with the blood of the sacrifice made before them. To a passerby, the boys were screaming in agonizing pain. Within their minds, they were experiencing the most incredible joy ever imagined. As the souls left the bodies, a new pain emerged. The energy that was their essence violently ripped from the proper path it was supposed to follow.

Sara had usually enjoyed this part of the sacrifice the most. It was the moment when the soul became a part of her being; this was what the former goddesses had longed for so often. The energy of a willing participant created an exhilaration that no mortal could ever come close to touching. Scott's soul fought hard to escape, but it was too late. The deed had been done, and his soul would forever be a part of her; it would forever be a part of her essence.

The ritual came to a close, and Sara eyed up her sisters. Both Rachel and Nicole appeared completely satisfied. She smiled in return, acting as if she had enjoyed the experience, but she felt a pang of deep sorrow within her heart. Sara understood and imagined just how disgusted Jared would be if he discovered what she had done. A sense of shame overwhelmed the former goddess. She found it terribly difficult to contain the all too human emotions.

"Sisters!" Rachel spoke up, covered in blood and high from having feasted on Bobby's soul; her dark blue eyes glowed with intense power. "We're stronger now than we were before. We move out quickly so that we can be rid of Valerie. She has a power within her; I've felt it. There's no mistaking she's suspicious of our true natures. As it stands, whatever power resides within her should be no match for the three of us."

"For nearly as long as humans existed, I have been one of the Sleeping: a god in slumber hiding in human form. That was the only impact the Distinction had on me. I didn't remember who I was while in this state, and that never mattered. I am Necessity; when a bond happens from a primordial need, that energy is given to me. I was sustained without effort on my part. Existence is never without necessity." – Ananke, goddess of bonding (necessity – primordial goddess)

9

SLEEP FAILED JARED as he sat on the far end of Valerie's couch, staring at the apartment door with fearful anticipation. Hours had trickled by since Valerie said she would return, and as each second vanished with no sign of her arrival, he felt increasingly lost and alone.

The near-death encounter with the water demon had forced him to remain clear of the bathroom and all other sources of the liquid. His bladder was pushing for relief after hours of holding it in. Jared realized how his fear controlled too much of his circumstances, and he was suddenly struck by Minx's words on accepting fear and letting it go.

The door began to slowly unlock. Jared jumped to his feet, moving comfortably in the clothing given to him by his new mentor. He crept up like a would-be ninja behind the door with a prop fire poker held so tight that his grip hurt and his hands were numbing. He found the iron poker while snooping about the living room and noticed it was used as decor for the main wall's faux fireplace. As the door opened, Jared found himself unable to move. A paralytic spell had been cast.

"A fire poker? Really? What exactly did you intend to do with that?" Valerie's voice was calm as she entered. She snapped her fingers and watched as Jared became delighted to have movement restored to his body.

"I have to do something to protect myself! What if it hadn't been you coming through that door?" Jared insisted.

Valerie sighed. "I told you that you were safe. I made sure of it before I left."

"Then what about that water demon that managed to get in here and try to kill me? You seemed pretty sure about me being safe before that happened." Jared crossed his arms to accent his point.

"It was a minor oversight. I didn't anticipate such creatures coming after you. The flaw was corrected before I left for Brightwood." She admitted the mistake with reluctance and was beginning to resent that she had to continually defend and explain herself.

"What's a water demon?" Carl asked as he entered the apartment.

"Carl!" Jared leaped toward his friend, overjoyed at seeing a familiar face. "You're really here? I'm not dreaming! You remember me, right? You know who I am?"

Carl couldn't help but smile. "Of course I know who you are. You're one of my best friends, Jared."

"Where's Joe?" Jared turned his attention back to Valerie. "You said you'd be back here with Joe. Did something happen to him?"

"Joe is on his way." She assured both Carl and Jared with a hand gesture before continuing. "We each left separately so as not to arouse suspicion. However, I fear these rogue spirits already know I know what they are. Rachel studied me closely tonight as I studied her. We were both able to see through each other's facades."

"Rachel?" Jared closed his eyes briefly, remembering how nice she had always been. *Was it all really an act?* "What are they exactly? Have they always been these spirits you keep talking about?"

"They've always been creatures of a supernatural nature - by them, I mean the rogue spirits that inhabit the bodies." Valerie's tone implied the youth ready themselves for an uncomfortable truth. "The three girls were once purely human, but I fear that each girl's original essence was eaten by the invading spirits a long time ago. The mask of the identities the rogue spirits use may be all that remains of who these girls used to be."

"Essence... Do you mean their souls?" Carl closed the door behind him and stood unsure; he didn't know where it was acceptable for him to go in the apartment. Valerie's home was alien to him, and Carl stood beside Jared. They both gazed upon Valerie, desperately needing her to make sense of everything.

She nodded in response to the question and regarded the two young men with slight pity as she sat in a chair perpendicular to the couch in her living room. Then, she gestured for them to be seated, watching them tiptoe to the empty couch. The exhaustion of the situation they were facing enveloped their physical senses like a rock abruptly submerged in water as the youths sat. Now in the company he wanted and needed, Jared felt his body demanding that he get the rest it craved.

"What is a rogue spirit?" Carl asked with calmness in his voice.

"Many of us used to be gods and goddesses. Some of us were among the first creatures when the Supernatural was born from the Founding Magic. Others followed shortly after." She spoke calmly in return.

"So, Zeus and Mars or Aries, or whatever he's called, and all of them... Valerie, are you telling me that they all really existed?" Carl couldn't believe what he was hearing.

She nodded. "Yes. Most of them still do. Odin, Loki, Thor, and others of the Norse pantheon roam freely, and even Izanagi and Amaterasu."

"Who are those last two?" Jared asked.

"They're of the Japanese pantheon. Your future encounters will likely be filled with many supernatural beings. Even creatures of the natural realm are to be treated with equal caution and respect. You're familiar with Natural Magic, mostly as science. Still, the science you know is limited compared to what it can yield." She explained.

"Science is magic?" Jared fought off a yawn as he asked the question.

"Yes, in a manner of speaking. It's the latest form. I must prepare both of you properly before you boys begin to venture off on your own. Hopefully, after this is all settled, you can go into hiding somewhere safe and live your days in peace. But we'll discuss more of this in the morn-" Valerie abruptly became silent and exuded a face of extreme concentration.

"Valerie? Valerie, are you okay?" Jared posed the question while inching closer with caution.

Carl remained seated, unsure of the proper course of action but wanting to aid. A flash thought of calling 911 raced through his mind, but he soon felt like an idiot for having even considered that a viable option. He doubted that there was a service available for supernatural creatures.

Jared waved a hand before Valerie's face as he moved closer. "Hey!"

"Don't distract me right now!" Valerie barked. "They're here! If my true nature was in question to them before, it no longer is! They can feel my magic, and they're testing it as we speak!"

"What do we do?!" Jared turned to Carl for an answer and received a dumbfounded stare in return.

Valerie's voice strained. "They must have had some type of sacrifice made to them after they left the country club tonight... They're much stronger now. I can feel the change in them. They're pushing through the barriers I set up to ward against uninvited intruders."

"I don't understand!" Jared moved his hands through his hair in panicked desperation.

Her impatience at his understanding grew. "Rachel, Nicole, and Sara are outside of the apartment building and are attempting to break through the barriers of protection I put in place. Breaking through the barriers requires a great amount of energy, and they've amassed lots of potential for that kind of energy. It's only a matter of time before they're successful."

"We should run!" Carl's fight or flight response kicked in. He shot up and waited to see if Valerie and Jared agreed.

She shook her head. "Running isn't an option. Right now, the only thing protecting us is the safeguards, and it's taking more out of me than I have to keep those barriers intact. I'd be able to fight off just one, but chances are I'm going to fail against all three of them."

"What can we do to help?! There has to be something we can do!" Jared reached for the fire poker and held it close.

"I must become stronger than I am. If I had my former status, this wouldn't be an issue. Carl." She remained focused; her gaze was on nothing in particular.

"Yes." Carl was desperate to help.

"Are there any creatures in the area that you can summon? Did your animal guide help you understand what you can do?" She asked.

Carl nodded quickly. "Bandolar helped me understand a little bit, but we haven't had a lot of time! He said he'd find me later - I'm not sure I can do what you're asking!"

"Relax. I need you to extend your mind." The strain from the power struggle wore on Valerie. Her voice began to waiver, and her body was barely able to keep itself seated.

Carl closed his eyes and concentrated. His mind reached out. He soon found himself connected to all types of creatures, from the tiniest insects to the larger rodents patrolling the alleyways and moving in and out of sewers. He could see with their eyes and feel what they felt as they moved about eating, sleeping, and fighting amongst other creatures. Carl pinpointed a small rat, in particular, to focus with. From its vantage, he saw the three girls standing across the street from the apartment building where he, Jared, and Valerie were.

"I can see them!" He was amazed by the sensations going through his body; Carl was connected to so much vibrant life. "All three of them are together right outside, just like you said. It looks like they're trying to cross the street, but something is blocking them. I think it's the barrier you were talking about. It's crazy, I didn't feel the barrier when we walked up, but the rats can feel it."

"The animals around you... Are there many of them near?" She asked.

"Yes. There's a nest of rats in the sewer right below them. They're a bit scattered about, but I can feel them. I think I can bring them all together." Carl's eyes remained closed.

"Do it!" There was satisfaction in her voice. "Gather them together... Have them attack... It will buy us time."

Jared was amazed that his friend had uncovered such extraordinary abilities. But then, he was snapped back into the moment by Valerie's firm hand reaching out and forcefully latching onto his forearm.

She looked him in the eyes. "Jared... I need to know the truth. Are you a virgin?"

"What? What does that have to do with anything?" Jared was flustered by the question.

"Carl is buying us some time with the animals, but it won't last much longer. I need your blood to get stronger." Each word was riddled with the pain of extreme concentration. "It's the only way that we can survive this."

"What do you need my blood for?!" Jared couldn't mask the growing fear.

"A virgin's blood is pure and powerfully potent when given as a sacrifice. Make a cut, drop some blood before me, and say, 'I give this blood sacrifice unto you.' And you have to *mean* it with every ounce of your essence. Believe... the words." Her command was forceful.

With closed eyes, Carl spoke. "The rats are moving in. You want them to attack?"

"Yes." Valerie maintained eye contact with Jared as she concentrated on holding up the barrier of protection around the apartment building. "Get a knife from the kitchen and drop that ridiculous fire poker!"

Jared dropped the fire poker, startled by Valerie's intensity, and ran to do as ordered.

Through the eyes of the rats, Carl could see the small creatures scurrying about beneath the surface of the streets; it was a vantage point that would be at ankle level to the eyes of a human. A swarm of rodents emerged, and every last member of Carl's army was intent upon assaulting the three female intruders. With sheer willpower, Carl pushed his rodent forces forward. They were ready to attack without question flooding the surface street with his intent.

He viewed as they began biting and clawing at the women poised with a concentrated effort to break down the protective barrier. The distraction worked as intended, and the girls were forced to deal with the creatures around them, causing their efforts to falter. The aspect of the connection that Carl had not anticipated was the intense pain the animals experienced as Rachel, Nicole, and Sara began eradicating them. Flames burst forth, charring the rodents alive. Other rats exploded from the invisible strain of force placed upon them. The physical act of stomping also put an end to others as the assault continued.

Carl felt every death, and with each death, he wanted nothing more than to break the connection. "When can we stop?" His voice quivered in pain.

"Soon." Valerie watched as Jared scrambled back into the living room with a knife in hand.

Jared held his left forearm before Valerie and pulled up his shirt sleeve. He grabbed the kitchen knife handle in his right hand with the tightest grip he could muster.

"Do it..." The weakness in her voice expressed just how drained her energy and power were becoming. Her body was on the verge of caving in upon itself, and her eyes cried for help.

With a deep sigh and a concentration he never knew he possessed, Jared spoke aloud, "I give this sacrifice of my blood unto you, Valerie." The knife went into his flesh, and he cut along his forearm. It was a small incision. He held the cut forearm before Valerie and allowed the blood drops to spill directly before her.

Valerie reached out with a weak hand and let the red liquid of life fall into her palm. The red droplets absorbed into her flesh, and she instantly felt the power of the sacrifice rush through her entire being. In a simple act of survival, she had regained most of her former glory; it had been ages since a mortal had sacrificed anything to the former Grace. She had nearly forgotten how much she enjoyed the rush of powerful energy that came from such a simple act of devotion.

"I can't take much more of this." Carl fell to his knees as his body began to shake. Tears ran down his cheeks, and his eyes were closed so tight they started to hurt. The pain he felt from each death grew unbearable, and he wanted nothing more than to sever the connection.

Jared went to his friend, holding him steady. "It'll be okay, Carl."

"We're almost done. I just need you to continue for a few moments long-er." Valerie stood from her seat and held her hands before her in a type of prayer position. She spoke a language long dead to humanity and, with those words, forced the will of her magic to be carried out.

Jared could almost see the ripple distort the very space around him. It flew outward in a large ring passing through him and extending beyond the apartment's walls.

Carl saw the ripple through the eyes of the rodent army. He watched and felt as the surge forced the girls to cower in intense pain through their per-spective. The trio now had no choice but to retreat. With much hesitation, Rachel finally conceded and vacated the area with her sisters.

"You can let go of the link now, Carl," Valerie explained; her tone was comforting.

Carl opened his eyes, realizing that Valerie's hand was placed on his shoulder. Jared aided in keeping him upright while on his knees. Carl rose to his feet, fighting for balance, and began wiping away the tears from the shared pain he had experienced. "I felt them, Valerie. I felt them die for me."

"I can only imagine how it feels to have a strong bond ripped away in such a manner, but you did well, Carl. You helped save us all." She remind-ed him.

"I feel so strange now." Jared sat down, sensing Valerie with a new eu-phoric perspective.

"The two of us are forever bonded. It was done out of necessity." Her tone implied another hard truth for the youth. "It was unavoidable, given the sac-rifice. You gave me your blood, which is a vessel of your essence; part of that essence is a part of me. You're now my subject, for lack of a better term. I'll always feel you and know where you are. In return, you'll always have a sense of wanting to protect me and know where to find me through that bond."

Jared opened his mouth as if to speak but closed it opting for silence. She was right yet again. He could feel the change within him and was bonded to her now, for better or worse.

Quite abruptly, the door to the apartment creaked open at a slow, steady pace. Valerie, Jared, and Carl stood ready to face whatever new possible threat entered unannounced.

"At first, they seemed helpless. They were just teenage boys with no direction thrust into a world beyond their understanding. They were then given incredible abilities and expected to use them as if they had honed these new skills their entire lives. Little did I know that a trinity of sorts had been born. A trinity of powerful individuals made stronger by the bond of friendship. This trinity helped to shape the new world."
– Aglaia, former Grace (known as Valerie during the birth of Vestor)

10

THE DOOR OPENED at a mind-numbingly slow pace and fell silent as it abruptly stopped moving. Joe entered, startled by the defensive reception. He stood with a bag of sour cream and onion potato chips while waiting for the group to relax and realize he was not a threat.

"Jesus Christ, Joe!" Carl exclaimed as relief filled his body.

"Where have you been? You were given specific instructions to return here immediately." Valerie stood with authority. It was the posture of a boss handing out discipline; there was nothing supernatural about it.

"I got hungry on the way over, so I stopped at a gas station to get a snack. I didn't know what kind of food you'd have here, and I figured entering the apartment wouldn't be a big deal since you said I was allowed to pass the barriers. Does anyone else want some chips? They're delicious, man; I mean really good." Joe held the bag out with an offering gesture and winked at Valerie sensing her frustration.

"I'll have some." Carl walked over, reached into the bag, and began eating as if it were any other day.

Joe scooped up more chips after Carl and munched loudly as he spoke with enthusiasm between bites. "The great thing is I didn't even have to pay for them. I practiced some of what Grandpa Chan taught me, and I con-vinced the guy that these were part of some kind of accidental overstock and were expired. I also made him believe I was an employee throwing away bad product. I can get used to this whole manipulator business."

"You're not supposed to use your powers in such a manner!" Valerie reprimanded.

"Calm down, Val. You sound just like my ma, and that ain't cool. I get enough shit from her as it is." Joe continued to devour the snack.

Valerie sighed and plopped her exhausted body down on the couch. She remained silent while studying the three young men and regarded the bond of true brotherhood they shared with a fond grin. Her initial reaction had been wanting to yell at Joe's ignorance. But instead, she decided to allow the boys to have their moment of joyful reunion. There would be plenty of time for disciplining later if she could manage to keep them out of harm's way.

"It's good to see you, Jared. I'm glad you're okay." Joe walked up to his lifelong friend.

"It's good to be seen and to be remembered. I'm sorry you guys got mixed up in all of this." Jared didn't know what else to say.

"Shit happens. As strange and messed up as it may be, it all really happened, and we're in this together. We'll figure it out, man." Joe reassured.

With his friends before him, Jared grew confident that things could be okay. He turned to Valerie; she sat in silence on the couch. Jared could sense her current mood and felt an incredible urge to help his goddess relax. The overwhelming desire to please her shocked him, and he realized how profound this bond of blood was.

After a shared group silence and sensing everyone's exhaustion, Valerie spoke up with heavy eyes. "We all need to get some rest. Tomorrow. More will be explained tomorrow. I promise."

PART SEVEN:

FINAL

PREPARATIONS

"Ever get a sudden feeling that there's something you should be doing? Have you ever had a strong inclination to carry out a task that is unlike you? Have you ever felt like there was something you should know or something you should do that you can't, for the life of you, remember? Chances are you've just been hit with a powerful spell and were lucky or unlucky enough to be within the radius because what you've forgotten was either supernatural bliss or the stuff of nightmares." – Special Agent Sionmen Repus of the Natural Magic Order.

1

DYSNOMIA ENTERED THE home, which once belonged to the original flesh and blood Rachel. The vessel the rogue spirit inhabited obeyed her every command. There no longer remained any essence of the young girl within the body's blood; Rachel's soul had been devoured by the former goddess that lived in the body. With angered steps, she led the way through the house as Nicole and Sara followed; they were all frustrated by the sudden failure of their efforts to put an end to Valerie.

The trio ceased movement in an open hallway and cast their unified gaze upon a middle-aged man and woman sitting in silence at the edge of a couch in the living room. The couple's legs were at a perfect ninety-degree angle, and their backs were stiff. They were the birth parents of the body Dysnomia commanded.

In a fashion in tune with that of a zombie, the vessel's parents turned their heads and regarded their master with blank expressions. Then, their gaze landed upon the three girls as they rose like marionettes from their seated position awaiting instructions.

"How may we serve you?" The male bowed his head to Rachel. The movements were lifeless.

"Have the two of you replenished your bodies with the required sustenance?" Rachel stepped forward, examining the parents of the flesh she inhabited for any physical ailments that would lead to their decay. Dysnomia had never even taken the time to learn their real names, but thanks to her crafty spell, they carried out her bidding. As a result, both acted as they were supposed to in the outside world. This precaution kept the illusion of Rachel with a happy family intact.

"I still don't understand why you didn't just have them cleansed from existence." Little Nicole scoffed, looking at the trinkets that adorned a shelf in the living room. All the items in the home were nothing more than remnants of a forgotten family that would soon be lost to time.

"It was necessary to keep them around to maintain our false identities. And you should be grateful I did the same for the parents of the vessels the both of you inhabit. I swear, without my leadership, the two of you would be lost." Rachel explained before returning her attention to the man and woman of late middle-age years. "You may both retire, allowing your bodies to rest. You'll wake up in the morning and resume your activities like normal. Are my orders clearly understood?"

"They are." Both the male and female responded in unison. They walked up a small staircase to the second level of the house like two well-programmed machines; each step was synchronized.

Once the bedroom door shut on the second level, Rachel turned to face her sisters. She looked to Ate (Sara) and Lethe (Nicole), releasing her rage. Her posture was on the verge of a violent outburst as she wanted nothing more than to demolish everything in sight. "She shouldn't have been that strong tonight!"

"I tried to warn you. We shouldn't have underestimated Valerie, Dysnomia." Sara spoke up, not caring if her comment were out of turn. Rachel was her eldest sister, but events could have conspired to be far more severe had they not retreated in time. The barrier of protection they attempted to breach spiked in strength out of nowhere. It was a counter that had been unanticipated.

Words were not spoken as Rachel glared at Sara. Little Nicole stepped between the two, attempting to break the tension with her presence. The seconds of silent anger that passed felt like an eternity.

Lethe cleared the throat of her vessel as she stood between them; her tone was diplomatic. "Ate. Dysnomia. The important thing to remember is that we now know Valerie to be a creature of power. She could even be of our own pantheon. How she manipulated the barrier is similar to the magic of our kind. Her magic, however, increased in strength when we attempted to breach. I thought we had her, though - I was certain of it! But, toward the end, something changed."

"We did have her, Lethe! She had help. Others must have been with her - they had to have been!" Rachel scoffed, irritated for having to state the obvious.

"What do we do now, Dysnomia?" Sara moved to the main couch in the living room. She sat down, allowing her hands to run over the smooth brown fabric.

"We change nothing. We make the grand sacrifice happen as planned. To miss the opportunity the nexus point grants us would be folly. It'll allow us to be powerful enough to set foot on Olympus without being summoned by Zeus." Rachel's eyes grew distant; an underlying sadness weighed them down. "He hasn't bothered to speak to us in so long. I miss his call – to be summoned and wanted... So we force our way back! It's the only way we can be as we were. It's our only way home."

"What of Valerie and the others?" Sara sighed, keeping her innermost thoughts confined. Her sisters hadn't noted the subtleness of Joe's answers when questioned about Jared, and they missed the quirky way in which Carl had been acting. Sara was confident that Valerie protected all three young men but refused to share this insight. A part of her wished for them to be safe, and she remained on the couch, allowing her sisters to stay focused on the sacrifice to come.

Jared...

A strange and very human longing overwhelmed her. Sara had felt an insatiable desire to be near him again and know his pure affection. She expressed love for Jared, and this was the catalyst that marked him. He had crossed over because of her, and at that moment, another very human feeling crept upon her. It was the burden of intense guilt. She felt responsible and desperately needed to somehow atone for her actions.

As Sara sat on the couch, it occurred to her that perhaps they had all spent far too much time in human bodies, but now she found she had grown too accustomed to the vessel. She wanted to feel how all mortals felt and to know Jared's kiss upon her lips at least one last time.

"Ate!" Rachel barked. "Are you ready to cast out the calling? All of us need to be connected and focused. We're strong enough to do this now. The time is right."

With a reluctance that went unnoticed, Sara stood from the couch and joined hands with her sisters. Together all three formed a circle in the center of the living room. As they held hands, they spoke in a language long dead to human ears, and their eyes grew an intense dark blue that glowed and rippled like the waves of a stormy ocean. Then, another glow began emanating from the center of their circle. A wave of willed energy expanded in all directions throughout the fabric of existence.

"Most people don't realize it, but we all have hidden admiration for certain individuals – even the ones we don't think we care about." – Ming Chan – descendent of Chu-Jung, the Chinese god of fire.

2

WORK RARELY ENTERED Mr. Drake's mind even when the pompous man was at the Brightwood Country Club that supplied him with the monetary means for the good life. The members had chosen him over a variety of candidates. To be perfectly honest, each one was far more qualified than him. Through domineering persistence and blackmail, he gained the desired position accompanied by exorbitant pay.

While enjoying a fine red wine on the rooftop patio of his prestigious high-rise apartment, he found himself fixated on his place of employment. A strange sensation blanketed his entire being, penetrating the elaborate blue and gold silk robe that adorned his body. It was as if the country club called to him like a long-lost lover returning with the promise of never again leaving. He felt a great desire within his essence to feel the embrace of this lover, and he knew that the following night would be ideal for a glorious grand gathering.

"Worship..." He whispered the word. It felt strange and foreign coming out of his mouth, and his voice sounded as if it were no longer his own. He belonged to that country club. It had granted him the lifestyle he sought, and for that, he truly did worship it. It was sacred ground, and upon that holy ground, three names emerged from the sea of desire splashing about within his mind.

"Rachel... Sara... Nicole..." Images of the young women flashed through his thoughts as he whispered their names. He felt a sense of gratitude to them like none other; they were three incredibly hard-working young women. They never bumbled about like most of the idiots that collected paychecks. They always knew how to perform the tasks given to them with the utmost proficiency. If it hadn't been for those three young ladies, his place of worship that he was so grateful for would have fallen apart. Without them, it would no longer be that sacred temple to the life he was given. He owed them, and he would show them how grateful he was on the coming night.

"A place is only sacred because of the energy we put into it. Our WILL feeds the belief. This is why a church can be absent God, and a cardboard box can be a true shelter and know His grace." – Matthew Gomez, the Forever Man.

3

OLD MERDITH LIVED a long and fruitful life, and the Brightwood Country Club had been a principal aspect of that existence. Long ago, she had chosen to reside near her place of employment and always felt an intense connection with the members and the club itself. Brightwood had sustained the old woman throughout the years. It had given her a purpose in life she would not otherwise have had, and for that, she would remain eternally grateful.

The house where she lived alone was very conservative in decor, much as Merdith had been all her years. A wild bone dared not exist within the woman's body. More often than not, she detested the inappropriate manner in which her beloved country club's young employees carried themselves.

The land upon which the club was built had been sacred to Merdith, and she felt that sacredness now more than ever. While getting ready for bed in her thick burgundy robe, she felt a warm desire wash over her frail old body. She had left the country club hours ago, ending a glorious wedding celebration that had exhausted her aged frame. Still, she yearned to be at Brightwood again nonetheless. She wanted to thank those who contributed to making it such a sacred and special place.

Rachel... Sara... Nicole...

The three names washed up on the shores of her sleepy consciousness. She viewed the three young women with great affection and knew within her heart just how hard they had always worked. They performed their jobs superbly, and without them, she knew that the club would not be as well off as it had become. The establishment would inevitably fall to pieces if they lost these particular employees. Merdith would then be forced to lose her special purpose.

"I need to give proper respect and worship...." Her voice sounded strange, but Old Merdith was too old to care. She attributed it to being tired, and she felt that she had to rest for the special night. On the night to come, she would give proper respect and thanks to these three young women. She felt a sense of loyalty she never thought herself capable of.

Yes. I must show respect.

Those three young ladies would indeed be given proper respect. Old Merdith would be there to ensure it was done flawlessly tomorrow night.

"Even a former goddess can suffer from the pitfalls of pride. I should have killed him when I had the chance. Instead, I played the game and watched him learn, adapt, and grow more powerful. I let it happen because I thought I could control him."
– Renee Dempsy, former Fury.

4

BEING WED TO Mr. Dempsy had transferred Renee into the social status of old money. Her doting idiot of a husband had inherited the family wealth at his disposal. Being in existence since the age of myth and carrying the title of a former Fury made Renee Dempsy old magic. This aspect of her long life, she had accomplished all on her own.

The former goddess could feel the fabric of existence shifting within the Brightwood Country Club she was a member of through marriage. She remembered Jared but knew he'd been marked and acted like she had never known the young man. She also knew that rogue spirits were plotting to their own ends at the club. But, like many magical creatures living in secrecy, Renee Dempsy often chose to mind her own business. Leave well enough alone was the unspoken motto of former deities and other creatures that existed on the fantastic side of the Distinction.

"I have the strangest desire to be at the country club, my love." Mr. Dempsy, obese in every sense of the word, looked over to Renee. He awoke to feel this odd need and shared it with his trophy wife. He sleepily gazed upon her as they lay in bed, nearly returning to the point of desired slumber.

The older yet attractive Renee smiled comfortingly at her husband. She sensed the rippling flow through the fabric of reality. A potent calling spell had been cast, and it demanded great worship. She remembered how such things felt during her days as one of the Furies.

"Do you think you'll go with me to Brightwood tomorrow night?" Mr. Dempsy asked. "You know, now that I think of it, three girls there have always worked so hard: Rachel, Nicole, and Sara."

"Is that so dear?" Mrs. Dempsy cast a polite smile and listened to her husband, who had succumbed to the spell of worship cast out by the rogue spirits. His mind was weak. She knew of ways to break him from the clutches of such a spell, but she grew tired of the overweight pervert in reality. Without guilt, she decided that he was on his own. With any luck, she would be rid of him once and for all. This would leave his remaining fortune all to her. After all, this was never a marriage of love. Love was dangerous magic all on its own.

"Yes, it is, Renee." He sighed. "You'll be with me to give them proper respect, right?"

Renee gave him a look of promise. "I'll try my best, dear. Unfortunately, I have prior engagements tomorrow night, but I promise I'll do my best to attend. I know how important this is to you."

"I wish you would just commit to it, Renee. But please do try and make it. It's paramount that we're there. I'm going back to bed now. I feel exhausted." While in the trance of the spell, Mr. Dempsy closed his eyes and returned to the world of dreams.

Jared...

Renee had known long ago that the boy was special. Aside from her marriage's monetary gains, being a member of the country club allowed her to keep close tabs on young Jared Hernandez. She followed his ascension in silence, knowing full well what he would become and that he would eventually grow into his role as a Time Bender.

She smiled, thinking of the captured source that gave her the information about the one that would be Vestor. Renee managed the impossible and put into motion a plan that caught her very own Time Bender. The mortal prophets that tell the future were always elusive; they were typically impossible to corner and take prisoner. Inevitably the sly prophets always saw the outcome. Still, her fortuitous encounters and special planning allowed her to succeed in her hunt.

Incredibly, the old crone is still alive. Her human body is pushing two hundred. But, then again, she hadn't expected to live this long in the first place. The thought of having such a valuable prisoner comforted the former Fury.

Renee pictured the frail old woman doting prophecy through the aid of what the natural science called drugs. The old crone's strands of thinning white hair barely held on to her scalp, and her sagging skin appeared to be a robe draped about the weakest of skeletons. The former Fury maintained this particular Time Bender's essence by keeping the body alive with the soul tethered to it and had been doing so for a very long time.

The elder prophet was secure in a location known only to Renee. Her visions were attuned to precisely what Renee asked of her. It had been challenging to break the proud prophet, but in the end, she obeyed Renee's will. Through these visions, the former Fury discovered how difficult the young Jared Hernandez would become. She sought to vanquish the youth on several occasions; the boy and his family considered the near-death encounters accidents in retrospect. Yet, even with the aid of the Time Bender, it was as if the universe protected its prophet.

Her mind shifted to the woman that had been keeping this boy secure. She went by the name of Valerie these days, but Renee remembered her for her true nature. It was nearly impossible for the former Fury to forget how it felt to be near one of the Graces. Their beauty always emanated no matter the form they took. However, Renee went unnoticed by Valerie even after all this time that she had been a member of Brightwood. It was understandable, considering the original form for which Renee was known. It had been far more hideous than the more appealing appearance she now showcased during this current age.

Vic, I hope the water demon you gathered was strong enough to carry out the given task. The thought came to the forefront of her mind.

If the plan were successful, Jared would die before he became Vestor. If it failed, the boy would live to become a powerful Time Bender, and the one Renee served did not wish for this to happen.

"Everyone can see what's about to happen to them. Unfortunately, most people tend to ignore it, and it seems sudden and unexpected when the time of change comes. The writing is always on the wall. Everyone shares the same order of experience: a beginning, a middle, and an end. Most people are oblivious as to when something begins. A handful seems lucky enough to catch it in the middle. The majority only see the end and treat it as unexpected. By then, it's usually too late." – Vestor, the Time Bender.

5

"SOMETHING IS GOING to happen tomorrow night," Jared spoke, unable to fall asleep. He rolled into various uncomfortable positions on the couch in Valerie's apartment, recalling the simplicity of a few days prior. That simple version of him felt like another life.

Joe lay beneath a blanket on the carpet near Jared and yawned as he spoke. "What makes you say that?"

"Right now, it's just a feeling. There's something important about tomorrow night. I can't explain it more than that. It's going to be something big, and I can't shake the feeling that it's the kind of something that will change me forever." The sensation growing within Jared was maddeningly ineffable.

"What the hell do you mean by that man?" Joe grunted, troubled by his friend's statement. He'd seen many strange things come to light this week, but his best friend changing into God knows what was something he could do without.

"It means what it means. It's something that will change us forever." Jared reiterated.

"No, you said something will change you, not us." Joe pointed out. "What did you mean by that? What'll change you?"

Jared tossed and turned on the couch some more. He kicked the covers around and took a deep breath, unable to find comfort in any position. "I don't know, Joe. I'm full of shit. I'm just tired, but I'm too damn scared to sleep. I have no abilities to fall back on like you and Carl. Everything is just so fucked up right now."

As a calming reflex, Joe reached out with the energy of his thoughts and tapped into Jared's mind. While within his companion's consciousness, he implanted a relaxing sensation. Jared soon felt as if everything was going to be okay. Joe knew the effects would not be permanent, but they would be enough for his friend to attain a much needed good night's sleep.

"Did you get inside my head? I feel very relaxed all of a sudden." Jared asked.

"And if I did?" Joe smirked.

"Thanks." Jared finally said.

Joe shrugged it off. "No worries. Go to sleep man."

Jared closed his eyes, allowing the relaxing sensation to penetrate deep within his body. His eyelids grew heavier with each passing second, and he was on the verge of drifting into the world of dreams. It was then that both Joe and Jared awoke to a sudden burst of loud snoring. Carl lay beneath a blanket on the couch opposite Jared. Joe and Jared lifted their heads up, startled by the motor-like rattling. They looked at each other, surprised Carl could even make such a sound.

"I didn't know he snored." Jared rubbed his eyes.

"Me neither." Joe's irritation grew. He was tired.

Jared nudged his head in Carl's direction. "I don't suppose there's anything you can do about that, is there?"

"You bet your ass there is." Joe reached near his clothes pile, grabbed a sock, and launched it at Carl's face. The sock landed on its intended target, and Carl woke up in a heart-racing daze. He held the sock in hand and looked around to see Jared and Joe lying sound asleep.

"What the hell, guys?" He spoke aloud, receiving no reply. Finally, tired and sleepy, he shrugged his shoulders and lay down beneath the blanket to find slumber again.

It took considerable effort to sequester the laughter, and Jared closed his eyes with a childish smile. He loved his friends dearly now more than ever. The looming fact that things would never be the same remained like a dark cloud above his head. Still, he also knew without a doubt that together the trials to come would be dominated.

His mind also shifted to intense thoughts of Valerie. When those thoughts surfaced, he felt an incredible loyalty that was inexpressible. He found her desirable and felt a sense of worship mixed with a great need to please the woman at all costs.

I hate being this connected to her! He chided himself.

Jared hadn't known that he would harbor these intense feelings when he sacrificed his blood to strengthen Valerie's magical resolve. She had taken some time to explain it to him thoroughly after the fact. So she would always know where he was, and he would still be drawn to her.

Go to sleep, Jared, he ordered himself.

Yeah, go to sleep, Jared. Joe's voice popped into Jared's mind.

Joe laughed while moving about on the floor of Valerie's apartment. "Just practicing. I have to stay sharp."

Soon all three young men were fast asleep, resting for the events to come.

"The waking world – that is the REAL dream. The realm I once presided over holds more truth than the creatures that touch upon it ever realized. The reality lived by so many in this waking world is just a bad interpretation of the dream realm. The dream is a bridge to the world of the dead, and the dead are only ever owed truth." – Morpheus, the god of dreams.

6

SLEEP FOR VALERIE maintained and rested her physical body. Still, the essence that drove her mind remained conscious and alert. She often felt like a projector manipulating her surroundings at will within the realm of passage to the land of the dead. She regarded what was left of the dream world as a safe haven to collect her thoughts and find solutions.

Most creatures that experienced dreams could now enact change to the realm if they were fully alert while within it. Valerie took advantage of this whenever in the dream world and stood naked within a vast forest of trees surrounding her. She loved every second of the experience feeling as pure as she had during the moments after her creation.

Morpheus fled his powerful kingdom of dreams long ago, leaving his father, Hypnos as the interim ruler. Hypnos, concerned with the nature of sleep rather than the dreams that came from slumber, soon allowed the dream world to fall apart from sheer negligence. Eventually, the remaining Oneiroi fought amongst each other, rebelled against their father, and fled like their sibling before them. The world of dreams was left to itself, where the universe kept the order as best it could, and other deities battled over the kingdom.

Valerie had known Morpheus once upon a time. She would indulge his creations by participating in specific dreams on his behalf. That was when the dreams he created influenced Kings. Now the dreamer changed this realm, and they were primarily clueless about how much they shaped it.

During that time, long ago, as one of the Graces, Valerie (Aglaia) would never have imagined that the dream world would become such a barren landscape of willed possibilities ruled by none.

What other new and unimagined things are on the horizon before me now? The former Grace wondered.

She allowed the question to float away like the leaves she envisioned that were swooped about by gusts of wind. Autumn had always been her favorite season. The changing colors of the leaves had drawn her in for as long as she could remember, and it was a beautiful transition she often recreated while in the land of slumber.

"That which is on the horizon is far more dangerous than your cute little naked butt could have ever anticipated." A voice as sinister and dark as Tartarus was carried by a loud gust of wind.

Valerie turned in the direction of the voice to see Develin. She noted the dark red suit and fedora to match. He appeared forever in the role of gangster though he had lived much longer than any man. He had survived to the present age with a deviant grace all his own. His magic was far darker and more dangerous than Valerie would have cared to admit. Her nakedness did not bother her as she stood firmly before the demon wizard.

"Why are you here, Develin?" She demanded.

The demon wizard took a few steps toward the naked woman and smiled as he admired every curve of her body. "You're quite fetching - truly stunning. It's the type of flesh that I could just eat up. But, of course, I'd expect nothing less from one of the former Graces."

She ignored the comment. "Answer my question."

Develin sighed. "You're no fun. Anyway, I'm here because of the kid you keep locked safe and sound in your humble little abode."

Which one? She focused on keeping her thought contained so it would not float away like the others had.

Develin smiled, noting the body language. "I'll tell you this much, hun. It's not the manipulator medium smartass chink kid, and it sure as hell ain't the not-too-bright animal speaker blond Ken doll. When you take those two out of the equation, all you have left is the so-called normal one; however, that won't be the case for much longer. He's not as normal as he may appear to be."

"What makes you say that?" Valerie had sensed something different about Jared but couldn't discern what it was. After all, the goddess inhabiting Sara's body had fallen in love with him. Having the genuine affection of a deity is no small feat for a mortal.

"Do you honestly believe the attack by the water demon was a fluke?" Develin flaunted that he knew more than Valerie realized. "Yes, I've been keeping tabs on you, hun, and I've been trying to figure out who sent that water demon. My reach is far, and my interest in the boy is great. But remember that I speak for myself right now as I stand before you. Dracien has absolutely nothing to do with my little visit."

That piqued Valerie's interest. "Does Dracien have a vested interest in Jared?" She asked. "I know the two of you are forced to work together these days, and every chance you have to undermine him, you take."

Develin smirked. "Dracien has no interest whatsoever in the young man. He couldn't care less about what happens to the kid. But, on the other hand, I think it's great that you're protecting Jared."

"Get to the point of your visit." Her irritation grew.

Develin bowed his head in mock apology. "I'm sure a beauty as tuned in to spells as you are felt the calling made by the rogue spirits you shelter the trio of do-gooders from."

She recalled the sensation of calling. "Of course I felt it. They're planning a sacrifice, and I intend to be there to stop them from carrying it out."

The demon wizard laughed. "I'm aware of this as well. You're all about protecting innocent lives, etcetera, etcetera... The only thing I care about right at this moment is the boy."

"Why would you care?" Valerie stepped forward, keeping her gaze level with the demon.

He sighed once again. "He's so fundamental, Aglaia, and you must bring him with you when you attempt to stop the sacrifice."

"Call me Valerie." She corrected.

Develin rolled his eyes. "I know the way you think, *Valerie*. I know that you'd feel better leaving him wrapped up within the safety of the barriers of protection you have set up in your pathetic one-bedroom apartment. But, the fact is he needs to be with you tomorrow night. The powers that be, as they are Praetor Projector Council and all, have become rather pragmatic. Ripples in the fabric of things make them very uncomfortable especially considering how our kind has slipped further and further since the Distinction of Realms was enacted."

Valerie considered his words.

The demon wizard continued. "Jared is crucial to the nexus point on the horizon. How do you think the ultimate Time Bender gets born anyway? He's going to be the prophet of prophets more powerful than any that have come before. Jared may even be able to see well past his death. If you decide to not take him along, then his powers don't manifest, and he befalls a horrible fate and premature death. This would alter the fabric of everything, and no one wins out. But, on the other hand, if you bring him along, the Time Bender within gets born, and he'll become a powerful one that could benefit us all. Events will happen surrounding the sacrifice at the country club to ensure this."

"So that's your game, then?" She knew there was more, but knowing this was a good start. "You hope to control a Time Bender so that you may have him at your disposal? Are your plans so transparent these days, Develin?"

"Come now, hun, who wouldn't want that kind of power?" He couldn't believe Valerie would have to ask such an absurd question.

Valerie stepped closer to the demon wizard, experiencing the crunch of leaves blanketing the forest floor beneath her bare feet. "Why warn me? Why tell me any of this? You know full well that I won't let you have him once his powers manifest. I'll do whatever it takes to prevent such a thing."

Develin smiled. "I tell you all of this because otherwise, you wouldn't bring him along. As far as stopping me goes, we'll just have to cross that bridge when we get to it. Make sure Jared is with you."

There was too much Valerie didn't know, and it bothered her. "I know you, Develin. This isn't just about controlling a future Time Bender. There's something else going on here, and I'll discover what it is."

"If you say so. I'll see you around, hun. You look great naked, by the way. You should try not to wear anything more often." The demon wizard faded away with a devilish wink, leaving Valerie to ponder the exchange of words within the dream world.

"I have no idea why she's kept me alive this long. Well, I'm not technically alive; I'm... I don't know what I am. I'm a curiosity to my sister. I'm a project that's around for her amusement. She loves me, yes, but I'm still aware of what I am to her. I don't mind, but it's draining. Existence is dreadfully exhausting when you aren't supposed to exist. There are days when I wish she'd simply let me die for good." – Edward Wols – created brother of Nina Wols.

7

NINA WOLS CONSIDERED her brother Edward with a fond smile that only a younger sister could carry. She did not fault him for being born without a gift. That's how she created him, after all. Still, often she wished he had abilities other than salesmanship. He spent most of his time conjuring up magical trinkets for sale to the lesser forms of supernatural and natural creatures that visited.

"How's the clean-up going, Eddy?" She called down to her brother, who was tearing through the concrete floor in the basement. It was deep into the night, and a soundproofing spell prevented the loud noise from escaping the confines of the lower level.

"It would go a lot smoother if you used your gift to dispose of these bodies." Edward Wols huffed and puffed and took a break from within the basement. He sat down on a crate and looked at the fresh corpses of bums and degenerates that his sister had recently fed upon.

Soul Eaters needed to feed. It was, by definition, in their nature. Not only was his lovely sister a Soul Eater, but she was also a Projector to boot. Her powerful magic kept him alive for far longer than he should have been allowed.

"I could, but I just fed, and you *know* how tired that makes me. And besides, this gives you purpose. You do like having a purpose, don't you, Eddy?" She smiled. She loved tormenting her brother occasionally and knew how loyal they were to each other. It was a bond that was deeper than any magic.

While sitting at the top of the stairs that led to the dank basement, Nina discerned a specific wave of magic. It flew past her in the fabric of reality. It was not intended for her or her brother and reeked of rogue spirits. The fact that the Praetor Projector Council had allowed such a spell to be cast surprised the young Soul Eater/Projector. Helping Valerie with her plan put Nina in opposition to the Council's ruling to allow the fallen deities to operate in the first place through their representative, Dracien. This made the sinister smirk on her face all the more apparent.

Nina despised her elder Projectors because of how they viewed her. She was a Soul Eater, while the Council was made entirely of pure Projectors. They didn't have to feed the way she did, and the Council made it clear long ago how disgusted by her feeding they were. That, coupled with how young she was compared to them, caused the Council to continually monitor and restrict her actions. Siding with Valerie on the Edict of Innocents, however, gave her some freedom.

Uncle Minx, how I love you for bringing this to my doorstep! She delighted in what would happen on the night to come.

"Oh my!" Edward exclaimed from the basement.

Nina stood from the stairs, intrigued by her brother's sudden alarm. Edward was jumpy on occasion, but the jumpiness usually came with good reason. She floated down the staircase and touched down alongside her sibling.

"Take a look at that." He pointed to one of the bodies nearest them. It was the corpse of a young man who had lived out his years as a drug addict. The dead body became animate, twitching about sporadically. "You didn't completely feed off of him from the looks of it. That's never happened before."

"Indeed, it hasn't." Having never known fear, Nina moved to the twitchy body without reservation. The flesh was mainly decomposed, and as she approached, the corpse sat up, looking directly at her with a devilish grin.

"Greetings, Nina." The voice spoke through the body.

A smirk formed on Nina's face as she studied the remains with a childlike fascination. "Hello, Develin. Resorting to meeting with me through the corpses of those I feed upon? Are you really that afraid of me?"

The corpse attempted to grin as it studied her; flesh fell from the lower lip. "I can feel what you've done to this body with your ability and how you ate its soul. So, yes, I'm that afraid of you. You're a Soul Eater and Projector. There aren't many with that specific combination left around - not even a handful remains. You might find my true form a bit too tempting, with my essence being far more potent. I can't let that be the end of me, can I?"

Nina sighed as she stroked the remaining hair attached to the little bit of flesh left upon the corpse's skull. "This is a good look for you, demon wizard. Perhaps you should make it a permanent one. I could always do my part to make it so."

"I would appreciate it if you didn't," Develin spoke through the barely operable mouth of the corpse.

Edward grunted and sat down upon the same crate as earlier. He pulled from within his pocket a pack of cigarettes. He lit up, allowing the sensation to relieve his current physical and mental tensions.

The corpse speaking for Develin glanced upon Edward and smiled. "Edward! It's great to see you! It's been a long time. I remember when you were a living human child, instead of whatever your sister has made you into."

"Hi, Develin. It's good to see you as well." Edward inhaled deeply and exhaled a few rings of smoke.

Nina cleared her throat and forced the head of the corpse to look at her. "Why are you here, Develin? Your visits are typically a sign of mischief to come. It's a wonder you and Loki aren't best friends."

Develin cleared the throat of the corpse. "I'm here because of the nexus point. It's an important one. I've discovered that this nexus point will be the birth of a great Time Bender. He'll be the *greatest* Time Bender, as a matter of fact."

"Really? Do go on." Nina's curiosity grew.

The corpse continued. "Valerie, as we all know her now, and the plan to which you will aid tomorrow night revolves around a young man named Jared Hernandez. No one else really seems to understand this. Creatures have attempted to create a premature demise for the youth, while others like Valerie fight to protect him. Once he becomes a Time Bender, bringing about his demise will become incredibly difficult. Other Time Benders will possibly emerge once the era of Vestor begins."

"What does the Council say about this?" Nina asked.

The corpse expressed disdain for the Council. "Your elder Projectors are clueless about the boy. Everyone seems to be, save those that are trying to kill him."

"Tell me, Develin, then what of Aglaia? Why does she insist on protecting him?" Nina stroked the few stands of hair left on the corpse's head.

"Valerie makes her own choices, hun. She hasn't involved herself with the Council in ages. If you knew the former Grace like I do, you'd know that, over time, she's become quite the protector. She's fond of humans and almost tried to become one herself. Unfortunately, she now has this silly notion that maintaining and keeping human life safe is in our best interests." Develin had the corpse shrug, not getting it.

"Is Aglaia aware of the boy's true worth?" Nina asked.

The corpse nodded. "She is now. I paid her a visit to explain as much. I come to you, however, because she's ill-equipped to handle the situation. Someone wants the boy dead. Someone powerful. You can *truly* protect him."

"Your information has always been suspect, at best, littered with loopholes and wiggle room. Yet, you've never been so forthcoming. What is your true goal in all of this?" Nina demanded.

Edward cleared his throat to remind the others that he was also in the basement. "If I were to hazard a guess, I'd put money on the fact that this young boy being a Time Bender benefits dear old Develin. He plans to use him, and he is here because he thinks he'll need your help at some point. It may start as simple protection for now, but it'll become much more about manipulating the young man later on. Again, if I were to hazard a guess, that is. But don't mind me."

Both the corpse and Nina turned to look at Edward, almost having forgotten his presence. They then returned their respective gazes to each other. Nina had a questioning expression while the corpse exuded naive innocence.

"How does the soon-to-be-Time Bender aid you, Develin? What games are you playing?" Nina demanded with more authority.

Develin held the corpse's hands up as if painting a picture. "Imagine having a Time Bender at your disposal, Nina. If you're around to guide him after his birth, you can use him as you see fit. He'd be in your debt. Jared is young and naive. He won't truly understand his powers when they come to be. Just because he'll be able to see all possible futures does not mean he'll truly understand the full scope of what he'll be able to do."

She smiled. "So after I aid the former Grace with her plan, you want me to keep a close eye on the young soon-to-be prophet? You want me to protect him?"

Develin made the corpse nod. "I do. Ensure the boy lives after his powers manifest. We can both share the immense benefits of controlling the young lad. Think of this as the beginning of a long-overdue partnership between us. I'll be seeing you around, Nina. You're as radiantly beautiful as ever, by the way."

The body returned to its lifeless state after yet another large smile was expressed on the decaying face, and the corpse collapsed before Nina like a rag doll.

"Eddy..." Nina levitated while pondering the proposition and pointed to the mess of corpses in the basement.

Edward put out his cigarette and stood from the crate where he sat. "I know, dear sister, I know. It's back to work for your dear old brother. Thank you kindly for the purpose."

"I wasn't always like this. I didn't care about anything for centuries after I was turned. All that mattered was the blood. Feeding. I was no better than a wild animal without a purpose. What happened to change me? Tell you what - if you buy me a drink, I'll be more than happy to share!" – Minx (centuries-old vampire – a supporter of the Forever Man)

8

MINX RESTED HIS small frame atop an extravagant skyscraper surrounded by a sea of large buildings in the central downtown district of New Gilead. More prominent skyscrapers rose above the little vampire and were illuminated by countless lights that cast long shadows on the city streets below in a futile attempt to fight the night. While perched upon the gray concrete ledge, with ornate statues of industry representing the might of Olympus Corporation's headquarters, his gaze focused below toward the dirty inner-city streets.

As the elder vampire viewed the nightlife, he enjoyed the gusts of wind from the high elevation that washed over his compact stance. The buildings' bright white and warm yellow lights and the flashing vibrant multicolored billboards took turns casting an aura around Minx as he brooded. Then, a wave of magic rippled past him through the fabric of existence. Any newly born vampire would have failed to notice, but Minx had the advantage of being centuries old.

It's a calling spell, and a powerful one at that. It must be part of whatever Valerie is up to. I hope she knows what she's doing. The little vampire mused.

Minx experienced sudden thoughts of Valerie and the young man she chose to protect. He always respected Valerie, which led to the mention of Nina as part of the solution to the former Grace's problem. The small yet menacing creature of the night had been indebted to both women for differing reasons. However, the situation brought them together in a way that wiped his debt on both accounts.

The image of the frightened young Jared continued to plague the vampire's thoughts. Minx regarded the boy as incredibly awkward. He also noted that he carried a strange aura atypical of what he'd seen throughout the centuries. There had been something intriguing in Jared's innocent nature that resonated from the boy's soul. It was an energy that forced Minx to ponder the old ways and recall the primordial gods and goddesses that were there shortly after all things began. It was, after all, because of them that he searched for the Forever Man.

Once upon a time, Minx, you didn't believe in any of this. Now it's all you have.

The information that led the vampire to New Gilead insisted that the Forever Man resided here. The hunt for the one who could never truly die continued. Minx would fulfill this quest until he was decapitated or his essence given to the blistering sun. A vow was made several centuries ago, and his devotion was just as intense now as it had been on that fateful day.

The bright star of the earth would be upon him in four hours, and he would find proper rest as sunshine showered this part of the world. When night returned to push away the day with their never-ending struggle, he would continue his search. He often wished for a companion to break his wanderings' solitary nature, but no stable connections had successfully been forged. Minx could always create a companion; a willing participant would welcome the gifts he had to offer. In this modern age, one only had to toss a rock and watch as it landed on someone wanting to become a child of the night.

The more he thought of it, the more the modern age irritated the little vampire to no end. The current perception of his kind usually left willing undesirables. A plethora of tattooed Goth kids and love-struck teenagers lining up and romanticizing what it meant to be a vampire in the first place was the last thing he needed. His old age made him impatient, and the idea of reeducating the young ones left a foul taste in his mouth. For now, he figured, he was better off alone.

Minx allowed a slight grin to form as he took in the ambiance of the vast skyline. He reached into his jacket pocket and pulled out a vodka flask giving a toast to the city. "Here's to you, old girl!"

The alcoholic beverage did little for the vampire. Its effects were minimal, but drinking the drink was perhaps his last remaining human habit. The vodka also gave the blood a flavor it wouldn't usually have. After the long swig, he stood up on the rooftop ledge. He spotted his prey walking alone in a filthy alleyway.

If a normal human eye had looked upon the scene, they would have witnessed a split-second blur. Minx returned the flask to his inner coat pocket during that minute span of time and flew down, cutting through the air like an arrow. His prey belonged to Dracien. The foot soldier would serve as an undeniable message; the vampire and elder demon have been in opposition for the better half of two centuries.

The unsuspecting thug was lifted from the ground against his will and whisked away into a dingy alley surrounded by darkening shadows. The fear grew exponentially in the thug; he could discern that a small shadowy figure held him up in the air with little effort. What added to the fear was the limited vision from the dim alleyway lighting, which allowed his attacker to remain covered by darkness.

The immense strength within the small body pinned the thug against a stained brick wall while forcing his head to the left. The feet of the small shadowy figure floated in the air defying the laws of gravity. Before the thug could scream, he felt sharp teeth bite into his neck with the immediate sensation of a mouth sucking upon effortless puncture. The blood flowed freely from the thug's body, and within seconds consciousness ceased. The vivid thoughts and memories that fought to be heard soon became as pitch black as the alleyway's shadows.

"My city was falling apart. Unexplained murders were taking place all over New Gilead. The dead were being found in strange places, with mysterious causes of death. None of it made any sense. At least, none of it made sense on my side of the Distinction. But, after I crossed over, it made too much sense. Once your eyes are open, there's no going back." – Detective John Lycros.

9

DETECTIVE JOHN LYCROS hoped he would never get used to the macabre imagery discovered in the abandoned house lost to time in a dense forest outside of New Gilead proper. The old rickety home had been untouched for many years and existed as an anomaly; no one knew this house was here, but somehow it hid among the ancient trees that were old before New Gilead was a city. Windows were broken, the paint on the walls had peeled away, revealing rotting wood of the frame, and dirty dishes inhabited a sink waiting for occupants that would never return. Old photographs lined a few walls, having yellowed and faded over time, granting a glimpse of a family long gone.

Lycros hadn't shaved in days, and his beard grew in revealing hints of gray. He'd shave in a day or so; this was his new cycle. Part of him felt just as unkempt as the house while he patiently waited for his partner to appear on the scene in the early morning to help him deal with the corpses of three teenage boys. Unfinished beer cans and an entire case remained off to the side as a sad reminder of adolescent ignorance.

The hearts had been extracted from the corpses' chests; no one had been able to find them in the house. Nevertheless, the bodies, just as they were, left a lasting impression Lycros could have done without. The look of pure happiness that remained on the teenagers' faces created a haunting image as disturbing as the house. The blood had been drained from their faces, carrying a paleness and texture that should have made a look of fright. But, instead, those faces bore an expression of pure joy.

While Lycros paced about the crime scene, forensic crews and other officers worked diligently around him, carrying out the routine bag and tag procedures. Footsteps gave a slight echo on the wood floor behind Lycros, and from the sound of the heels, he knew that his partner Diana Knight had finally arrived.

She approached in an elegant blue dress with black high heel pumps to match. The brunette's free-flowing hair added to the already impressive figure that people on the force rarely got a chance to see. The woman was typically more conservative with her wardrobe. She expressed a tough bravado, which conveyed a clear message that she was not to be crossed. Seeing her hidden feminine side this early in the morning was unexpected, to say the least.

Lycros turned and was pleasantly stunned to witness Diana's enticing allure. Being a detective, he could also tell she had put the dress back on somewhat haphazardly. She did what she could to keep it presentable. Her hair was combed as best as it could be given the rush to gather her appearance, and slight traces of dishevelment remained in the strands. This told him loud and clear that she hadn't been home when she got the call a half-hour ago, and she more than likely hadn't been wearing that lovely blue dress either.

Hope it was a good date last night, Diana. Lycros let the curious thought go; he never viewed his partner as the dating type.

She rolled her eyes. "You can stop gawking. I've been known to wear a dress. I was out having dinner last night, and I'm sure you've already figured out the rest. It would have taken me too long to get home, change, and head out here. You said it was urgent, that I show up immediately. Now, can you explain why the hell two New Gilead detectives were called out to the middle of nowhere outside of suburbia?"

Lycros nodded, getting to it. "Apologies for interrupting your downtime, but I needed your eyes on this while things were fresh. It's a strange one and similar to things we've seen lately. The local leos wanted to pass it along.

They aren't equipped for this kind of thing and know we've been dealing with a lot more of it."

She dismissed his words accepting the apology with a hand gesture. The job always took priority. That was merely the way it was. "So what do we have?"

Lycros turned his attention back to the teenage corpses. "We have three dead males in their late teens. We've identified the victims as Scott Riley and his classmates Derrick Reynolds and Bobby Morgan. Their hearts were taken from their chests, as you can see. It almost looks like some kind of wild animal reached in there and ripped them out."

As Lycros spoke the words, Diana studied the bodies and felt her stomach begin to churn. She had been around many gruesome scenes during her career. Still, the recent cases she had been walking into were far too overwhelming. The hard reality they were facing was that these types of murders were happening with higher frequency popping up all over the city. She yearned for the days of a simple shooting.

"Any thoughts?" John asked.

"This is absolutely sick, John. Were there any signs of a struggle?" She asked.

He shook his head. "None that we can determine. The happy-go-lucky look on their faces concerns the hell out of me, though. Going to have to wait for the toxicology report to come in, but I'm guessing they had to be on something pretty strong to look that happy while getting their damn hearts ripped out."

"What about the house? What do we know about it? Who owns it?" Diana stepped closer to the bodies; her eyes were both curious and disgusted.

"It's been abandoned for the last fifty years in the middle of nowhere. We found the bodies by pure luck. A man's car broke down near here, and his cell phone died. He got lost walking through the trails near the road, came upon the house, and thought he could ask for help. He discovered the door was left open, popped his head in, and found this instead. Miraculously this old ass house still has power somehow. So he was able to charge his phone while panicking about the bodies and call for help. We cut him loose before you got here."

Diana sighed. "I'm at my wit's end here, John. I don't know what to make of these killings anymore. They're getting stranger and stranger. Are they connected somehow, or are people just that screwed up?"

"Fortunately for you, we can take it from here." A female voice spoke up from behind the two detectives. It was a strong voice that demanded respect.

Diana and Lycros turned their heads to see two somewhat intimidating agents dressed in black suits. One was a woman, strong in every sense of the word. The other was a bald man with thick musculature that threatened to break through his suit; his posture gave a distinct hint of deadliness.

Lycros grunted in disgust, already knowing where this conversation would take him. "And who exactly are the two of you?"

The woman gave a quick flash of a badge as she spoke. "I'm Special Agent Della Myer, and this is my partner Special Agent Sionmen Repus."

"You guys Feds, I take it?" Lycros hadn't been able to look at the badge as well as he would have liked and had a strange feeling about the two agents. They weren't like any agents he'd been forced to deal with in past encounters. On a purely physical level, the two almost seemed as though they were superior by design. One could even argue that they came across as perfect human specimens.

Della nodded. "In a manner of speaking. To be precise, we work for the government on special cases like this one."

"How does this rank as a special case?" Diana moved closer to her partner. She could feel Della sizing her up and caught a flash of disgust on the agent's face for having shown up to a crime scene dressed as she was.

"Well, it just is. This house is also considered a historical site and is protected by several federal laws. So, in case you were wondering, that was my way of saying it falls under our direct jurisdiction." Della walked closer to the bodies as she spoke. She studied the open chest cavities without so much as a flinch.

Lycros noted this behavior as he kept his gaze on her and Special Agent Sionmen Repus. *She's seen this kind of thing before. Maybe even worse by the way she's prancing around the bodies.*

"We never came across this house as being a historical site. The records we found don't show any of that." John took a step toward Della.

"The documentation will be brought to you. The records we have access to happen to be a bit more extensive. Also, the rest of my team is on its way here as we speak. When they arrive, I ask that you and your people clear out immediately. This is no longer a matter for the local authorities. You and your partner don't even have to stay. We can handle the transition." Della looked to the two detectives and gave them as polite of a smile as she could muster.

"If it's okay with you, we'll wait until your team gets here and help over-see the transition - as you put it." Lycros returned his attention to the dead bodies. He reminded himself that they were the victims. He was here to find the truth on their behalf. This entire case was wrapped with perplexing cir-cumstances. Still, it was necessary to remember why he was doing any of this in the first place. He was the voice for those who no longer had one: a mes-senger for the dead.

"Have it your way. Any evidence collected will be transferred over, of course, and this whole mess won't be your concern after that. Then you guys can move on to more prevalent caseloads that require your kind of experi-ence. And yes, that's my way of saying you'll see more of me and my people. It appears that there are connections between these murders and other un-solved cases in New Gilead. I'm here to help clean that up and make sense of it for you." Della continued examining the bodies.

Lycros refused to take his eyes off the special agent as she soaked in the entire crime scene. She had an experience about her that was admirable. He found himself respecting her ability to stay focused while dealing with the politics of the situation.

Diana leaned closer to John with her arms crossed in a defensive posture. Her anger about all of this was quite evident.

"Don't worry, Diana. This isn't over for us." John assured his partner.

"It doesn't look like we have much of a choice." Della countered.

Lycros sighed. Something about this particular case and the others were speaking to him. It was the type of something that would drive a man insane if he attempted to ignore it.

"What do we do now?" Della asked.

Lycros stood firm. "We wait, we cooperate, and then we dig."

Diana was somewhat startled to hear John say as much. "We dig?"

He nodded. "There has to be some kind of record of these agents. They're not normal. Something is definitely off, and the fact that they're here in full force taking over doesn't sit well with me either. I don't like any of this, and you know how much I hate not knowing. Think about it. Our caseloads get incredibly bizarre, and now these guys show up. She just told us they'd be looking into other cases that we haven't been able to close. There's something they know, and they're not going to share it willingly. So, yeah, we dig."

"Okay. Sounds like a plan." Diana grinned with smug satisfaction while keeping her arms crossed.

Due to the superior hearing granted by genetic enhancements, Della Myer could listen to the conversation while examining the lifeless bodies. She knew without a doubt which supernatural creatures had carried out this sacrifice. Della also knew that her job had been to contain the fallout of the sanctioned events set to take place at the country club when night returned. Those were her specific orders, and she and her partner would follow them without question. She only hoped that Lycros and Diana would do the same when given orders by their superiors to stay out of it.

The sun began to rise, casting new light into the dimly lit abandoned house from dirty uncovered windows and an open front door. Dust particles danced in the beams of sunshine as they gradually emerged all at once. The way the light bathed the joyful faces of the dead teens kneeling in a state of rigor mortis left more of a haunting impression than witnessing the scene under cover of night. People continued to work, barely noticing the change.

Detective Lycros noted it, however, as the haunting image seared into his mind. He felt his entire world change within the span of a few heartbeats. A new day was upon them all. What it would bring remained to be seen.

PART EIGHT:

BEFORE NIGHT

FALLS

"Being imprisoned for so long didn't break me. Not the way people think it did. Being alone was maddening at first, but it sharpened my powers. I learned how to create complex illusions and put them in my mind to take me away from the isolation. I also learned how to call upon spirits far away from where I was to keep me company when I needed to speak out loud. In that way, I was never really isolated or trapped, which was the intent of those that imprisoned me." – Joseph Chan, Medium/Manipulator.

1

JOSEPH CHAN KNEW full well that he was standing in his bedroom. The paraphernalia depicting his identity to this point in time were within the proper confines of this space, representing a sanctuary to the male teenage soul. All those items were precisely where he had left them, oblivious to the life-altering events of the last few days. However, there had been a lingering sensation that washed over his body, creating an uneasiness that was difficult to identify. This was his room, but it was no longer his room.

The drive back home from Valerie's apartment that morning carried a loud silence. His life had changed in days, and the people he observed going on about their business were none the wiser. The beautiful yet frightening nature of magic and science was unknown to them, and he drove shrouded in the nothingness of his predicament. There was an undeniable urge in his soul to scream at the masses. But, deep down, he knew it would do no good; people believed what they wanted. His perspective on life and the universe had undergone such a dramatic change that there was no explaining it to an outsider with mere words.

Joe had always expected a drive home from the apartment of an alluring older woman such as Valerie to have the lingering memory of an encounter more suitable to the libido of a late teenage male in his prime. Knowing his grandfather had been intimate with the woman also left an unsettling feeling in the pit of his stomach. He quickly did away with viewing her as a possible sexual conquest.

Joe's eyes continued to pan his bedroom as if he were seeing it for the first time. It was messy, unorganized, and littered with random items commonly found in a young man's bedroom; he even had a collection of pornography hidden away in a secret compartment of his sock drawer. Remembering the secret stash made him laugh, and he always wondered why he preferred the old-school material to the readily available free internet content. There was just something about the care put into it. But then, the smile faded as the room no longer gave off the aura of welcome he had expected. No matter how much he yearned for it, this entire house no longer felt like home.

He packed a small suitcase with various outfits at the ready after having showered and changed for the day. Joe took in the bedroom walls reminiscing on the blissful simplicity of what was; posters of movies were set up haphazardly. There was no turning back now, and he'd decided on the drive over that he would travel after helping with Valerie's plan. Joe felt comfort knowing he could return whenever, but he thought the change was far too significant. With a determined sigh, he grabbed the suitcase and exited the bedroom for the last time.

He descended the stairs, walked through the small living room, and entered the kitchen to find his mother. Ming rummaged through the refrigerator for a meal to satisfy her current hunger. She took a plate of leftover lasagna and set it on the countertop before her; a smile showcased how she was happily satisfied with her choice of sustenance. She peeled back the plastic wrapping that kept the food freshly secure while smiling at her son.

"I'm going to be leaving here in a sec, Ma," Joe explained; there was a sudden heaviness to his tone.

Ming nodded, accepting the statement. "I know Joey. I always knew you would eventually. Are you hungry? Do you want to eat something before you leave? I know lasagna typically isn't eaten this early in the morning, but I figured, what the hell? Food is food. What does it matter what time it is when you eat it?"

Joe shook his head. "No thanks. I'm good. I'm just trying to stay focused on this whole plan of Valerie's. I hope I don't mess anything up tonight."

"You won't." Ming hesitated.

"What is it?" Joe asked.

"I'd be lying if I said I wasn't worried. I want to help, but Valerie assures me it won't be necessary and that she'll keep you safe. Do you want my help?" Ming was eager for a specific response.

As much as it pained him, Joe shook his head. "I can't explain it, but we have to do this alone. It's important. It's mostly because of Jared."

"How?" Ming asked.

"He's got a feeling. A strong one. And I felt it when I tapped inside of his head. That feeling is true. It's not just his gut; it's something guiding him. Like he can sense what's going to happen. So the people assembled as is; that's how it has to be. Otherwise, I'm afraid it won't work and..." Joe left the sentence unfinished.

"Okay." Ming accepted even though she was disappointed. She looked at the plate of cold lasagna and placed her hand above it. The magic emanating from the woman made her hand appear elegant with its slight movements. A moment later, a small flame shot downward and heated the meal to the perfect temperature. This all took place within a second.

"Mom! Did you really...?! I... I had no idea you could do that! When the hell were you going to tell me?" Joe was amazed. "And how the hell have you kept something like that secret from me for so long?"

She smiled. "I've always used my abilities, Joey. I just made sure to use them when you weren't paying attention. Our magical blood comes from gods who decided to procreate before the Distinction of Realms was made final. After the Distinction, it was forbidden for the gods of old to have children."

Joe said nothing; he was still in awe.

Ming continued. "There's the blood of Maya, the goddess of illusions. She's of the Hindu pantheon, by the way, and there are a lot of fascinating characters there, although I've only met a few personally. Then we have Chu-Jung, a powerful god of fire, amongst other things. It's why you're so good at creating memories within the minds of others and why I can warm my lefto-ver lasagna to perfection." A smug smile adorned her face before she contin-ued. "The mixture of the magic in the blood also yields unexpected abilities, such as your status as a medium."

"That's some pretty heavy shit to lay on me right now, Ma. I mean, I was coping with the fact that I can now do what I do, but the god thing is... really? That's where our family comes from? Grandpa forgot to mention that part." Joe took a deep breath.

Ming smirked while nodding. "Yes, really, and there's a lot your grand-father didn't mention, I'm sure—all in good time. Just be proud of your her-itage. We should make t-shirts or something, but instead of a flag of nation-ality, maybe have a picture of Maya and Chu-Jung."

"I'm glad to know that the smartass aspect of our family also runs through the blood," Joe commented.

Ming kissed her son on the cheek. "Oh, that's how we can tell that we're all related. It's by far a test greater than any magic."

Joe smirked this time. "True enough. I better get going. Have to go to the country club to stop three rogue spirits from sacrificing innocent people. Never thought I'd say something like that and mean it."

"And after?" Ming's eyes were hopeful.

Joe felt a pang of sorrow that formed his expression. "Ma, I... I just need to go. I don't know why. I have to see what's out there and travel for a bit. I hope you can understand that."

She nodded. "I do. I went through a similar phase around your age. Good luck with everything, Joey, and stay safe."

Joe moved to his mother, giving her a tight hug. "Thanks, Ma, for every-thing. I'll stop back again to visit."

She lightly touched his cheek. "You'd better. If you need help with anything, let me know. And don't forget that since you're a medium, your grandfather is only a summons away. He can help and give advice with just about anything."

"I know, Ma." Joe looked about the kitchen with a thoughtful gaze. "I never expected life after high school to be like this. I thought it would be more like drunken dorm parties and scantily clad women."

Ming slapped the back of her son's head. "Things are never what we expect."

"Do me a favor, Ma, and try not to burn the house down while I'm gone. With your age and magic combined, you add a whole new dimension to hot flashes." Joe jumped backward with a wink to avoid another slap on the head and smiled at his mother as he exited the kitchen's back door.

Just like his grandfather, Ming thought while eating her breakfast lasagna. *I only hope he doesn't make the same mistakes.*

"Bandolar was my first guide to the animal world. He was the first to speak to me. There have been others since then, but none quite like him. That corgi knew me better than anyone else, even my closest friends. That is the bond between an animal speaker and their guide. I've lost count of how many times that dog saved my life." – Carl Remington, Animal Speaker.

2

AGAINST VALERIE'S WISHES, Carl ventured to the mansion estate that had been his home before the world changed. As he approached the grand entrance resting on lush greenery, the familiar wrought-iron gate saddened him. He knew this would be the last time he'd ever be at this house. The sweet fragrance of blooming flowers wafted through the air, mingling with the sounds of chirping birds; a gentle breeze rustled through the leaves. Carl wasn't sure if it were his new powers or nostalgia, but he felt nature around him in a more profound way. The manicured lawn was alive with flowers in full bloom, providing a riot of colors.

His parents would not recognize him. Carl struggled with this fact knowing those that cross over are forgotten. He'd been cast into the realm of magic due to his true nature; his brotherly bond with Jared Hernandez also facilitated this. Carl's transition had been slower, having developed without the aid of Valerie's magic, but it was still occurring. The reality struck even harder when his key failed to work in the deadbolt lock at the front door.

Damn it! I didn't even get a chance to get clothes or any of my stuff! The frustration only made matters worse. He still wore the ridiculous waiter uniform.

By this point, Carl's room had literally ceased to exist in the physical form that had been familiar. Valerie explained the process in great detail before he left that morning to fetch what possessions were still salvageable. However, each item was reshaped and changed to fit a world that never knew

Carl as an average human. The odds of his parents being marked were also unlikely, considering the startling revelation by his animal guide Bandolar. The people that raised him weren't even his actual birth parents.

"Who the hell are you, and why the hell are you sauntering about on our property?" The gruff yet professional voice of Henry Remington boomed from the end of the long driveway where it met the posh upper-class city street. The limo drove off as he and his wife, Elizabeth, made their way to the front entrance.

Carl turned to face the two as they approached with a walk of entitlement. They're *not even my real parents, but they raised me all the same.* Carl still felt loyal.

Henry was a tall man and carried the charismatic bravado of a natural leader. His unyielding determination forged his company's mighty empire, and his physical appearance betrayed the fact that he was younger than he actually looked. The stresses of building such a financial empire had taken their toll on Henry's body. He moved a few steps ahead of his wife and looked at Carl with a slight hint of recognition.

"Hello." Carl cleared his throat. He hadn't expected this and had assumed they'd be out of town.

"Do I know you?" Henry studied Carl.

Carl shook his head. "No. I don't think we've ever met before."

Elizabeth stepped forward with a posture that demanded attention. The woman was older but fought to maintain her youth. Upon studying her more closely, Carl realized that a woman so intent on appearance would never have actually put her body through the rigors of childbearing. The reality of having been adopted kept hitting him at every turn.

"Do be kind to the young man Henry. He's handsome, and I don't believe he means us any harm." Elizabeth finally said.

Henry scoffed. "You think all young men handsome, darling. There is something familiar about this one, though. I can't quite explain it. Are you sure that we have never met before?"

Carl shook his head again. "I just have that kind of face, I guess. Sorry to have disturbed the two of you. I must have mixed up the address. I'll be on my way now. Sorry about the whole mix-up again."

"Utter silliness. Be mindful of where you are and what you're doing." Elizabeth barked.

It was a phrase that had been directed at Carl time and time again. Hearing it at that exact moment grated his polite sensibilities infuriating the young man. "I have always been mindful of what I'm doing and where I am! The two of you were the ones always going off wherever you pleased and doing whatever the hell you wanted!"

Henry puffed out his chest. "Excuse me, young man, but that's no way to speak-"

"For once, you will both just shut the hell up and listen!" Carl towered over his adoptive parents with a confidence he had always seemed to lack. "Looking back on things, yes, you both gave me a good home. I'll always be thankful for that, but in the end, I guess I was just another thing for both of you to own. I was the son you bought to be proud of and show off at parties - but that's okay. I did just fine on my own. The both of you were never really around anyway. And *knowing* that you aren't my true parents makes leaving all of this behind that much easier."

Elizabeth and Henry cast puzzled gazes. They then directed them to the strange young man.

"Carl..." Henry whispered the name as if his body acted on its own impulse.

A glimmer of hopefulness shined through the frustration as he saw the recognition on his father's face. "Yes?"

"What?" Henry snapped back into the moment. "You're speaking nonsense, young man. You appear to have gotten the wrong address, as stated, so please be on your way. We want nothing more to do with this ridiculous conversation."

Carl ran his hands through his long blond hair. He soaked in how Elizabeth and Henry appeared, cataloging the two people who raised him in his mind. "Have a good life - both of you."

A real sense of closure formed within Carl, and he darted off with determination down the long driveway to the city street. It occurred to him that perhaps that was why he felt the need to return to the enormous house one last time. The items lost to the cleansing of his old identity could always be replaced; starting fresh and knowing that a chapter in his life had ended was something that needed to be experienced.

The familiar bark of the corgi took Carl's attention away from the moment of inner peace. He looked down to see Bandolar a few feet away on the sidewalk as he stood near his old beat-up station wagon. "I could feel you nearby. I haven't seen you since the night I could start talking to animals. Where have you been? I don't even know what I'm supposed to be doing with this – I don't know - power? What do you want now?"

Found proper... smell. Smell... like you. Where you are... from. The feelings and thoughts were transmitted to Carl's mind as strained words.

Carl's face lit up with excitement. "Show me!"

"Of course I think Valerie is beautiful. She's Valerie! A goddess, for fuck's sake! I was a teenager. My hormones were out of control – that's what it was like for all of us. The turning point was when I learned she had been in love with my grandpa. That kinky shit is all good and well in porn, but it leaves you feeling a little different in real life. So no, we never got involved. Sorry to disappoint you." – Joseph Chan, Medium/Manipulator – conversations with Minx

3

"SO, TO BE completely clear about the matter, you and my grandpa were in love? You were both together and never had any children *at all*?" Joe rummaged through Valerie's kitchen, intent on finding adequate sustenance. He prowled through the cupboards like an enraged predator hungry for any prey.

Valerie rolled her eyes, annoyed; the interrogation regarding her past was tiresome. She took a refreshing sip of coffee before speaking. "For the last time, Joseph, yes, your grandfather and I were together. I almost married the man. We were in love, and I also renounced my godhood for him. I thought we could truly be happy, and we were for a short time. Things changed. Things always change."

Joe returned to Valerie's apartment moments after departing his childhood home. That act of leaving his former life was still fresh in his mind. Joe considered his mother, and at that moment, the idea of never seeing her again flashed through his consciousness, creating a momentary panic. He had no idea what would become of him, and the reality of the dangers he faced hit him for the first time. The collected snacks from scavenging were comfort food for the intense emotions brewing in reaction to the unknown.

Valerie shot a curious glance at Joe while raising an eyebrow. She continued her close study of him as he sat on the couch near the coffee table. A bag of potato chips and chocolate chip cookies lay on his lap like a security blanket. A joyful grin formed in anticipation of the instant gratification the snacks would grant, and he wasted no time tearing open the bags that kept his palate from experiencing pure delight. He devoured and savored each bite of junk food while sitting across from Valerie.

"Not exactly the breakfast I would recommend." She sipped her coffee with elegant grace.

"It runs in the family. Food is good any time of the day. And besides, I take what I can get." He spoke between taking bites of food.

"Apparently so." Valerie didn't bother hiding her disgust.

Joe smirked. "So, where did Carl go this morning? He seemed like he was in a hurry. You send him off on an errand or something?"

Valerie shook her head. "No. The choice to leave was his own, despite my protests. I suppose it's understandable that you boys require some kind of closure. Still, I'd rather you were all here and safe until we finish the business at the country club tonight. However, he felt that some personal matters couldn't wait."

This confused Joe. Valerie was a powerful goddess. "Why not make Carl stay? Why did you let him go? You could have forced the issue. It's not like he could have stopped you."

She sighed after another sip of coffee. "Certain things have to be experienced no matter what anyone tells you. Advice from others wanted or not, can only go so far."

The combination of chips and cookies was highly gratifying. Joe ate with furious speed when thoughts of Valerie's past resurfaced. "I still can't believe how much you let me hit on you knowing full well that you could have been my grandmother! Why the hell didn't you stop me?"

Valerie controlled her irritation. "Joe, once again, I can't have children, and it has been this way for ages. The Distinction of Realms forbids it. Therefore, there is no way that we are or could have been of blood relation."

"What about my blood? I'm descended from old gods. My ma told me the whole damn story earlier this morning." Joe picked a piece of chip from his teeth and swallowed it once it came loose. He enjoyed seeing how this bothered Valerie.

She relaxed her shoulders and refused to let Joe get to her. "That happened before the Distinction was made law and before the Praetor Projector Council forbade the birth of new bloodlines from old gods. The Council polices these matters. It would take quite a bit of power to hide it from them. Your family history stretches back quite a ways, Joe. I'm sure your mother explained that too. Whether or not you were listening is another matter entirely."

"Okay. I get that. But if you would've married my grandpa like you intended to, that technically would have made you my grandma, regardless of whether or not you guys could have had kids. And to be honest, this whole thing just bothers the hell out of me! It's fucking ridiculous!" Joe scarfed down more chips feeling an even stronger surge of emotions run through his body. Eating pushed those feelings back down to nothingness.

"Why does this particular aspect of my past upset you?" Valerie placed the coffee cup on a coaster on the table and leaned closer, studying Joe's angst. He angrily crumpled up the empty bag of potato chips tossing it aside on the clean couch.

Emotions erupted as he slammed the cookies on the coffee table. "It bothers me because he was my grandpa, and you were in *love* with him, and you still are, as far as I can tell! It bothers me because my mom knew about you and what would happen to me, and she never told me about any of it until after the damn fact! If people were upfront with me, then maybe I could've been prepared for this, and maybe I could've stopped some of it from going down the way it did! Jared could still have a normal life, and Carl too! And..." His voice trailed off. "...being a medium means I could have made contact with my dead father a long time ago."

"Fixating over the past prevents you from living in the present and ultimately kills your future. So you have to let it go." Sympathy grew in her voice.

"You don't understand," Joe continued. "I tried to reach him. There was... nothing there. Why can't I contact my dad's ghost?"

More sympathy emanated from the former Grace. "I can help you in contacting him. As can your grandfather."

"That's not good enough. I need to fixate on it. If I'm going to do better for the sake of what happens after tonight, then I need to remember the why." Then, with reluctance, he admitted one more thing. "And I shouldn't still be attracted to you after finding everything out." Joe shoved more food into his mouth. "I mean, I always had a thing for older women, but this is taking it to a new level. Ten to fifteen years is one thing, but thousands of years? That's something else."

Valerie retrieved her cup of coffee and used a white napkin to wipe the spots that spilled over when Joe slammed the cookies down. "Attractions are natural, Joe. It's the way the universe works."

"Then maybe I'll start boycotting the universe. How about that?" He scoffed.

"You're stubborn, just like your grandfather," Valerie smirked.

Joe ignored the comment and studied the apartment, just now realizing that Jared was nowhere in sight. "Where did Jared go? I thought he was strictly under house arrest until later tonight when we do our supernatural mission impossible thing."

"He's taking another stab at a shower. He was rather hesitant, given what took place last time. I can't say that I blame his reaction." She sipped more coffee.

"He told me all about it. So what's with this water demon calling him Vestor? What the hell is a water demon anyway?" Joe took his time with the last cookie in the pack savoring the chocolate chip flavor as he bit into it.

She thought about how best to explain. "Water demons can be very deadly. I wish I knew why this one was forced to go after him. Unfortunately, Jared is new to all of this, and as far as I can tell, he yields no special talent, although recent developments point to the contrary."

"I don't like the sound of that," Joe said, slowly eating his next chip; the crunch shattered the silence after his comment.

While drinking the rest of her coffee, Valerie recalled her visit from Develin in the world of dreams. That vile demon wizard spoke of Jared's importance, explaining how he was to become a rather powerful Time Bender. "All I can say with certainty is that there is more to Jared than originally thought. Time will reveal such things about the young man. But, until then, we stick together and look after one another. That's how all three of you will survive the days to come."

Joe nodded in agreement letting out a loud belch.

Valerie rolled her eyes in disgust. "I have to admit you were far more charming when you thought you had a chance of bedding me."

Joe belched again as if to prove a point. "Anything I can do to get rid of that image or idea, consider it done."

Valerie smirked at Joe's remark and subsequently thought of Jared. His presence was strong through the bond of sacrifice, and she knew he was in the next room alone and scared. She could feel the fear festering within his mind. But then, she couldn't help but wonder how so many legends began with a scared and uncertain youth.

"I have certain matters to attend to." She spoke abruptly as she stood.

"Okay. What do you want me to do?" Joe crumpled up the empty bag of cookies while slouching with lazy comfort onto the couch.

"Stay here with Jared. Make sure he's okay and look after him." She commanded.

Joe laughed at this. "I've been doing that for years now, and I'm not planning on stopping anytime soon."

Valerie grinned with approval. "Good because things will only grow more dangerous from this point on. You'll have to excuse me now. I'm off to have a conversation with the smartest person I know."

"Every sentient creature wants to know where they come from. They want a line connecting them to a past that makes them feel larger than themselves. When a thing is born, there is great pain because it is cut off from the line it was connected to – most violently in some cases. That pain is a reminder that you were a part of something that spans eons. You are CONNECTED. For some, that is enough. For others, they want more. They want the truth of that connection to the past: to their origins. Unfortunately, this usually leads to madness." – Chaos – High Primordial god of the Void.

4

THE MIDMORNING SUN shined upon the cemetery with a majesty that Carl had never appreciated until now. He continued to relish the heightened as he saw through the eyes of all the creatures around him, both large and small. The birds viewed the sky with brilliant perception, as did the insects that buzzed about. His little companion Bandolar was no exception to the wonder he experienced at seeing and feeling from the perspective of other living creatures.

The canine led Carl to an unmarked grave in a section of the cemetery where the city buried the forgotten that no one claimed or cared for. Carl had been standing before the headstone for nearly a half-hour at an utter loss for words. He felt baffled about how his small companion could determine that it was his birth mother, dead and buried beneath the earth.

Still, you... not trust... my smell? The corgi came across as somewhat offended.

"It's not that. I just..." Carl felt his eyes begin to tear up. When he sensed the truth behind Bandolar's message of Elizabeth and Henry not being his real birth parents, immediate hope was born that he could find his true mother and father. As it turned out, one of them was dead.

Smell same. You smell of female. You come from female, Bandolar explained.

Carl knelt beside the grave and closed his eyes, sensing what his companion did. He immersed himself in the corgi's feelings and was able to match scents in a way he never thought possible. At that moment, he realized just how wrong the smell was that came from Elizabeth and Henry Remington.

He abruptly opened his eyes and looked at the corgi that pushed up against his leg in a somewhat affectionate manner. It was the equivalent of a sibling placing a caring hand on a shoulder. Bandolar then sat down on Carl's left foot, offering protection to the animal speaker in his own way.

"I wish I could just speak to her for a moment. If there was only a way that I could do that." Carl thought out loud.

Scent... weak... Scent going back... to where scents go... No one here to make sound with scent. Bandolar explained further.

"Wait! I might know someone that can actually do it!" The sudden realization returned hope to Carl that he thought was forever lost.

I go. Bandolar seemed troubled.

"What?" Carl shot a confused glance at the corgi. "Why would you go? You brought me here."

The dog barked as it stood on all fours, ready to run from the cemetery. *Better if go... dead talk... not like... not of life... not of nature.* The corgi paced from side to side, wanting the approval to be on his way.

Carl nodded, understanding his friend's unease. "Okay. How do I find you?"

I... find... you. With another bark, the corgi known as Bandolar trotted off on all fours, leaving Carl by his true mother's grave.

"For as long as there is affection and friendship in the world, I will always have my place. When a long-lost companion arrives, I am the smile that overwhelms you. When you embrace and feel the warmth of your lover as they hold you, I am the joy that electrifies your body. When you feel fond of someone, I push you to make it so. So I ask: are these not among the greatest things that people fight for?" – Philotes – goddess of friendship, romantic friendship, and affection.

5

AFTER DRYING HIS body with a warm towel, Jared gingerly stepped out of the bathtub pushing the shower curtain aside. He dressed and emerged from the bathroom, fully clothed and grateful that this bathing experience was without incident. *Am I always going to fear taking a shower? Large bodies of water are definitely out of the question now.*

"Jared, how ya feeling?" Joe sat on the couch yawning while stretching his arms and felt the immense weight of tiredness from the boredom of nothing to do rather than the fatigue of being physically exhausted.

"I'm doing okay. Where did Valerie go?" Jared asked.

Joe gave his friend a half-shrug. "She said she had certain matters to attend to. She mentioned something about meeting with the smartest person she knows. So I guess she's trying to figure something out. But, hell if I know, I'm mostly in the dark, just like you."

Jared was troubled by the news. "What else is there to figure out? The plan is set for tonight, right?"

Joe responded with another half-shrug. "That's what I thought too, but apparently, there's some other serious shit going down that relates somehow. She failed to go into detail. It's her way. But she'll be back with even more cryptic info, I'm sure."

Jared nodded as he sat across from his friend, melting his body into the couch. "Is Carl back yet?"

Joe shook his head. "Nope. He's still gone. I'm worried about him. I've been worried about both of you guys. Everything has been so damn crazy, and we're all so easily accepting it because we have no choice. Doesn't it all make you want to stop and fuckin' scream or something? I mean, there are things we should be questioning, and maybe the path we're going down isn't necessarily the right one despite what the woman whose a few millennia old says."

This time Jared shrugged, signifying the defeat he felt. "I'm as frustrated as they come, Joe. I thought Sara was normal, but I fell in love with a former goddess, for fuck's sake. Do you know how batshit crazy it sounds to say that out loud?"

"Look at it this way: you might as well go big if you're going to be in love, and a goddess is as big as it gets, right?" Joe smirked.

"Yeah." Jared chuckled. It always amazed him how Joe could extract laughter. "I guess I haven't had time to think about any of it in depth, mostly because it freaks me out. I've just been going with it because I don't have a choice. What else am I going to do? I'm dead on my own."

Joe shook his head, unwilling to accept this. "That's the thing, you aren't alone. We could get out of here: all of us. We could go our own way. My family will help you and Carl. We could be safe and not get mixed up in any of it."

Jared considered. "I'm not sure that running is the best thing either, Joe. We have to learn how to face these things. I have to learn to protect myself too, and Valerie is my best bet."

A frustrated sigh escaped Joe. "She's interested in you. She mentioned there might be more to you than she originally thought. Plus, there was that crazy talk you had going on last night."

"I was talking stupid. I'm just paranoid about everything." Jared wished he believed his own statement.

Joe shook his head vehemently. "No, you weren't. You always trust your instincts, and yours are telling you something important. I don't care what

Valerie or anyone else says, and I'm sick and tired of all of us being forced one way or the other. Why would that water demon want to kill you? Who the hell sends a water demon? I mean, what the fuck is a water demon?! Can you really wrap your mind around all the shit that's been happening to us lately?"

For a split-second, Jared relived the experience reacting with a momentary shiver. The feel of the water tightening around his body like ropes was something he would not soon forget. He looked at his longtime friend and sighed, defeated. "I don't know, Joe. I wish I could answer those questions. The damn thing called me Vestor."

"You still have no idea what that means?" Joe asked.

Jared shook his head. "No. But there is something I feel that is getting stronger. Something will happen to me, Joe, and I can't shake the feeling that Jared, me, the way I am now... It just feels like there's this echo saying that I'm going to die - that this version of me will die. It's like a voice so far away you can barely hear it yelling, but that voice is there, and it's screaming at full volume. It's bellowing out that Vestor is coming, and Jared won't exist anymore."

Joe studied his companion, uncertain of how to give comfort. "I won't let anything happen to you. You know that, right?"

"Of course I do. But no matter what happens, I have to be there tonight. I just have to." Jared was clear on this.

Joe's phone buzzed, breaking the flow of the conversation. He looked at the text message with curiosity.

"What's up?" Jared asked.

"It's Carl." Joe kept his eyes on the text. "He wants me to meet him at a cemetery."

"Did he say what for?" Concern grew in Jared's tone.

"No. He just said to hurry up and meet him." Joe was torn. He was supposed to stay with Jared, but Carl needed him.

Jared summoned his strength. "I'm going with you."

"Oh no..." Joe took a defiant step back, shaking his head. "Valerie was pretty specific about you staying put."

"Joe, I'm tired of hiding out in here, and I'm tired of being afraid of what's out there. I may not be able to do what you or Carl can, but I won't be afraid anymore. You guys are all I have right now. You're the only people that remember me." Jared stood tall, confident in his decision.

Joe smiled, happy to see the strength in his friend. "Fine. Let's go see what Carl wants."

"That thought that comes to you when you least expect it, that moment of insight or wisdom that hits you with a physical reaction to the realization you've just had – all of those things are me. I am wisdom. I am intelligence. I'm the unseen force that guides you to the proper conclusions. If you'd just stop ignoring me, then you'd be further along with everything." – Omoikane, the Japanese god of wisdom.

6

THE LOUD SILENCE mixed with the hum of whispered conversations and the rustling of flicked pages by a motley variety of avid readers and researchers was the picture-perfect scene one came to expect at the Central Gilead Library. Valerie stepped within the sacred temple of knowledge with a sense of ease and an underlying reassurance that she was relatively safe. Libraries were sanctuaries. The knowledge contained in print upon countless pages led to the power derived from belief. No creature that fed on that pure energy would dare cause harm to such a magnificent treasure trove of knowledge. It was the kind of information that gave rise to and maintained the life essence of many deities.

Valerie stepped through the main lobby, immediately struck by the intricate patterns and colors featuring shades of rich burgundy, deep navy blue, and sparkling gold. The tiles were arranged in a geometric pattern that created a sense of depth and movement that drew one's gaze to the grand staircase several paces ahead of her. Feeling the energy shift, she adjusted her sensibilities to the quiet, polite decorum. A steady stream of patrons checked out, returned, or renewed books and other media at the circulation desk.

The familiar silence was soothing as she passed the desk and reached the base of the elaborate marble staircase, taking one easy step after another to the second level. This was where the more dedicated students researched and referenced, attempting to put a new spin on old ideas; the low hum of voices as huddled groups discussed and debated texts and peer-reviewed journals brought a smile to Valerie's face. She admired, to no end, the tenacity of humans when they wished to learn. One silent figure, however, was no mere student. This man was a god now living in the realm that gave him the most significant power he could ever have asked for; he was drowning in pure knowledge.

From an outsider's perspective, he would appear to be a middle-aged man of Japanese origin. However, those living on the Distinction's magical side knew this former god as Omoikane. In the days when his pantheon was held in high regard by the people that believed, his counsel was sought after by fellow deities. His knowledge was vast, and his advice well-informed. As time passed, he continued to amass that which gave him power and always found himself traveling from library to library, expanding his reservoir of information.

He cleared his throat with light ease after having been silent for most of the morning and cast a gracious smile as Valerie approached him between two large bookshelves. "No one has sought my counsel in ages. I gather it must be important, especially since you're not of my pantheon, Aglaia."

Valerie issued a polite smile in return and bowed her head accordingly. To anyone walking by, it appeared as if two old friends had reunited by chance.

"I sense that you have true power again. That is odd. During your travels throughout the East, it was made clear that you gave up godhood. Your powers faded as you became more and more human." Omoikane pushed a cart along the aisle between bookshelves and began placing each book in its proper place.

Valerie acknowledged this with a nod. "A minor sacrifice was given to me. There were people in my care that required protection, and I needed more power to ensure that protection. It was based on necessity."

"Ah, yes." His childlike grin betrayed his actual age making him seem even younger. "I recently learned of your current crusade. You seek to save innocents by invoking an old edict that not even the Praetor Projector Council can overturn. Unfortunately, you've also displeased Dracien. The rogue spirits have already paid proper tribute to the old demon, but he dislikes when others meddle with what he has already allowed in his city."

"Enemies can't be helped." She admitted.

"The Distinction of Realms certainly saw to that." Omoikane agreed.

She nodded. "Indeed it did. It changed things for us all." A brief pause giving thought to events passed was shared by both ancient deities. Valerie then looked at the Japanese man, ready to discuss the reason for her visit. "Omoikane, I come to you because I require counsel."

"Aglaia, you have always been just and kind to me and others you have encountered over most of your life. Of course, we have all had our transgressions, but you, for the most part, have learned from them. So I offer my counsel to you freely, for I know it will be put to good use." He smiled at her.

"I thank you." She bowed her head again.

He continued. "I already know what it is that you plan to do. So what troubles you is not what is seen, but rather that which is hidden in plain sight."

Valerie nodded. "Yes. A boy has crossed over to our side of the Distinction; he got himself involved with a rogue spirit. What troubles me is that Develin came to me in the realm of dreams. He spoke of this boy in particular and named him Time Bender. He said the boy is to become a mighty Time Bender."

Omoikane considered her words. "What did the vile demon want you to do? Kill the boy or hand him over, perhaps?"

"He wanted the opposite, actually." She answered. "He wished that I keep the boy alive and see that his powers fully manifest."

Omoikane raised a curious eyebrow as he transferred books from cart to shelf. "There is something the demon wizard wishes of the Time Bender to be."

"I agree." She crossed her arms. "The problem is I can't figure out what it is. This boy has a good soul. He knows what is right. I don't wish to see him corrupted by things that mean to do him harm."

Omoikane closed his eyes for a split second, and during that time, Valerie could swear that she saw the workings of many minds at once. The focus and concentration were beyond anything a human could attain. This god most certainly lived up to his name. While he concentrated, Omoikane continued to take books and place them on the shelves without looking. Valerie smirked with an eye roll, knowing he was showing off a bit.

"To know the demon wizard's future plans, we must delve further into his past." Omoikane opened his eyes, radiating supreme clarity. "In the past is where you'll find the answers you need to ascertain what he is planning presently for the future."

"So much of Develin is a mystery. He's a lie wrapped in an enigma covered with misdirection." She grunted, disgusted with the demon wizard.

"That is how it has always been with that vile creature. Has anyone else shown an interest in this boy?" He asked.

She nodded. "A water demon was sent to kill him."

He pondered further. "That is most curious. Some wish him alive, and some wish him dead. And you say he is to be a Time Bender?"

Valerie nodded. "Yes. What conclusion have you come to?"

Omoikane looked directly at the former Grace. "I see opposing realities converging to specific points in the past. We exist in a universe where time moves in a way we experience as forward. However, some powers and magic move contrary to our way of experiencing things; some sentient beings completely live outside of time. A powerful creature could tap into that backward flow of magic and use it to try and alter what has already happened by the will of Chronos."

"Wouldn't that create new realities? Are there not laws against it, such as with the Distinction of Realms?" The idea disturbed Valerie if there weren't.

Omoikane sighed. "The problem is, Valerie, none have been powerful enough to do such things since the Founding Magic. Whatever is trying to alter this Time Bender's path is extremely powerful. It is of the caliber of a High Celestial, High Primordial, or even above that station. Perhaps it is two great powers in a future far ahead battling for a desired outcome. It may even be one great power in different versions of futures trying to change conflicting outcomes in parallel realities. Whatever is doing this is a force of great magic, far beyond what we are capable of. It exists beyond time itself, and that is a terrifying prospect."

"And you believe this to be tied to Develin?" She asked.

"Again, I believe the answers are tied to the demon wizard's past. Develin is cunning, but we all answer to someone in the end. At some point, the vile creature was made a true servant to a great power." He concluded.

Valerie sighed, considered her options, and bowed to Omoikane once again. "Thank you for your council Omoikane. It is greatly appreciated."

The former Japanese god cast another friendly smile. "It was my pleasure Aglaia. Feel free to visit any time you wish." Nonchalantly he returned to the task of shelving books.

With elegant grace, Valerie took her leave. She exited from between the large bookshelves sauntering off through the sitting tables where students, fans of literature, and researchers went about their business. She headed toward the marble staircase with a pensive expression and soon found herself in the grand main lobby on the first floor. From the outsider's perspective, the two old friends finished their brief conversation as the catching up dictated by social contract ended.

"Animal Speakers are rare. The universe created them this way for a reason. Imagine having the power to influence every living creature on the planet other than your own species. You could control the majority of nature. It takes a special person to wield this power; they typically come from an honorable lineage. Every so often, one among us abuses this power and must be dealt with by the others." – Edison Rockwell, Animal Speaker and great-grandfather to Carl Remington.

7

THE SUNSHINE FILTERED through the oak and maple trees, casting dappled shadows on the ground; this brightness also illuminated the gravestones with a warm glow. It presented a serene yet somber atmosphere in the cemetery as Joe and Jared approached Carl, who stood before the unmarked grave with eager anticipation. The reasons behind the sudden meeting were not clearly explained via the text message Joe received. Still, from the look on Carl's face, it was evident something crucial had transpired.

Carl shot a disapproving glance as he noticed Jared walking alongside Joe. Reflexively he brushed his hands through his shaggy blond hair. "Why the hell is Jared out here with you? I specifically asked for you, Joe. You know he's not safe outside the apartment."

"I needed to get out of that damn apartment. What's going on with you anyway? Joe said your message was urgent. I wasn't going to just sit by like I have been and do nothing to help." Jared crossed his arms with defiance. Nothing was going to change his mind.

Carl returned his focus to the unmarked gravestone before them. "My real mother is buried right here. When I started being able to talk to animals and see what they see, well... I... I was informed that the parents that raised me weren't my real parents. That little dog that talks to me, Bandolar, he told me that this one was my mom. I believe him. I could feel what that corgi felt, and he picked up on the scent. There's no denying it. I don't expect you to understand all that, but it's true. You have to believe me."

Jared uncrossed his arms, allowing the defensive posture to dissipate. A week ago, that explanation would have sounded like complete madness. It would have been met with ridicule and sarcasm. But, as he heard the heartfelt explanation, it dawned on him why Carl had desperately wanted Joe to be present. One of Joe's newfound talents was that of a medium. He could focus his magic and talk to the dead.

"It's okay, Carl. Joe and I are here for you." Jared said.

"Thanks. I know it's asking a lot, but I figured it was worth a try. Joe, I hate to put you on the spot like this, but can you make it so I can talk to her?" Carl looked to his friends with eyes that pleaded for the yes he was desperate to hear.

Jared studied Joe, attempting to grasp the abilities his friend had. "Do you think you can do it?"

Joe shrugged. "I'm not sure. When my grandpa showed up to talk to me, it was because of a spell he placed to be set off when certain things happened. He told me how to be a medium. I tried. I tried to reach my father. It didn't work. I couldn't do it."

Carl and Jared remained silent, nodding their heads.

Joe looked around the cemetery. In the distance, mourners paid their respects, oblivious to how the rest of the world had moved on the instant their loved one died. He looked back at Carl. "And then there's the fact that we're in a cemetery. What if I end up calling all of them out of the grave? That would be one hell of a mess. I mean, we'd be looking at many angry dead people taken from their peaceful slumber."

"Can you at least try? You had answers lined up for you when you changed and crossed over. Your family was waiting for this to happen. I didn't have anyone. All I had was that damn dog, and I can't even understand what Bandolar tells me half the time. Maybe my real mother knew something more about all of this. There just has to be more to it." Carl continued pleading with his eyes as he spat out the words.

Joe nodded, empathizing with his friend, and moved closer to the un-marked grave. "Okay. I think I can make it so you can talk to her directly. I'll be able to see and hear her too. I'm not sure if you'll be able to, Jared. This summoning the dead thing is kind of new to me. Some spirits are stronger than others; some can be seen because they *will* it and don't need someone like me to make it happen. That's what I got out of the explanation given to me anyway."

"Don't worry about me. Just help Carl." Jared watched with hopeful eyes. In a way, he needed this to work as well. A positive experience would be a vindication of the hope he carried that this new world he was a part of wasn't all that bad.

With ease, Joe placed his left hand on the unmarked gravestone and put his right hand along Carl's left temple. Joe closed his eyes when Carl closed his and concentrated his abilities by focusing on the medium aspect of his powers. A vastly different sensation took hold of his entire body. The magic was similar but varied enough to require an alternative approach to sum-moning the strength needed.

Jared watched with amazement as Joe grew shaky from the exertion of energy. For a moment, it appeared as if nothing was happening. Then, in an instant, he witnessed the change as Carl and the gravestone connected through the conduit that was Joseph Chan. Jared soaked in the brilliant hue of energy and colors that emanated around them in elegant swirls. At that moment, the magnificence of the experience caused Jared to forget his trou-bles.

Carl grew a new awareness from the more powerful and potent connec-tion than that of the Animal Speaker. Instead of merely being connected to a living thing, he was now connected to a ghost. That type of energy was strongest in the realm of the dead. His eyes were closed as he focused his entire being on maintaining the connection that Joe had created for him.

"Carl. Open your eyes." Joe sounded as if he had just finished running a marathon.

Carl's eyelids parted slowly as he let the visual information process within his mind. Eventually, the somewhat translucent image of a woman stood atop the grave of his birth mother. Her physical appearance phased in and out of the space it inhabited; she took a step closer, recognizing Carl for who he was. Upon her face was a mixture of sadness and joy. The sight pulled at Carl's heart so immensely that he couldn't help the tears that trickled down his cheeks.

"You have a few minutes, if that. Not sure how long. It took a lot out of me to bring her here, so get to it." Joe stepped back, walking away from the gravestone, and stood next to Jared, exhausted from the experience. "Let's give them some privacy."

Jared nodded in agreement, amazed at the reunion taking place. He took a few more steps back with Joe until the two were out of earshot.

The blonde apparition moved in front of Carl and reached her hand out to touch her son's face. The essence of her form went through Carl, unable to make physical contact with the realm of the living, and she expressed a scrunched face of disappointment.

Carl decided to speak. "I'm Carl. Carl Remington. Not sure if Carl was the name you gave me when I was born, but that's what I've been called for as long as I can remember."

The ghost nodded. "Carl was the name I gave you. You were named after your father."

Carl wiped a few tears from his eyes. "My father was named Carl? Who was my father? Why am I the way I am, and why did you... why did you give me up?"

The ghost of Carl's mother looked away, ashamed. "I wanted to keep you, Carl. You have to believe that."

"I don't even know your name!" Carl bellowed.

She looked into his eyes. "Raylene. Raylene Winter. And your father was Carl Rockwell or still is. He may still be alive."

"Raylene..." Carl's lip trembled as he whispered the name.

"Your abilities have surfaced, I take it?" Raylene's ghost asked.

He nodded.

A terrible sadness weighed Rayelene down. "I was always hoping that would never happen. That's partly why I gave you up. I wanted to keep you away from the madness of the world on this side of the Distinction."

"It didn't work. I crossed over anyway." Carl explained.

She nodded. "It sure looks that way. You look good. You seem very strong. I can sense the Animal Speaker in you. Just like your father."

"He could do what I do?" He was barely able to contain the excitement in his voice.

She nodded again. "Yes. Your father was a compelling Animal Speaker or still is. It's hard to tell who is still alive being on this side of things."

Carl stepped closer. "What happened to him? Where can I find him?"

"Carl, there's something you need to know about your father. He..." In an instant, Raylene's ghost began to phase out. Her words turned into strained mumbles as her essence faded in. A desperate concentration took hold as she tried in vain to remain where she was.

"No!!" Carl bellowed, reaching a hand for the empty space where his mother's ghost had been.

Joe and Jared ran to Carl's side.

"Bring her back, Joe!" Carl demanded.

Joe gave his friend an apologetic expression. "I wish I could, Carl-"

"Just do it, Joe!" Carl raged louder than before.

Joe kept his voice calm. "I can't. I'm not strong enough. But maybe I will be someday. Right now, I'm just not."

"Please, Joe!" There was a desperate madness in Carl's eyes.

Concern filled Jared as Joe once again attempted to be a conduit between the living and the dead. Unfortunately, this time the brilliant hue failed to emerge. The focus and energy simply weren't there for the medium.

"I'm sorry..." Joe fell to his knees, exhausted. "She's not here anymore. I'm not sure where she went. It's like she fled the grave."

"What?" Carl didn't understand; he had just seen her.

"Her essence, it found somewhere else to be. I don't know how else to explain it. She went away or was taken away." Joe stepped up slowly, aided by both Carl and Jared.

"My father is still alive. At least she thought he was." Carl said.

"That's good news, right?" Jared asked as the three began walking away from the gravestone.

"I don't know. She was going to tell me something about him before vanishing." Carl sighed and regained some composure. "Thanks, Joe, for doing this."

Joe waved it away as if it were nothing. "No problem. I'm sorry I couldn't give you more time with her."

"You did great, Joe." Carl smiled. "You did great."

"Now what do we do?" Jared studied the endless sea of gravestones; the style varied from simple flat markers to elaborate statues and monuments. An eerie feeling crept over him as he realized how many souls could be summoned from their resting places. So many mysteries could be solved with the right questions directed at the proper spirits. It wasn't until this moment that he realized how much power Joe had.

Joe cracked his neck and stretched as if he had just woken up. "Right now, we should head back to Valerie's apartment. We have a lot of work to do tonight. I guess you can look at it as our final shift at Brightwood, and it's one that we aren't even getting paid for. You'd think that money wouldn't matter now, but it still does. I mean, look at Valerie. She still works. She insists that we have to work regular jobs again too."

"It's all part of blending in," Jared remarked.

"Well fuck that. I'll make my own way, which won't require a chump job. That's all I have to say about it." Joe stretched again as the three exited the cemetery. "Fuck that."

PART NINE:

WHEN PLANS
COME TOGETHER

"My brother is often given much credit for war, but he only represents the conflict. He is the physical manifestation of what war is. He is violence. They forget me easily because they forget there is another side to war. A campaign must be planned; the moments leading up to the conflict should be considered. The strategy and tactics are implemented and adapted as the battle unfolds. This is the backbone. Violence is universal, and violence in war is well known. But do not forget the planning. Do not forget the intelligence. Do not forget me." – Athena, goddess of wisdom.

1

AS NIGHT FELL, the atmosphere of the Brightwood Country Club gave off a sophistication not felt during the daytime hours. Soft ambient lighting illuminated the well-manicured lawn and gardens, casting a warm and inviting glow. The clubhouse was a bustle of activity; members and staff ran around as if fueled by a drug they couldn't get enough of. Chilling classical music wafted through the night air, adding weight to the fact that the people arriving in droves were about to be sacrificed. The members piling into the club were controlled participants lining up to be offered to creatures beyond their understanding. What they believed to be *free will* was a spell that exploited their affection for Brightwood.

Jared walked in step with his companions and newfound mentor, experiencing equal parts excitement and trepidation. He harbored no powers like Carl, Joe, or Valerie; from the feelings brewing within, however, he came to fathom his presence was of the utmost importance.

He turned his gaze from the establishment that had employed him only a week prior and laughed as though it were the greatest joke in the world. Life had unfolded in so many unpredictable ways, and he could only begin to imagine what lay on the horizon throughout the uncharted territories of his new universe.

Jared's eyes casually fell on Valerie. He was bombarded by that sense of intense loyalty and devotion. He thought he would have to argue with the woman for his attendance on this night to be entirely accepted, but Valerie gave no resistance to the idea of him joining the group. Instead, with a stern voice, she imparted to Jared that he was meant to be with them no matter what unfolded. This only added credence to the premonition that something important would happen.

The night air cast an aroma of varying possibilities. There was a strange hue to the glow of moonlight, and Jared sensed that they were coming upon a crucial point in time and space. He could almost feel himself changing as they walked through the parking lot.

Jared's eyes shifted to the black pavement as he trailed behind his three protectors. For a brief moment, a vision of Valerie, still young and beautiful, with a man he had never met before, flashed through his mind. This man had raven-colored hair, and Jared's body suddenly felt incredibly aged. Within the blink of an eye, the vision was gone.

He shook off the imprint of the vision while touching the clothing on his body to ensure he was here and now. His shirt and jeans were given to him by Valerie and had fit his slender frame like a glove. Carl and Joe were also dressed in more comfortable clothing; their fashion choices perfectly matched their personalities.

"You okay back there, Jared?" Joe turned to face him. "You don't have to be here tonight, man. It's just another friendly reminder."

"He's well aware, Joe, and he's prepared to deal with whatever happens tonight," Valerie spoke up so Jared wouldn't have to explain the strange sensations within him. She could feel it through their bond. "We move quickly and get into position. Once we're ready, we make our presence known. These three women know who we are, and we know who they are. Open battle is the only real option left to us, and we can prevail if we stick to the plan. They're far too confident in their abilities. We use that."

"Do you trust these other people to follow through like your friend said they would?" Carl chimed in.

Valerie nodded. "Minx would not betray me, Carl. The debt owed is too great. His input was invaluable."

Valerie turned her attention to Jared and gave him a smile of reassurance. When he smiled back, she recalled her visit from Develin while she was in the realm of dreams. *A powerful Time Bender stands before me.*

The group made their way closer to the main entrance. The distance granted by the parking lot was near its end, and the time to act was now at hand.

"Carl. Are the animals in place?" Valerie asked.

Carl seemed to look off into another world as he mentally checked. "Rats, stray dogs, some stray cats, a few lone raccoons, and a couple of coyotes too. Did you guys know there's an alligator in the sewers? She's forty years old... anyway; I can sense them waiting for me to let them know what to do next. And Bandolar is somewhere around here too. I can feel him. He's on his way."

Valerie nodded in approval. "Utilize the corgi if you need help, Carl. The dog was trained by Nature to aid you, after all. Joe. Are you ready to do your part?"

With confidence, Joe winked at Valerie. "We're all about to find that out."

"Then let's not keep them waiting." Valerie led the way to the main entrance; the group mixed in with a sea of people under the spell of rogue spirits.

"Madness. There are several forms of madness. Most assume the madness and insanity of a crazed rage is the only kind that really exists. But let me assure you, there are other forms of madness to partake in. The madness of repetition. The madness of blind devotion. The madness of loss and even the madness of love. All of these simple forms of madness that have crept into the modern world are all the sustenance I require to stay relevant. They are strong enough to touch me where I am, in the realm of the Formless, where I help carry out the will of the Messengers." – known in the early age of Vestor as Annalisa – last of the Maniae.

2

EVERY MEMBER AND employee that belonged to Brightwood scurried about getting last-minute preparations together for the grand sacrifice. The formal dining hall was transformed into a magnificent altar designed to please the three girls they knew and loved, Rachel, Nicole, and Sara. The large crowd of mesmerized humans carried on as expected from the mass-induced spell beyond their comprehension. Mr. Drake and Old Merdith led the anxious group of members and employees as they willingly tottered about, ready to be sacrificed in the name of their three magnificent goddesses.

"Oh no! That floral arrangement is all wrong!" Old Merdith barked at Mr. Dempsy. He defiantly continued placing whatever decorative pieces he could find at the base of the stage where the children of club members were usually betrothed.

"What would you have me do then? It's all I could find, and we were told to use everything we could find!" Mr. Dempsy barked in return. "I hope my wife makes it tonight. Renee is better at arranging things like this anyway. If she were here, it would look a million times better than anyone else could make it. I wonder why she isn't here yet."

"Now be calm," Rachel said while standing atop the stage. She viewed the mass of people gathered for her and her sisters with extreme satisfaction; Nicole stood by her side, emulating Rachel's smugness.

The devoted group of worshipers setting up for the sacrifice recognized the powerfully alluring voice. They turned to face Rachel, hanging on her every word, and bowed their heads in deference to the one they cherished; it was a strict devotion that went beyond fanaticism. Then, one by one, like a wave of properly placed dominos, silence blanketed the large crowd gathered in the formal dining room.

Rachel's voice boomed as she addressed the gathered sheep. "You are all so loyal! I feel your devotion and love, which brings me so much joy! Your sacrifice will be great and allow my sisters and me the power to go where we please without summons!"

"We would do anything for you, Rachel." Mr. Drake's joyous smile beamed as he looked up at her.

"I know you would, and we're all so very grateful." A devilish grin formed on the corner of Rachel's mouth. "Please continue! Time is paramount! The nexus point is upon us, and we must all be ready to proceed!"

Without hesitation, the large crowd of members and employees returned to their assigned duties. Like a colony of synchronized ants, they swarmed specific areas, ensuring the altar was perfect. They were determined to make sure the sacrifice would not disappoint the most influential women in their lives.

Rachel watched with growing amusement as Old Merdith and Mr. Dempsy fought over floral arrangements again. She panned her vision to the others gathered within the large dining hall. Tall skinny Chef and muscular Memo worked diligently, bringing about a banquet fit for the gods of olden times. Ana sat by herself, staring at Rachel's fellow sister Nicole with a loving admiration that rivaled her one-time feelings for Joseph Chan. All was going according to plan. The humans summoned were ready to be slaughtered and give up their souls.

"I wasn't just cut off from Olympus. I was cut off from my family. It's true; they were there with me, inhabiting those human bodies. But I wasn't TRULY there with them. I couldn't relate to them anymore. I love them, but my sisters were strangers to me. The human emotions of the body I inhabit continually remind me of how tragic it is to view family that way." – Ate (goddess of mischief and blind folly)

3

INTERNAL CONFLICT WAS something Ate had never experienced until taking over the physical form of Sara White. The former goddess existed in her human vessel for so long that she had grown accustomed to *feeling* specific ways. The memory of existence before human form had nearly been forgotten; the days before she was banished from the abodes of the gods cried out like a distant sound barely recognizable.

Of course, Ate had been in exile far longer than her sisters; she had been banished before the Distinction of Realms was enacted. Dysnomia and Lethe wanted no part of the forced Distinction. As a result, they, too, had been stripped of their status within the echelons of their own pantheon and forced to depart. Already an exile, Ate found her siblings and survived in a new world with her sisters.

Sara sat alone in the linen room as she recalled those moments after the age of myth. The solitary storage space was the only quiet area where she could escape reality, and it had served as an adequate rendezvous with Jared before his unfortunate crossing over.

She thought fondly of the young man recalling their countless conversations. The emotions stirring within the human body were indeed her own. Sara had denied them as much as she could, but in the end, she knew they had not stemmed merely from existing in this form. She, a former goddess of renowned glory, had fallen in love with a mortal human. There was only one other time in her past when this had happened, and it had been with a Time Bender, no less. The human body she controlled was different in those days; she inhabited a woman in her prime during the eighteenth century. Jared reminded her of that man so long ago...

Sara twirled her hair as she sat, imagining Jared across from her, seated as they used to be. He had dreams of living an everyday life. He had wanted to go to school and make his father and mother proud of their sacrifice for his education. She was painfully aware that such choices had been stripped from him and that she was the reason. Her love had marked him.

The linen room door opened, and little Nicole poked her head about, searching for her sister. She appeared annoyed and relieved when she spotted Sara huddled alone in a corner. Nicole took note of the melancholy look on her sister's face. She scoffed as she realized the root cause of Sara's frivolous emotional state.

"Go away, Lethe. Leave me be. I'll be ready when the time comes for the sacrifice." Sara spat out.

Little Nicole shook her head with pity. "Where did you go wrong, Ate? How is it that you can wallow over such an imperfect creature?"

"Are we so perfect?" Sara asked.

Nicole couldn't believe the question. "We're so much more than they can ever dream of being."

Sara stopped twirling her hair and looked at Nicole. "We *used* to be so much more. The nexus point is powerful, but Dysnomia overestimates how much power this sacrifice will grant us. We'll never reach the status we once held, let alone surpass it. She believes we can set foot upon Olympus again without summons. It was never our role, and Zeus will never take me back - not after how I influenced him to make such a rash choice."

Nicole said nothing, absorbing the words.

Sara continued. "I was alone for so long until the two of you found me. I was happy to be with my sisters again. It still shocks me that your opposition to the Distinction of Realms caused your banishment. We've survived for so long, existing in human form since. The truth is I'm tired of it. I'll always remain with you both. You're my sisters, but I tire of it all, Lethe. Can you possibly understand that?"

Nicole struggled. "If Rachel heard you speak in such a way, she'd have your head. She won't tolerate any of this behavior - not when we're so close to attaining our former glory. It'll work in our favor, Ate, you'll see. We'll be more powerful than before."

"And where is our sister now?" Sara asked.

"She is making sure the altar is properly put together. Watching Mr. Drake and Old Merdith squirm about and jump at every command is a lot of fun. The entire country club is acting this way. They'll do whatever we want. But the sacrifice tonight is going to be glorious! You have to believe that Ate and you have to stop this foolishness. I'm your sister, love you, and want you to be what you once were. We'll all be better than we were. Can't you see the truth of this?" Little Nicole hoped she was getting through.

"I love you too." Sara smiled. She meant the words as she spoke them, but she knew their endeavor was foolish. When it was all said and done, Ate was still the goddess of blind folly.

Nicole calmed her demeanor once she realized her sister did not share her growing enthusiasm but was also grateful for the words of love given in return. Then, with disappointed steps, little Nicole walked to the linen room door and exited, leaving Sara to sulk in self-pity.

I can't even relate to them anymore, Sara thought. Over the years, Lethe and Dysnomia had become more alien. She now felt she had completely lost touch with what it meant to be connected to them like in the olden days. The isolation of flesh often led to such feelings, but Sara knew it was true in her heart. Her love for them, however, remained, as did her love for Jared. The confusion continued to grow, and she hadn't a clue what the proper course of action should be.

"Is it fun? Sure! Messing with people's memories is fun; at least, that's how it was at first. I was a kid! What did you expect? I was going to try things. But I kept it above level. Nothing too crazy. I'm much more responsible than people give me credit for." – Joseph Chan, Medium/Manipulator.

4

JOE KNEW ALL the critical locations in the Brightwood Country Club. He still remembered the placement of all the tables, the numbers assigned to those tables, and how the various areas were divided. However, this time, he did not feel like an eighteen-year-old high school graduate finishing up his first job before college. While making his way through the central kitchen, the past week's experiences weighed down on Joe, forcing him to stand like a man with a purpose. He was a manipulator and a medium, and he would ensure his role on this night would be carried out to the best of his newfound abilities.

"Joe, is that you?" Memo towered behind Joe.

For a split-second, Joe jolted; the large man had been stealthy in his approach. He turned to face Memo, knowing he had to acknowledge being spotted. He made sure to pay particular attention to the look on Memo's face; the man was possessed and in a deep hypnotic trance.

"What's going on, Memo?" Joe smiled, playing the part. The last thing he wanted was to openly be called out as someone that stood against the sacrifice.

"I've never felt better, Joe! You're here for the sacrifice, right? We're all really excited about it! We can't wait! I'm just getting the plates ready for the final meal, and then when the time comes...! I'm telling you, man, it's going to be amazing!" Memo pranced about like a child on Christmas morning.

"You're damn right! I'm here for the sacrifice! I'm just so happy to be a part of it." Joe attempted to dance about like Joe to no avail, and his lack of enthusiasm went unnoticed by the large man.

Filled to the brim with uncontainable excitement, Memo slapped Joe's shoulder in a gesture of comradery. Memo may have still been under the spell of the rogue spirits, but the man was powerful trance or no trance. Nevertheless, Joe felt the sting of that slap and did his best to appear unfazed.

Memo beamed with joy. "Man, tonight is going to be so great. None of the stuff that happened before matters one bit. I don't even care that you tried to hook up with my little sister!"

"Tried? I did-" Joe regretted the words the moment they escaped.

"Come again?" Memo opted to take a harder look at Joe. The anger Memo directed at him somehow began to break down the hypnotic spell.

Shit, Joe panicked, remembering more of his grandfather's lessons. *A strong emotional reaction could break the spell if focused on something else.*

Joe made a quick note of Memo's struggle. He witnessed the blind rage burrowing through the euphoria of the former cook's sacrificial duties. Memo could very well likely go about killing anyone and everyone in his immediate path if the trance were to lose its hold. The immense eruption of anger would take complete control.

"I don't think you heard me right, Memo." Joe put his hand on Memo's shoulder and reached within his mind. "I never hooked up with your sister. As a matter of fact, she and I have never even met, as far as you're concerned. And this whole conversation we're having right now never even happened. I was never here."

Memo looked around the kitchen as if waking up from a dream. He realized he was standing alone with an intense feeling of forgetfulness. His gaze panned about at the hustle and bustle of people gathering food and beverages for the grand sacrifice. A fierce certainty that he had to finish his dish duty pulled on him like gravity. The fanatical loyalty to please Rachel, Nicole, and

Sara resurfaced. He eagerly ran back to continue working on his assigned tasks forgetting everything just as Joe had intended.

Joe watched Memo run; a smirk formed as he witnessed this through the glass window on the door that led to the main wait station. This was his assigned spot for the plan that Valerie and her small vampire friend laid out. The girls had no reason to enter this particular room, and neither did anyone else. No one would be up for tea or coffee after having their blood spilled and sacrificed to three former deities.

A yawn forced its way out. Joe opened the refrigerator door next to him, and a nice cold soda was ready. After pulling the tab and hearing the all too familiar fizz, he engaged in a few refreshing sips. Then, like he had done so many times before, he placed the aluminum can behind a stack of plates on the top shelf. Some habits just couldn't be broken.

"Hoomans... always smell funny. Emotions are strong in how... smell. Lots... smell bad. Better emotions. Better smell." –
Bandolar the Corgi – first guide to Animal Speaker Carl Remington

5

TO EXERT THE amount of concentration needed to call forth the army of animals demanded, Carl needed to be in a secure location where no one could harm his physical body. Since all the parties involved in the plan required separate areas, Carl's only logical place to stand his ground was in the often-forgotten basement of the Brightwood Country Club.

The underground of the luxurious club was anything but elegant. The constant thrumming of the boiler system rumbled beyond the insulated room and heavy fire door, providing heat for the century-old Brightwood. The mechanical room's HVAC system spread the heating system's warmth and the air conditioning's coolness through mazes of engineered ventilation. In both chambers, the equipment took up the majority of the space. Finally, the electrical panels, switchgear, and transformers that were the central nervous system of Brightwood buzzed on a frequency you could feel when standing near, providing power to the club.

Carl waited, standing in the musty storage area surrounded by forgotten tables and chairs and the constant noise of the three main rooms that brought the building to life. Then, finally, he reached out with the full extent of his newfound senses as an animal speaker. Through the haze of the spell that held the club members in a trance, Carl could feel the rats, dogs, cats, raccoons, and coyotes waiting patiently for him to give the order to attack.

The pitter-patter of tiny footsteps on the cold cement floor ran toward him with an eager cadence and broke through the usual sublevel noises. Carl knew the steps weren't human, and through the darkness, at the end of the large basement corridor, a small corgi approached. Bandolar regarded the animal speaker nonchalantly and trotted up, sitting by Carl's side.

"I could sense that you were close by. How did you find me down here?" Carl asked.

Magic bond... you and I... joined. Bandolar whined with joy.

"Really? There's a bond beyond us being able to talk to each other?" This hadn't been explained to Carl by the animal guide.

No. Follow scent smelly hooman. Bandolar looked at Carl and came as close as a dog could to a joking smile.

Carl groaned. "I already have to get smart-ass comments from Joe, but now I have to get them from you too?"

The corgi barked and playfully bumped into Carl's leg like a friend patting a shoulder in jest.

Carl peered into Bandolar's mind viewing imagery through the corgi's perspective. He felt an intense sense of loyalty and devotion. He could see the dog being trained by a particular aspect of Nature that was shown to him as more of a feeling of what was connected instead of being an actual entity; it was incredibly potent and old magic. However, Carl could also sense the difference between this magic and how it shaped life. There was more to it. He could almost make out the figure of a woman – a divine woman who gave birth to the Earth. A woman named... *Sophia...* The name slipped away, and Carl couldn't remember it anymore.

"You really are man's best friend, aren't you?" Carl knelt down and pet Bandolar as the corgi moved closer.

The bouncy corgi barked with eyes on Carl. *Be ready... stay speaking... to others... I watch... let know... if trouble here...*

The message conveyed was not in the form of language but as images and feelings translated into words that Carl could comprehend. Carl nodded, understanding.

"Alright, Valerie. I'm ready when you are." He spoke out loud for the comfort of hearing his own voice and closed his eyes, immersed in the connection. Sifting through so much imagery was dizzying at first. Still, he felt he was beginning to get the hang of being an animal speaker.

"He looked the same, but he wasn't. It was the eyes. Jared's eyes had changed. So much age and experience in eyes meant to be in a young man's body. It was unsettling at first." – Carl Remington, Animal Speaker.

6

VALERIE LED JARED through the maze of winding back halls designated for staff. With speed and stealth, they crept about like spies avoiding contact with the spellbound fanatics. The former Grace suspected that Rachel and the girls would be gathered in the formal dining hall preparing for the grand sacrifice. She approached that location, and Jared followed with a growing sense of unease.

"Carl and Joe should be ready soon." Valerie checked her watch, taking note of the time.

A dizzying sensation took a firm hold of Jared as he stood next to his mentor. The feeling that encased his senses was so powerful that he nearly collapsed while standing beside Valerie. Luckily, she was there to steady the youth, grabbing him by the arm and holding him upright, concern on her face.

"Thanks." Jared regained his balance as the invisible force that broke into the forefront of his consciousness urged him to take the next available left. "I think we need to go our separate ways. I need to take a left here."

"What just happened to you right now? I could feel something change. I think it'd be best if we stayed together." Valerie noted a slight difference in Jared's eyes. The youth wasn't under any spell, but she could discern that there was an outside force guiding his actions. *It must be near the hour of his birth as a Time Bender.*

A sense of knowing filled Jared as he spoke. "You know I'm always going to be loyal to you; my blood was given to you. I feel that bond no matter what, but I *have* to go left right now. Something is going to happen soon. I can't explain it, but it's important. I have to do this. I need you to trust me; I will be okay."

Valerie nodded, finding it difficult to accept. "I understand. Do what you need to do. I'll always know where you are. Just be safe for the time being. This will all be over very soon."

Jared's eyes studied the bowl Valerie held close. At first glance, the receptacle was quite dull and rather ugly. This vessel, however, was ancient, and countless sacrifices had been carried out with it. "I'm going to be okay, Valerie. Something's telling me that you won't have to worry about me anymore."

Valerie nodded again and placed an affectionate hand on Jared's shoulder. She had grown fond of the young man and knew he would never be the same after tonight. Develin had somehow learned of this as well and was counting on the transformation about to take place. Whether that was good or bad was yet to be determined, but she held on to the recent memory of young Jared Hernandez for this brief moment.

"Are you going to be okay?" Jared observed the strong emotions Valerie expressed. Of course, it was out of character for her to let her guard down, but he was grateful she had done so with him. After everything that had taken place, it was relieving to know with certainty that she genuinely cared.

"Yes. Thank you for making me stronger with your blood. And whatever happens tonight, remember the good. Remember the balance and know that I am always here for you." Valerie lifted her hand from Jared's shoulder, turned, and began walking in the opposite direction.

"I thought I was in love. At times, that is enough to spark change – thinking you are something until that is what you ac- tually become." – Vestor, the Time Bender – thoughts on being Jared Hernandez.

7

THE PULL THAT had taken hold of Jared returned with even greater in- tensity. He turned left and followed the hallways' path until he arrived at the all-too-familiar linen room. The door was closed, which was expected, but he knew that what lay behind the door was more than linens. He reached for the handle with a gentle grip, opened the door with excited caution, and en- tered to see Sara curled up against the wall on the carpet, alone and de- spondent. She hugged her legs close to her chest and waited in the room like a hopeless prisoner with only moments left to live.

Her eyes lit up for a brief second as she saw Jared standing across from her. "What are you doing here?"

Jared shrugged. "I'm not exactly sure, but I know this is where I'm sup- posed to be."

He recalled a similar scene in the country club parking lot only days ago. Jared had been sitting on the black asphalt much as Sara was now. She hugged her legs close to her chest with a similar intensity. This time he walked to her, and this time she was the one confused and lost.

"Is it okay if I sit down next to you?" A rush of emotions ran through Jar- ed; his feelings for her were still valid.

"If that's what you want. I imagine the truth of everything has been re- vealed to you. You know what I really am now, don't you? I'm Ate. I was once a goddess; this human body isn't my own." Sara wiped a few stray tears from her eyes and fought the urge to look directly at him.

"Like the number, right? That's how you pronounce it? ey-tee?" Jared took his time sitting down next to her and, with a gentle hand, brushed her hair behind her ear to get a better look. He wiped a tear from her eye with his free hand and guided her face by the chin so that they made eye contact.

Sara nodded. "Yes. That's how you pronounce it."

Jared forced a smile. He didn't know what to do but was glad to be near her again. "If it's all the same to you, I'll stick with Sara. I know you're powerful, and I have an idea of what you're capable of, but that doesn't change how I feel. Things around me have obviously changed. What was real isn't, and what is real is more fantastic than words can describe. The only thing I've learned that I can rely on is how I see things and feel about them. I still feel that you're good and that I really do love you."

Sara reached out and held Jared's hand. "It frightens me. I blamed it on being in this human form for too long, but I do *feel* it. I marked you by allowing those feelings to be expressed. I changed your life forever because I love you, and for that, I'm sorry."

Jared shook his head. "Don't be. I'm glad it was you that changed me." He smiled again – this time not forced, and a sudden strain of gravity yanked at his mind pulling him down. He felt the weight of time and space manipulating how he interpreted the world around him. Linear ceased to exist, and nothing made sense. Yesterday was today, tomorrow was the past, and the present was nonexistent; it all was happening at once.

"Are you okay?" She reached out to him, sensing the beginnings of a puissance. He was getting stronger, somehow, and there was magic in him, after all.

Jared concentrated on speaking. "I don't know. It's like everything is counting down backward yet simultaneously moving forward - in sequence. Things are meeting up like they're synchronizing, and it feels like my mind is trying to make sense of the backward and forward flow of things, but it isn't quite there yet."

"It might be a result of the nexus point," Sara suggested.

Jared's expression urged her to clarify. The pain of time came and went.

"The nexus point is the reason Rachel and Nicole wanted the sacrifice to take place tonight." Sara continued. "You see, they're my sisters from a long time ago. The one you know as Rachel is truly Dysnomia, and the one you know as Nicole is Lethe. We were goddesses of what you know as the Greek pantheon."

Jared continued to listen; her voice was an anchor from the distortion of time he felt. "You really are a goddess. I mean, I knew, but to hear you say it... it's something else. So this nexus point is important?"

She nodded. "Very. A nexus point's raw energy allows us to become more powerful because that energy is channeled through a proper sacrifice. These nexus points are notable instances in time when all realities that exist seem to merge for the briefest moments. The blink of an eye is too slow compared to how quickly these nexus points align. To carry out a sacrifice during the right moment can channel the energy of all realities into the sacrifice. It will make my sisters very powerful but not powerful enough to do as they wish, and that is to go home. Ultimately, this is all about returning to where they think we belong. They're fools. Zeus will never allow it."

"You don't agree with them," Jared noted.

Sara kept her eyes on Jared as she spoke. "I don't know what to do, Jared. I'm not even sure that the sacrifice will work as intended. I suppose I can give it all up, but then I'd be stealing this body permanently, which wouldn't be right either. The real Sara remains locked away within the mind of this vessel. Rachel and Nicole did away with the essences that originally inhabited their bodies. Still, I kept the true owner of this human form around. I figured I would give it back when we were done. The others don't even know that I did this."

Jared sighed, weighed down by the complexity of it. "I had no idea that it was like that."

Sara nodded. "That's how it works for us now. After the Distinction of Realms, many quarrels and schisms existed among the gods and goddesses of all pantheons. Some fled to the lands of their origins, while others are content bouncing between realms. Some stay hidden in this realm, giving up what they once were; others try to return to some type of former glory, like my sisters and me. Dysnomia and Lethe were exiled after the Distinction of Realms was agreed upon by the Praetor Projector Council. My sisters disagreed with the terms. I was exiled long before that."

"Why were you exiled?" He asked.

Sara looked off, remembering. "I used my powers at the time to influence Zeus. He made a decision he otherwise wouldn't have. When he discovered the truth of it, he banished me. I've been paying for that mistake ever since. Not long after the Praetor Projector Council banished my sisters, they sought me out. I'd already been alone for so long, bouncing from body to body, that it was a relief to be with my own kind again. We struggled, hiding within the mortal realm for a very long time. We jumped from body to body through the ages until we found the bodies we now inhabit. We were waiting for something like this nexus point to save us. It was supposed to be our salvation."

Jared was afraid to ask. "Did the real Sara ever know me?"

She shook her head. "No. She never met you. I took control of her a long time ago, and she's been a passenger ever since."

"You can help us stop them." He eagerly suggested.

"No, Jared. I can't help you with that. In the end, they're still my sisters." The conflict tearing at Sara grew more potent by the second. "You understand that, right?"

Jared nodded and thought of Joe and Carl. It would be nearly impossible to stand against them if he were forced to.

Ate had come to a decision. "I have to give Sara back her body. If I leave it in this condition, I won't last long as a rogue spirit. I'd have to find another body to inhabit, and I don't want to do that anymore. I don't want to participate in this sacrifice either. These people are being forced. In the past, others gave us our glory willingly. We could feed on the energy they created from lawlessness, oblivion, and blind folly. My sisters don't care about human lives, but I can't grow more powerful like this. These people deserve their freedom."

"There has to be another way." Jared pleaded.

Sara looked at Jared and smiled as best she could through the sadness. "There is another way. I can't exist as I am any longer, and I'm ready to move on."

"Move on to what?" He asked.

"To whatever it is that lies next. Energy never goes away. It simply changes form. I'm ready to change my form." Ate was adamant.

"How?" Jared was still confused.

She locked eyes with him. "I want to give myself to you, Jared. Sacrifice can work both ways. I want to sacrifice my essence for you. It will make you more than a normal human, for a while at least. You'll live longer than most and perhaps even gain a few abilities that can help protect you in the years to come."

Jared stood up from his seated position next to Sara, at a loss for words. "I... I don't understand how that would work."

"Do you accept my offer? Do you accept me as I am?" Sara stood up, moving closer to Jared. The level of her seductiveness rose in an instant.

He fell prey to the allure and cupped the back of her neck, moving in for a gentle kiss. The passion grew, and he allowed himself to get lost in that moment where two lovers were connected. He then let go and took a slight step back, locking eyes. Their matched desire for each other was insatiable.

"Say the words to me. Say that you accept my offer. I give my essence to you, Jared." Sara (Ate) spoke with such conviction that it startled her. She wondered if her followers, over the countless years, had felt as she did at this moment.

"I accept your offer. I accept you." He said, meaning it.

With a loving touch, Jared helped her disrobe from the waitress's uniform. The vest came off one button at a time, and soon enough, she stood before him naked. He kissed her again, and as the passion between the two grew more intense, he released himself from the confines of his own clothing.

"I love you." He spoke the words after a shared silence where they stared into each other's eyes.

"And I love you." Sara (Ate) held him close with their bodies intertwined, and she proceeded to give him all that she was.

"The ability to adapt and change inherent powers as a deity while maintaining a connection to the original powers one was granted is a fascinating study in adaptation. Survival of the fittest indeed!" – Sir Charles Darwin, Council Member of the Natural Magic Order

8

THE GLORIOUS HOUR was upon them. The large crowd of loyal souls gathered eagerly as everything was in place for the grand sacrifice. Upon the main stage, the altar stood as an excellent example of worship. It was a testament to the beauty that those being sacrificed saw in what they were willing to give up. Rachel stood atop this altar with Nicole by her side. The two smiled with satisfaction as they felt the adoration from those waiting to offer up their blood and souls grow stronger with each passing second.

Rachel turned to her sister, noting that the trio was short one member. "Where is Ate?"

Little Nicole was afraid to answer. "Last I saw, she was in the linen room. Do you want me to bring her here?"

Anger peppered Rachel's tone. "She should be with us. Something isn't right with her. I've felt it for a while. Has she changed that much? Has exile made her want to become one of them? She's been surviving this way far longer than you and I."

"She is troubled. What if she chooses not to partake? What do we do with her then?" Nicole knew this to be the likely outcome.

Rachael considered. "If that truly is the case, then we shall be forced to let her go, and we continue forward as planned. The nexus point is upon us. These people are ready and eager to slaughter themselves in our names - in our *true* names. I say we let them and let our sister decide her fate."

Little Nicole licked her lips and closed her eyes, doing her best to remember what it was like to be a free-flowing entity that fed upon these mortal creatures' raw energy. She was a goddess and would become even more significant after tonight.

From the back of the formal dining room, the main doors opened as if they chose to move on their own and called attention to their existence. A woman that radiated grace took one casual step after another toward the altar. She moved through the crowd now amassed and, with her presence, parted the people like a shark fin rising from the ocean. As she moved closer, it became evident that Valerie was the woman with the confident stride.

"What is she doing here?" Nicole stepped forward, acting as a barrier between Rachel and Valerie.

"I'm here for the sacrifice. That's why we're all gathered here tonight, isn't it?" Valerie continued walking through the people blinded by forced fanatical worship. Her voice boomed throughout the formal dining room, carrying a weight that was impossible to ignore.

Rachel smirked; her arms were crossed. She stood unafraid of the intruder. "Then you've come to give yourself over to us as well, I'm assuming? Your blood would be most appreciated."

Valerie chuckled, shaking her head. "Actually, my blood will remain my own, and the two of you will be sacrificed instead of these innocent people."

Rachel began to laugh. "You're delusional. You've no right."

"I have the right. The Edict of Innocents is on my side." Valerie revealed the bowl she held close and placed it on the altar. Then, she stepped on the stage, appearing as Rachel and Nicole's superior in every way. The sacrificial bowls chosen by the rogue spirits weren't nearly as potent or old as the one Valerie had attained; Minx had indeed done an excellent job in fetching it for her.

"How dare you bring that here?" Rachel barked, taking a startled step back. "What right do you think you have to interfere with our sacrifice?"

"What right do you think you have to take all these innocent souls without their consent?" Valerie asked.

"Our sacrifice was sanctioned by Dracien. He is the authority in these parts of New Gilead." Nicole stood ready to strike. She wanted nothing more than to tear Valerie's head from her body.

The former Grace's voice roared throughout the hall. "He is part of the authority but not the entirety. Yes, he sanctioned this, but you forget I do not answer to Dracien. He is merely the force that offers you safety from his minions that control most of this area. That old demon doesn't control me. My actions on this night are cleared by the laws of balance set forth after the Distinction of Realms. I have the right to step in as I see fit in this matter, and not even Dracien can stop me. It sickens me to see how quickly you girls have forgotten about balance on this night! I can't allow mass slaughter, especially during a nexus point."

"We have the right to regain our former glory!" Rachel shook her head angrily; her red hair flailed about, accentuating her frustration. "We have the right to return to our true natures and live in the realm from which we were banished! Olympus will know lawlessness, oblivion, and blind folly again!"

Valerie smiled. "So that is your true nature then? I knew there was something familiar about you girls. Allow me to give you my real name: Aglaia. I will not allow these people to die. They are innocent. Your former glory be damned!"

"Do not stand in our way Aglaia!" Once again, Nicole spoke up, ready to take action. "I won't hesitate to strike you down even though we come from the same pantheon."

The three women were at a standstill on the stage set up in the formal dining room. The calm before the storm was near its end, and the battle would soon ensue. All the while, the members and coworkers under the hypnotic trance of loyalty were none the wiser.

"In a weird, screwed-up way letting me have some abilities af-ter she left my body was some kind of payment. She didn't get rid of me – Ate, that is. She kept my soul around as a prisoner instead of feeding on it. When she gave herself to Jared so Vestor would be born, she used my body without my permission. It wasn't the first time. There were a lot of bad people she made deals with - experiences I'd forget if I could. And Jared, well, he willingly took my body. Vestor, as he now calls himself, is sup-posed to be on the side of right, or so I'm told. We may be on the same side, but I do not forgive him for the violation." – Sara White, in conversation with Aglaia (Valerie)

9

THE MOMENT OF climax reached the two lovers; their bodies inter-twined, and two hearts beat as one. Time became irrelevant as ecstasy con-trolled all aspects of awareness. They orgasmed in unison, and Jared wit-nessed Sara's (Ate's) sacrifice come to fruition at the moment of pure re-lease. The bright energy that was Sara's (Ate's) essence lit up the linen room with a brilliant glow, focusing on Jared's naked body. The pure spirit of Ate entered Jared, elevating his sensations to a level no average human could ever hope to attain. With that release, Jared heard Ate's final thoughts. *Goodbye Jared. I'll always love you.*

Jared's mind was without thought and immersed in the present. He was connected with everything and nothing and felt the raw power of a goddess become a part of him. When it was over, he slowly came back to reality. He was in a linen room naked with a scared woman his age. She backed into the nearest corner and pulled some discarded clothing over her naked body.

"Am I really free?" The true Sara White looked around the linen room. It had been so long since she could control her own body that moving her head astonished her and, in many ways, was challenging to master. Her voice was shaky at best, and one could tell she hadn't used it herself in years.

He nodded. "Yes. You're free. The goddess inside of you, controlling you – she isn't with us anymore. She's gone, and you're all that's left. Your body belongs to you again." Jared reached out to hold the frightened young woman but stopped as she cowered in fear. She didn't trust him.

"You... We... You were *inside* of me, and I... she was controlling everything. It wasn't the first time. She had me do so many horrible things." Tears began to run down Sara's cheek as her body visibly shook from the trauma.

"I'm sorry you were forced to experience that and all the other things." The reality of what the actual Sara was going through weighed down on Jared. She had been a prisoner in her own body for however long the rogue spirit Ate held on to it.

"Whatever was inside me told me that it would be okay. I'm just glad it's finally over. I'm really free?" She looked at Jared in disbelief. She was sure that the control she now had would be taken away at any moment.

Jared nodded comfortingly. "Yes, you're free. And there are good people here that can help you. These people have helped me."

Sara studied Jared, her eyes not used to her commands. "That thing inside me said you would help. She really did love you. Before she left me, she told me that you were a good person."

"Do you believe her?" He asked.

Sara shrugged, struggling to maintain a steady breath. "Do I have a choice?"

"There's always a choice. Stay here for now. In a little while, you'll have the urge to explore. Embrace that urge and follow the path you *feel* is right. I'm not sure how I know that, but trust me when I say it's true. You'll run into a woman named Valerie. You can trust her. She'll help you." Jared could feel the clock moving forward and backward within his mind zeroing into a specific moment. The pain was gone leaving only awareness.

Driven by the same power that caused him to enter the linen room, Jared dressed hastily. He put his clothes on and waited until Sara had done the same before moving toward the door. He didn't want to leave her naked and alone and felt a measure of responsibility for her now.

"Shouldn't I just wait here for you or something? Are you sure I should leave the room?" The thought of being abandoned terrified the young woman.

"You won't be forgotten, Sara. Just do what I say, and things will work out. You'll see." Jared turned and exited the linen room, guided by the countdown and lead in with time that was simultaneously happening. Two powerful clocks continued to move forward and backward within his mind's eye, and his true nature would soon come to fruition; his true magic would be brought to life.

"The events at the Brightwood Country Club were sanctioned. The area in question is currently controlled by Dracien and his contingent of creatures from beyond. Our orders were simple. We would only intervene if the agreed-upon sacrifice spilled beyond the permitted radius. It was contained, and our duty demanded we clean up the mess. But I do grow tired of cleaning up the mess. All this training – the enhanced abilities - I... I just want to make a true difference. I want to be the reason no one needs to clean up." – Special Agent Della Myer of the Natural Magic Order.

10

VALERIE STOOD FIRM while on stage where the makeshift altar had been constructed. Rachel and Nicole looked upon her with contempt as tensions rose before a captive audience.

"You go too far. Can't you see that all of this is for us?" Rachel gestured to the crowd of people watching events unfold. "You're not one of *them*. So don't stand in our way."

"I have no choice." Within her mind, Valerie gave the signal Joe had been waiting for.

Finally! Let's get this thing started. He responded through the telepathic link.

The large group of humans edged closer to the stage and surrounded the three women. They watched the altar with childlike fascination. Some were confused by Valerie's presence, while others were outraged by it; most of them anticipated the sacrifice to take place at any moment, as promised by their goddesses.

"Valerie, what are you doing up there? Where did you come from?" Mr. Drake asked. His three-piece suit had never looked so disheveled. His loyal eyes paid close attention to the girls, and his face of loving worship bordered on deranged. The fanaticism was unbearable.

"You don't belong on that stage! That's for the girls only! They're the special ones here, not you!" Old Merdith chimed in, upset that Valerie would do anything to disrupt the great night they had worked so hard to prepare. "They deserve to be up there! This place would fall apart without them, and you know it!"

The murmurs within the large crowd began to spread like a rushing wave. The volume of conversation grew to a distracting level. Valerie lifted her right hand for all to see, and silence blanketed the entire formal dining room the second she closed that hand like a mouth being shut. They stood staring at each other, wondering why the ability to speak had been taken away. Panic would have engulfed an average crowd, but since they were already under a powerful spell, the trance kept them docile. They merely awaited further instructions from their goddesses.

"Nice trick." Rachel stood unimpressed.

"I'm only just beginning." Valerie smiled.

Rachel stepped forward, moving past Nicole, who stood as her sister's shield. "Why? You've allowed your body to become of this realm, Aglaia - mortal to a point. Why would you do that? Why would you not only give up your glory but also your power? You were one of the three Graces!"

Valerie sighed. "It was out of love, and that's something I daresay you wouldn't understand."

Nicole grew tired of the banter. "We have love! All of these people gathered here love and adore us!"

"You have blind devotion! You have followers manipulated to care. The real thing is as close to perfection as anything in this universe can ever become." Valerie crossed her arms with disgust.

Rachel soon observed that a second Valerie appeared with them on the stage. The second version looked at the first, and both smiled at each other as if they knew a great secret. Then, Valerie number two proceeded to cross her arms and stared at the girls like a disappointed parent.

"What is this?" Rachel did her best to focus as a third Valerie approached the stage.

"The truth is I'm much more than what you believe me to be." The second Valerie spoke up.

"Don't you mean that we're much more than what she believes us to be?" The fourth Valerie chimed in, walking in from another direction of the large dining hall.

"Come now, girls, we mustn't fight amongst ourselves." The second Valerie uncrossed her arms and began walking toward the two rogue spirits.

The number of Valeries in the room began to multiply exponentially. Determined to survive whatever onslaught was pointed in their direction, the two former goddesses started throwing wild magic at any version of Valerie that approached them or the stage. At that moment, Nicole and Rachel both realized they felt something they had never honestly felt before. The emotion was strong and had been imprinted upon their essences as a result of their human bodies. They were afraid.

In reality, there was only one correct Valerie. She had jumped off the stage and placed a protective shield over the silenced group of people intended as the sacrifice. The wild bursts of energy from the rogue spirits bounced off the barrier like ricocheting bullets. Valerie was mindful to stay low in case the violent kinetic blasts moved in her direction.

The former Grace closed her eyes and concentrated her thoughts on Joe. He was strenuously working his new-found ability to fool Nicole and Rachel into believing that Valerie could multiply herself. *Joe, you're doing great. It's working beautifully. Keep it up.*

I will. Their minds are entirely human, even though the souls controlling the bodies belong to rogue spirits. So getting into their heads was easy. It was a bit of a strain to communicate and keep the illusion going.

A smile of satisfaction formed on Valerie's face as she shared her next thought. *Let Carl know now is the time for his part.*

"An ant against a lion – some would say that's not a fair fight. An army of ants with a purpose against a lion – that's a different story. When you give something a purpose, you can make it very formidable and dangerous." – Carl Remington, Animal Speaker.

11

CARL KNELT IN the Brightwood Country Club's basement; his knee was on the cold cement, and the hum of the various mechanical rooms kept a soothing rhythm in the background. He scratched behind Bandolar's ears as the corgi snuggled against his leg and felt a tremendous kinship with this creature beyond words. The dog's uncanny ability to communicate with him sometimes left Carl speechless, and he appreciated the guidance and perspective the animal had to offer. After all, that was what the dog had been trained for by the Supernatural Magic responsible for giving Carl his abilities.

Carl, are you hearing me in that noggin of yours? Joe's voice appeared quite suddenly in Carl's mind.

Carl focused on sending his thoughts as a response. *Yes, Joe. Is it my turn?*

It sure is. Joe responded.

The corgi mentally chimed in. *Focus. I... protect.*

Thanks, Bandolar. Carl shot the thought his animal guide's way.

There was mental confusion from Joe. He asked: *Bandolar? What are you talking about?*

I was talking to the corgi. Carl realized Joe's powers didn't allow him to read the animal's thoughts even when they were within Carl's mind.

Carl stood and straightened his posture as if he were a concert pianist about to perform before a grand audience. He closed his eyes, concentrating with all of his being. Carl could feel every single animal awaiting his command to attack. He saw through their eyes and felt the anticipation and their devotion to him. These brave and loyal creatures were ready to die for Carl, and he respected them in a way he had never respected any living thing before.

It's time, he called out to them. *Attack!*

The rats were the first wave and began bombarding the Brightwood Country Club from every angle imaginable. Through their point of view, he saw as they ran from the sewers, through the parking lot, and into the establishment gaining access through any window, door, or opening that could be utilized. Some snuck in underground, and Carl could feel them rush past him, intent on their mission. He also felt Bandolar watching out for him as he used his gift to the best of his abilities.

The stray cats and dogs in the area also began their assault. Carl viewed the different paths each took and saw precisely as each creature did; doors, windows – any opening was subject to the full force of these creatures. Carl was in many places at once. The sensation of being connected to and seeing so much nearly overwhelmed the youth.

Consciously being aware of and monitoring so many perspectives simultaneously while maintaining a hold of his own identity was a daunting and very exhausting task. However, Carl's fortitude remained strong as he kept his objective in focus, calling in the remaining coyotes and raccoons. He could see the rats approaching the makeshift altar in the main hall with the other animals trailing right behind. They would attack suddenly and with great force.

"The true breeding ground for Time Benders are nexus points. These points that connect all timelines spark Chronos' power and the Chronos within those touched by the Founding Magic. This power is primordial, and though there are other Time Benders out there, this power is truly mine. I exist beyond my lifespan in a way others do not, and cannot." – Vestor, the Time Bender.

12

RACHEL (DYSNOMIA) AND Nicole (Lethe) had never been so frightened or confused as they had been while on the erected altar in the formal dining room. Valerie after Valerie continued to appear. No matter how much of their power they called upon, the two former goddesses could not eliminate all the Valerie duplicates as they bombarded the altar with devious smiles.

The powers used against Dysnomia and Lethe were beyond the range of combined experience held by the two ancient deities. Having only ever truly experienced the energy of ordinary mortals and the gods and goddesses of their own pantheon meant that crucial information was missing. Moreover, the former deities lacked knowledge in other areas. It was only recently that they had dealings with demons like Dracien. They were formidable creatures when it came to the raw energy of magic. Still, the human minds of their vessels had made them easy targets for manipulation.

"You can't win." Valerie, number twenty-five, laughed.

"You're both rather pathetic, come to think of it." Number thirty-two chimed in.

"Shut up! All of you just shut up right now!" Rachel's rage grew more intense, and she began expending violent energy with greater zeal.

"Sister! Look!" Nicole pointed toward the sea of rats that moved upon them like a devastating tsunami.

"More of these vermin?! Who is controlling these infernal creatures?!" Rachel channeled her powers and began eliminating the rodents as the army of rats charged the stage in full force.

The sheer number was overwhelming, and she began to feel bites as they ran at her legs, climbing as high as they could. Dogs and cats quickly followed, pouring over the stage, knocking items off the altar from the large volume of creatures, and biting and scratching at any flesh upon the nearest two girls. The final wave of coyotes and raccoons washed over the previous two, and the formal dining hall had been invaded by an army of animals unified with a single purpose.

"What are these damn creatures doing?!" Nicole sent a burst of energy that exploded a few dogs and cats as they ran upon her. The blood and guts of the rats, dogs, and cats were all too real. Some of the red liquid landed upon the girls as they fought tooth and nail for their survival and the glory of the sacrifice they still intended to carry out.

Lost in a haze of anger and bloodlust, Rachel did not even realize that the animals were biting and scratching to collect her and Nicole's blood; the raccoons were the most tenacious, clawing at the ankles. Each creature took a turn scurrying back and forth between the rogue spirits and the sacrificial bowl set up by Valerie. The blood quickly accumulated as the animals spat what they attained and returned to gather more.

It was at that moment that Jared entered the formal dining room. In all his years, he had never experienced the euphoria that enveloped him as it had at that precise point in time. He felt as if he was floating through the room and lazily watched as Valerie ducked down, shielding the crowd of people from the wild energy blasts cast about by the girls on stage.

He looked with dreamy amusement as Rachel and Nicole struggled to kill the creatures attacking them. He chuckled as they exploded more deadly bursts of magical energy at imaginary targets in the process. Jared was unable to see what the girls were seeing, but he knew that Joe was behind the ruse, for that had been his part of the plan to take them down.

In the background of his mind, Jared could scarcely make out a familiar voice. He was soon able to ascertain that the voice belonged to Valerie. She was yelling at him to duck for immediate cover with frantic arm gestures. He smiled at her and waved as if they had run into each other at a casual gathering. It was all so amusing to him, and he knew he wasn't in danger even though she thought that was the case. He was touched, yet again, that Valerie had cared for him so. Their bond was powerful, after all.

What is that idiot doing?! Valerie's anger at Jared's idle state frustrated her beyond words. She wanted to tackle the youth, but she would lose contact with the group of people she had been shielding if she were to do so.

"I certainly do hope that my arrival isn't too late," Nina's dramatic tone preceded her as she also entered the large formal dining room with casual amusement. Her entrance was grand, and she moved as if she had all the time in the world; Nina's feet hovered ever so slightly above the ground as she took steps to appear as if she were walking on air. She sat on a chair near one of the large round tables and looked at the scene with a curious smile. "Now, this certainly looks like a good time. I'm sorry I missed most of it."

Nina's black dress fit her body nicely, accentuating the curves of her figure, and she crossed her legs while absorbing every detail of her current environment; her pale white skin appeared as smooth as porcelain. Then, a wild burst of energy flew in Nina's direction, and she deflected it with a snap of her fingers.

"Good of you to join us. You go by the name of Nina, I presume. You look exactly as Minx described." Valerie struggled to speak as she concentrated on the task at hand. It took much energy to shield such a large group of people.

"I am. It's a pleasure to make your acquaintance. Uncle Minx always has the nicest things to say about you. Well, as nice as nice can be for him, I mean, you know how he is. But, if I'm not mistaken, given what you used to be, I believe there was a time in your life when a task such as this would have been easily dealt with. It *pains* me to see you struggle so. You used to be a powerful Grace, after all." Nina smiled with sympathy and looked at Valerie as if she had suffered a terrible malady whose effects were irreversible.

"Is there enough blood for you? Will you be able to control them?" Valerie continued to struggle and ignored the condescending tone. She had never actually met Nina previous to this night. Still, she had heard countless stories from their mutual vampire cohort involving the soul eater and projector.

Nina closed her eyes and reached out with her senses. She could feel the warmth and slickness of the blood within the sacrificial bowl and knew that the precious liquid of life was flowing aplenty. The simple creatures had done their jobs well, thanks to the animal speaker commanding them.

"All is as it should be, Valerie. We may proceed." Nina's smile was that of an excited child.

Valerie closed her eyes and concentrated on the link Joe had made with her mind. *Joe! We're ready! Call it off right now!*

Thank God. I wasn't sure I could keep it up anymore. Joe's thoughts communicated his struggle and exhaustion.

Nicole and Rachel gazed upon their surroundings in confusion as the army of animals began to retreat. They were also relieved when the multiple Valeries that had manifested upon the altar vanished as quickly as they had materialized.

"What happened to them? Why are they leaving? Was it because of us? Did we stop them?" Nicole spoke up, tired from having expended so much energy. The confrontation had taxed the human body she inhabited greatly, and she could barely stand.

Nina rose from her chair and walked to the stage until she actually began levitating toward it. "Please allow me to explain. Upon this night with the nexus point approaching, you've both been kindly sacrificed to me." Her smile was charming as she studied the two girls.

Rachel and Nicole looked at the bowl and realized it had been filled with their own blood. The bites and scratches all over their bodies suddenly stung not only with physical pain but also with the agony of defeat. They exchanged desperate glances with each other and then regarded Nina, sensing just how powerful this woman was. Even with their combined strength, they didn't stand a chance; a petrifying fear took hold.

Valerie maintained the shield around the group of innocent humans. She spoke loudly, believing the words with all her being as she said them. "The blood upon this altar belongs to Nina! She is a great projector and soul eater! And the creatures whose blood this sacrifice is made with are given to Nina, essences and all!"

Unable to speak, Rachel struck out with all her might in a blind rage. The burst of energy deflected off Nina as the powerful projector glided to the bowl of blood. The redirected kinetic magic flew directly toward an indifferent Jared Hernandez, who stood as an amused spectator.

The wave rippled through the air on a collision course with Jared's body. The power of the energy burst could easily obliterate his flesh, but time itself came to a complete stop before it could touch. Jared observed everything with wonder as the entirety of his surroundings froze perfectly in place. He found himself to be the only moving aspect of a photograph that encompassed all of the action in the room.

Hello Jared. A voice within Jared's mind spoke up. It was an oddly familiar voice that was old and weathered.

Who are you? Jared sidestepped the burst of energy, able to feel its trapped power. The momentum of the blast stood next to him like a frozen blur of displaced air.

I'm you from a very long way into our future. This is a crucial moment in time for us. It's a nexus point. This is where we're truly born. Vestor explained.

Jared didn't know what to make of this. *If you're me, then what do I call you? Jared, part two? Older Jared? And what am I being born into?*

Future Vestor continued to explain. *Vestor is the name of choice. It'll become our new and common name. We are Time Benders. We live backward and forwards simultaneously. We're of older magic: primordial magic. It's a direct line to Chronos, the primordial god of time. We're needed every so often in the manifestation of physical form to instruct and guide the proper course of things. We're commonly referred to as prophets.*

How is that even possible? Young Jared asked.

With a voice of wisdom, future Vestor continued. *It's what we are, Jared. It's who we are. We are time. Time is constantly changing. The balance of time must be maintained. Some forces attempt to abuse what we can control. Everything that can happen does happen. But occasionally, a nexus point is created where all realities merge at a single point for the tiniest fraction of time imaginable.*

Is that why I feel so strange right now? Jared noted the odd sensations throughout his body.

Yes, the future Vestor confirmed. *You can feel the power of the nexus point, as do all creatures that deal with the magic of the universe.*

Jared took a moment to absorb with his mental faculties the portrait of events that surrounded him. He could see Old Merdith and Mr. Drake holding each other tightly beneath Valerie's protective shielding. Chef, Memo, Ana, and others Jared recognized were with the blind mass of devoted followers beneath that same shield. He also noticed that Valerie gazed upon where Jared had been standing. Even though time was frozen, Jared could still feel the bond he now had with the former Grace.

He decided to speak to his future self out loud as he examined Valerie's statuesque pose. She truly was beautiful. "Can I freeze time like this when I want to?"

No. This is just how you're born - how we're born. The universe has to reset itself to account for our abilities. The older version answered.

Jared struggled with how to phrase his next question. "Is my... Is our ability with this magic like Valerie's?"

No. We're of the Founding Magic. It's primordial, as I stated before. It's powerful magic much older than anything they know. The age of myth from which they were born came to be much later.

Jared nodded, accepting the answer. "I guess that makes sense. Time has always been around."

Yes, it has, and you've been awakened to your true nature as was intended. So we'll be communicating from this point on. Future Vestor explained.

"What do you mean by that?" Young Jared poked at frozen Mr. Drake. The man looked pathetic. How could Jared have been so intimidated by him? And Old Merdith seemed so frail and weak in his arms.

I mean the future you, that is I, and you as you are now. I'm the future you, and you're the me that is to be and has been. Our lives are a loop, and we influence one another. Also, we'll have to look into the Forever Man soon. He's important in what happens later on down the line. We have to groom him for Eternity's Endgame. Old Vestor seemed tired as he explained. It was like he didn't have much time left.

"The Forever Man? Eternity's Endgame?" The terms stuck in Jared's mind.

He's of the Founding Magic and is one of the first to be of Chronos' line. He's the physical manifestation of eternity. He takes varying forms and travels at will. There are times when his identity is known to him and times when he's lost. We deal with him quite a bit, given that time and eternity are related. He is continuously reborn. Future Vestor answered.

Jared sighed. "Okay. I'll just have to take your... *my* word for it. What do we do now?"

The impression of future Vestor smiling was felt by young Jared. *Now you accept that Jared is dead and that from now on, we live as Vestor. Jared will never exist again.*

Jared took a deep breath and exhaled. He concentrated on his breathing, and it was as if he could finally let go of everything he used to be. The flow of living backward hit him as Jared continued to move forward through time. He realized he had been many people living in many realities as different versions of Jared Hernandez. Jared Hernandez was now changed forever as Vestor. They all had happened, but at the same time, they would continually change to protect the fabric of time itself. It was a crucial balance that maintained all of existence.

With a new perspective on the universe, Jared returned to the action of the present. He had stepped out of the way of the energy burst, allowing it to be absorbed by Valerie's shield. He watched as Nina drank the blood from the sacrificial bowl dedicated to her. Rachel and Nicole were powerless while standing before the mighty projector and soul eater; tears of defeat slowly swam down their cheeks.

"Kneel!" Nina demanded, and the two girls had no choice but to obey.

Valerie released the protective shield over the crowd of spellbound people. They stood in shocked awe of the calamity. The spell that held their simple minds in a state of worship began to lose its effect. With forlorn faces, they studied the dead animals and bloodied animal parts that engulfed their immediate surroundings. Complete and utter horror soon blanketed the crowd that had amassed before the altar. Blood from the slain creatures had stained most of the contents within the dining room, and the crimson color had landed on many people as well.

"Oh my God..." Old Merdith felt like she would vomit; she fainted where she stood.

Mr. Drake moved to hold the old woman as gravity pulled her down; he stared at Valerie with eyes that questioned the reality of the situation. He remembered doing things for Rachel, Nicole, and Sara. He recalled a feeling of great devotion to them and couldn't understand why he had willingly carried out the now strange desires for the three young girls.

"Mr. Drake, I'm afraid that this is all very real. I can assure you of that. But it's over now." Valerie answered the unasked question.

"How?" Drake held Old Merdith and made sure that she was still breathing. "How can any of this have happened?"

"I wouldn't worry about that for much longer. Very shortly, you'll all forget the events that took place on this night. Your minds will be cleaned. The powers that protect the balance and Distinction of Realms will make sure of it. This will all turn into a dream until you're left with a feeling of having known something that isn't there anymore. Eventually, that will pass, and you'll continue living your lives." With those words, Valerie made her way to Jared, leaving Mr. Drake to wonder in silent horror about the things he had experienced.

"My greatest enemies never understood one simple fact: they could always use my powers against me. They couldn't see the future, but they knew I could. That alone has always been enough to set a trap – limit my choices in what I see coming and create impossible situations. Develin and Renee came very close." – Vestor, the Time Bender – Conversations with Matthew Gomez – the Forever Man.

13

"VALERIE, I KNOW what you're going to say." Jared/Vestor smiled at her with wisdom that hadn't been present before.

"Is that so?" Valerie smiled in return.

"I was never in danger, and you don't need to warn me about Develin. I know your encounter with him in the dream world was cause for concern, but I'll be ready for him. He'll try to control me for his own ends and try to kill me. I'll see it coming unless other Time Benders make certain choices on his behalf. That's always a possible outcome if I don't tread carefully. A lot of changes are coming, and there are many variables to account for. So much is already off-balance. It'll be hard to contend with the unknowns, but there's always a way. At least, I hope so. That's what my future self and I are counting on anyway." The remaining pieces of Jared Hernandez were melting away into Vestor.

Valerie looked at him with reverence; even a goddess could be in awe. "You truly are a Time Bender. You know what will happen next?"

He nodded. "I know what is possible and what must be maintained. There is an infinite number of possibilities. I wish you could see them the way I see them now. It's so beautiful how the fabric of the universe and time are entangled. Joe and Carl will be up here soon. In a few moments, I'll be leaving. None of you will see me again for a while."

"What? Why?" Valerie harbored many questions, and she still felt responsible for his safety. "You should remain with us, Jared. Time Bender or not, you're still very new to everything."

Young Vestor looked at Valerie like a teacher that knows better. "It's the best choice I have. If I stay, Nina will attempt to manipulate me and will likely succeed, given how new I am to everything, like you said. Her actions tonight were for two motives: there is the obvious one of gaining power from the blood sacrifice, and then there was trying to win favor with my newfound abilities. I see no other way around her getting to me. There are things I must do before I can adequately mold her to my needs. Once that is done, she'll be indebted to me. I have to leave now."

Valerie remained silent, taking in the information.

Vestor continued. "My leaving shouldn't be too much of a concern for you. You'll always know where I am. We're connected because of my blood. So when the right time comes, you'll find me. Also, remember that I'll always be loyal to you and that Jared Hernandez no longer exists."

She accepted his declaration. "Then who are you if not Jared?"

Vestor seemed taller as he spoke his following words. "From here on out, Valerie, you can call me Vestor. And please make sure that Sara is looked after. She's no longer controlled by the rogue spirit of blind folly, Ate. Ate's essence was given to me by sacrifice. The essence of a former goddess made me stronger, able to live longer, and has granted me the ability to carry out a few tricks outside of time-bending. It was also the catalyst that allowed me to realize the link to Chronos I have within my blood."

"That's remarkable." Valerie half grinned, accepting the transformation and understanding that a boy no longer stood before her.

He nodded. "Like I said, the body of the girl, the real Sara, has been relinquished to the rightful soul. It's very confusing for her. She has yet to discover that being controlled by a magical creature left residual powers within her blood. You have to guide her and teach her how to properly use them. She has her part to play in things as well."

Valerie nodded a heartfelt farewell and watched as Jared, now Vestor, exited the formal dining room of the Brightwood Country Club with a casual wave, smile, and wink. He moved with a calm demeanor that merely *knew*; his easy-going gait carried real wisdom. Finally, he disappeared around a corner, smiling the entire time, making it seem like he had never been there in the first place.

The cries of Rachel and Nicole caused Valerie to turn her attention back to Nina. She watched as the projector and soul eater forced Rachel and Nicole's chests open with an invisible force that emanated from Nina's hands. The rogue spirits' life energy spilled forth from the hollow cavities of flesh like fireflies that swarmed Nina with anticipation. The projector/soul eater grew stronger with each second of absorption and smiled as she heard the former goddesses' final pathetic cries. Their essences were now a part of Nina, making the already powerful creature even more so.

Carl and Joe ran into the formal dining room from the wait station where Joe had positioned himself. They slowed their run to a stunned walk as they approached Valerie and studied the altar in amused horror. They witnessed a delighted Nina feasting on the blood and flesh of the two dead girls with disgusted expressions.

"So, um, do we just let her continue doing her thing up there?" Joe asked Valerie feeling as though he were about to empty the contents of his stomach.

Valerie nodded. "Yes, we do. This is Nina's sacrifice. And besides, what else would you expect from a soul eater? The name says it all."

"Sorry, Val, I never had the pleasure of seeing one up close before. I didn't think the title would be that literal." Joe turned away, feeling his stomach churn from the amount of blood on stage.

Joe's eyes panned the crowd, and he spotted Ana standing alone with a group of confused employees. A numbing pain filled his chest as he wanted to run and ensure she was okay. But, in the end, he knew it would be a pointless gesture. Her mind would be cleaned of this night soon enough. He had already taken care of her feelings for him with his unique abilities as a manipulator.

Carl gazed upon the dead animals that sacrificed themselves for the greater good. They were noble creatures that had trusted and followed his command without question. He would forever be grateful to them and found himself reciting a prayer that shot to the forefront of his mind from the magic that now defined him.

Valerie smiled as Joe looked at Carl dumbfounded. Before Joe could interrupt, Valerie grabbed the manipulator/medium by the arm and spoke so that only he could hear. "It's an ancient animal speaker prayer. It's ingrained in his blood and a part of who he is now. It connects him with the creatures that serve him."

"If you say so, you're the expert. So where did Jared go?" Joe asked, sensing that something was very different with his longtime friend. "I tried to feel for him, but I couldn't get a good hold of his mind. It's like his mind just isn't there anymore. It was all jumbled up like it was everywhere at once."

She smiled. "That's because Jared isn't there anymore, Joe. Not in the way that you would normally understand it."

"Is he dead?" Carl asked after finishing his prayer. He felt a horrible pang of dread fill the pit of his stomach.

Valerie shook her head. "He isn't dead. He's very much alive. But he isn't who you knew him as any longer. The next time you see him will be as Vestor. That is his new name, the one he chose."

"What the fuck does that mean? Isn't that what that water demon called him?" Joe grew frustrated. "Where the hell did he go?"

"When the time is right for him to do so, he'll come back to us. I'll always know where he is in the meantime, but you have to understand that right now, Jared, or Vestor, I should say, can protect himself. He has the benefit of foresight." Valerie closed her eyes, sensing Jared/Vestor with the bond of blood that connected them.

At that moment, a small corgi ran into the dining room and sat next to Carl in a posture that stated loudly he belonged there. Bandolar looked at the group curiously as he stayed near his animal speaker.

You run... with... them? Bandolar asked.

Yes. You can run with them too. Carl replied.

"I'm guessing that this little fella is with you." Joe looked at the dog and took a step back as the corgi lightly growled at him.

"His name is Bandolar. He's a good dog." Carl reached down and began to pet the corgi.

Joe responded with his usual sarcastic tone. "Good for you, Carl. Glad to see that you can still make friends." He then looked back to Valerie. "How do we clean up this mess, or do we even bother with that?" Joe moved his gaze back to the frightened crowd of people and the dead bodies on stage being eaten by Nina.

"A cleaning this big needs to be done before the normal cleansing magic has time to spread. These days the Natural Magic Order takes care of that. Others with supernatural abilities that work with The Order will no doubt assist. I'm certain they've been monitoring and waiting for their moment to step in." Valerie explained.

"The Natural Magic Order? Who the hell are they?" Joe grew tired of the influx of new information. His mind was taxed as it was from having to stage the distracting illusion for Rachel and Nicole.

"You'll find that there are organizations within organizations, Joe." Valerie yawned, acknowledging the exhaustion her own body felt. "Right now, the two of you need to make a choice. You're both more than welcome to stay with me. I can offer up guidance while the transition into your new life continues. I can assist both of you until you're ready to be on your own. Of course, you may also go your separate ways now if that's what you want. Joe, you also have the option of staying with your mother. I'm sure Ming wouldn't mind teaching you herself. She's skillful."

"I remember my Ma trying to teach me how to drive a car. That didn't go so well." Joe said.

"Maybe you're just a shitty driver? Ever consider that?" Carl interjected.

"Hey, don't start talking shit just because you want to impress your little doggie friend there." Joe attempted to pet the corgi, only to be growled at again. "I don't like you either."

"I think I'd like to stay with you," Carl said after briefly laughing at the exchange between Bandolar and Joe. The dog at his side barked excitedly as he communicated his feelings to Carl. "I think Bandolar would like that too."

"This Bandolar is the most curious of companions you've found, Carl. I look forward to getting to know him." Valerie smiled as the corgi bowed before her.

Carl regarded Joe. "What are you going to do?"

"I might as well stick around. Someone needs to keep an eye on you, Carl." Joe winked at Valerie. "And you too."

Valerie scoffed at Joe's arrogant comment and noticed that a timid figure entered the formal dining room peeking in. The woman staggered about with careful steps and studied her surroundings like a helpless child.

Joe's attention fell on the young woman, and before he could make a move to strike her down, Valerie held his arm with gentle firmness. "Joe, it's not the Sara you think it is. It's the original Sara. The rogue spirit released her. The true Sara has control of her body again."

The authentic Sara White made her way over to the trio. She followed Jared's instructions without question and stayed true to the feeling that led her to her current position. "Are you Valerie?"

Valerie nodded with a warm smile.

"Jared said that you'd help me." Sara cringed as she saw the carnal bliss Nina was having at the altar upon the stage.

"Don't look at her. Just stay focused on me." Valerie reached out both hands so she could hold Sara's within them. Her touch was gentle and reassuring. "We'll help you. I promise."

Joe allowed his anger to dissipate. He studied Sara, realizing that she wasn't the same girl that had marked Jared. "You don't really remember us, do you?"

Sara shook her head; the motion was weak. "I saw my body interacting with you, but I've never met you before."

"I'm Joe. This is Carl." Joe forced a smile while Carl nodded with a smile of his own. "I think maybe we should get out of here?"

"That is a splendid idea." Valerie took the lead, guiding the group toward the exit. Sara walked alongside her with unsure feet as Carl and Joe watched their surroundings. From the corner of her eye, Valerie saw Mr. Drake reaching a desperate hand toward her.

"You can't just leave us here." Mr. Drake bounced his gaze between Valerie and Nina, who reveled in her sacrifice. Fear and horror danced upon his face as he witnessed Nina drink and lick the blood of her victims. The projector/soul eater was in a state of extreme delight.

"All will work out as it should, Mr. Drake. But, for now, do your best to get these people home, and very soon, this will all feel like a distant memory until there's nothing left to remember." Valerie assured him.

"So what do we do now?" Joe asked, nearly tripping over the small corgi as Bandolar did laps around the group while traveling to the country club's exit.

Valerie sighed, allowing her body to relax. "How about we relocate? Could we all start somewhere fresh? I could use a new job anyway. I'm not saying we must leave New Gilead, but a different part of the city might not be a bad idea."

"Are you seriously going to get a regular job again? I think I'm understating things when I say you're overqualified for pretty much anything out there." Joe was put off by the idea of employment. The more it lingered in his mind, the more disgusted he felt. "I gotta be honest here. I can't see myself working some shit dead-end job again. There's so much I could do with these new skills of mine."

"Balance Joe. It's all about balance and fitting in. That's how we live." Valerie's voice was stern.

"Whatever. I'm not getting a regular job. So you can forget about that." Joe's tone was adamant.

"That shouldn't change things much. It's not like you did any real work at the country club. If you could find a job where you're paid to avoid work, then I think you'd be a perfect fit." Carl chimed in.

"Keep it up. I'll get inside your head and make you think you were a little girl with pigtails for the first ten years of your life." Joe warned.

Bandolar barked in defense of Carl and threw another growl at Joe.

Joe pointed a stern finger at the small corgi. "You're lucky I can't get inside of your head."

Carl chuckled. "I wish you could. The insult Bandolar just threw at you was hilarious!"

"Are they always like this?" The real Sara asked as she clung to the security of Valerie's presence. She watched with amusement as Joe and Carl cracked jokes at each other while they exited the country club.

Valerie lifted a curious eyebrow. "I do believe that they are."

While Joe and Carl continued to argue, Valerie took the opportunity to explain the new life in store for the real Sara White.

PART TEN:

AFTERMATH

"So many worlds exist with versions of the same city, and other worlds have cities that are unique to it. Take New Gilead, for example. This version of Earth is the only one that has it. What do you suppose that means? How do you think that impacts the various timelines and versions of existence? How do you think this impacts the Distinction of Realms within those various timelines? Make no mistake, they all exist. Nexus points bring them together. So how can a city that doesn't exist in other timelines suck up all the power of a nexus point? My people have answers. We are here to spread the truth. We are here to bring an end to the Distinction. We are the Messengers." – Recording from the Avatar of the Messengers – the one known to Vestor, The Time Bender, during The Messengers case – Natural Magic Order archive 2282

1

DETECTIVE JOHN LYCROS had grown familiar with the third shift rhythm at the downtown New Gilead precinct. The multi-story building in the city's heart was a second home to John; the activity in the patrol area, officers responding to calls, and the dispatchers working to prioritize incoming calls served as comfortable background noise. Nevertheless, it allowed him to delve deep into unsolved caseloads that were as mysterious as Scott Riley and his friends. Bodies found mutilated in strange ways were on the rise, and the encounter with Special Agent Della Myer left Lycros unsettled. It pushed his drive for answers harder than ever, and like a bloodhound, he would find what he was searching for.

While hunched at his desk, Lycros soaked in the emptiness of where he sat; Lycros was alone in a sea of empty workstations. The night detective was out on a call, the desk sergeant intermittently cleared his throat between monotone responses to conversations with walk-ins, and patrol corralled the late-night disorderly citizens to holding cells. During a brief moment of respite, the lack of audible distractions struck. His department's usual hustle and bustle only shrouded him with a loud silence that reminded him of the empty house awaiting his return.

Determined to avoid unwanted feelings, his mind snapped back to Della Myer. He'd been unable to access a single file on the supposed Special Agent and her bald partner. But then, anything relating to the Riley boy and his death at the abandoned house became instantly classified. The information on the case was now filed away as sealed documents John Lycros wasn't privileged enough to even glance at.

His partner, Diana, suggested in her own way that the entire endeavor was a dead-end unworthy of an intensive follow-up. Nevertheless, the fact remained that too many strange occurrences had been taking place under his watch. John's obsession with not having answers was too much to handle. He needed to find the truth. The untold stories had to come to light for the people no longer able to tell their side. Unfortunately, his wife was one of those people, and her death left one too many unanswered questions.

A picture on his desk was all that remained of the life that once was, and it was the only picture he held on to of his departed wife, Jennifer Tollan Lycros. A random car accident left Jenny without the use of her eyes, forever changing her world. She could not adjust to the disability; the lack of physical vision proved detrimental to the defining purpose she had discovered as an artist. Then, amid what seemed to be a critical case, the love of his life decided to commit suicide. He was no closer to understanding it than he was on the night it happened; he continued to blame himself for choosing the case over his wife.

"I had a feeling you'd still be here," Diana said as she approached John. The man was still hunched over his desk, exhausted and worn out beyond his years.

"Did you..." Lycros stopped the question in progress as Diana handed him a cup of coffee. She sat down next to him in an empty chair. "You're the best. Thanks." He cast a warm smile her way before sipping the hot beverage.

"I take it you still haven't been able to find anything concrete on this Special Agent Della Myer?" Diana spoke the name with disdain. Their first encounter with the woman left her just as unsettled as Lycros.

Lycros nodded. "I've turned over just about every stone, called in a few favors, and I still keep coming up empty. Whoever Della is, and whoever she works for, is higher than anything I or anyone else I know has come across before. She's a special agent, but for who? What kind of branch grants that authority and keeps such a tight lid on itself?"

"Maybe she's a part of something new or something we're not even supposed to know about in the first place." Diana noticed the picture of John's wife and concealed a sad sigh with a sip of coffee.

"It just doesn't add up. I can't even look at the files from the Riley case anymore. Magic hands swooped in and sealed them. Only people with high-security clearance can take a look." Lycros drank his coffee. Diana knew precisely how he liked it, and he was grateful for a partner like her. She always seemed to know what he needed.

Diana sighed, about to say something she knew John wouldn't like. "I think we might have to let this one go. I know I sound like a broken record, but we have enough to deal with as is. These murders we're looking at are getting worse. We have our hands full."

Lycros shook his head. "No, Diana. There's something wrong with this. I can't walk away. It's just too damn strange. I mean, there has to be a way to learn more about what's happening. My gut is screaming at me that it's all connected somehow, and Della's organization is a part of it."

Diana considered. "What if we reference other cases where Della Myer took over as lead investigator? We had to have written it off in our own reports somewhere along the line. Besides, given the scope of things, we can't be the only detectives on which she's pulled her jurisdiction. And you remember what she said the last time we met - she made it clear that we'd be seeing her again. So the more we learn about what she's worked on, the more prepared we'll be in figuring out what she's going to be working on once she and her people swoop in."

"That's a good idea. How about we get started?" Lycros stood up, ready to get to work.

"No." Diana also stood, placing a hand on John's shoulder. "First, you go home and get some proper rest. The mystery of Della Myer isn't going anywhere. It'll be here when you get back. Eat something and get some sleep. You're no good if you're burnt out."

Lycros nodded and surrendered a smile to Diana in agreement. "We'll pick up on it tomorrow. And thanks."

"For what?" She was confused.

"For making sure I don't burn out." He smiled.

Diana gave him a wink and a nod. "That's what partners are for."

Lycros trotted off, making his way past the uniforms at the desk with an intense stretch followed by a yawn and a lazy wave goodbye. Diana watched until her partner was out of sight and reached within her pocket for a cell phone. She sat back in the empty chair, keeping her eyes on the picture of John's dead wife, and looked away as the phone rang. After the third ring, labored breathing could be heard on the other end.

"Hello? It's me." Diana cleared her throat. Making contact with *her* had always been unsettling. She thanked God she didn't have to do it face to face.

"How is he?" The raspy female voice finally asked, breaking through the eerie silence.

"He's troubled, there's no doubt about that, but he's also more determined than ever. He wants answers more than anything. He's fanatical. I don't know how else to sway him. I've tried. Over the past year, I've tried. You have to believe that." Diana pleaded.

"I do..." The voice took a moment to contemplate. *"His wife's death should have been the end of it. It should have changed his path."*

"Was her death for nothing?" Diana asked.

"No. Jennifer Lycros was meant to die. John was too close." An eerie pause interrupted the cadence of the conversation. *"It is a delicate balance we play at here. Lycros must cross over, but he must do so our way. We need total control for him to be of use to us. We can't let that crossing be premature and must ensure he suffers... madness."*

"If the death of his wife couldn't drive him into madness, then what could?" Diana struggled with this.

The labored breath turned into a chuckle as the raspy voice spoke up. *"His wife's resurrection, of course."*

Diana couldn't hide her shock. "What do you mean? Hello?"

The line disconnected, and Diana was left with an unsettled stomach. Walking the line had never been easy for the woman. She lived in two worlds for most of her adult life, given the magic of her true bloodline. Most of that time was spent as an ordinary detective in the world of humans. However, secrets had to be protected, and it was no accident she had been assigned as a partner to the man that nearly uncovered them.

She placed the cell phone in her pocket and stood up. The picture of Jennifer Tollan Lycros almost looked at her with despair. "I'm doing my best to protect him, Jen. But madness may be his only way out of this."

"How she lived was more important to her than dying. Doing right because it was right was etched into her soul. She was the strongest, bravest, and best partner I ever had. She was the best of us." – Special Agent Sionmen Repus – the funeral of Special Agent Della Myer after 122 years of service.

2

SPECIAL AGENT DELLA Myer was the epitome of the warrior spirit. The woman was an expert in physical combat with heightened genetic attributes; she carried a vast knowledge of spells and how they worked though she was unable to conjure the majority of them, and she held great pride in the fact that there was no trace of Supernatural Magic within her blood. Instead, her powers came from Natural Magic referred to by the ordinary world as science. Genetic manipulation was well known in the everyday human world, and on the magical side, the practice had made incredible leaps and bounds.

When Della was just an infant, she was forced to cross over to the magical side of the Distinction and raised by The Order's monks, representing the major policing force within the significant circles of supernatural activities. These monks that believed in maintaining balance, had given her the education, genetic enhancements, and rigorous training needed for survival in a world where monsters lurked in every shadow. She served The Order and the greater good without question, for she was a true believer.

Special Agent Myer, like most agents, understood the need for simplicity in everyday life. Upon entering her apartment, you would be greeted by an open layout that maximized a strong sense of space. Every room was furnished with a minimalist aesthetic, for she considered clutter in any form negative and sought clarity in everything; that concept was crucial to her life. It was that mentality that kept her sharp and allowed her to stay focused. Della's job wasn't easy, and she always needed to remain vigilant.

She sat in a lotus position, meditating on everything and nothing. Thoughts regarding several months ago flowed through her mind. It was when she had been in charge of a mass clean-up. A large group of individuals needed cleansing. The appropriate measures were taken to ensure that everything experienced was forgotten. They'd witnessed a sacrifice at the Brightwood Country Club, and all those that had attended nearly ended up being sacrificed themselves. The events were permitted by Dracien, but a woman named Valerie stepped in, protesting the authenticity of the sacrifice by invoking the Edict of Innocents.

Valerie had left an impression on Della as she reflected upon their brief encounter. Her instincts told her that they would meet again. Della began keeping a file on the woman, discovering her true nature as the former Grace Aglaia. This former deity had crossed paths with The Order on several occasions since the organization's inception.

As of late, Della's meditations grew increasingly difficult to maintain. While seated in a lotus position, she breathed in a way that passed the breath throughout her entire body. Her mind was stubborn. A way to cut through the murkiness was beyond her, and the clarity she sought was out of reach. Something was disturbing her personal balance. Then, as she meditated, two names kept appearing at the forefront of where the unconscious and conscious minds met.

Vestor... The mystery Time Bender's sudden appearance shook The Natural Magic Order and the Praetor Projector Council's authority. His presence was being felt by all in power as he began to reshape events to unknown ends. Even Dracien's organization grew unsettled. Della's latest task involved her attempting to find this Vestor and bring him in.

The second name came to her as strongly as the first. "You play a dangerous game John Lycros." She said out loud, visualizing the stern features of the detective. To say the man was tenacious was an understatement. His investigation into the strange was insatiable; nothing seemed to deter him. "If you're not careful, you'll end up on my side of the Distinction, or maybe even worse."

She relaxed her pose, fully aware of her surroundings. The stillness was comforting as she realized how difficult the road ahead was going to be.

"Capturing Time Benders was nothing new to me. I'd done it several times before. They are nothing more than glorified prophets doomed to repeat a cyclical life wrapped around a nexus point. Vestor.... He is something new, somehow. He continues to elude me. It is infuriating, to say the least. But I will bend him to my will. I will do so or die in the attempt." – Alecto (former Fury – known as Renee Dempsy during the time of Vestor)

3

TO SAY THAT Renee Dempsy was disappointed was an understatement. Her task to eliminate the Time Bender that became Vestor ultimately failed. She had been close to the boy on several occasions. Still, she could not commit the act of assassination without arousing the wrong kind of suspicion. This led to the employment of outside forces, which also ended in utter failure. Her master was not pleased by this one bit.

Damn that water demon! She contained her emotions while sitting in the lobby of an extravagant office in the most prominent building to reside in the business district in downtown New Gilead. It had just so happened to be the principal office of the demon that all inhabiting the realm of magic referred to as Dracien.

Dracien controlled most of New Gilead and was charged with watching over the day-to-day transactions of anything that dealt with the darker aspects of Supernatural Magic. By visiting Dracien, a mighty demon born from those of the fall, she knew she'd have to break her everyday cover as the perfect trophy wife. Of course, her true identity as a former Fury of old would be revealed, but that was precisely her intention.

Her idiotic husband somehow managed to survive the fiasco of the sacrifice at the Brightwood Country Club several months ago to top it off. Mr. Dempsy showed all the signs of a faded memory of the events of that night. But, in truth, that was all for the better. She was confident that one of her extracurricular activities would bring about his demise eventually; she just had to be patient on that front.

The lobby she was forced to wait in welcomed her with false comfort with an underlying sense of raw power. The arrangement of furniture and the use of space made anyone waiting to feel minuscule and powerless in the presence of the man to whom this lobby belonged. Renee could sense that a spell had something to do with that impression while reaching out with her senses.

The large ominous black double doors opened with a sharp dominant display. A woman in a black business suit stood looking directly at Renee. There was a tinge of amusement in her voice as she smirked in her direction. "Mr. Dracien is now ready to see you, Mrs. Dempsy."

Renee stood with a pleased smile while walking to the open doors. "Thank you, my dear."

As she entered the office, a large man stood with his back to her. He towered over Renee, and she realized that he had to be nearly seven feet tall. The man's burgundy suit was a finely tailored cut that fit a physical form of raw power. She studied Dracien as he gazed out of a sizeable stained glass window that gave a crystal clear view of his city. She then noticed how his office was lavish yet conservative in a strange mix of the two styles. Finally, the dim lighting served its purpose by creating a need to get toward the illumination that surrounded Dracien, and she stood waiting to be addressed by the powerful demon to be brought into his light.

Dracien's voice boomed with a deadly bass after a few heartbeats of silence. "Mrs. Renee Dempsy. I know that you were once a Fury of great influence. I know that you have been hiding, as many of our kind have been, with a mortal disguise. But, nevertheless, your true nature was never secret from me; try as you might to conceal it."

Renee stepped forward and bowed her head to the demon before speaking. "I thank you for granting me this audience Lord Dracien."

"The old ways are obsolete, so you may do away with the formalities." Dracien turned around. He looked down at her with a menacing yet handsome face. It was another contradiction that worked in his favor, and he took a few more steps in her direction.

"You have me at a disadvantage, then. It appears that you know more about me than I had anticipated." Renee admitted.

"I know what I must. You tried to kill the Time Bender before his birth as one of those annoying prophets. How you managed to gain control of a water demon is beyond me, but that speaks to your skill. In hindsight, I should have supported you in his demise, given the trouble this Vestor is *now* causing. Even the forces that cater to the lighter aspect of things are having trouble with him. Unfortunately, it appears the newborn prophet's agenda is greater than anything we can discern." Dracien cleared his throat; the stained glass window vibrated from the bass.

"There isn't a circle of creatures out there that doesn't now utter his new self-appointed name," Renee added.

"This Time Bender has earned some reverence for having proven himself formidable in such a short amount of time." Dracien stalked over to his desk chair and sat down with a kingly air. Even seated, he still towered over the former Fury. "Why are you here?"

She stood tall. "I seek aid."

Dracien considered this. "Your pantheon has never sought out my kind on purpose, and I take great offense to that. So much could have been accomplished so long ago had we been able to look past origins and ideologies. So make your next words worth the risk of this visit. I could easily make it so that you no longer exist in any form. The void is far worse than any version of hell out there. In the void, there is simply an eternity of conscious nothingness."

Renee cringed at the idea of ending up in the void. The thought of not existing frightened every creature. She wondered at how some of their kind had actually chosen it. She shed the idea and spoke up, confident in her mission. "Everyone believes this Jared Hernandez, now named Vestor, to be a future asset. Everyone believes that he'll be their tool like many of the prophets before had been for others. Still, he is far more dangerous than anyone realizes. You view him as an annoyance right now, but mark my words when I say that this annoyance will soon become unstoppable if not handled with care."

Dracien let out a dismissive gesture. "How could you possibly know any of that? Develin and other conjurers of equal or greater status have done the magic. They were unable to foresee any problems other than the obvious pain he'll become to certain business ventures, shall we say?"

"With all due respect, they're not Time Benders. They can't know the future as surely as one of the prophets can." She stood her ground, not giving in to the intimidation even though her essence wished her to scream in fear.

Dracien cast a casual gaze upon Mrs. Dempsy. It was more than intimidation. Looking into the eyes of the demon left her unsettled to her core. Evil incarnate reached out from those eyes and touched her essence in ways she could not describe and did not care for.

She cleared her throat, attempting to get back on track. "Vestor is dangerous."

"Are you telling me that in conjunction with your skills as a fallen Fury and dabbling in the magic within your reach, you're also a Time Bender on top of it all?" He smirked at the idea, chuckling. The bass of his voice rattled the room and its contents.

She shook her head, thinking of Clara. "I'm no Time Bender, but I have one in my possession. She's held captive and has been sedated. Her drug-induced state allows us to tap into what she sees, with her being none the wiser. She has seen what Jared, or Vestor, will come to do in the days ahead."

Dracien's eyebrows rose in cautious surprise, and he leaned forward in his chair. "Are you telling me that a Time Bender of old still exists and that you have her under your control?"

Mrs. Dempsy nodded. "Her name is Clara."

The demon sat back. "I find that hard to believe, considering that the Time Benders of the last generation are long dead to this world. How is it you have one in your possession? Clara, is it? She would have to be well over two hundred years old."

"Clara had friends throughout her travels. They did their best to protect her and helped extend her life with the magic they offered; my magic keeps her alive still. She was far older than any normal human and outlived the other Time Benders of her generation as a result. As to capturing her, well, there are ways to shield one's self. Time is magic of old; it is of the Founding. It harkens back to the primordial age of Chronos, as you well know. There also exists other Founding Magic, which can be used to counter what a Time Bender can do. The exact details I'll keep to myself." Renee smiled.

Dracien nodded, showing the slightest hint of respect. "It appears that you have everything under control. What would you require of me?"

Renee's smile deepened, relieved that the conversation was finally going her way. "We use Clara to capture Vestor, and then we kill him. The people I work for are far older and more powerful than your superiors. They come from the old magic as old, if not older, than the Founding. They care nothing for the trivial ideas of balance that have governed our lives for so long and led to this wretched Distinction of Realms."

"Vic," Dracien called the name with penetrating eyes that remained on Renee.

She watched as the werewolf stepped forth from the shadows in complete human form. Vic looked to Mrs. Dempsy with a slight bow of the head and returned his full attention to Dracien.

If he knew what he needed to know, he would know of my hold over his prized werewolf. Renee allowed the thought to satisfy her.

"Develin," Dracien called out again with his powerful gaze still unwavering.

From the same shadows, Develin appeared, almost forming from the darkness of those very shadows. He carried a mischievous smile and wore a red suit covering his lean physique from head to toe.

"How may I serve?" Vic asked while keeping his head down.

"I want you to go and verify the claims made by Renee Dempsy. Then, if she truly has a Time Bender in her possession, we'll discuss what possible options can be taken from there." The demon ordered.

Vic nodded and stepped to where Renee stood like a predator, ready for the hunt. "Let's look and see if what you say is true. I'll drive." Renee nodded in compliance playing up the ruse of not knowing the werewolf. Vic followed her out of Dracien's office without speaking another word.

Develin waited until the doors were shut and privacy guaranteed before sauntering to Dracien's desk. "Do you really believe she has a Time Bender all to herself? The last recorded prophet was before the 1900s. I know because I killed the bastard."

"That's what we've been led to believe, Develin, but you know just as well as anyone that things aren't always as they are supposed to be. She claims to have captured a Time Bender, and I know that you have managed an impossible feat by killing one." Dracien cracked his neck while seated behind his desk, allowing his posture to relax. He rotated the chair he sat in to view the skyline of New Gilead from the large glass window.

"What would you have me do about it?" Develin asked.

Dracien kept his gaze on the skyline. "I want you to find out who she's working for. She said they were more powerful than our superiors. Find out the identity of these creatures that make such demands of a former Fury. Above all, find the best way in which this can benefit us. We've prospered much because of the full knowledge granted to the Time Bender you killed. Let's make sure we continue to prosper."

An evil smile formed on Develin's face. "As you wish." He turned from Dracien and began walking back toward the shadows of the office.

"Develin," Dracien called out.

The demon wizard turned his head. "What is it now, dear brother and fellow child of the fallen?"

Dracien eyed the demon wizard. "I know you meddled in the events that led to Jared becoming Vestor. You've given ample warnings to most of those involved, including Nina and the former Grace that initially protected him. Nina's involvement has forced me to sequester the soul eater and infant projector at the behest of the Praetor Projector Council. But that is beside the point. Tell me: why would you want him alive? What are you up to?"

Develin shrugged. "I figured I could gain the full knowledge from another Time Bender and get a better idea of things to come. Time is always changing after all, and information is the only currency and power worth having."

"Why don't I believe you?" Dracien asked.

"You question my loyalty?" Develin feigned offense.

"I would if you had any." Dracien smiled.

Develin scoffed. "I'm bound to serve you as per my release from hell, the main incarnation of it, that is. Am I up to something? Of course, I am. The day I'm not is the day you should truly be worried." With those words, Develin melted into the shadows and exited Dracien's office.

"Because of his sacrifice when he was a youth, I've always been connected to Vestor by blood. This has allowed me to always know where he was and be able to locate him if needed. His abilities let him know when to show up when I needed help. The most frightening time I'd ever experienced – concerning Vestor – was when I couldn't FEEL him. You see, the only way to sever the connection of blood is death." – Aglaia (former Grace known as Valerie during the time of Vestor)

4

FIVE MONTHS HAD passed since the Brightwood Country Club incident. During the weeks following the sabotaged sacrifice, Valerie found herself saying a sarcastic yet sincere goodbye to Joseph Chan. The youth grew restless while living within the strict parameters set up by the former Grace. Finally, when satisfied Carl would be adequately cared for, Joe vanished headfirst into his unknown destiny.

Joe's mother, Ming, wasn't surprised when Valerie relayed the message of her son's insatiable need to travel. Ming asked that her Stepmother keep her apprised of current developments regarding Joseph and her son's companions. Valerie was more than happy to oblige the woman that was the closest thing to a daughter she would have during this era.

The former Grace had tendered her resignation, putting in her two-week notice to Brightwood shortly after Joe's exodus as a lone wolf. Mr. Drake and Old Merdith were sad to see her leave the country club and protested her resignation with a sincerity she hadn't anticipated. Nevertheless, Valerie stuck around long enough to ensure that no residual effects of the nexus point lingered within its walls. She knew the Natural Magic Order would have taken care of such things, but she felt it necessary to make sure of it with her own eyes.

While living off a decent sum of money saved over many years and existing between jobs in the "normal" world, she also felt the need to do her best when training Carl. On top of that, she tasked herself with acclimating Sara White to her new life. Like it is with any students, there were good days, and there were bad days.

She stood within the expansive studio space furnished conservatively for the three of them. Giving up her old apartment had been an easy enough choice. The former Grace had lived far too long. The idea of being partial to one set space seemed absurd compared to experiences traveling the world and beyond. Using funds stored away, she purchased the studio space outright. Some walls had been put in, a training area secured, and separate sleeping quarters had been arranged for herself, Sara, and Carl. All and all, it was a comfortable and large living area, and she had been more than satisfied with the outcome.

The hour was late. Valerie stood peering through the clean glass of one of the large black windows focusing on the vastness of the city skyline. So many lives interacted in what appeared to be complete randomness, and so many choices were made regularly, with the majority of those decisions going unnoticed.

Vestor...

She still had difficulty getting used to the name change that Jared had placed upon them all, and what kept her up at such a late hour was the fact that she could feel him in New Gilead. He had returned after these long five months. The blood connection was never wrong; if she wanted, she could go to him. Valerie would, however, refrain from such action. She knew the Time Bender could take care of himself and was aware that when the time was right, he would seek them out.

Carl had progressed much in five months since his powers first manifested. His abilities as an animal speaker had grown considerably as he focused every second on perfecting every aspect of what he could do. He had become one with Nature in a way most humans could never appreciate.

Sara kept him company through most of it, and the two youths grew very close, considering they had no one else or nowhere else to turn. It was inevitable. Valerie couldn't help but feel that Sara was another reason for Joe's decision to travel alone. Joe knew she was not the rogue spirit that had inhabited her body, but every time he looked at her, he saw the girl that changed their lives forever. They all had to give up who they used to be, and that reminder was too much for him.

The unexpected residual effects of being inhabited by a former goddess came to fruition, just as Vestor had predicted. Valerie hadn't anticipated Sara's new ability with elemental spells and energy manipulation. Sara was eager to learn more now that she tasted what she had been forced to only witness as a hostage of Ate. Valerie hoped that this thirst for knowledge was pure and that she could steer the young woman away from corruption.

The rustling of the bedsheets came to Valerie's attention. She preferred Carl and Sara to sleep in separate rooms but knew there was little she could do to control it. She was secure that pregnancy wouldn't be allowed unless Sara undid the magic that prevented conception. She could hear Carl telling Sara he would be right back, and Valerie could picture the jealous face the young woman carried. It had become a cause for more concern. The closer she and Carl grew, the more resentful she became of Valerie's presence.

Youth... The thought flew through Valerie's mind as she awaited her pupil.

Carl exited his room and saw Valerie standing on the second level of the large studio apartment. He put on a shirt that matched his pajama bottoms and walked up the stairs to stand next to Valerie. She wore her favorite red robe and smiled in an almost motherly fashion as Carl approached.

"Trouble sleeping?" He asked as he also gazed upon the magnificence of New Gilead through the window.

"He's back." Valerie finally said.

"Jar... I mean, Vestor?" Carl's expression brightened and then returned to one of seriousness. He knew his friend had changed perhaps more radically than he and Joe combined. He wondered how much of the former Jared remained and how different Carl would appear to this newly named Vestor persona.

Valerie continued. "It doesn't mean that he'll seek us out."

Carl didn't understand. The first thing he would do upon returning would be to look up friends and loved ones. "What other reason could he have?"

She shrugged. "I wish I knew. He's a Time Bender. The battle for balance never ends with their kind."

"I was just excited at the idea of seeing him again." Carl sighed and cracked his neck. He had maintained his strict workout regimen in conjunction with his new training, and they were balancing each other out nicely.

"How is Sara doing?" She asked, changing the subject.

Carl sighed. "She still has bad moments. Anxiety will hit her when she tries to sleep, and she worries that she won't have control of her body when she wakes up. I can only imagine what that must have felt like."

"I'm sure it wasn't pleasant," Valerie added.

"I was thinking about something else." Carl took his gaze from the city and looked directly at his mentor.

She met his gaze. "And what was that?"

"We've been training for a while now. I'm just not sure what we're training for." Carl asked.

This time Valerie sighed. "It's best to always be prepared to face whatever comes. If you feel it's time to move on, I won't hold you back. You've always been free to do as you wish."

He nodded with an apologetic gesture. "I know. It's not that. It feels like something is coming for all of us. Am I imagining that?"

Valerie shook her head. "No. I've had the same sensations these last few days. It started when Vestor returned."

The patter of paws was soon heard, and Carl smirked as Bandolar raced up the stairs to join them. The dog panted and bumped into Carl's leg before sitting on his foot.

"We haven't seen him for several weeks." Valerie looked at the creature curiously. "And how does he manage to get in this building unhindered?" This always fascinated the former Grace.

Carl laughed. "He won't tell me." He took a moment to take in the information from Bandolar. "He says there's been a lot of man-wolf activity. What does he mean by man-wolf? Is he talking about werewolves?" Carl looked at the small corgi posing the question mentally and looked to Valerie when he received his answer. "Yes. Werewolves. He's concerned about the growing number of them that are entering the city."

"That is strange." Valerie raised an eyebrow and looked back to the sky-line, focusing on the downtown area. She could feel Vestor more strongly now that she was concentrating all her thoughts on the bond.

"Is it because of Vestor?" Carl knelt beside Bandolar, petting his back.

She nodded. "It more than likely is. You should go back to sleep. Get some rest."

Carl yawned at the mention of sleep and looked Valerie in the eye once again after returning to his full height. "What about my birth father?"

"I'm still investigating that, Carl. Please be patient. These things can take some time." She explained.

Surrendering to her words, Carl nodded. "You make sure to get some rest too." He smiled before descending the staircase back to the first level.

Valerie gave a dismissive nod and continued to focus on her view of the city's downtown area. *What are you up to, Vestor?*

"I have a plan. That plan involves saving all realities, and to do that, I have to make choices. I have to play with the variables at hand. Those choices will not make sense to a lot of people, and I will be considered extremely dangerous. I will do things you will not agree with and sacrifice those closest to me. It will be hard for you to understand why, but I need you to trust me anyway and know that it all serves a purpose: the preservation of life and freedom for all that live on both sides of the Distinction."
– Vestor, the Time Bender (conversations with Valerie (Aglaia))

5

WHILE PERCHED UPON a rooftop next to a stone gargoyle, Minx viewed the human masses roaming about the metropolis of downtown New Gilead's Lower East Side. Most of the mortal fools gallivanting about were lost souls with nothing better to do than prowl the nighttime hours for some form of excitement that added to the experience of their mundane lives. Some found more than they could handle, while others saw nothing but disappointment at every turn. How the dice landed was left up to chance, and chance was notorious for dishing out the surprises that people seldom expected.

The Forever Man was out there in this city, and Minx knew that his mission to seek out and protect was of the utmost importance. He'd been searching for the physical manifestation of Eternity for centuries now. Prophecies had been left by long-dead Time Benders, and they spoke of the Forever Man returning to human form in this era. Minx had been searching for so long that he began to lose hope in ever finding the one that could never truly die; eternity was forever.

"I know exactly what you're thinking right now." A voice spoke up.

Minx found it disturbing that he could not sense the approaching human body. The voice had a familiar tone, and he could now smell the blood of the person behind him. The fact that such a warm body had stood undetected made the vampire wonder if he grew weak in his older age. Minx kept his back to the mystery man feigning that he knew he had been behind him the entire time.

The voice of the mysterious human chuckled as he spoke. "And there's the classic body language. It reeks of someone acting as if they knew someone was behind them, even though the truth of the matter is I snuck up on you. Just eats at ya, doesn't it?"

"And who exactly are you?" Minx finally asked.

The stranger cleared his throat. "I'm someone you've met before. When we first met, I must admit, you frightened me a lot more than you do now. Probably had something to do with the fact that I was just so damn new to everything."

Minx turned around to gain a visual. He was surprised to see the boy that Valerie had been protecting not so long ago. He stood before Minx, only eighteen years of age, but the vampire could detect that something was very different. Minx could see it in Jared's demeanor. His posture spoke of confidence that hadn't been there before. A transformation had occurred, and the boy standing before Minx was no longer a boy but a man who knew who he was. There was also a magic about the young mortal that Minx felt upon closer inspection with his senses.

"You knew me when I was Jared." Vestor took a few casual steps closer. He placed his hands in the pockets of his black jeans. The pure nature of the black clothing that adorned his body allowed him to blend in with the night that shrouded the city.

"When exactly did you stop being Jared?" Minx asked.

Vestor smiled. "The very second that I was born as Vestor."

Minx wasn't sure about the name. "Vestor? So you're the face behind the Time Bender that's causing so much chaos. Not sure if I like the name change, but I must admit it is a strong name." Minx moved his neck to the side, cracking it.

"I didn't know that vampires got stiff necks," Vestor commented.

Minx rolled his eyes. "Well, now you're aware. Guard the knowledge carefully. We mustn't let it get around."

Vestor chuckled. "Yes, of course. Your secret is safe with me."

Tired of the conversation, Minx lunged out at Vestor with lightning-quick speed. To the average eye, he would be nothing more than a blur. But, when he stopped moving, the vampire realized that he was grabbing at the air before him and that Vestor was standing behind him; the youth was calm as if he hadn't just been attacked.

Minx smirked. "You learned how to move quickly. It appears that you have magic in your blood after all."

Vestor shrugged it off. "It's an ancient type of magic that courses through my blood. It has nothing to do with speed and everything to do with timing."

Minx leaped at Vestor again and found that there was only more air for him to grasp. He turned around to see the young man smiling and sitting on the edge of the building where the gargoyle was perched.

Vestor yawned. "We could do this all night, but this is the part where I tell you I'm a Time Bender and that I'll always see what you're going to do before you do it."

Minx's eyes widened with surprise. "You're a real Time Bender? Your kind has been gone for a very long time if you'll excuse the redundancy in the usage of the word."

Vestor leaned closer from his seated position to explain. "There was a nexus point a while back - five months ago. It was my birth. I'm the first of a new batch. Others are going to be born with similar abilities. It seems that my kind will be needed in the days to come. We'll be crossing paths with the other Time Benders. Eventually, the two of us, that is. I'm afraid that some won't be as friendly to the cause. Not to mention that I have a ridiculous amount of enemies already trying to kill or control me."

"What do you mean by us?" Minx levitated from the ground of the roof and floated over to where Vestor sat.

The Time Bender looked at the vampire as if it were obvious. "I meant exactly that. It's going to be you and me. You aren't the only one that has business with the Forever Man. From this point on, Minx, our fates are intertwined. I can help you find him very quickly. It was, after all, my kind that told of Eternity's return to physical manifestation."

The little vampire crossed his arms. "Okay, Time Bender, so what happens now?"

Vestor reached inside his coat pocket and pulled out a silver flask. He opened the flask and took a swig of the vodka within. The liquid still had a powerful effect on him, and it felt no different from when he used to drink it straight from the bottle with Joe and Carl. Regardless, he held the flask out to Minx, knowing the little vampire would appreciate the gesture of a drink between comrades.

"I might as well." Minx grabbed the flask and drank the vodka as if it were water. "I believe things are going to get a lot more interesting with you around. So tell me, how does this whole time-bending thing work?"

"It is what it is," Vestor answered, sitting next to the vampire.

"How bloody Zen of you." Minx took another drink instead of passing the flask back to Vestor.

The Time Bender settled in for an explanation. "Time is an illusion, Minx. It's one I've just begun to learn how to manipulate, and eternity is a limiting word placed upon an abstract idea that willed itself into creation. That physical manifestation is crucial to Eternity's Endgame, an event that remains far down the road all life travels. Every so often, the balance is threatened. You're already aware of that fact. Luckily, those on both sides respect that balance enough to stand together, but I get ahead of myself. First, we must find the Forever Man."

Minx perked up. "You know where he'll be? You said you can find him quickly."

Vestor nodded. "Our magic is linked." He held his hand out, and Minx reluctantly gave up the flask. Vestor took another swig of the vodka and smiled.

"Why are you smiling?" The little vampire had a terrible time trying to get a read on the young man.

"Minx, I'm smiling for no reason at all, and that's the best reason to have." Vestor leaned forward and pointed down at the street toward a crowd of people moving along the sidewalk. "There."

Minx searched through the crowd with his enhanced vision and spotted a young boy a few years Vestor's minor. He appeared no older than fifteen years of age. His hair was scruffy as he roamed the nighttime streets, moving through them like he'd won the lottery. But, when it was all said and done, he was just another boy with teenage angst sneaking out at night to try and act older than he was.

Vestor took another swig of the vodka before speaking further. "That's him, Minx. That is the Forever Man to be."

"What?" Minx was dumbfounded.

"I told you I'd find him quickly." Vestor gave the vampire a wink.

"You're not right in the head. I don't believe you or believe that it would be that easy to find the Forever Man. I've been searching for centuries, and you're just going to come along, point your finger, and say you found him?" Minx snatched the flask from Vestor's hand, drinking most of what remained with large furious gulps.

"He doesn't know what he'll become yet. The mortal name he goes by is Matthew Gomez. For now, it's our job to protect him while staying hidden. When his true nature as the Forever Man is revealed, we'll be there to help guide him." Vestor sighed, seeing the possibilities that were ahead. "You see, Minx, if we play our cards right, young Mr. Gomez will help maintain the balance."

"You don't have to recite the prophecies to me!" Minx snapped. "Your life is just the blink of an eye compared to how long I've been around. I'm well versed in the words your previous Time Bender friends left behind. Are you certain he's the one?"

Vestor looked at young Matthew Gomez, having seen this moment happen. He nodded for Minx's benefit without taking his eyes from the young man prowling the streets in childlike wonder. "I'm very sure." Another smile formed upon Vestor's face.

"Do you still have no reason for that smile of yours?" Minx asked, finishing off the last drops of vodka in the flask. The alcohol always did have a way of making the blood taste sweeter.

THE BEGINNING...

Join our side of the Distinction.

We have magic!

www.ingramcontent.com/pod-product-compliance
Lightning Source LLC
Chambersburg PA
CBHW072023020726
47501CB00006B/1930